ENDLESSLY

Elizabeth Stokes

Little Acorns Publishing

Little Acorns Publishing

Copyright © 2011 by Elizabeth Stokes

First published in Great Britain in 2011 by Little Acorns
Publishing

ISBN: 978 0 9568080 0 4

Cover designed by Elizabeth Stokes and Vic Bearcroft © 2011
www.vicbearcroft.co.uk

A catalogue record for this book is available from the British Library

Little Acorns Publishing
78 Grove Street
Balderton
Newark
Nottinghamshire
NG24 3AS
01636 651699

www.littleacornspublishing.co.uk

Printed and bound in Great Britain by Lightning Source

For Vic, who put up with the rollercoaster ride and supported me completely…as always.

And for Maria, my number one fan and close friend, whose constant enthusiasm and support pushed me to get Endlessly out into the big wide world.

Thank you also to my cold readers, your feedback has been invaluable.

And Deborah Anderson, your professional input was hugely appreciated.

We meet extraordinary beings rarely
throughout our lives

Chapter 1

There were so many of them sitting around the fire: faces I didn't recognise, talking quietly and laughing easily. Amongst those faces of native origin, one person stood out. But it was not his face that caught my attention; it was the fact that I could not see it. I could see every face but his, hidden under the wide brim of a Stetson hat.

I tried to push my body forward towards the group so that I could bend down to see him or lift the hat to expose the face that eluded me. But my body was numb, paralysed. I was unable to move a muscle or utter a single word to draw attention to myself. I was an invisible, silent bystander.

I closed my eyes tightly, desperately trying to summon the strength to move, to say something out loud and make him look up at me. But when I opened my eyes, I found myself being forced backwards by a wind so strong that it drove me into the surrounding woodland, my arms flailing as I tried in vain to grab onto branches to stop myself.

When at last I landed painlessly in the earth amongst the leaves, I stood up, brushing the woodland carpet from my clothes. The paralysis was gone, and I let out a barely audible gasp of relief. Slowly I looked around, wondering where I was. All I knew was that I needed to get back to the group of people. I had to find them again, even though I didn't know why.

As I looked over to my left, I saw smoke billowing through some distant trees and my body involuntarily started moving towards it. Soon, I was running, running so fast it felt as though I was skimming the ground. A charred smell filled my nose before I saw anything; it was an acrid smell, the smell of burning flesh.

My body suddenly left the ground and I floated high into the air, slowly moving forward towards the smoke. As I moved out of the trees into the clearing, I caught sight of a familiar Western hat lying upturned in the dirt. I looked at it as I passed overhead and, when I turned back, I was hovering above two strangers.

I knew immediately that the man crouching below me was the one I had been desperately trying to see, and now I was floating only twenty feet above him, watching. I could see his shoulder-length dark-brown hair, which hung in unruly curtains around his face, blocking my view of him.

Then I heard him scream the word 'no', sending shivers down my spine, such was the anger and violence in his voice. I focused my attention on what lie on the ground beneath him, my body hovering slightly to one side to see more clearly.

Lying motionless was a woman with the most beautiful face I think I'd ever seen. She was staring up at me with deep, glistening brown eyes that bore deeply into mine. I blinked, and in that split second every part of her native beauty disintegrated before me, into the charred remains that truly lie before him.

I found my own voice right then and let out the loudest scream. He became completely still and slowly started to look around, as if he were following the movement of a bird or butterfly on its flight into the air.

'Soon,' he muttered, a hint of a smile appearing on his lips. Just as he was about to lift his face enough for me to finally see him, everything went completely dark.

Chapter 2

What is it about dreams? Dreams that are so vivid, so real, and yet had nothing to do with what was in your mind before you fell asleep.

Dreams bugged me; *my* dreams did anyway. And for the last year or so they had plagued my sleep, often leaving me in a trance-like, sleepy state for the whole of the following day. My dreams hardly ever meant anything to me either. I rarely had a place in them, and many of the faces that I saw I didn't recognise.

This last dream, though, was terrifying. It woke me with a gasp. My eyes flashed open and my heart thumped in my chest in rapid, nervous beats. When I finally realised I was awake, I lay still, concentrating on slowing my heart and taking deep breaths.

I stretched out and rolled onto my side to gaze out of the tall, arched window – which ran the full height of the lodge – into the hazy early morning light. I sighed deeply. I had only been in Manzano for four days, and already a light depression had started to creep over me, numbing my spirit.

As I thought about Luke and Anna, the heat of unwanted tears pricked at my eyes. What had I done? I'd left behind everyone and everything I knew and moved thousands of miles away to a place where I knew no one, bar one person.

I also missed mom and dad more than ever, and would have given anything to have them alive again. My sudden grief became over-whelming.

I felt my body start to overheat as the anxiety and stress built up inside me, but with perfect timing to interrupt my chain of thought, I felt a nudge in my back. The tension eased from my face and I peered over my shoulder to see Ember, my black and white Siberian husky, whose paw was jammed in my back as he woke from his deep sleep and stretched.

'Hey Ember,' I said, reaching my hand back to scratch his chest.

Ember looked at me for a second then stood and shook the sleep from his body. He bounded onto the floor and made a beeline for the stairs, excitedly anticipating his early morning yard exploration.

I looked over to Ned, who was lying on the small floral sofa near the mezzanine railing. He was curled up into a tight ball, watching my every move. He too stood, his silver tabby form arching at the spine as his body vibrated in his stretch, then jumped down and trotted towards the stairs in hot pursuit of Ember.

My strange little Ned joined me just over a year ago. Luke and I had returned from a meal in Boston with Anna, my best friend, and her husband, Cam. I had already let Ember out for his last pee before bed and was taking a bag of trash out when I saw his dark form sitting neatly and precisely on the bottom step under the porch light, totally unphased by my approach. He was an adult cat already and I smiled at his blatant cheek as he perched in front of me, staring into my eyes. He then sauntered up the steps, brushed his tail against my leg and walked through the back door.

That was the last time Ned would be homeless, and he quickly became even more of a shadow than Ember. Wherever I was, I could always guarantee he would be somewhere in the same room; sleeping, watching me, or staring at invisible objects.

In the silence of the bedroom I became lost in thought again. But this time I didn't think about running back to Boston and the man who had hit me, and I didn't think about the fact that I had no job and was living off of savings, or even about Anna, my best friend, who I missed heaps; instead, I was thinking about the strange man I'd seen in Manzano the previous day. The man who'd frozen completely still when I pulled up on the other side of the road from him. The man whose stark profile was deeply embedded in my mind and the man who, somehow, seemed familiar, even though I'd never seen him before in my life.

I sighed again, but this sigh was a determined one. *Just get your sorry ass out of bed, Meg,* I thought and kicked the covers from my body.

Since arriving four days ago in Manzano – a small, western-style seasonal tourist town set in the mountains of San Diego – my depression had been creeping over me. But, for those four days, I had gotten up and busied myself so that I could stay positive. I was okay through the day in the sunshine with lots of things to keep me occupied, but when the nights drew in and I was alone again, I let myself spiral deeper into despair.

This morning was no different. I took Ember around the yard then washed and readied myself and headed into town to stock up on some food.

As I entered Manzano, just a couple of miles from my new lodge on 'Whispering Pines', I slowed to the obligatory thirty miles per hour, glancing as I passed at the people idling around the town in the steadily rising temperatures, in no hurry to get anywhere.

I parked up and went to buy some soft furnishings and candles from Hearth & Soul, then to the bakery for some fresh bread and finally to the supermarket for food and pet goods.

Financially, I was fairly comfortable. I had some decent savings: money left by my parents in their will and proceeds from the sale of their house. I also didn't expect it to be too long until the money came through from Luke for my share of our Boston property.

Back at the lodge, I let Ember out as I unloaded my shopping and packed things away. Then, with a glass of juice in hand, went to sit on the rickety old wooden bench next to the bunkhouse, listening to the distant occasional noises of human life; muted voices down the hill, a lawn mower buzzing in the distance, and the birds noisily going about their business in the yard.

I went inside to get my camera and set about taking photos of the lodge, yard, and the views of Manzano, so I could email Anna and show her my new home.

When I'd finished, I decided to take a better look around the bunkhouse. I wandered inside to get the keys and tried and tested them until I found the right one. I had to boot the jammed door hard and the last kick sent the door flying open, the room revealing its dark, dusty self. The furniture was draped with navy sheets, which I started to pull off, causing dust motes to fly into the air, glistening where the small windows threw hazy sunlight into the dark wooden interior.

There was a mix and match selection of furniture and an old sleigh bed. I hadn't noticed from outside, but beyond the bed there were double patio doors leading out onto the decking.

As I moved forward, turning to look around the rest of the bunk-house, my eyes were drawn to a painting on the wall in front of me. I was instantly struck by the simple, yet striking oil painting that depicted a wide lake with green, cold-looking water. Dense trees flanked the lake on all sides and at the far end were two dark silhouettes: one was a person, the other a dog.

The perspective of the painting suggested it was painted from the small woodland pathway between the trees in the foreground, whose branches framed the painting. It looked peaceful, yet a little haunting. The scene appeared somehow familiar and, as my eyes relaxed, I found myself being drawn further into the setting, my imagination almost taking me to the far side of the lake before I blinked and breathed sharply, bringing myself back again.

I looked to the opposite side of the room and found a second painting. It was of a similar style to the first but had softer, more peaceful and much warmer tones. It depicted dense woodland surrounding an old wooden cabin. Random patches of delicate pink and yellow wild flowers led from the foreground towards the narrow door of the cabin. Smoke escaped through the chimney in hazy chuffs, and logs were stacked deeply beside it. I pushed up onto my tiptoes to get a closer look at the details and also saw what appeared to be horse tack hanging up next to the door.

Both paintings held a strange artist's signature, but no date:

Γαβε Λετενιερρε

I looked at both paintings again for a few minutes and then walked once more around the room before I turned for the door.

I grabbed my gardening gloves and went to work in the yard. The land on the property stretched to about an acre and surrounded the lodge, and from its elevated position on the hillside, offered a fantastic view down towards Manzano. I pulled weeds and collected dead wood for the fire, with Ember's assistance, which meant helping by grabbing the bits of wood and lying down on the ground to chew on them.

Ember, like Ned, was an unplanned 'child'. I had taken him on as an unwanted pup from my old veterinary practice, where I had worked for three years as a technician. He was only five-months-old at the time. He had been a perfect companion; never phoning me to say work was hectic and that he wouldn't be home until after midnight, again. He never argued with me or ignored me or lost his increasingly bad temper and hit me. He always wanted to eat a meal with me and he was never too busy working to have a little fun or just chill out and watch a movie. That had been someone else. It was quite simple: Ember was holding me together.

After a long, hot day of chores, I ate a ready meal for one and grabbed the fresh bedding from the line. With Ember insisting on jumping on the bed and helping me, the whole bed-making experience had taken me a lot longer than I intended. But it was fun and entertained both of us while we each fought to take control of the cover. I dropped on the bed afterwards laughing as Ember happily circled and dug the covers, carefully stamping his authority to show that this was now his side of the bed. Once happy with his nesting ritual he dropped down and lay facing me.

I looked at him and clenched my jaw, my laughter subsiding as it was replaced by the sudden realism and sadness: all I knew was gone. I lay looking at this endearing black and white face with eyebrows spotted white and comical. His amber-brown eyes bore deeply into mine confirming what I already knew; that he *did* understand that my messing around and smiles were fading into sadness and worry.

I stretched forward to run my fingers through the dense fur on his neck, sliding my hands over his ears and under his chin. 'I think I'm a bit lost, Ember,' I muttered, gazing into his eyes. His next reaction brought me right back to earth.

Ember sat bolt upright staring towards the stairs.

Chapter 3

As soon as he did it I pushed myself up into a sitting position, twisting to look at the stairs. After a few seconds I turned back to his motionless face for some idea as to what he'd heard or sensed. Suddenly, Ember shot off the bed and raced downstairs towards the front door.

My sadness and tears gave way to a nervous fear. I slowly followed Ember down the stairs and went to peer through the blinds into the yard. It was just light enough to see that there was nothing different outside. Everything was still. Quiet.

I made my way to each side of the lodge looking out of all the windows. I felt silly being so cautious and scared in this peaceful town, which my internet research had convinced me was one of the quietest, safest places in California.

My turbulent and nervous state of mind stayed with me, however. This was another downside to living alone; there was no one else there to be tougher and braver than I was. Well, except for Ember, but then there is a fine line between being brave and being plain stupid!

As I traipsed around the lodge checking through the blinds, I noticed Ned sitting quietly on top of the kitchen table staring at the door, his tail swishing and as thick as a toilet brush. I followed his gaze but saw nothing. I gulped. 'Oh, enough!' I said out loud, breaking the silence. 'This is silly.'

I switched the outside light on and opened the door with a new-born confidence. The failing light enabled me to see there was still nothing unusual out there. Ember, though, had decided that the danger was not enough to warrant any further investigation and turned his attention instead to detaching the legs off a cricket.

I relaxed the furrow on my brow and stood still as I looked through the trees into the distance. I turned in a slow circle, taking in the view, and stopped where I'd started, watching the deep-red sun fall behind the distant mountains. I closed my eyes and listened to a dog barking in the distance and the nearby crickets starting their evening chorus. I felt the tickling of loose hair around my face which was helped along by a light breeze whispering through the trees.

I took a deep breath and opened my eyes. A solitary tear sat carefully balanced beneath my eye. I blinked and sent it tumbling down my cheek onto the ground. After a few minutes, I walked back with Ember into the lodge, making sure I locked the door behind me, and hung the keys up.

I switched my laptop on and made a coffee while I waited for it to boot up. With my camera connected I started looking through the photos I'd taken that afternoon, selecting the ones I wanted to email Anna. As I clicked onto one showing a view of the yard, which was taken from the lodge, I noticed a dark shape that had no reason being where it was. 'Hmm,' I muttered, zooming in on the picture. I scrolled around to find the area I was searching for and saw a dark shadow that resembled a man. The shape appeared to be peering out from behind one of the distant trees.

I zoomed in again but the shape showed no detail. I moved back from the screen hoping that the distance would help my eyes focus better, but it looked the same.

It was dark outside so I knew I'd see little if I went to look at what might be forming the shadow. It was eerie how the shape exactly resembled a man and yet, with the clarity of the photo along with the bright daylight, it seemed odd that any shape would look so dark and unfocused.

I continued preparing the photos then attached them onto an email and sent them to Anna, with a few lines telling her we'd all settled in fine and that we couldn't wait for her to come and visit.

I continued to sort out my possessions until it started to feel like home. The lodge had been rented to me on a long-term lease and was pretty well furnished with all the main things I'd need. Although it was a small A-frame, it was perfect for one person and had a simple open-plan layout.

Looking at the details while sitting with only Ember for company in the office of our Boston house, I knew I had to get this place. I was sold as soon as I saw the photos on the website, drawn to it somehow. I was on the phone to seal the deal within minutes.

In bed that night I picked up my battered book to occupy my flaky mind, set the alarm, then started from where I'd left off the previous night. After about half an hour my eyelids became heavy and my blinking slowed. I tapped the lamp off and nestled under the warm quilt.

In the darkness outside, the distant house lights twinkled through the trees as they wavered in the breeze. It was a soothing sight and I started to drift into sleep, thinking about the photos and listening to Ember's quiet little wimps as he slumbered in his canine dream.

I idly wondered what dogs dreamt about and imagined them being far less complex than my own disturbing dreams. On that thought, I fell straight into my own restless slumber.

I was up at 8 a.m. and slid on my flip-flops and robe, put the tea-kettle on, grabbed the keys off the counter and headed outside for our morning wander. I realised it instantly; I was *sure* I'd hung the keys on the towel rail after I'd locked the doors the night before.

I strolled to the front door and glanced inside, puzzling over where I'd actually picked the keys up from. I passed it off as my bad memory and then walked back out into the yard with a mug of coffee, and headed straight towards the place where I had seen the shadow in the photo. As I walked towards the trees, Ember happily trotting along with me, I saw nothing that resembled the shape in the picture. The only thing hanging on the tree in question was a metal dreamcatcher wind charm, which had small silver charms depicting wolves, bears and cougars dangling on wire and tapping on the dreamcatcher in the breeze to create the sounds. I'd never noticed the pretty trinket before.

I headed back inside and into the shower, emerging fresh and clean a while later into a steamy bathroom. I zigzagged my hand across the mirror to clear the steam and wasn't at all surprised by the pale, drawn reflection staring back at me. My dark green eyes had completely lost their sparkle, the ugly shadowing beneath making me look tired and flat.

As I continued examining myself more closely I noticed my sallow, sunken body hadn't fared much better. My once athletic physique was now puny, my stomach inverted. I continued the process of trying to make myself look alive and, as I dried my hair, made a mental note to find a hair salon in town. The deep-red highlights were desperately in need of attention and had all but blended back to their natural dark-brown tones.

I also planned to look for a local animal shelter in the hope that I would be able to spend some time volunteering with the animals and hoped my friend, Olivia, would point me in the right direction. Liv was a fellow veterinary technician and past colleague of mine from Boston, who now worked in Manzano in what she told me was a small but busy practice.

With everything I needed to hand I left the lodge, rummaging in my bag for my cell phone as I went. I'd only had it switched on until the day I'd arrived, after which I'd decided I didn't want to hear from anyone. Not yet, anyway.

I was absent-minded as I locked up, thinking about what I needed to get from town. I'd just climbed into my car when the familiar recording of Ember's howl sounded in my purse, notifying me that I had a new message or voicemail. I slid the phone open to see I had four new text messages.

The first was from Anna, worrying about me, and asking me to call her. The next, and following two texts, were from Luke asking me to call him to talk.

My face dropped. That was *not* what I was expecting. I lowered my phone wondering what he wanted then quickly looked at the next two messages. They were from Luke again, saying that we'd made a mistake splitting up. I sat in the car staring through the windshield, surprised and lost in thought. After a few minutes I started the engine and set off towards town.

The parking on the west side of town was all road-side, offering easy access into the buildings' front entrances. Once I'd parked up, I glanced around to familiarise myself before I got out. Straight away my attention was drawn to a silver Jeep I recognised with darkened windows parked right outside the veterinary practice. This time the strange man was nowhere in sight.

I wandered into town and crossed the road when I caught a glimpse of a small store up a side street with throws hanging outside on the porch. Many of the businesses in Manzano looked like people's homes from the outside, with each room offering an array of merchandise.

I headed up the side street towards the store, and as I reached the steps to the entrance I looked up onto the porch at the variety of throws showing images of Native Americans, wolves and other mystical scenes. Full moons were very prominent on most of the items, but all the merchandise made the store seem inviting, if a little touristy.

I made my way up the wooden steps onto the porch and opened the door, a small bell announcing my arrival. The strong and fragrant smell of incense wafted out and, as I started to look around, a woman appeared from behind a small beaded curtain. She met my gaze and smiled.

'Hi there!' she announced, walking to the small counter in front of the curtain.

'Hey,' I replied, my eyes flicking around and taking in little pieces of this treasure trove.

'Can I help you with anything today?' she asked.

'Well, I'm new to the area and just checking out the local stores,' I replied.

'Oh great! So, how long have you been in Manzano?'

'Just a few days,' I replied. 'I moved here from Boston.'

'Well, it's lovely to meet with you. Welcome to Manzano,' she said, putting her hand out to formally introduce herself. 'I'm Abigail.'

'Nice to meet you, Abigail. I'm Meg,' I replied. 'You have some great things,' I said, making a move towards the shelves and rails.

'Well, feel free to browse around,' she said.

Abigail looked to be in her early to mid-forties with poker-straight, deep-red hair which sat just above her shoulders. She wore a small stud in her nose and had tanned yet smooth and wrinkle-free skin, an amazing complexion for her age.

As I scanned the bits and pieces, shuffling through jewellery, clothes, purses, books and candles, I stopped at the tarot cards.

'If you'd ever like a reading feel free to call in,' she said suddenly, drawing my attention away from the cards I'd found on the shelf. 'I'm the local reader in town. Let me know if you're ever interested in a little insight,' she continued before shifting her attention back to the newspaper she was reading on the counter.

'Oh, great, thanks,' I replied, knowing it was an offer I would refuse. I'd never be brave enough to take her up on that, even though psychic phenomena were something that had always intrigued me. I had a morbid fascination with the unknown. I loved it yet feared it at the same time. However, I was also a factual person, someone who needed to have proof. I wanted to believe in something spiritual, I think I needed to believe in it because of losing my parents, but I resisted because there was no hard evidence for it.

I was sceptical of psychics and readers, but still my weird dreams and the bizarre feelings I'd had on occasions when I was younger seemed very real. I got my first *weird* feeling when I was seven years old. My grandpa had passed away, unbeknown to any of my family. I had been playing with my toys on the upstairs landing of our house and my friend was playing a whistle, blowing mindless tunes into it. As I played, the sounds he made suddenly started to go through me, making me dizzy and light-headed. My vision became blurred and I was shaking so violently inside that I had to sit down on the top stair to stop myself falling.

Minutes later the phone rang and I heard my mother talking quietly to someone, followed by her quiet sniffling as she wept. I crept downstairs and looked through the rails on the staircase, peering into the kitchen where my dad stood next to my mom, his arms wrapped tightly around her as she cried into his shoulder.

That was the first of several such events. Each time I'd had an *episode* like this, something bad was announced shortly afterwards. It wasn't always directly associated with my close family but, sadly, it often was.

As the years passed and I grew up, I learned to understand what was happening when my dizzy spells came. I knew how to deal with them. I just had to wait for the aftermath of misery to follow. I had never once had a funny turn for no reason; something bad always happened.

The last time this feeling struck was the day my parents were involved in a fatal road accident. They had gone out on their motor cycle on a fine, sunny day in Portland, planning to camp out for a few days. I had just celebrated my eighteenth birthday and was pleased to have some time on my own with my then boyfriend. The elderly driver of the truck had not been paying attention as he pulled out of the junction, taking them both off their bike. The worst part was that he'd barely hit them: it was the type of impact – a sideways shove – that had killed them, throwing them both into the path of an oncoming vehicle. My dad had lived for three days in the critical care unit, but his injuries had proved too much for his body and he died. My mom had been killed outright. With no siblings or close relatives for support, I was pretty much left alone.

I suspected there was more to our souls than we'd ever know but, on the rational side, I'd never heard from either of my parents. I only wished I had; I could have taken comfort from it.

'I'll take these for now,' I said, heading towards the counter with a book on the history of Manzano and the surrounding area and a couple of chunky scented candles. 'You have some great things,' I said, placing the items on the counter and taking out my wallet.

'Thanks,' Abigail replied, wrapping the items in bags. 'I hope to see you again soon,' she continued, smiling and fixing her gaze on me a little too long for my liking.

'Sure. Bye for now.' I took my paper bag from the counter and turned for the door.

After another hour shopping I headed for the bookstore and spent the next half hour inside buying some novels along with a book on Californian wildlife and one on local hiking spots. After satisfying my shopping needs and feeling pretty tired, I headed home.

I reached the steep drive and started the climb up to the parking area, happy now that the clearance on my old Toyota SUV was ample. At the top I looked through the passenger-side window towards the lodge and saw Ember watching my return through the window, his head stuck between the slats of the blinds which, thankfully, were still hanging up.

As soon as I opened the door Ember shot out, swishing his tail in excitement and anticipation, sniffing me to check where I'd been. I gave him a chew stick and went to offer Ned one of his treats. He was sitting on the back of the couch with his tail high in the air, twitching, looking past me towards the door.

I smiled as the kids entertained themselves with their treats, took my cell out of my bag, and perched on one of the kitchen chairs. No new texts, one new voice message. *Here we go,* I thought as I slid the phone open.

I clicked the retrieve button and lifted the phone to my ear, waiting uncomfortably for the message to filter through.

You have one new message, received today at 11:46 a.m.
Hey, it's me, again. Please can you call me, I really need to talk to you. I know you probably don't want to but, please, call me. Love you.

I pressed the end call button and put my cell on the table, staring at it as if it were about to jump up and bite me. To hear the familiar tone of Luke's deep, intense voice threw me right back to Boston and our old life together.

I idly rubbed my fingertips on the table, thinking, wondering, and then picked the phone up. I ran through the contacts list and hit the button when I found his name. My finger hovered over the green call symbol as if it were willing me to press it. My eyes blurred as I imagined the expected conversation in my head and I just stared unblinking at his name on the screen.

I didn't dare press it. I didn't want to hear the voice that would bring him whooshing back into the forefront of my mind. I was torn between wanting to call him and wanting to ignore him at all costs, for fear that hearing him would throw me all the way back to the beginning and exactly what I was trying to escape.

No, I was not calling him. It was the wrong thing to do right now. But my finger overrode my brain.

Nervously, I pressed once, and waited for the call to be answered.

'Meg,' the relieved voice said. It'd barely rung once before he picked up. 'Thanks for calling me.'

'What is it, Luke?' I asked, desperately trying to sound uninterested.

'Are you okay?' he asked.

'Yeah, I'm fine. What do you want, Luke?' I had to keep up the facade.

'I…well, where do I start? At the beginning, I guess. Okay, well, I think we made a huge mistake,' he replied.

'Oh. Well, I think it's a little bit too late since I moved to California already,' I said sarcastically.

'I just think we should still be together, and I don't think that place is right for you either. It's all wrong you being there. We both made mistakes; I have, and will, regret mine for the rest of my time.' His voice wavered off, as if he were trying to control his emotions.

Control and patience had not been one of Luke's most endearing features over the last year, the highlight being about a month before I left Boston. That night he came home well into the early hours stinking of booze and with a ripped and blood-soaked shirt. By that point I'd had enough of his erratic mood swings and stressed outbursts. I had let rip at him, the worry and anger getting the better of my honest but sharp tongue. His reaction? Well, he landed me a quick and solid right hook which threw me a good distance across our kitchen and turned me into an unattractive, swollen, cut-mouthed ex-girlfriend. There and then it was all over. That one – but by anyone's account – vicious second was all it took for me to make my final decision.

'Please Meg, forgive me. I will do anything you ask. I'll sell the business. We can move away somewhere else, anywhere you want, anything. Please just give me another chance.'

'Well, you know what Luke; I think we're a little late for all that. I'm living thousands of miles away now, the legal stuff is going through, the deal's done. Not even to mention the months and months of shit we went through when you made no attempt to repair *us*.' My voice started to waver at the *us* part, a shame as it'd been such a promising start at the beginning of my spiel.

'But we just got it a little wrong along the way. It happens, and I've realised that.'

That did it. The tears flooded and stung my eyes. All the tension and sadness I'd been holding back so well for the last month had found an exit, and his voice was the only trigger I'd needed. I forced myself to sob silently. I could not let him hear me hurting; I couldn't waver now.

He kept his silence on the other end of the phone. I didn't know what state he was in but I could imagine. It took all my will to halt the tears and bring my voice back to a normal tone.

'Luke, I...' I stopped, regrouped and took a deep breath.

'I think we had our time. I think we miss what was familiar more than we miss each other. It's over now. We can't go back. Too much has changed.'

'No, no, it can't be. I can't function without you. We are two halves of the same whole,' he said, his usual persuasive tone coming through. 'Please, let's give it another go. Please, Meg.'

'But it all went so horribly wrong, Luke. We...*I* need to change too much to go back now and that isn't fair on either of us. We've both been through so much,' I said, trying my hardest to be sincere.

'Okay, look. I know this is hard and not a decision to make lightly, and, believe me, I hear what you're saying, but promise me one thing,' he asked.

I took a deep sigh, preparing for what was to come. 'What, Luke?' I asked, my voice coming out more like an annoyed breath.

'Just promise me you'll think about how we were in the beginning, how happy we were together. I promise it could be like that again, better than that. Think about it. Take our life together through your head from the start and *then* answer me,' he said with more confidence, more defiance in his voice.

'Okay, okay. Yes, I will think about it. I promise you that much. I still care enough about you to consider it, but right now I need this time alone to evaluate things for myself, away from you, to decide what *I* want and make sure I'm doing the right thing,' I said, gaining a little strength in knowing I held the deciding cards.

'That's all I ask,' he said. 'I'll leave it to you to ring me but please don't leave me suffering too long, Meg. I can't bear this.'

'Okay, I'll call you. Just give me time,' I said, prepared to say anything to stop what almost seemed like him begging me.

'Okay, well, later then. I love you,' he said, knowing he could say or do no more.

'Take care, Luke. Bye,' was all I could muster. I quickly pressed the end call button.

I remained sitting at the table, tossing the whole conversation around in my head, trying to decide what hearing his voice did to me. But I didn't cry again for Luke. Why didn't I cry? I sat for ages before deciding that to stick to my end of the bargain, and to really think about *us*, I needed to think about *me* first and take some time out, on my own, in my new home.

I could be wrongly influenced at times, led by my heart more than my head, and this could so easily have been one of those occasions. But whenever I thought about the many fantastic times we'd shared over the last six years those thoughts always became darkly overshadowed by the one *bad* time. The fact that he had completely lost his temper and hit me.

That side of Luke had been brewing, building up before my eyes for months, only I figured he'd sort his head out as he always had in the past when stress got the better of him. He'd changed; he'd let himself go, and the drinking and staying out was only one small part of the problem. His eyes became angrier and distant and he got into fights at bars. Exhibit (a) a blood-splattered shirt and a busted nose. Only three days later, exhibit (b) two broken fingers and another ruined set of clothes. Could all that stress and pressure really just go away? That bad-tempered new side of him? Inside I really doubted it could. Maybe that's why I didn't cry again for Luke.

My attention was drawn to Ember as he jumped onto the couch, rubbing his face on the cushions in post-treat pleasure before collapsing with a contented, yet stupid, grin. Ned jumped onto the window sill and sat gracefully with his tail wrapped around him as he peered through the blinds.

With little resistance I made my way upstairs and lay on the bed. My head ached. The soft duvet moulded itself around my heavy body and, as I pushed all the worry and thoughts out of my head, my breathing deepened. I got one more vision, one more flash in my head before my eyes shut. It was of the strange man from town. Behind my eyelids I could see his profile so clearly: his white skin and dark hair.

Repeatedly I thought of him, his face following me as I fell into the nothingness of sleep.

Chapter 4

I woke with a start and let out a barely audible gasp. I'd slept for over six hours; it was almost dark outside. I tapped the light on and stretched before I looked around the room. No Ember, no Ned. Hmmm.

I lay for a moment feeling disoriented, but much more rested and relaxed. I twisted up and sat on the edge of the bed looking out of the window towards the twinkling lights of the houses on the hillside. I got up and strolled warily downstairs to check on the kids. Ember looked to have slept as long as I had, but Ned was seated in the same position, watching out of the window.

With my hair tied up, I went to work on the remaining boxes, renewed and adamant that I would unpack them all before I slept again. It was after midnight before I had everything out and in place, and as I looked over the rooms, it hit me that it actually looked like my home now and not just a holiday rental.

I leaned against the kitchen counter to drink a cup of hot chocolate as Ember wandered around outside, paying his last visit of the night. After a few minutes, I peered through the little porthole window in the front door expecting to see him waiting to be let in. No sign. I grabbed my sweater off the back of the couch, sliding it over my head as I went, and opened the door to peer around the yard. 'Ember, come on,' I called, pausing to listen for any sign of him. A no show.

With the door closed behind me, I headed down the path to search for him, expecting to find him either in a major sniffathon and refusing to obey, or lying down somewhere, detaching the legs off an ill-fated cricket. Still no sign.

I walked up to the highest part of the yard where I parked the car, which allowed the best viewpoint, and looked around for any sign of him. He was standing facing away from me a few feet down the drive, his head dropped low and his hackles raised; his eyes were locked onto something at the back of the lodge.

I gulped but didn't dare call his name. He didn't hear me approaching, or at least he didn't acknowledge hearing me, anyway. As soon as I was alongside him, his attention broke, and he turned and bolted back over the path and behind the trees towards the bunkhouse.

I ran after him and as I turned round the corner I saw his face following something as it moved down the hillside. The way his head shifted, whatever he'd seen must have moved fast. I tentatively walked after him, my eyes flitting all around to see what he was looking at, my heart racing as I moved.

As I got closer, he ran over to the bunkhouse decking and peered through the railing down into the trees, tail raised, body stiff, watching. I saw nothing and wondered if he'd spotted a wild animal, something that was maybe too big to investigate close up.

I walked up behind him and took hold of his collar, turning to drag him back to the lodge. As I walked away, I glanced back once but whatever it was had long gone.

Once all safely locked inside, I chastised him, mainly for scaring me more than for disobeying me, and grabbed a couple of my new books to take upstairs. I changed and jumped into bed, instantly picking up a novel as a weapon to keep my mind occupied.

Ned stayed downstairs, but I knew he would make his way up sometime through the night. By the time I switched the lamp off, it was after 2 a.m. I turned onto my side, yawned, and sleepily stared towards the distant lights. I stared, numb and still, listening to the steady tick of the clock above the fireplace before sleep, thankfully, took me.

I woke in the night to a loud solid thud, and a cat yowling and hissing. I lay completely still, my eyes wide as I stopped breathing to listen. But the noises had stopped. Ember was gone, and there was no sign of Ned. As I stared through the darkness, trying to let my eyes adjust, a large shadow came into focus, making its way slowly up the stairs. It appeared to be hunched over itself, keeping low, heading in my direction.

I gulped and watched the shadow through the railing until it reached the section of the stairs out of my line of sight, around the corner. I moved my hand to the bedside table reaching for my cell; I'd left it downstairs. I tapped at the touch light constantly, but it didn't come on. As the dark figure reached the top of the stairs, it started to unfold, growing slowly taller and facing my direction.

I scrambled back across the bed, getting caught in the sheets as I went, trying to create some distance, but the shape effortlessly and fluidly moved towards me, as if it were floating. It was in front of me in a split second. I stared at it, gasping for air, seeing nothing but a black silhouette hovering before me.

A rush of cold air hit my skin, freezing me instantly. I leaned back as far as I could, lifted my eyes upwards and saw two distinct glistening eyes looking right at me. I felt the slightest tickle across my forehead and stumbled off the bed, backing frantically towards the wall, screaming as loud as I could and hoping that in this sparsely populated place someone would hear my cry for help.

I kept screaming until I jolted upright, turning my head towards the stairs, my heart racing, my whole body wringing wet from sweat. There was nothing there. I tapped the base of the light hard; it came on. I had sweat pouring from my whole body, yet I was freezing cold and shivering.

I searched back to the bed to see Ember lying beside me. He was staring at me, puzzled by my behaviour even though my dreams didn't often startle him anymore. I started to calm down, realising immediately that I had been dreaming, and ran my hands over my face and through my soaking hair, trying hard to regulate my breathing.

I glanced at the clock. 4:20 a.m. I tapped the light down to the dimmest setting and lay back down, hoping to settle with the light on. The next thing I knew, it was 7:35 a.m. The morning sun was glaring in through the window. The lamp shone dull in the daylight that outshone it, and Ember was stretching out beside me.

I lay in bed remembering the dream, recalling in detail the horror of the night. I quickly put the thought aside, and tried to think of nothing but what I was going to do that day. I had already found a local park about twenty minutes drive away for Ember and me to go hiking in.

I ate a small breakfast and readied myself for the walk, gathering Ember's travel dish and filling a plastic bottle with fresh water. I loaded my backpack with my usual walking accessories and camera, and slipped some cash and my cell into the side pockets before changing into my walking boots, ready to go.

With the map on the dash to show me the way, we set off through the estate, taking a right onto the highway. Ember sat in the passenger seat with his head out of the window, his lips flaring in the wind, to my constant amusement.

We travelled about twelve miles with the sparse traffic until we reached the turn for Ysabel National Park, and spent the morning enjoying our first of many hikes in our new home.

About an hour later, we were back at the car. I poured Ember some fresh water, which he drank instantly. I shut the trunk and got back into the car. I swung the car round, leaving the way I'd come, and headed out along the long track back to the main road.

Once home, Ember, with renewed energy, skipped into the lodge and straight up to Ned, who sat on the table awaiting our return. I unloaded my gear from the backpack, and busied myself refreshing water and putting the teakettle on. I grabbed my cell off the counter and searched for Anna's home number. With coffee in hand, I headed to the couch, mentally preparing for our conversation.

'Hey, you,' the voice said after a few rings.

'Hey,' I replied, thrilled to hear her familiar voice.

Our conversation lasted about half an hour, covering Cam, the kids and how I was doing in my new place. When the inevitable subject of Luke came up, I changed it quickly, snapping a little at Anna for even mentioning it; she knew not to push the discussion.

With another necessary conversation out of the way I relaxed, knowing I had the rest of the day to myself, and pottered around until it was time for dinner. Before the light gave way to dark again, I gathered some logs from the back of the lodge and set the wood burner going. I dug out a bunch of DVDs, showered, changed into my warm, thick nightclothes and fleecy robe, and set the washer going. I tidied the kitchen and, armed with chocolate, went to settle on the couch next to a tired but contented husky. Leaning back into the deep couch, I relaxed, watching one of my ultimate chick flicks, Sweet Home Alabama, wishing my life could be more like that of the female lead.

Not long after the movie was over, I made my way to bed, tapping the lamp down to the dimmest glow and settling back to read. I only managed a dozen pages or so before my eyelids grew heavy and I began re-reading the paragraphs. I slid the book on the bedside table and tapped the light off, so exhausted from our hike that my mind didn't have time to conjure up anxiety about more dreams. Thankfully, I had the best night's sleep since I'd arrived, dreamless and peaceful.

The next day passed in a flash. Ember and I headed out to the same park, this time following the orange route, taking us into deeper woodland territory on a longer, harder hike. In the afternoon, I text my friend Liv, who replied instantly, and arranged for us to meet up the next day for a long lunch in town.

Liv was a bundle of fun – too much fun. She was three years younger than me and we'd hit it off immediately when she came to work with me in Boston, quickly becoming inseparable. She had a habit of following boyfriends around the country and enjoyed being young, free and single, which meant she never stayed anywhere for too long. We hadn't seen each other in almost two years, since she'd left Boston and moved to the town practice to be close to her then boyfriend, who lived in San Diego. It was never going to last, but Liv didn't give a shit; she just enjoyed him while it lasted and moved on to the next cute ass.

I think I saw in Liv what I wanted to be – well, at one time anyway. But I never had the confidence to be as free and unconcerned as she was. The one bit of permanence in her life, though, was California; she loved it and that's why she was still here.

I made my way into Manzano just before noon the next day, after making great effort to look like I was fit and well, and had spent no time getting ready, even though it had taken me a good hour applying tons of makeup to give me that natural, un-made-up look!

When I arrived at the veterinary practice where I was meeting Liv, the sweltering heat hit me as I opened the car door. I nervously wandered through the door into the air-conditioned reception and approached the desk. A smiling face looked up at me.

'Hi, I'm here to see Liv,' I said to the deeply tanned receptionist.

'Oh, Hi. You must be Meg. Liv mentioned you'd be calling in. Take a seat and I'll go tell her you're here.'

'Thank you,' I said, looking around the practice and making my way to the nearest chair. I looked at the posters and displays while I waited and, a short time later, the same smiling face returned.

'She's just finishing up out back. She'll be with you in a few minutes.'

'That's great, thanks,' I said, grabbing a magazine and settling into my seat. As I flicked randomly through, I heard a door opening.

'Mr Miller, please,' a deep voice said, and I turned to look towards the direction of it.

All I could see was the back of a very tall, dark-haired man, holding the door open for a client and his German shepherd to go through. He wore a black, fitted polo shirt, which was tucked into a pair of navy cargo pants. His dark brown hair was just above his shoulders, unruly, almost windswept.

As I looked over at him, I realised who I was looking at: it was the same man I had seen previously leaning into the trunk of his car. After the client walked through with his dog, the veterinarian paused in the doorway and twisted his head ever so slightly down and to the side, allowing me to catch another glimpse of his pale, gaunt profile. He stood like that for no more than a second, his mouth slightly parted, almost as if he were about to mutter something to himself.

As he moved into the room, the last thing I saw was a long, muscular arm, with leather binding wrapped around his wrist below his watch. I sat looking towards the door with a vivid mental picture of the pale profile embedded in my head.

'Hey, you!' a familiar voice said, making me jump as she brought my attention back to the present.

'Hey!' I said, standing up and heading towards Liv, opening my arms in preparation for our embrace.

We chatted animatedly for a few minutes in the waiting room, with Liv commenting on how well I looked (thank God my great attempts at looking natural had paid off) and asked me where I wanted to go for lunch. We both agreed on Italian and Liv said she knew a nice little place just on the edge of town so we left the practice and headed out towards the restaurant.

Liv looked great, as usual. She'd always had the funkiest of hair styles known to man and this time was no exception. Her almost black hair was cut short at the back, lengthening to choppy long points at the sides, one much longer than the other, with a thick, edgy fringe to one side. She was the one girl I knew who could pull off just about any hairstyle – even a shaved head would look great on her. I was pleased that she'd bagged an extra half-hour that she was owed to lengthen our lunch.

We walked through town, talking constantly without pausing for breath. Once inside the restaurant, we didn't stop. The restaurant was fairly busy but we managed to grab a small table near the window, and both ordered pasta and ice cold drinks.

'So,' I started 'how are things? Work, men, tell me all.'

'Ah, you know, same old, same old,' she said, bobbing her head smiling. 'My job's the best and, I know you won't believe me, but I'm single so I've been spending loads of time in the city with friends. Seriously Meg, California is awesome: the shopping, the nightlife, the climate – what more could a girl ask for!'

'Well, that sounds like you. So, I take it Rob is long gone?'

'Rob?' she asked, puzzled.

'You know, Rob, the guy you originally moved to California for?' I could not help a wry smile at her, shaking my head in despair.

'Oh, Rob, yeah, I'd forgotten about him. Well, that lasted, like, two months or something after I moved out here. You know, San Diego has a lot to offer so I kinda got bored,' she said, grinning wickedly at me. I knew exactly what she meant; I always did. 'Anyway, so you're here and Luke isn't. What's that all about?'

'Long story,' I said, looking down at my newly delivered soda, 'and one better saved for another time.' I knew there would be another time; Liv would not let that conversation go. She'd thought we'd be together forever.

'You got it,' she replied. One thing about Liv, she always knew when to leave something alone.

'So, you, single…how did *that* happen?' I asked, actually pretty surprised.

'Well, yeah, I am…for now. Not been seeing anyone for at least a few weeks,' she said, shaking her head. 'Wow! I'm gonna be an old spinster soon, taking home loads of stray cats from work.'

'Liv, you're 25 years old!' I started laughing, uncontrollably. It was a great release, and one I desperately needed.

'I know! But in California, you're like, over the hill by thirty,' she said.

'Great!' I said, rolling my eyes and slamming back dramatically into my seat. 'I've had it then; I'm 29 in November. I should just go ahead and move to Florida!'

'Well, you know, I feel sorry for you, babe, I really do, but going for nights out with someone your age bodes well for me with the men,' she said, leaning to pitifully and playfully pat my arm.

'Oh, whatever!' I said, laughing harder.

By the time our food arrived, my stomach was aching from laughing. 'So, tell me more about your job. Any cute guys there you plan on stealing from their girlfriends?'

'Hey! I only did that once…Okay, twice, but what can I say? If they were happy, they wouldn't have strayed, would they? Anyway, are you kidding me? My boss, William, he's the best, but at 76, even *I'd* be setting my personal best if I went after him! The only other man in the practice is Gabe, and he's pretty hot but he's not my type. He's the distant, mean and moody type; I couldn't be bothered with all that. I like the shallow, easygoing types.'

'Ah, right. I think I saw him while I was waiting for you in the practice. Tall, dark hair, pale?' I asked, knowing only too well that was him. So, now I had a name for him at least.

'Yeah, that's Gabe. He's a little on the lean side for my liking, but, oh my, he does have a smoking body. When we're doing ranch work, or physical stuff in the practice, you can see his muscles tensing. That's why I never complain about going out to see the horses with him, or watching him lug a heavy dog around on his own. Anyway…' she said, realising she was talking too fast and becoming a little flushed in the face.

I laughed again. Liv never could grasp the fact that a great personality counted for a lot – more than looks sometimes – in my book, anyway. But, even having only seen him a couple of times, I already knew exactly what she meant.

We chatted non-stop as we ate our lunch and by the time we'd finished we'd arranged a night out in town the following Saturday with one of Liv's work colleagues, Maria. We agreed that I would meet them outside the practice at eight and then we would head to the bars in town. Liv had also given me rough directions for the local animal shelter, where I planned to offer my services as a volunteer, helping however I could.

When we got to my car, we hugged and giggled, and then she darted back to work, ten minutes late. I jumped in my car and headed home, ready for some fresh air with Ember.

As we walked around the local park, just outside of town, I decided that, if I were to be going out in public, I needed some new clothes, and planned a trip to the mall in Chula Vista on Friday.

The evening passed quickly, and I even pushed my limited culinary skills to new heights, grilling a nice well-done fillet mignon with all the trimmings, Ember and Ned naughtily enjoying the leftovers.

I settled down in my fleecy robe on the couch, twisting up and around Ember's curled-up body, with Ned alongside on my cushion, and watched another movie. It wasn't much after ten when I called it a night, and, within five minutes, was comfortably tucked up in bed, my sidekicks in tow. I managed about four pages of my book before I flicked the lamp off.

I woke in the dark to Ember's low grumbles. Listening hard, I could make out what sounded like the creak of a wooden door. I lay listening for several moments before I crept down to the wide step halfway down the stairs and peered out into the yard. I saw nothing; the only wooden door outside belonged to the bunkhouse. As I looked in that direction, everything was still. I pushed my ghoulish thoughts to the over-imaginative back of my mind and went back to bed.

On Friday, I headed to the mall and bought too many clothes, all going-out pieces, along with some new makeup and a couple of perfumes. I found the cutest top (which had cost a small fortune) that would look fantastic with my jeans.

So, by Saturday, I was completely hyped-up for my night out with the girls and started to get myself ready far too early.

With the CD playing loud in the kitchen, I showered, using a little bit of every product I had lying around to buff and moisturise my skin. I clambered out into the cool, shaded bathroom and dried off, feeling excited about the coming evening.

When the mirror was cleared of steam, and with my hair bundled into a towel, I went to work, starting with my eyebrows. It was going to take some time. 'It's a beautiful lie,' I sang to myself, rubbing foundation into my skin. 'It's a perfect denial,' I continued, enjoying the old routine of getting ready.

I hadn't bothered with myself in months and it was starting to show. But with the extended pampering time, things were starting to improve. I worked on some smoky eye shadow, defined with black eye liner, and added a slick of mascara to finish off my look.

With my long chocolate hair in ragged twists, the gray eye shadow complementing my green eyes and the black strapless top, I felt pretty pleased with how I looked. A first in a long time.

I spent the final half-hour seeing to the kids, letting Ember out for a wander about, while Ned nervously watched me move round the lodge. I sprayed perfume over me – again – and applied a slick of natural tinted gloss to my lips. Ned twitched his tail, as he did when he was anxious, and followed me around meowing and pestering.

I gave him and Ember each a treat, then loaded my cash, card, and cell into my purse and made for the door. As much as I wanted to have a drink, driving was probably the best option for me. I did not need a few drinks inside me right now, bringing suppressed emotions to the surface. I'd managed to barely think about Luke since our conversation the other day and needed to keep it that way. The last thing I wanted to do was call him in an inebriated state, swearing undying love and pledging to go back to Boston, only to wake up the next morning, or afternoon, and have to crawl beneath the sheets at what I'd done.

No, I couldn't allow that to happen. No men. No hassle. Just *me* time with no distractions.

Although, if I knew Liv, I might not have a choice.

Chapter 5

I drove past the crossroads to the far end of town, where I was meeting Liv and her friend, Maria. I glanced at the clock; it was ten to eight. A little early, but not so early that it made me appear desperate. Manzano was surprisingly busy, buzzing with people, and so the car parking spaces were limited. I swung into a space a little way up from the practice and turned the engine off, looking around nervously for her familiar face. I pulled my cell out, checking messages to pass the time.

Saturday June 30. 6:02 p.m. Sender: Anna
Hey honey, how are things? Got some dates to come stay, call me to arrange. Miss you. A xxx

I smiled at my phone, thinking about Anna, and almost jumped out of my skin as someone loudly tapped on the passenger window. It was Liv, beaming at me as she caught my startled expression. I smiled back, returned my cell to my purse, and jumped out.

'Hey, made you jump,' she said, walking around to the driver's side of the car. She reached out and hugged me as I got out, still giggling.

'This is Maria,' she said, stepping aside to introduce her friend.

'Hey Maria, great to meet you,' I said.

'Hi, nice to meet you too,' she replied, her huge white smile dazzling me. Maria looked a little older than me, probably in her mid-thirties. She was dressed in a coral top and jeans, and her curly dark-blonde shoulder-length hair sprung out all over, looking unintentionally wild. She had very chiselled features, high cheek bones and the prettiest hazel eyes. Her accent didn't ring true to California and as we all chatted walking towards the first bar a slight New York twang came through in certain words.

We arrived outside the bar at the far end of town and, as we walked in, it reminded me of a bar I'd visited in New York the previous year with Luke: private booths along the walls, high stools around the bar, music playing and a baseball game showing quietly on the big screen. There were quite a few people inside and I instantly went into my self-conscious mode, lowering my head and following at the back of Liv and Maria.

'Hey, Tom,' Liv said to the barman.

'Hey, Liv, Maria. How's it going?' he replied, smiling widely at all of us.

'Good, man. It's all good. I'd like you to meet Meg. She's an old friend of mine who's new in town so I thought we'd come have a drink, you know, show her the local haunts,' Liv said, smiling widely back at him.

'Hi Meg. Great to meet you,' he said, leaning forward to shake my hand.

'Great to meet you too,' I replied, smiling as best I could and trying hard to mentally block out the staring eyes. I returned the handshake, feeling shy and nervous as several people looked directly at me to see who this new girl was that Tom was talking to.

Maria seemed to sense my discomfort and leaned in to whisper in my ear: 'Don't worry. They'll get bored of staring real soon,' she said, smiling so warmly I couldn't help but exhale nervously and smile back.

Liv and Maria were about the same height, both about five foot four, making me stand out even more at five foot nine, with nowhere to shelter and hide from snooping eyes.

Tom was a fairly tall, well-built and muscular man. He looked to be in his late thirties, with very short light-brown hair and deep-blue eyes.

'So, you girls hitting *both* bars in Manzano in the one night then?' he asked, grinning. Little did he know it was still more bars than I'd visited in the last six months.

'Well, hell, yeah,' Liv said, turning to me. 'It won't take us long,' she added dryly.

I laughed along before Tom asked us what we would like to drink.

'Maria and I will have the usual, please, Tom, and Meg...'

'Erm, a Malibu and Coke, tall glass with ice, please,' I replied.

The eyes of the strangers in the bar had thankfully tired of this far-from-exciting newcomer and their interest had returned to the game on TV, much to my relief. Tom told us to grab a table and he'd bring the drinks over.

We sat at a nearby booth where I shuffled around, getting comfortable. It was a really nice bar, something I didn't expect to see in Manzano, very inviting and relaxing.

Maria slid in next to me rather than Liv, in an attempt to offer security, I thought. We all chatted easily about trivial stuff and I got the impression Liv had told Maria a little about why I had moved here. I was sure she would have done this in order to save any awkward questions.

Tom brought the drinks over and placed them in front of us, on top of the paper coasters he'd laid out. I was dying for this drink. He'd barely put my glass down when I tilted it and tipped the brown fluid down my throat, half-gone already.

'So, you'd be thirsty, then,' he said, grinning.

'Sorry,' I replied, 'Just ready for a drink, I guess,' I said, smiling subtly back before he left us to it.

'Well, why don't you leave your car in town and I'll drop you off at home?' Liv offered. 'That way, you can drink all you want tonight.'

'It's a tempting offer. I'll see how I feel after the next one,' I smiled, knowing I could drink all night long but that it was best not to.

'Well, it's no problem. You're only a couple of miles at most out of town. You can walk that in no time or I can collect you early in the morning before I start work and drop you off for your car,' she said.

'Okay. That'd be great,' I agreed, a little too eagerly. Bang went the no-drinking rule.

As we chatted on about clothes, music and movies we'd seen, all easy non-prying topics, something turned their conversation towards work. My ears pricked up.

'Hey, so what was Gabe's problem today?' Liv asked Maria. 'He was in such a foul mood; I don't think he spoke to anyone.'

'Ah, who knows,' Maria replied, tilting her head to one side and shrugging. 'He's gotten even more distant in the last few weeks, if that's possible. Did you see his friend who stopped by today?' she asked Liv.

'No! When was that? Where was I?' Liv replied, suddenly distraught she'd missed something going on.

'Late morning, this really tall blonde guy came in with Gabe. They headed into William's office and Jen heard raised voices. Five minutes later, the man came storming out. Jen said he was as white as a ghost when he left. Must have been some argument,' Maria said, leaning in towards Liv as she told the tale, pleased that Liv had not witnessed the incident herself.

'Nooo! I wonder what all that was about?' Liv stared at her drink for a few seconds, probably trying to think up the wildest explanation she could, knowing her. 'Was he hot?' she asked quickly, her one-track mind kicking in.

'Well, not my type. He was tall and skinny and had the deepest blue eyes. He had an accent, too, and he wore this black leather jacket, which looked a bit out of place in eighty-plus-degrees Manzano,' she said.

'Ooh, an accent. I like a nice accent,' Liv said giddily.

'You like a nice anything, Liv,' I said, smirking at her shallowness when it came to men.

We huddled closer together, chatting and giggling like high school girls. As the chat flowed, so did the drinks. I didn't miss the odd fleeting 'look' between Liv and Tom every time he delivered our order, which I planned on bringing to her attention later in the evening.

After another half hour, we all decided to move on.

We downed the last of our drinks and stood to leave. I put on my jacket, having already learned how chilly the evenings got in the mountains, and we all headed for the door.

'See you later!' Liv and Maria called to Tom, waving and also saying their goodbyes to others in the bar they knew.

'Later,' Tom said, looking at us, raising his hands and giving a smiling nod, adding, 'nice to meet you Meg.'

'You too,' I replied, smiling back, as I followed Liv and Maria towards the door.

It was a much cooler night, the coldest I'd felt since I arrived, which was surprising considering it had been such a hot day. As we wandered over the road and back towards the practice side of town, I saw in the distance the subtle sign of another bar, the one we must be headed for. The Budweiser sign swung gently in the evening breeze.

'So, you and Tom seem quite familiar,' I said to Liv, raising my eyebrows.

'Ah,' she replied, smiling and leaning towards me. 'Well, we kinda had a thing a while ago but, to be honest, it wasn't really leading anywhere,' she continued. 'Is it that obvious?'

'Erm, kinda,' I replied, smiling.

'I actually really like him, but he got divorced, like, two years ago and I am a little unsure about things,' she said, in a hush, as if he could hear her.

We chatted more as we walked and I learned another thing that put me at ease. There was never any crime in Manzano, certainly nothing big-scale, just the odd alcohol-fuelled fight and a few loud car stereos as the high school kids drove around looking for something to do.

We walked into the next bar and the warmth hit me as we swung through the saloon-style doors. It looked a lot less city-like inside. The low wooden booths were less modern and more rough-and-ready in appearance. It had an inviting feel to it, though, and was also quite busy with locals, young and old alike, chatting and watching the game on TV. The music coming from a jukebox was more prominent, with a country song being the current selection.

We wandered over to the bar, with me following Liv and Maria as before and again feeling a little stared at. I had not yet had enough drinks to gain confidence and raise my head from my typical shy pose. I took a deep breath and followed them through the groups of people.

'Hi, Ed,' Liv said, in a familiar tone. 'How are you?'

'Hey, Liv, Maria. I'm good thanks. How are you guys doing tonight?'

'Great, thanks,' Liv replied. 'This is Meg. She's new to the area, so I'm showing her around,' she said, looking at Ed and then me.

'Hello,' I said, a bit too formally, my nerves kicking in again.

'Hi, Meg, It's nice to meet you,' he said.

'You too,' I replied, starting to carefully eye around to see if my entrance had been noticed. People were coming and going, and I could hear the sprung wooden doors opening and scratching a little as they closed.

'So, guys, what can I get you?'

'Can I get a Coke, no ice, a white wine and…' Liv looked towards me for my answer.

'Malibu and Coke with ice, please,' I finished.

We looked around for somewhere to sit, spotting a free table around the side of the bar, and waited for our drinks to arrive. As Ed placed the drinks on the bar, I retrieved mine quickly and took a massive swig.

'I'll get those,' an easy, deep voice said from behind us.

Liv turned quickly towards the voice, her smile wide with recognition. I lowered my drink slowly to the bar and tentatively turned my head, looking straight up into the darkest pair of eyes.

'Gabe,' Liv said in a flirty voice.

'How's it going, Olivia…Maria?' he asked, looking towards each of them in turn and nodding. As the three of them spoke, I found myself staring at his face, unable to turn my eyes away. I was transfixed by his pale, gaunt skin and his dark brown eyes, which were deeply set and framed by heavy brows. Something about his odd look was mesmerising.

'Well, it's nice to see you out in town,' Liv said, still grinning widely.

Ed hovered in the background, which caught Gabe's attention. 'Can I get two beers, please?' he asked.

'Coming right up,' Ed said, turning to go get the order.

As soon as he'd ordered, Gabe turned his eyes in my direction, instantly meeting my gaze. I flicked my eyes away and took hold of my glass, taking a long drink. I began to feel unwell, almost dizzy, in a similar way as I'd felt as a child when something bad was going to happen, the shaking happening deep inside my body.

'Oh, sorry guys,' Liv apologised. 'Gabe, this is Meg. She is, sorry, *was*, a fellow technician and friend of mine from Boston; she's just moved here. Meg, this is Gabe, one of our veterinarians.' When she looked back at me, she widened her eyes as if to say 'this is him.'

'Meg…nice to meet you,' he said, nodding, his mouth twitching at the edges into a small smile. His eyes looked guarded, distant as he stared down at me, completely motionless as he'd been the previous time I'd seen him.

'You too,' were the only words I could find before I averted my eyes and took another drink.

I looked towards Liv, searching for some kind of reassurance in a familiar face, but her eyes were on someone else now: the tall, blond man who stood silently behind Gabe. I saw a flicker of recognition on Maria's face as she too looked towards the stranger.

He had short, thick, dirty blond hair and dark blue eyes. He was very slim and sunken in his frame, yet strangely, he had a strong appearance, as did Gabe. His side burns grew low down his jaw, which he clenched constantly, like he too was feeling uncomfortable about being a newcomer in the bar. This must have been the man who'd been at the surgery with Gabe earlier that day; the same one Maria said had left speedily after an argument.

'I must apologise,' Gabe said, turning his body towards the blond man. 'May I introduce my friend, Sebastian. He's visiting from out of town,' Gabe said, not making eye contact with his friend.

We all acknowledged Sebastian but it was Liv who, as usual, did the talking.

'So, Sebastian, out of town. Where would that be?' she asked.

'I am from France, originally, but I live in Sacramento now,' he said. His accent was distinct but he had very good English. 'Gabe and I go back a long way,' he continued.

'Cool,' Liv replied, 'you here for work or vacation?' she asked. I'm not sure if it was just my own impression, but he seemed to look a little annoyed by her questioning.

His face finally crumpled into a faint, knowing smile as he replied, 'A little of both, I fear,' he said, glancing over to the side of Gabe's face, which remained poker-straight. He was still staring right at me.

'Oh, well, if you'd care to join us, you're welcome,' Liv said, much to my discomfort. *Please don't say yes*, I thought.

Gabe kept his eyes on me as he replied to Liv's question. 'Thank you for the invite, but, no, we have business to discuss and not very interesting business at that,' he said, smiling slowly, and showing just a tiny bit of his white teeth, his full lips stretching over them in almost a smirk. Liv just grinned.

'Well, okay, thanks for the drinks, anyway,' she said, quickly, followed by Maria's thanks. I just smiled shyly, focusing on Liv, and uttered weak appreciation.

'You're welcome,' he muttered, before he turned and headed for a table near the doors.

I regulated the deep breath I'd exhaled so nobody would hear it and followed Liv and Maria towards a table in the opposite direction. As I moved away, I heard the faintest sound, almost a whisper, which rang in my head. I didn't understand the words I'd heard; they weren't English and I searched round quickly, looking straight towards the backs of the two men walking the other way.

Liv herded us to another table across the room where more people were hanging around. I slid into the seat first, with Liv following me and Maria on the other side.

'Hot as he may be, they're both really weird,' Liv said.

'I'd say,' Maria replied, taking a sip of her wine.

'Nice of him to buy us a drink though,' I added, trying to appear nonchalant about them.

Just then, Maria spotted a man at the bar who she'd liked for some time, and the conversation took a complete turn. I felt they were going to continue on this subject for a while. I sat back and picked up my drink as Liv and Maria chatted and giggled. I kept sipping at my drink, adding the odd comment to join in, but really trying desperately to tune out. And that's when I did the one thing I was so conscious that I shouldn't do. It was an involuntary reflex, as if I was being forced to do it: I looked over in the direction of Gabe and Sebastian.

At the exact moment that I casually glanced over, Gabe looked up and right at me. His eyes looked even darker from a distance, sunk into his porcelain white skin. I flicked my eyes away within a second and felt how taut and defensive my face had become. I gulped and felt my breathing becoming heavier again.

As I tried to push the image of his face out of my mind, I tried to re-tune into the conversation, but my mind was muddled. I'd never been one to flirt, or chat constantly about men, mainly, because the good-looking ones were nearly always egotistical assholes.

I'd found an exception with Luke. Although he was not what I classed as a stereotypical 'handsome' man, he had always attracted attention from other women, mostly due to his wicked sense of humour. He was six feet tall, of athletic build and I always thought he had a 'different' look to him. He had the most amazing dark green eyes, and his hair was dark brown, almost black, styled in a kind of roguish, choppy way. He had the most perfect white smile and, with it, always came a sparkle in his eyes, one that enabled him to get away with most things. He'd bagged a first date with me on the basis of that smile alone.

The man I'd fallen for, along with the carefree, compassionate personality he'd once had, disappeared in the last months we shared together. He'd let himself go big time. His hair grew longer and he was happy to go to work with a couple of days of stubble, something he would never have done before. His eyes lost their constant sparkle, and instead they became darker, duller and more distant. Stress and pressure, along with the nights out drinking, had been at the root of the temper that spiralled within him.

As I remembered Luke, I fought hard to clear my mind of the images of him. I inadvertently looked up again, but I was safe this time. Gabe and his friend Sebastian were deep in conversation. Sebastian was leaning forward, cradling his beer, while talking to Gabe, who sat back in his chair shaking his head and clenching his jaw hard.

I carried on watching, trying to keep a tab on the conversation at my own table in case I was called on to add something. Gabe had become animated, his hands moving as he talked, his eyebrows raised, causing his forehead to wrinkle. I was intrigued to know what they were discussing. If it was work they were talking about, then they must have been hammering a lot of things around.

I dragged my eyes back to my table and threw everything I had left back into the conversation, which had now turned to shopping. All three of us got on so well and being with them was easy, even though their conversation was a little uninteresting to me at times. Very little of me fell into the 'normal' category and so I often felt the odd one out.

We started to make plans for the following weekend, which would give me something else to look forward to. We were going to head into one of the big malls outside San Diego, make a day of it: shopping, lunch – the works. In the evening, we planned to head out for a meal at a place Liv raved about before making our way to the next, and much larger, town of Antala, where we would make more of a night of it, hitting the many bars there.

After another drink, I felt the yawns coming and suppressed them as best I could. Liv seemed to notice and, after several jokes at my expense, mainly because I was a lightweight, we drank up and stood to put our coats on.

Stretching my arm into my jacket, I attempted one more sneaky glance in Gabe's direction and was caught out again. This time, both he and Sebastian were looking over at me in complete silence. I caught their stare and Sebastian looked away quickly, his face poker-straight.

Gabe's eyes did not move from mine and, again, I felt like a deer caught in car headlights, unable to break my trance-like stare as my eyes became blurry. My breathing slowed, like when I felt tired and warm and ready for sleep, only as my body relaxed, I felt a strange kind of dizziness again and I heard the faint whisper of the voice I couldn't place, saying something in my head. I started to gently rock on my feet, a hardly noticeable movement, as the voice whispered constantly. I stood in my trance and there was only one word making itself clear, one out of the many whispered words. 'Dream,' the voice said, more of a breath than a word, just as Liv's voice brought me back to the present.

'Meg, hey, you okay?'

I looked at her face and I could feel the colour drain from my cheeks. It took a few seconds to bring myself around enough to break the spell and give her my best attempt at a smile. 'Yeah, sorry, think I'm dropping off here,' I said, which was not far from the truth, in an odd way. 'A few too many drinks,' I laughed as Liv broke a cautious smile.

'Okay, Miss, let's get you home,' she said, linking her arm through mine and waving to Ed as we walked past. 'Night Ed.'

Maria trailed slightly behind us and, as we reached the table where Gabe and Sebastian sat, I drew my eyes up again. They both stared at us and nodded as we walked past. 'Night, Liv, Maria…Meg,' Gabe said.

'Nice to meet you all. Goodnight,' Sebastian continued without looking at us.

'Night guys, and thanks again for the drinks,' Liv said, smiling her 'reserved for the hot guys' smile.

'Thanks,' Maria and I muttered, 'Night.' As we walked past, I kept my focus completely on the door, desperate to escape into the cool air and the direction of my home.

Chapter 6

I waved as Liv's car disappeared down my steep drive, its tail lights heading out of sight around the corner. I wandered slowly up the path, my body and mind tired. The breeze was starting to build again. 'The Santa Anas' Liv had said when I'd asked about the odd winds in the area.

I was too tired to pay much attention to the crackling in the dark trees surrounding the lodge, no doubt the wind or some small critter searching for food or passing through. I paused momentarily to look towards the noise, my eyes squinting to make out the shadow I saw. I gave in, too tired to care, but still hastened my way to the door.

I opened the door to a hyper-excited Ember, who fussed me more than normal before going to relieve himself in the yard. I pulled the door to, staying outside to watch over his wandering. As he skipped around and threw himself into sniffing the trees where the noise had been, he stopped and wagged his tail eagerly, before losing interest and brushing past me back inside the lodge.

I went straight up to the fire, placing more logs on before it became too low, and rubbed my hands together, trying to rid myself of the chills that covered me.

Ned came sauntering from the downstairs hall near the back door, stretching his back legs out as he paused to look at me. I went and tipped some biscuits into their respective dishes, then slumped on the couch. It was just after 11:30 p.m. and I felt absolutely exhausted, alcohol no doubt the cause of my tiredness. I went to the bathroom and cleaned up before switching the light off and going to check the doors. I grabbed my cell and made my way upstairs with Ember leading the way. I slung on my nightwear and grabbed my book, throwing it on the duvet as I slid under the cool covers.

Ned settled onto the couch, watching me intently, his nose sniffing and whiskers twitching. I smiled at them before finding my page and settled into my book, listening to the crackling logs on the fire and relaxing in the dull light.

As tired as I was when I got to bed, I became so engrossed in my book that I read for a long time, losing myself completely and managing to forget most of the things that had swirled around my mind earlier in the evening. I suddenly felt my head bob and jolt, and realised I was dropping off. I slid a bookmark in the page and glanced at the clock before I tapped the lamp off; it was just after 1 a.m.

I turned to lay on my favoured right side, snuggling further down into the covers with just my face peeking out. I closed my eyes, blanking out the dancing glow from the fire, and my breathing instantly fell into deep, heavy breaths. As I fell asleep, I listened to the peaceful sounds of the crackling fire far below and the slow yet relaxing tick of my old clock downstairs.

I woke naturally in the depths of the night, feeling a light tickle across my left cheek. I sleepily and contently turned over to a fresh sleeping position, then saw the silhouette of Ember's face as he sat upright on the bed, peering towards the mezzanine.

It was 3:35 a.m., and the fire still bravely fought on, the light all but extinguished. As I lay watching Ember, my eyes became more questioning as they focused and I caught sight of a dark reflection in the small facing window. Something was moving down the stairs.

I gulped, hardly daring to breathe. Nervously, I stretched my head around to peer over my right shoulder. I saw nothing, and gradually twisted my whole body towards the mezzanine, moving slowly and deliberately so that my movements would go unnoticed. I lay there quietly but my eyes were wide and searching. My silent breathing allowed my ears to be more vigilant as I listened for something, anything. I heard nothing. No sound of anyone in the lodge, no movement, yet there *was* something, one sound that was missing. My old clock was no longer ticking.

I looked back at Ember, who sat excitedly looking towards the stairs. I quietly and slowly slid my arm backwards, taking hold of his scruff to hold him in place, and looked back towards the stairs. I didn't know what to do. I was scared and yet at the same time I wanted to protect myself and my family. I remembered the knife I'd brought upstairs that lay in the top drawer of my bedside cabinet. I tried to think rationally. What if the reflection had sprung from a dream as I woke, a product of my tired mind? But Ember would not have sensed that.

As I was trying to think and listen, Ember shot up and out of my grasp, bouncing off the bed and hitting the floor with an almighty thud. I cringed and looked straight towards the stairs and the back of Ember as he confidently trotted to the top of the railing and peered though. 'Ember, wait,' I whispered, praying he would heed my command. He looked round at me before he turned back, and made his descent towards the living room.

I slowly slid the drawer open, taking the knife in my left hand, and tried not to move too much, causing anything to creak. With the blade facing out, I slid my legs sideways out of the bed and let my feet drop silently to the floor.

I made my way on tiptoes to the rails of the mezzanine, stretching my neck to peer over and see the main part of the living room. No Ember, no intruder. I stood motionless for a few more seconds, looking and listening. I turned to look at my phone, but it was switched off. Great. By switching it on, the stupid tune would play, alerting anyone down there that I was awake and had no signal for several minutes until it had started up fully.

I gulped and started towards the top of the stairs, looking over the railing and down into the living room as I went. I tried to move extra quiet but the creaks in the floorboards of the old wooden lodge were inevitable; as each one announced my position, I paused and listened, widening my mouth to bear my teeth, grimacing.

The glow of the fire was brighter in the living room, no longer blocked by the ceiling and railings, and as I approached the bottom of the curved staircase I caught a glimpse of Ember's tail sticking out from behind the wall, swishing slowly from side to side. I peered around the room, the knife in a defensive position, searching for any sign of movement.

As I crept forward, Ember's whole body came into view. He was sitting in front of the door, wagging his tail slowly, with his head cocked and looking up expectantly at the door handle. I leaned to switch the kitchen light on and a sudden rush of fury passed through me, making me shake with a mixture of anger and adrenaline.

I was sure someone was or had been inside. I searched downstairs, checking the bathroom, and made sure the back door was locked. I walked back into the kitchen and grabbed the front door handle. It was still locked. I stepped back and took the key from the rack, then went to open the door. As I placed the key in, I tried to twist it round to the left to unlock it but it wouldn't move. I twisted the key a few times but it wouldn't budge an inch. I grabbed hold of the handle and pushed down, causing the door to open slightly under my weight.

A cold breeze drifted in through the gap and a shiver went down my spine. The door I know was locked only seconds before, *definitely* locked, was now open, with no need for the key.

I opened it wider, feeling terrified inside. I took a tentative step onto the porch and Ember shot past me and straight into the dark night, disappearing from my view within seconds. With only a few dim lower street lights shining up through the trees, and the half-dozen solar-powered lights making my land visible in the distance, I could see very little.

I walked out onto the porch, giving myself a better, unobstructed view, and looked around the part of the yard I could see. The cool breeze brushed my skin and I could feel goosebumps rising on my arms. The bunkhouse door was still closed and I took another few steps onto the path, listening for any sounds. A gust of air swirled a few fallen leaves around my feet, distracting me, and I looked down to watch the movement, then back up in time to see Ember trotting happily back towards me, wagging his tail.

In the distance, from the area Ember had just left, I saw a large, dark shadow hovering behind the trees. I squinted to try and see better but the shadow started to move backwards. I ran in its direction, shouting, 'I know who you are!' even though it was a lie. 'If you ever come on my fucking land again, I'll kill you!'

The volume of my voice should have woken the neighbours, but as I looked around through the trees for any sign of lights being switched on I saw none. I frantically scanned the trees where the shadow had stood seconds earlier. 'I will kill you if you come on my property again, you hear me?' I continued wailing, my anger flowing naturally and unharnessed now, as branches became tangled in my hair and scratched my face.

As I stood looking through the trees, another strong and unexpected gust whirled up fast around me and whooshed around my body, before tunnelling away in the direction of the shadow, rocking and pushing the branches as it passed through.

I lingered for a moment before turning to see the door open where I'd come out. 'Ned,' I called, panicked that he'd come outside. I ran back into the lodge, slamming and locking the door behind me. I searched for Ember too as I raced upstairs. Ned was sitting on the bedroom window sill staring out, probably entertained by his loony mum running and screaming round the yard in the middle of the night. To my surprise, Ember was curled in a ball on the bed, asleep, as if nothing had disturbed or rattled him, unlike me.

The rest of my night's sleep was fitful. As a precaution, I placed the knife with the handle ready to grab on the bedside cabinet and switched my cell on.

My disturbed night did not deter me from visiting the rescue centre the following morning, though. With my usual lack of sleep, thanks to my dreams and the night time disturbances, I was up and about just after seven, feeling a little more than shattered.

I decided to attempt my first run into town to collect my car. It was only two miles and I figured it was an easy start with quiet, flat roads. If I headed out soon, I would surely miss the bulk of traffic and people – as well as the heat – which sometimes became stifling by mid-morning. I could then get back home for a quick shower, grab some breakfast and ready myself before I headed to the shelter.

I grabbed my running gear, dressed quickly and slung my hair into an untidy ponytail. I had a couple of glasses of water and put my car keys and cell into my wrist pack, before sliding my sunglasses on. With Ember attached to his short bungee leash around my waist, I locked the doors and walked out into the fresh morning.

I set off at a light jog, taking it easy. I hadn't run in a long time, easily four or five months, and needed to feel how my body would react. After about half a mile of slow running, I felt okay so I notched it up a gear. Ember complied and sped up with me, obviously thrilled at being out and about running again.

The freedom of running came back easily and my mind gradually left its worries behind, focusing only on my breathing, the scenery and the road ahead.

We reached town in good time and, as I passed the gas station, I slowed to a fast walk, then to a steady one, easing my body and heart rate down slowly. There were a few people in town, heading into various stores to prepare for their day's work. As I hit the crossroads, I looked towards the other side of town and the distant veterinarian sign. I just caught sight of my car when the practice doors swung open and out walked Gabe.

I halted Ember and turned quickly to look into a store window, a few doors up from the practice, so I wouldn't have to speak if he saw me. Oh great, talk about awkward situations. I had decided to stop and look in the window of the one store which would look completely odd since it sold and leased equipment for the disabled.

I glanced into the window, searching for his reflection which would confirm it was okay for me to go get my car. All I could see was Gabe loading bags into the trunk of his darkened-out Jeep before he walked around to the driver's side and climbed in. I looked at nothing in the window again, listening for the engine to start. Within a minute, it started, and I looked for the reflection showing him reversing out. Seconds later, he was driving out through the west end of town. The chances of him recognising me were slim anyway; I had my sunglasses on, was dressed in running gear, with my hair up and with a dog he wouldn't know.

I walked to my car, taking the keys out of my wrist pack, and opened the door, letting Ember jump in and onto the passenger seat. I reversed a little faster than I should have out of the parking space and drove home.

Once inside, Ember took his fill of fresh, cold water and went to chill out on the couch, panting to cool off. I took a shower and spent a little time on my makeup and straightening my wavy hair. With a pair of jeans and a vest slung on, I set about making breakfast.

Half an hour later and I was carefully following the directions Liv had given me for the animal rescue centre, glancing between her poor attempt at a map and the road. As soon as I'd turned off the main highway, I started looking for the sign for the shelter and, sure enough, a little further up on the right I saw a dirt track approaching, with a large wooden ranch sign hanging over the entrance.

As I reached the turn-off, the sign declared that I'd arrived at 'Manzano Mount Animal Rescue'. I drove the mile or so down the narrow track, the loose dirt kicking up from my tires, and pulled up in front of a fenced corral alongside a handful of other cars.

I twisted in my seat to look around at the small groups of people milling around outside and climbed out, locking the door behind me. I headed towards the large wooden cabin marked 'Reception', past several corrals filled with all manner of animals, from horses to donkeys and goats.

I looked beyond the large extended office building and further down stood several blocks of kennels, presumably housing the domestic animals. The whole setting was serene and beautiful, with long meadows and more horses grazing far in the distance, towards the mountains.

I entered the office, where a couple of women stood chatting to visitors. I passed time until they were free by looking through their well-stocked store, which sold everything from food to gifts to an array of educational literature.

'Can I help you?' a women's voice suddenly asked.

I looked up towards her voice. 'Oh, Hi. I wondered if it was possible to speak with the manager,' I said, looking into the face of a blonde-haired woman.

'That'd be me,' the woman replied. 'How can I help you?'

'Oh, great. I'm Meg, a veterinary technician. I've just moved to the area and would like to do some volunteer work in a local rescue, hopefully put my skills to good use,' I said. 'That is, if you could use any more volunteers right now,' I added.

'Well, we're always grateful for volunteers and, with your skills, I'm sure we'd have lots for you to do here. I'm Caitlin, by the way,' the woman said, extending her hand towards me. I accepted the gentle shake.

'If you could just give me ten minutes, we can have a chat,' she asked.

'Sure,' I replied. 'Am I okay to have a look around?'

'By all means,' she answered, gathering papers from the desk. 'I'll come find you.'

'Great!' I replied. 'See you soon.'

I headed out the door and into the balmy heat of the morning, where the animals seemed to be taking it easy in the fields. I made my way towards my car, near the first corral, which contained a variety of horses.

The horses grazed in the field, paying no attention to me whatsoever. I ambled along to the second corral where my presence seemed to cause more of a stir. A dozen or so donkeys looked towards me when I pursed my lips and made a clicking sound to get their attention.

As the first ones looked up and started to approach me, the rest followed suit, meandering towards the fence, obviously inquisitive about another visitor who might have food to offer.

I leaned on the top rail of the fence, dangling my arms over and placing the heel of my boot through the lower bar, waiting for them to come closer. As the first of the group arrived, I extended my arms, raising my palms so they could take in my scent.

After some serious muzzle rubs, in which they slyly checked out if their effort had been worth it, they started to disperse as slowly as they had arrived, once they realised that I did not hold the key to their initial interest – food. One old brown and white donkey stayed, seeming to enjoy the rub I was giving him.

I was rubbing my hands up and down his long ears, lost in peaceful thoughts and fully enjoying the interaction with the old, gentle donkey when a voice came from behind, startling me. I'd not even heard any footsteps approaching.

'He'll stand there and let you do that to him pretty much all day,' the deep voice said.

I kept my hand in place and twisted my head round into the glare of the sun to see who was speaking to me. I was surprised that I hadn't recognised Gabe's voice, although in the bar the previous night I hadn't really paid much attention to it. 'Yeah, I think I'm of no use to them without food,' I replied, squinting to bring into focus the weathered, pale face barely four feet in front of me.

'That's Bill,' Gabe said, nodding towards the object of my attention. 'He's an old timer, one of the permanent residents here,' he continued.

I momentarily looked back at Bill. 'Hi, Bill,' I said, giving him an extra little scratch on his nose.

'So, are you here looking for another pet?' he asked.

I looked back towards him before moving into his shadow to enable me to speak without having to squint. I hadn't realised just how tall he was and, looking up at him now, I guessed he was about six foot three, easily dwarfing my five foot nine inch frame.

What struck me again, as it had the previous night, was the depth and colour of his eyes. They were so dark and intense, and they focused directly on mine as we chatted. He had quite thick eyebrows which sat low above his eyes, making them appear deeper still. It surprised me that in the sun, where people's eyes normally gathered the sunlight and looked lighter, his remained a blackish-brown.

'No, I'm here to offer help as a volunteer,' I said.

'I'm sure Caitlin would appreciate another pair of hands. There's always something to tend to, something that's got into trouble,' he continued, making his way to the fence to my right. He leaned his forearms on the top railing, hunching slightly forward and staring into the distance, towards the donkeys roaming around in front of us. His thick hair looked a little unkempt, whispering at the edges of his face, and sat in no particular style or order just above his shoulders.

'So, what are you doing here?' I asked, moving my attention back to Bill.

'Oh, I work here some of the time. Check over the new intakes once a week, carry out necessary or emergency procedures, that kind of thing,' he said, taking in a deep breath and clenching his jaw constantly. 'Nice to get out in the fresh air.'

'Nice work if you can get it,' I said, reluctantly smiling as I looked over at him.

He looked back at me, and there was a glimpse of something in his face, as if he were thinking about asking me something but had decided against it. 'Well, better get to work,' he finally said.

We stared at each other for a few seconds, and although I felt a little uncomfortable as his eyes caught mine, I also felt a sense of calm wash over me. It was like when you've had a really hard but rewarding day and you sit down at the end of it with a nice glass of wine in the late afternoon sun, all warm and fuzzy and relaxed.

'Nice to see you again,' I said, turning my eyes away, back to the safer expression of Bill. I'd always felt a little uncomfortable with direct eye contact; it made me feel so self conscious. But his eyes didn't move. They stayed on me and out of the corner of my eye I saw him standing completely still, his face fixed on mine.

'Take care, Meg,' he said. 'Have a good day.'

'Yeah, you too,' I replied, keeping my eyes fixed firmly on Bill.

He headed off, completely out of sight, and I had no idea in which direction he went. I just waited and nervously flitted around stroking Bill to pass the time.

I casually turned to look around and exhaled when I realised he'd gone. With the way clear, I headed towards the kennel buildings. By the time I'd finished the first block of kennels, sticking my finger through the bars to offer a hello to all the dogs needing homes, I had brought myself down to earth, just in time to see Caitlin approaching.

We talked for about half an hour, going through my skills and what I was able to offer, and she discussed the rescue, their missions, and the areas which they needed help. By the time I was ready to leave, we'd agreed on me coming in to do the weekly admission checks on Mondays, the first being tomorrow. This was something that Caitlin had done up until now but her resources were desperately needed in other areas, like re-homing. I'd also agreed to come in for ad-hoc help with emergencies.

I said my goodbyes and returned to the car, carrying far too many unnecessary items that I'd purchased in the shop. My mind was full of only one thing driving home, one person. His face was somehow etched in my mind and I knew it would be him I was helping every Monday; I just wasn't sure how I felt about it.

Part of me was pleased, really pleased. On the positive side, I'd be helping a fantastic cause, keeping my hand in with my nursing, and it just so happened that I would be working with an extremely attractive man. On the negative side, I was vulnerable and in no position to be having thoughts or feelings, however small they might be, about this strange man. I already had alarm bells ringing from what I'd seen of him, not even considering what Liv and Maria had told me.

The journey back passed quickly, lost in thought as I was. I couldn't remember passing the mental landmarks I'd identified on my way to the shelter only a few hours earlier.

I got home just after noon and the rest of the day flew by. I headed into town to the DIY store, where I gathered some colour charts and paint. I flitted around doing random jobs, barely stopping to eat. The paint charts gave my mind something else to focus on, something other than Gabe, Luke, and my new, scary life.

I had no further text messages from Luke, which I was grateful for since it helped slowly push him further to the back of my mind. I replied to Anna's text, confirming the third set of dates she'd given me. I had put her off until then, wanting to settle in a bit more, and get some work done on the lodge. So, I had about five weeks before she came to visit.

By the time evening came, I had re-painted the family room and my bedroom a light hessian, keeping all the colours earthy and natural. I had bought some accessories, vases, cushions and mirrors for both rooms, and it all came together nicely.

I headed into the bunkhouse to look through the leftover boxes for some old work clothes for the next day at the shelter. As I stood up, clutching my jeans and polo shirt, my eyes caught sight of the painting hanging on the wall. I was drawn again to its peaceful yet haunting setting, the beauty of the lake and trees, and the people with the dog. I then glanced to the other painting of the log cabin in the woods. I stood looking at the lodge in the painting and as I stared into it my breathing became sleepy, heavy and my eyes fixed in a daze, unable to blink out of it. I had gone so tired, almost light-headed, as I floated into the painting, feeling as if I were there, standing beside the house, almost smelling the wild flowers and feeling the breeze swirling through the trees. With some effort, I freed myself from my trance and tucked the legs of my jeans over my arm before locking the bunkhouse up and returning inside.

Lying in bed that evening, my mind wandered from one thought to another: about what work I would be doing the next day, what ideas I had for painting the other rooms in the lodge and the same thought that had been stuck in my head for days, the local veterinarian. I had tried to shut him out but the harder I tried the more his face became clearer and stuck in there, stubbornly refusing to leave my flaky mind. I grabbed my book, frustrated with myself, and read for a short time before I fell into a deep sleep.

I woke in the dark again, gasping for breath, beads of sweat spilling down my forehead. I sat up and leaned forward, grabbing hold of my knees, desperately trying to breathe normally and bring myself down to earth. 'The paintings,' I muttered, almost involuntary, straight out of my dream. I sat for a few minutes calming myself. The paintings in the bunkhouse were vivid in my mind, every inch of them, as if I were looking at them right then on a screen. 'The paintings,' I said again, twisting my legs from under the quilt and sitting on the edge of the bed.

I threw myself out of bed and pulled on my sweater before switching the main light on. I set off downstairs, hanging onto the banister, still half-asleep and panicked by the dream. My eyes squinted against the brightness, easing only when I reached the bottom of the stairs.

I hadn't even stopped to wonder where Ember was and, just as the thought of him crossed my mind, I saw him. In the dim glow of the light from upstairs, I saw him lying upside down on the couch, lolling on his back with his front legs in the air, patting at something. I rushed to switch on the living room light, my heart racing, and looked towards Ember. The second the light came on, he jumped up and glared at me over the back of the couch in surprise, obviously startled.

I ran to the drawer in the kitchen reserved for 'any old crap' and grabbed the torch. I flicked it on to check it was working and unhooked the bunkhouse key from the wall. I switched the outside light on and unlocked the front door. I shut it quickly behind me so that Ember and Ned couldn't follow me out and paused momentarily on the porch, trying to let my eyes adjust to the darkness. I looked around, as much as my sight would allow, and fixed my eyes on the bunkhouse door. I took a few deep breaths, trying to tell myself that nothing lay waiting in the dark, the cold air sending shivers down my arms and back.

I took another breath and began the short walk to the bunkhouse, my eyes flitting around constantly. I stuck the key in the latch and twisted, hearing the click as the door unlocked. I made my way to the first painting of the house in the woods and stood staring at it, looking for something, anything. The paintings were still so vivid in my mind. I then swiftly turned and took the few steps towards the lake painting but as I stared into it I saw nothing obvious.

I looked to the floor as I tried to think about what else had been in my dream and it suddenly hit me. I knew something was different, very different. It was so obvious, staring me in the face, literally. I didn't dare move and, as my breathing increased, my heart pounded its usual double beats. I knew which one it was and I knew what it was, but I didn't dare look for fear of confirming it to myself.

I slowly lifted my head towards the painting of the lake and that's when I saw it. I focused and refocused my eyes to check that I wasn't seeing things. The trees were the same, the water was the same and the overhanging branches were the same, all but this one thing. On the day I had arrived and checked out the bunkhouse, I had clearly seen all of the painting, including the silhouettes of the person and the dog standing at the other side of the lake. Yet, I was now staring at three silhouettes: *two* people and one dog. I stood there with the hairs on my arms rising to attention. My heart gave a giant thump, making me feel queasy.

I stood looking at the painting for several minutes, trying to comprehend what I was seeing. There was no way to understand it. I walked straight to the door in complete shock. Seeing what I had made one thing clear in my mind: someone was hanging around the lodge and that person had, for whatever warped reason, altered the painting. What other explanation could there be?

I had to dare myself to leave the bunkhouse and go back to the lodge. Only twelve or so steps and I would be at the door; seconds later I'd be inside, with the door locked. I kept going through the steps in my head, talking myself into overcoming the deep fear I was feeling inside so I could force my legs to move.

I gulped several times, trying to lubricate my dry mouth. I *had* to get inside.

I looked around and grabbed hold of a sharp piece of broken wooden curtain rail and readjusted it into a strong grip, the sharp snapped end facing forward. I gently pulled back the curtain covering the window next to the door, just enough to peer outside. Everything looked the same. I took several deep breaths and swung the door wide open, making a frantic dash towards the lodge.

The bunkhouse door sprang back and made a loud crack as it hit the frame. I sprinted barefoot towards the front door and hit it running, panicked when the handle didn't open straight away. I pressed harder and the door finally gave way, just as I dived through it and into the kitchen. Ember, who was still on the couch, looked over at me as if

I were mad, his head cocked and eyes wide. I slid the bolt and locked the door before I stepped backwards into the kitchen.

I kept the curtain rail in my hand and walked to the cutlery drawer. I opened it, grabbing a large steak knife in my right hand, before moving towards the light switch. The lodge must have looked like a power surge had hit it as I switched every available light on, searching around to make sure nobody had got in while I was in the bunkhouse.

I continued checking every room until I was satisfied I was alone, tugging and pulling both doors to make sure they were locked tight. With my weapons and cell in hand, I made my way upstairs, leaving the downstairs light on, and grabbed Ember's house collar to drag him with me.

I contemplated calling the police to report the incident but, after a few minutes, thought better of it and decided to report it in the morning.

I couldn't get to sleep, worrying about someone loitering in the dark around the property, so instead of forcing myself I went and collected a couple of boxes of photographs from the spare room. I placed them onto the bed, along with the photo albums I'd bought in town, knowing I could keep myself busy for a few more hours, until dawn would be on my side and I could get on with my day.

I slouched on my elbow, flicking through photos, the fear of the night starting to leave me. As I glanced through them, I knew they would take my mind elsewhere, but I half-thought a different nightmare was about to start as I flicked through photos of Luke and me, some in happier times and some in not so happy times. We put on a great facade in our last few months together.

As I peered into the photos, I noticed how much younger I looked in them even though some of them had been taken only a year previously, in the happier times part of our relationship. Had I really aged so much? I looked more tanned, healthy and glowing. My smile was wide, my eyes sparkling as Luke stood laughing and looking at my face, his arm around my neck. What had gone so horribly wrong? Why had things changed so drastically? As much as I was slowly easing my way into this new life, I missed him so much. I missed the good times with him. I felt numb looking at the photo but I needed to see it, so I slotted it in front of the lamp, facing the bed.

I flicked through photos of Ned and Ember, and photos taken at Christmas with Anna, Cam and their two boys all laughing and smiling. It was only last Christmas. The one I came across of Anna and me was my favourite of both of us. We had been on a night out in Boston with Luke and Cam, and Cam had taken the photo of us made up to the nines, both grinning our heads off.

Tears spilled uncontrollably down my face. I had lost them all, the only family I had. I knew at that point, or at least accepted, that life could never go back to what it had once been. I felt a wave of grief pass over me as I sobbed hard, the tears stinging as they trickled freely, following the lines of my cheeks, jaw and neck, rolling on down to my chest.

I had no idea what time it was – easily three or four – but at last I managed to fall asleep, in a mass of upturned photos.

Chapter 7

I was up at seven, my mind still addled from the night's drama. I cautiously went downstairs, following a bouncing Ember. The morning was still and bright, and the distant sounds of car engines and people talking helped me relax. Everything was so much easier in the daylight. I looked in the mirror at the haggard, sleep-deprived face looking back and made the best attempts I could to repair the damage.

I aimed to be at the rescue for ten but found myself ready to go a good half hour early, so decided I had time left for Ember to have some fun outside. As he wandered off, cocking his leg and picking up who knows what, I tentatively went and pushed open the bunkhouse door, gulping hard as I did. I walked towards the painting, wondering if I had been dreaming again. But it still hung defiantly there, with all three silhouettes in place.

As I set off towards the rescue, my mind wasn't all there; I was preoccupied, wondering who could have changed the painting and when. I knew one hundred percent that there had only been one person in the painting before. I knew it. My mind was sure, clear, and now there were two. The thought sent shivers down my spine, the hairs on my arms bristling. There was no logical explanation. Whatever was happening, I didn't like it.

I pulled up at the rescue and looked around at the other cars scattered near the main office. To my surprise, I saw Gabe's Jeep parked between the main building and reception, almost out of sight. 'Great,' I mumbled, taking a few deep breaths. 'Shit.' I got out, dressed in casual ripped jeans, old hiking boots and my navy polo shirt, and twisted my hands into my hair, tying it into a ponytail. I headed towards the main entrance with my bottle of water in hand and my messenger bag slung over my shoulder.

Caitlin was standing in the reception area talking to another woman and she looked up and smiled warmly when I went in. I hung around for her to finish talking and then she came over.

'How are you?' she asked, giving me a friendly kiss on the cheek.

'I'm great, thanks, you?'

'I'm good,' she replied, 'just preparing everything for the new bunch we have in today. We have Gabe here giving the shots and checking them all over. There are six dogs, two cats and a couple of ferrets in since last Thursday,' she continued.

'Okay,' I replied, a little nervous and hesitant about if I would be the only one working with him.

'Come on, I'll show you through to the prep room and we'll get going,' she said.

I followed Caitlin, taking everything in, and when we reached the prep room, there he was, sorting out all his equipment and getting shots ready.

'Hey, Gabe, I'd like to introduce you to Megan,' Caitlin said. 'She'll be coming in to help out with the weekly intakes.' Gabe looked up to meet my inattentive gaze, my attempt at looking casual.

'Ah, we've already met,' he replied politely, but acting uninterested in acknowledging me, and looking back to what he was doing.

His response surprised me, especially after we had chatted briefly when I was with the donkeys. But I figured he was in working mode now, there to do his job, still, I was surprised at his flat reception.

The plan for the day was to vaccinate all the animals in the holding kennels, give them full health checks and carry out any necessary treatments. My job, as Caitlin had just explained, was to take her place and assist Gabe with the animals.

When Gabe had everything ready, Caitlin showed me through to the holding area so we could plan the work and see what needed to be done. I followed, keeping a discreet distance at the back, asking only necessary questions. It was obvious Gabe had done this many times before and I just tried to take it all in.

We brought the first dog through and Gabe effortlessly lifted it onto the table. I held it while he examined it thoroughly. Caitlin watched on. He commented to her about the dog, his attention focused on his work, and kept his comments factual and professional. Caitlin made notes in preparation for treatment and adoption, and Gabe gathered all the necessary medication and made a start on treating the dog. I asked Caitlin general questions about the processing of the animals, and made light conversation, though Gabe never attempted to join in.

Once I was happy with taking all the necessary details and my assisting role, she excused herself and left us to it. As I held the dog so Gabe could check its teeth and eyes, I casually glanced up to him, relieved that he was not aware of me staring. His eyes were the darkest brown, darkened further by the dim lights inside the small prep room, and they still held a deep, distant look, as if he were there physically but not mentally, carrying everything out automatically. I moved my attention back to the dog and, once we were done, I went to lift it off the table, something I was physically more than capable of doing. As I did, he slid his arms underneath it, catching both of my arms in the process, and scooped it up to place it on the floor, my arms becoming redundant.

'Don't want you hurting yourself on the first day,' he said, still paying me no attention but with the smallest patronising smirk on his lips.

'I think I can more than manage a medium-sized dog,' I shot back sarcastically.

There it was again, a little smirk, only he clenched his jaw and let a little laugh out through his nostrils. This seemed to lighten the mood, a tiny bit anyway, and as we moved onto the next dog, he started to ask me for instruments and make comments about the animal so I could note down the details.

A good two hours later, all the animals were checked and back in their respective kennels and cages. The lists were complete and Caitlin was thrilled not only with my work, but with the chance she'd had to get other things done.

'This takes place every Monday, if you're free to help out?' she asked, smiling in hope.

'Sure, I'd love to,' I replied. 'Same time next week then?'

As Caitlin continued talking to me, I noticed Gabe looking at us both out of the corner of my eye, as if he were casually listening to our conversation. When we finished, I took my car keys out ready for a quick escape. As I followed Caitlin towards the door for the reception area, I heard his voice.

'Thanks for your help today,' he said, looking directly at me. He really did have the most mesmerising voice: deep and raspy, and utterly captivating.

I took a breath and looked back in his direction. 'You're welcome,' I replied, forcing a shy smile from within, unable to shift my gaze from his.

His eyes changed then and it was if he was forcing himself to look away, to stop our stare there, to break the contact. His smile disappeared and his eyes darkened, a frown creeping onto his forehead as he looked towards his bag, pausing, and not actually doing anything.

I blinked my way out of the trance I'd fallen into and followed Caitlin down the corridor, noticing as I walked how fast my breathing had become, the quivering obvious in my chest. I drove all the way home with the image of his face in my head, again, and his voice ringing in my ears. It was those eyes; those dark, deep eyes transfixed on mine.

After almost the whole journey home thinking about him, obsessing over the face that haunted me, I stopped myself. In that second, I made the right decision. I would not allow those visions to invade me again. I would never let his voice or face swirl round in my head, I was not in the right place for him, or any other man, and something deep inside me told me I needed to keep away from him.

I woke just after dawn the next day and lay stroking Ember, looking out through the lodge window towards the distant hills, mentally planning my day. As I got up, Ember slinked downstairs, Ned not far behind, flicking his nervous eyes around, checking things out as he moved. I gave Ned his breakfast – Ember would eat after our exercise – and put the teakettle on, coffee being all I needed to get me up and running, literally. I went to put on my running gear and returned a few minutes later, wearing my vest, thin fleece, shorts and sneakers.

I drank coffee while getting Ember's drinking kit together and preparing his harness. I planned to try another route, about twelve miles east of town. Five minutes later, Ember sat in the passenger seat, waiting patiently for us to get going. I slammed the door, set the satnav and waited for it to kick in as I took my map out. After a few minutes we set off down the steep drive on our way.

Reaching the entrance to the park, Ember's interest peaked as he stared into the woodland. I parked away from the other few cars in the lot and took a long drink of my water, looking into the trees. I hooked Ember onto his harness and gave him a drink before we set off, which he lapped up eagerly.

I was a little out of shape and the previous runs had caused me some stiffness. I needed to run more often, get my athletic shape back. I hated the sunken body that had crept over my bones in the last few months and, as much as I was trying to eat more, I simply couldn't; I seemed to be barely eating enough to keep a sparrow alive. Even my favourite food in the world, chocolate, seemed to turn my stomach, and that in itself proved I was not myself.

As Ember finished his drink, I put my cell and keys in my wrist pack and grabbed my water. I attached Ember to my waist on his long bungee leash and we wandered to the recreational signpost showing all the different routes to take. I opted for one of the orange ones again, maybe a little ambitious, but I needed to push myself and free my mind. It was an eight-mile route and had some uneven terrain and a stream to cross.

I turned to find the beginning of the trail and we started out. I began slowly, the morning sun not bothering me much as it lay low in the sky, dappled through the trees, hitting my eyes on and off through the leaves. It was nice. We ran steadily and I picked my pace up well, to a point where I felt comfortable and easy in my stride. Ember ran alongside, happy with the speed too. He'd gained the weight I'd lost over the last few months. The freedom of running had been my saviour many times in the past and I now started to feel exhilarated by it again.

I ran, listening to the birds high in the trees and watching the butterflies flitting into the air. I inhaled deeply, taking the fresh pine air into my lungs. How free did I feel: to run, to forget, to push myself and make my body work hard. I needed this run today and I ran thinking of nothing but the life going on around me, glancing into trees, at birds, at Ember and the pure, breathtaking beauty of the woods.

The terrain became a little rougher and I concentrated hard as I passed over the many raised tree roots, trying to balance along the slanted earth. The trail led gradually down towards the stream over a distance of about half a mile. As we reached the water, I slowed to a halt to let Ember drink. He happily paused, lapping up the fresh flowing water, and then looking up with droplets dripping from his chin like a fountain. I panted hard, trying to catch my breath a little, my forehead glistening with a light sweat, my heart pounding through my chest. I took a long drink from my own bottle, letting it slowly refresh my dry throat.

After a couple of minutes, off we went, not wanting to let my loose muscles cool down. The pedometer showed we'd covered just over three and a half miles. I was pleased with my progress so far, although I had run much faster in the past. As we moved on another mile or so, I saw two people approaching, hikers. We greeted each other as we passed and carried on our separate way. My body was feeling a little more tired now, but I pushed on and started to think about what I was going to wear for my next night out to pass the time and push the tired thoughts out of my mind.

I began to look down more and more, checking how far we'd gone, my body tiring, and, eventually, as I strung things through my weary mind, I saw we were reaching our eighth mile. I pushed harder, looking for the parking lot, and felt so relieved when the first car finally came into sight up the rise of the hill. I slowed to a fast walk, puffing and panting, letting my body regulate slowly.

A short while later we reached the car. I opened the back door, and re-filled Ember's dish, then collapsed into the back feeling exhausted. After a few minutes I sat up and sipped the water from my bottle, staring towards the road. My attention was suddenly alerted when I saw a darkened-out silver Jeep passing the entrance to the parking lot.

I squinted as my eyes followed the familiar looking car, trying to make out the driver, but it was too far away and only a faint silhouette was visible. 'It can't be,' I muttered, following its direction. After it had gone out of sight, I did something I didn't expect myself to do. I jumped up, grabbing the keys from the carpet in the trunk, and emptied the remaining water from Ember's dish. With Ember safely shut inside, I slammed the trunk and jumped into the car. As I jammed my keys into the ignition, the one person with a darkened-out silver Jeep I knew sprung into my mind effortlessly. I whipped the gear shift into reverse, wound my arm around the passenger's seat to get a good view behind me and flew backwards with such speed my tyres skidded on the loose earth.

I slung the gear shift into first and set off in the pursuit of a whim, wanting to confirm it was who I thought it was in the car. As I swung out onto the road, not slowing as much as I should to check the traffic, my rational side kept trying to reason with my crazy side that maybe, or, actually, it was probably just a tourist in one of the thousands of silver Jeeps in the county looking for somewhere to hike. But my crazy side said I had to be sure.

As I sped down the winding lane towards the main highway back towards Manzano, I reached the open junction and, after looking briefly to check I was clear to keep going, I took the left turn a little too sharply, looking guiltily over my shoulder to see Ember hanging on for dear life in the back. On this particular road trip, even he wouldn't dare climb up front as usual to ride shotgun.

I remembered this stretch of road being long, with few bends, and slammed my foot hard to the floor. The car must have been no more than a mile in front and at this pace, if he was driving normally, I would catch up in no time. I was pushing eighty as I glanced at the speedometer and saw an old green pickup ahead. I approached from behind much faster than it was travelling and swung out wide to get past before the next small bend, a left-hander that I could easily gain a racing line on, allowing me to maintain my speed.

I hit the earth a little on the far side and saw the dust skip up from the tires in my rear-view mirror, before pushing into the bend and back onto my side of the road. The pickup flashed me from behind, obviously disgraced by my erratic driving. As I hit another straight, I saw a large silver vehicle up ahead, no more than half a mile or so. I kept my foot down and reached ninety easily, leaning forward as if the extra inches would help me focus on the silver dot up ahead.

I saw the approaching junction, where the silver vehicle took a fast right turn. Several seconds later, I came up to the same reasonably open junction, which had allowed me to see well in advance that no cars were coming in either direction. I swung out right onto the main highway and picked up speed again. The road here had more bends and I struggled to see the car again, desperately trying to get a glimpse of the licence plate. As I swung round the bends, the silver car was always one step ahead, just passing the next bend, making it impossible to see who was driving it.

I passed another bend, dangerously cutting the blind corner to close the distance, and opened up onto another long straight. At this point, I was sure I would catch up with the car. But it had completely vanished out of sight, even though I had only been following about fifty feet behind, a distance which made it impossible for a vehicle to leave the road without me seeing it do so.

It was not possible for the car to have gotten ahead so fast, not when I had been so close behind. I hadn't noticed any turnings as I'd passed and, again, to take the turnings in one piece, the car would have to have slowed to get round them, enabling me to close up behind and see where it was going. I would have seen it turn off, surely. 'Dammit!' I cursed, angry to have come so close but still lose sight of the car. 'Shit!' There was no point me turning round to find any side roads; I would have lost the car now, travelling as fast as it was.

But the very fact that whoever was in the car tried so hard to get away, so hard not to be caught, made me wonder why. 'Argh,' I grumbled, slamming my hand onto the steering wheel in temper. Ember's face appeared through the two front seats, looking at me and wondering what the hell was happening.

A few miles later, I saw my turn-off up ahead and drove the rest of the way at the legal speed. As I bounced up the drive, confident of the clearance for the bumper now, I felt so frustrated. I would never know if it was him.

Ember drank his way through another dish of water and I made my way to the shower, sticky and clammy from the run. I undressed, throwing my running gear into the washer, and grabbed a fresh towel from the cupboard.

I ate breakfast with a towel wrapped around me and one covering my hair. The shower had eased my tight muscles but I still expected stiff joints by the next morning.

When I was all ready to leave, I grabbed my purse and headed into town, parking up in the small lot outside the police department.

I sat in the car, wondering about the best way to explain about my recent concerns. There was no easy approach, other than to list everything that had happened over the last week or so. I would have to figure the precise words out when I got in there. I locked the car and headed inside, appreciating the air-conditioned building as I opened the doors.

It was a small building and a few officers milled around the open-plan office, which extended from behind the low-security main desk. A young guy was standing at the main desk, leaning forward and writing. I approached the counter and he raised his head to greet me.

'Morning,' I said.

'Morning, Ma'am. How can I help?' he asked.

'I'd like to speak to someone about a few disturbances I've had on my property recently,' I replied.

'Oh, okay, sure. If you'd like to take a seat for a moment, I'll get someone to come speak with you.'

'Thanks,' I said, making my way to one of the seats. I sat waiting no more than a few minutes before a plump and ruddy-faced man, who looked to be in his mid to late fifties, walked around the counter towards me.

'Morning, Ma'am. Sheriff Ellis. How can I be of assistance?'

'Oh, Hi,' I replied, taking a deep breath. 'Well, I want to report a few disturbances I've had on my property over the last week. They've all taken place in the night and two nights ago I noticed some things had been altered in another building on my land. I've also seen a shadow outside, someone hiding behind a tree, but they disappeared when I went out with my dog.'

'Oh,' he replied, seeming surprised by what I was telling him. 'Okay, well come on round to my desk and I'll take some details.'

I followed him around the main reception to his desk and sat tensely in front of him. He leaned down to get a book from his desk drawer, obviously the official book for noting incidents, and I could see by the amount of pages he turned through, about three, that the book was not used often. The previous entry before mine was dated five weeks earlier. I wondered on what date the book had actually been started.

'Okay, so if I can take your details first,' he said.

I went through all my basic details: name, address, contact numbers, etc., and he wrote them down on the form. Once the main parts where completed, he asked me to date and list all the events that had occurred. I dug deep into my pathetic memory and, thankfully, remembered all the things that had happened.

Listening to myself reel everything off, I realised how odd it all sounded. Everything, except maybe the painting incident, could have been completely innocent and rationally explained. He wrote everything down, then asked if there was anything else I could recall, obviously following procedure for these reports. I said that was it and he signed a copy and dated it, tearing off and giving me the top sheet.

'Well, we have notes now so make sure you log anything else, and if at any time you feel threatened or in immediate danger, just ring 911,' he said, handing me his card showing all the department details.

'Not wanting to dismiss these events,' he began, 'but there are a lot of wild animals out and about these parts, with us being so close to the mountains and national parks, and they're especially active of a night-time. When you're not used to somewhere, their presence takes a little getting used to,' he continued. 'You're new in town. You'll settle into things but, remember, call if you're worried, and in the meantime I'll have a patrol car do a few rounds up at Whispering Pines over the next week to show our presence. Okay?'

'Okay, thanks, I appreciate it,' I said, shaking his hand and standing to leave.

'Nice to meet you, Ma'am,' he said, as I turned to leave.

'You too and thanks again,' I repeated, turning and walking towards the main entrance, feeling every bit like the annoying nutty resident that would be the butt of their jokes for at least a few minutes.

I was furious as I left; not at the sheriff, he couldn't have been any nicer. No, I was angry with myself for sounding so stupid. He really had treated me seriously, yet I must have sounded like the typical woman having a hard time settling in and getting the creeps for no reason. I even started to wonder if I had seen the paintings correctly in the first place. But as I climbed into my car, I *knew* that something weird was going on.

I bounced up onto the drive and jumped out the car, slamming the door as I ran towards the lodge. I went in and Ember trotted up to me looking a little surprised. *What's she up to now, my loony tunes Mom,* I was sure he was thinking. I slid the keys across the counter and headed straight for the teakettle.

I spent the rest of the day moving dust sheets around as I painted the walls in a variety of neutral shades: some walls in warm stone, and the lower walls under the rails in a pale taupe.

In a matter of hours, I had finished the kitchen and the hallway. Noticing the time, I finished off and put the teakettle on before cleaning all my rollers and brushes. I'd eaten a little bread and cheese with some fruit for lunch, and that was all I'd had after my small breakfast. Now, just after eight, I was shattered, clammy and ready for a rest.

I lay on the couch with Ember behind my legs and watched an old movie before calling it a night just before eleven. The last few days had really caught up with me and I had a much needed rest, waking not once to any disturbances.

Driving into town just after ten the next day, I felt refreshed but nerves and anxiety soon started to twist my stomach. For whatever reason, against all my sceptical instincts, I had decided I wanted Abigail to do a reading for me. Maybe she could shed some light onto the weird events taking place and maybe I would get a little insight into my life and future. Either way, I thought it was worth giving it a try.

I parked higher up on the same street as the store and headed slowly downhill to the porch, trying to talk myself out of feeling embarrassed and forcing the scepticism out of my mind. The store had only a few people inside and a woman I had not seen before was serving behind the counter.

I walked in and automatically started looking around, too afraid to ask for Abigail. I looked through the books casually until I heard the door go and saw two people leave out of the corner of my eye. I brought my attention back to the books on display and suddenly changed my mind. I was just about to leave when I heard a familiar voice behind me.

'I knew it would only be a matter of time,' she said, as I turned to see Abigail smiling at me.

'Oh, Hi. Well, I figured a little insight might be what I need. Is this a good time for you or do I need an appointment?' I asked, feeling my face reddening.

'This is a perfect time. Come on, honey. Follow me,' she said, turning towards the counter. I followed her through to the back of the store, leaning sideways to slip through a beaded curtain into a long, narrow storage room, which led onto another room at the rear.

'Okay,' she said, 'what can I get you to drink?'

'Water or juice would be great, thanks.'

'Take a seat,' she said, not bothering to look back at me as she headed into the kitchen.

I looked around the brightly painted room, a perfect extension of the shop, with an array of weird and wonderful carved ornaments of wolves and Indians, alongside dreamcatchers, which wavered in the breeze coming in through the opened windows. I sat down on a spongy couch and leaned back onto a thick-filled, tassel-edged cerise cushion, waiting nervously and playing with my fingers anxiously. The room smelled of light incense and heavier oils, and I was pleasantly surprised when, after a few minutes, I actually started to relax.

Abigail walked over and placed my glass on a coaster for me and went to take the opposite couch, grabbing the tattered pack of cards from the table between us.

'So, how've you been? Busy settling in, I suspect,' she said, staring right into my face.

'I'm settling in fine, thanks. Just finished lots of painting and getting the lodge sorted out, making it a bit more homey, you know,' I replied.

Her face searched mine for several seconds before my eyes shied away. I looked back towards my glass, picking it up for a long drink to give myself something to focus on.

'Right,' she said, breathing out loudly. 'Now, I need you to shuffle these cards real well, until you're happy and ready.'

I looked at the pack and leaned forward to take them, starting the shuffle.

'Now, when you're happy, cut them and place the top cards to the bottom of the pile,' she said, taking a sip from her glass.

I did as she instructed and passed them back to her waiting hands.

In an instant, she was throwing the cards face-up in a pattern on the table. The images meant nothing to me as the colours flashed in front of my eyes. I looked at a few of the wordless cards and sat back, watching and waiting for what came next.

Abigail started to move each card slightly as her eyes flitted across them, moving some on top of others, singling some out on their own, but moving most into a different position.

'He was worth the years, you know. He was a good man. If you'd never met him, you wouldn't be here now,' she said, unexpectedly.

'Who?' I asked, feebly, instantly searching her face, but she did not look up at me.

'I read what I see, but you can't ask any questions and I don't want you to tell me anything,' she said, keeping her focus, a different woman now.

I sat forward, frowning, listening.

'The one you miss, the one you're grieving for, he's grieving for you,' she continued. 'Only, you're grieving for the change, the loneliness, the loss in that sense, not for him.'

I sat instantly dumbfounded by her statement. I'd guessed who she meant and she had my attention. Luke.

'You need this time alone, to gain a little perspective on your life and find yourself. You sometimes search for the very thing you fear.' Her eyes scanned more cards while she moved others around.

'And you need to open your eyes from time to time, to properly see what you're being shown,' she said, her eyes flitting over the cards, searching for more information.

'Stay away from him,' she said, more seriously. 'The one in your mind, he's not right for you. There's no match there.'

I wondered if she knew then who she was talking about as my face heated and reddened.

She looked up then, staring into my face for the first time. 'Take heed of warnings; don't put yourself in danger by letting go of your temper. And control your dog,' she said, as the thought of Ember's innocence filled me with a protective fear. What did *that* mean?

'Well, that's it for now,' she said. 'More will come as you change direction, make decisions. Then, I will see more.'

I sat, staring at her, taking in the small but astonishing amount of information she'd given me. She'd scared me shitless.

I couldn't say any more to Abigail. She knew that; she saw it in my face. I reached for my wallet to pay her but she leaned over to me, covering my hand.

'This one's on me,' she said, 'a welcome gift.' Just think about what I have told you, only don't allow it to make decisions for you. Just open your mind to the possibilities.'

'Thank you,' I said, smiling weakly back. My reddened cheeks must have been ashen white by now.

So, I was thanking this woman for scaring me shitless and for pushing my mind out of fourth gear and straight into fifth. But I was the one who thought this would be a good idea. What an idiot.

We chatted more casually about what I'd been doing, both ignoring the reading she had just given me, like that was her in her clairvoyant's role and now she was just someone I was getting to know. I really did like Abigail; I saw myself in her edgy quirkiness. I hated 'normal'. All my teenage and adult life I had strived not to be normal – from dying my hair a variety of colours, to piercing my navel and ears several times, to the rocky edge I held now – all to my parents' disapproval.

When we were back in the store, I went to browse again. I picked up two books that I'd seen on my first visit: one about the local history of Manzano and the surrounding area, and the other, a stunning photographic book containing images of Ysabel National Park.

I carried both books to the counter where Abigail put them in a paper bag for me. I paid for the books and said my goodbyes, desperate to get outside for some air.

As I jumped in my car, my cell rang and the caller display showed Caitlin's number.

'Hello,' I said.

'Hi, Megan?' the voice asked.

'Hi, Caitlin. Yeah, it's me. How are you?' I asked.

'I'm fine, thanks, you?'

'I'm good, thanks,' I said, waiting for the reason for her call.

'Great. Well, I was wondering if you could give us a little time tomorrow. We've got an additional intake of about half a dozen animals, five dogs and a cat, and I wanted to see if you could possibly help Gabe with the checks again?'

'Sure, not a problem. What time would you like me there?'

'Same as before,' she said, 'about ten?'

'Yeah, that's fine. I'll see you in the morning.'

'Thanks a million, Hon, see you then,' she said, ending the call.

I really had enjoyed the work last time, doing some of what I was used to doing, knowing I was helping a cause close to my heart. The downside, the bit I really wasn't sure about, was working with Gabe again.

After lunch, I slumbered on the couch alongside Ember, watching TV and looking through some of my wildlife photos I wanted to get enlarged. Ned decided this was the time to bring me one of my bed socks down from upstairs, carrying it in his mouth and shaking it from side to side to ensure his prey was dead. I chuckled to myself and he strode off looking for somewhere to hide it. I knew I would be searching for that everywhere later.

In the early evening, I got ready for what would hopefully be a cooler walk with Ember in the first park we'd visited. I grabbed my camera and all my usual walking gear and headed out the door. Ember knew the routine and positioned himself in his spot. I stuck on one of my favourite CDs in the car and we headed off to the park.

We walked for just over an hour, taking the shorter of the two orange routes and stopping periodically to take photos of the wild flowers and the landscape through the trees. The walk was just what I needed, steady and peaceful.

We drove home happy, content and tired, ready for a nice dinner, a hot shower and, hopefully, some sleep.

Chapter 8

I woke early after another deep and restful, undisturbed sleep. I bounded downstairs to ready myself for my few hours' work and felt a mixture of excitement and nerves, knowing I would see Gabe again.

Our daily routine had taken shape and I had it down to a fine art now. As Ember went about his business outside, Ned fussed around my legs, his tail tickling my shins. As always, I was never far from Ned's sight. Breakfast for everyone came next but I could only stomach a small bowl of cereal. Even then, most of the milk was left, for which Ember and Ned were always grateful.

I spent a little more time than usual readying myself, attempting a natural daytime look but using makeup to achieve it. From a practical standpoint, my hair needed to be in a ponytail to keep it out of the way, but I fluffed it with mousse as I dried it to glamorise the thrown-together look. Rather than the completely scruffy clothes I wore before, I slung on my low-rise jeans and skinny T-shirt, adding only a fleece round my waist and my usual low-heeled comfortable boots.

As I ran out the door, I saw Ember disappearing to his window position, waiting to see me leave down the drive. I slowly passed the window, looked across, and waved at him. I swear to God that dog would wave back one day.

I arrived at the shelter just before ten and caught sight of Gabe and Caitlin standing at the fence to one of the corrals as I pulled into the parking lot. Caitlin stood with one hand casually on her hip, looking up and covering her eyes from the sun with the other as she chatted to Gabe. He leaned back against the fence, talking animatedly to her while stroking one of the horses.

I sat in the car to catch my breath for a few seconds, the nerves kicking in big time. I got out, locked the door and headed in their direction.

As I got nearer, I casually looked around at the horses behind the fence next to where they stood, which were obviously expecting food. Caitlin looked round first and gave me a wide smile. Gabe kept his position, turning slightly to stroke one of the horses.

'Morning,' I said, in the cheeriest voice I could manage, my insides fluttering.

'Hi, honey,' Caitlin said, turning and giving me her usual hug.

Gabe looked round, still rubbing the muzzle of the horse and nodded, 'Morning.'

'Well, we only have four dogs and a cat today but I wanted to get them sorted as soon as possible so we can keep the ball rolling,' Caitlin said. 'We've re-homed well this week; good job with all the little ones coming through.'

'Really? That's great. Let's hope it continues,' I said. Gabe said nothing else. He just turned away from us and walked to the back of his Jeep, collecting the two bags he'd placed on the floor behind it. Now I felt like I'd interrupted their conversation. He walked into the main entrance and Caitlin and I made small talk as we followed on. As we went into the prep room, Gabe was taking things out of his bag, placing them on the table ready to start.

'Okay. I'll leave you kids to it,' Caitlin said, heading for the door.

'No problem, it won't take too long,' Gabe said, sorting things into order on the table.

'Just holler if you need me for anything, okay?' Caitlin said, as she turned and walked through the passageway to the reception.

I took a silent breath. 'What are we starting with?' I asked.

'We'll do the dogs first,' he said, making no attempt to look at me.

'Okay,' I replied, keeping it light, 'I'll go get the first one.'

I wandered off into the kennels and took the first dog out. It was a really scared-looking black lab mix so, as I took him out, I bent to my knees and gave him a few strokes and a kiss on the head. I took his paperwork from the front of the kennel and walked back through to the prep room.

He was a reasonable size dog, about fifty pounds, so I knelt on the floor to hold him steady instead of lifting him onto the table, waiting for Gabe to start the examination.

He turned and bent down and started to examine the dog, checking his ears, eyes and mouth. He reached up to the table to grab his stethoscope and silently checked his heart. The dog was wagging his tail the whole time and a little wriggly.

'Can you keep him still?' he asked, abruptly.

'I'm trying, but you're a wriggly boy, hey?' I said, stroking the lab's face.

'Maybe less fuss will help him calm down,' he muttered, barely audible.

'Oh, I'm sorry. There I was mistakenly thinking that I was helping the poor creature relax in this strange place, while you prod and poke him. Please accept my apologies,' I said, in the most cutting, sarcastic tone I could muster, which was not difficult. I meant every word.

I stood up, restraining the dog by his short leash as Gabe continued the examination. He didn't even seem to care that he'd been rude to me. What an asshole. It looked like it was going to be easy to stick to my no-men rule.

From my standing position while he bent below me, I took the chance to look at him from the closest perspective I'd had yet. His face stayed poker-straight and his dark eyes appeared elsewhere, as usual; they certainly weren't on his work. His hair fell slightly across his face as he leaned over to check the dog.

He stood up, and lifted him effortlessly onto the table, as if he weighed only a few pounds. I held the leash, standing to the front and stroking the dog's head slowly. I didn't want to piss the veterinarian off again, for whatever it was he thought I'd done.

Gabe turned away to an adjacent table to prepare the injections. As I held onto the dog, I looked at him again, knowing he wouldn't see me doing it, and noticed how muscular his lower arms were under the rolled-up sleeves of his pale blue shirt. The pronounced veins worked their way up the insides of his arms and his long fingers, which moved fluidly with their work, didn't look like they belonged to a working class man's hands.

I noticed a small dark mark on his right inner wrist. From where I stood, it looked like a letter or a symbol tattooed into his skin. I squinted to try to see it better, but couldn't tell exactly what it was.

He turned back to the dog so fast I had to avert my eyes quickly from him, and I made out I was casually picking something off of the dog's face. After a few minutes he put the needles back. 'Done,' he said, and scooped the dog from the table, placing him gently onto the floor.

Before I left the prep room, I gave the dog – which had been named Ollie by the shelter – a huge fuss, exciting him like crazy and sending his tail off into a wagging frenzy. 'Good boy,' I said loudly before leading him back to the kennels. Let him tell me off for that.

I brought the next dog through. It was a small cross-breed, weighing no more than twelve pounds, and I watched as Gabe readied his next injections, waiting until he cleared the table. He automatically turned and lifted the dog up onto the table. I stood there, like a robot, carrying out only what I was there to do, saying nothing more to him.

My ways to rebuff someone were basic; I only had two. I would either lose my temper completely and go hammer and tongs at them, or give them the silent treatment, festering inside until my temper was under control. This time I was using the latter method. I was so angry at this rude man and was going off him fast. One thing I could not stand in a person was rudeness and plain bad manners.

I continued this way for the rest of the hour, as did he, and we only exchanged the odd necessary word that related to the animals. When the final cat was safely back in its kennel, I walked back into the prep room, grabbed my keys and walked out, ignoring him completely as he packed his things away.

I pulled myself together to face Caitlin. Once I was out of there, I could seethe about him all I wanted. As we said our goodbyes, I agreed to the next Monday, unsure if I could actually bring myself to come back and be within a mile of the man.

I headed towards my car, cussing under my breath. But then I saw a little face that softened my mood, forcing a small smile to cross my lips. I reached the fence and slid my hands over Bill's old, soft face, and started talking to him in my quiet, gentle voice. 'Hey Bill, whatcha been up to? Feeling a little better in the cooler weather today, huh?' I asked.

I didn't hear the footsteps coming up behind me. The voice was far too close and I closed my eyes temporarily, deciding how to speak to him.

'Caitlin asked if I'd exercise a couple of the horses for her before I left,' he said, his voice low, softer.

I stood there stroking Bill, unable to speak, knowing my reaction to him now would be harsh.

'I don't suppose you'd have time to take one out with me?' he continued. How did he even know I could ride?

The guy just got better. *What a shit*, I thought. 'I'm busy. Besides, I might excite the horse too much if I pat it,' was my choice of reply. My holding-back and restraint had failed in an instant.

'A couple of the horses could really do with a good run out. It would help Caitlin if you could do this. I'm sorry I come across a little off-hand at times,' he said, before pausing. 'It's just…well, I'm not the best with people.'

'So, you think that excuses you, allows you to be rude?' I snapped.

'No,' he said quickly, moving from behind me to a couple of feet to my right leaning on the fence. 'I am sorry. I don't mean to be rude to you. Please accept my apologies. It won't ever happen again.'

I stood for a few seconds, clenching my jaw, looking into Bill's gentle face. Out of the corner of my eye, I saw him turn to face me. 'Please, I am sorry,' he said again.

'Fine, I'll accept your apology this time but don't you ever speak to me that way again. I'm helping out here because I want to. I'm struggling enough without getting hostility from you, someone I barely know,' I said, before stopping. I didn't like letting anyone know too much of what was in my head; I had my tough facade to maintain.

I thought I heard him say something quietly. It sounded like he'd said, 'still feisty'.

'I understand and I am truly sorry,' he said. I would love to know how *he* could understand anything *I* was going through.

I did, however, like the idea of riding. I hadn't ridden in a long while, actually, in many years, and I had hoped it would be something I could get back into once I moved and found somewhere suitable to do it. Another route of escapism.

'Okay,' I said, turning to face him. His eyes looked straight into mine, searching, apologising. 'But I only have what I am wearing.'

'Your clothes and boots are fine,' he said, looking me up and down to check. His eyes creased a little, showing the fine lines that surrounded them. It was the first time I'd seen him smile; a small, but genuine, smile. I forgave him instantly and looked away quickly into the safety of Bill's expression.

'I'll go get them ready over there in the far block. If you want to leave your keys with Caitlin,' he said, before turning and wandering towards the far stables.

I hung around, thinking about what had just happened. The guy was so bizarre: social and chatty one minute, utterly rude the next, and, then, wanting to go out riding! I didn't know what to make of him. I was torn between being completely annoyed by him to being a smitten kitten.

I was intrigued to know if by going for a ride with him it would break the ice completely, once and for all, and he would stick to his apology. Or, would he be like the fire and ice I was used to by now and go back to being rude again, pissing me off.

I also wondered if it was a good thing for *me* in general. The last thing I needed was to start liking this man too much, let him inside my head. And if he stayed true to his word and we got along well, I wasn't sure if that was a good thing for me emotionally. I doubted very much that it would be.

I traipsed slowly along towards the office, my mind full again, yet I was really looking forward to taking the horses out. I left my keys in the office and nipped to the restroom, re-tied my ponytail and concentrated for a few minutes on keeping the butterflies from somersaulting in my stomach.

The day was much cooler than the previous ones, and a light breeze, thankfully, freshened the air. I reached the stable block, separated from the public area by a 'Staff Only' sign, and slipped through the slightly open door, my eyes straining to adjust to the dim light inside. I saw that the stable door at the far end was open, and could hear movement inside, the familiar creak of the leather as the girth was tightened on the saddle around the horse within.

I walked slowly towards the noise, stroking a few of the interested noses that peered over the doors on my way. There were about eight stables in all, half of which were occupied. As I approached the furthest stable, Gabe was inside, bending across to collect the bridle off the hook it hung from.

'This is Warrior,' he said, busy placing the bit through the horse's mouth and reaching over his head to strap the bridle in place around his neck.

Warrior stood at least seventeen hands high, a striking black horse with sleek, well-toned muscles. His mane flowed long and untamed around his left eye and he stared down at me as I inched through the stable door.

I walked slowly towards his watchful, nervous eyes, my hand facing up and reaching towards him as an offer of friendship. My breathing accelerated. He was stunning.

'It's okay, friend,' Gabe whispered in his ear. I heard the air pushing through his nostrils as I approached but, with Gabe's gentle words, he started bowing his head and stretched his neck slowly forward towards my hand. He began sniffing my scent, making his decisions, and I could tell Gabe had his complete trust.

I stood very still, letting Warrior sniff me, then moved slowly towards and under his towering head. The smell I loved came rushing back to me as I raised my cheek to his muzzle, letting the aroma of warm hay and earth flow into me as well as the heat from his nostrils.

Gabe, who was standing just ahead of me to my right, had paused in his preparation of Warrior and was studying our interaction. I turned towards his stare, whilst continuing to stroke the velvet nose of Warrior, and had to catch my breath. His brow furrowed and a look of deep torture crossed his face. He wanted to say something, I was sure of that, but he offered nothing.

He took a step back and turned to walk soundlessly from the stable. I felt confident Warrior was at ease with me as I turned my face back to his, hearing another stable door being unlatched and opened. I stayed where I thought I needed to remain for the time being.

After a while, I heard the nearby door close and I knew Gabe had come back to the stable where I stood with Warrior. In that very second, I sensed his stare upon my back. I didn't need to look around to check; I knew he was there, watching.

'All set to go?' he asked. I turned towards his voice, with my hand still attached to Warrior, and saw him in the doorway of the stable, leaning against the wall, his arms crossed tightly over his solid chest. He stared at us, his face straight and taut.

'Who am I riding?' I asked, staring back at him and gulping hard as I felt my heart unexpectedly win the fight over my head.

'You'll be riding Mouse,' he said.

'Mouse. Cute name,' I said, smiling.

I walked tentatively towards the door, sliding my hand away from Warrior's muzzle, and hoped Gabe would move out of my way before I passed. I kept my eyes to the ground, desperately trying to avoid his intense stare, but I knew he was following my movement with his eyes. As I reached the door, I turned slightly sideways and paused, waiting for him to step aside. My breathing became harder, more obvious, and I forced my eyes even lower, towards my chest. I gulped again; my throat was so dry.

But he didn't move. His eyes were searching for mine, looking down and sideways at me, as he stood completely still, blocking my exit. The gap was not wide enough to pass through and I paused less than a foot from him, waiting for him to move and let me through. I was so close I could smell him. It was not the hot, working, outdoorsy smell I expected but a fresh, cold scent. It had something different to it, almost earthy. His towering frame filled my peripheral vision and it was like my eyes were being unwillingly dragged up to his.

I stretched my neck back to look up at him. His face remained completely numb, giving nothing away, and the few seconds that I looked at him was all it took to get the full mental picture of his face in its entirety. That would be the vision that stayed in the forefront of my mind for the rest of the day.

His face had an unfaltering strength to it. His dark, searching eyes bore into mine and the hardness of his face was chiselled with pure determination. His lips parted, as if he were taking a breath, about to say something, but he didn't.

As I stared back at him, waiting, trying to give him time to say whatever it was he wanted to say, I heard the faintest whisper, like words coming out through laboured breaths. It broke my attention and I looked away from him, over the door towards the entrance, partly expecting someone to come walking in. I looked back at him and he blinked slowly, moving his eyes to the ground.

'Excuse me,' I said, forcing my voice out. He slowly and silently moved aside, allowing me to pass, with his head bowed low. I'd broken *his* stare.

I walked to the next stable, unsure if I should go ahead with the ride now, feeling too uncomfortable. But, even so, I was desperate to hear what he had to say. Something was sitting on the tip of his tongue and I needed to slowly encourage it out.

'Mouse is perfect if you haven't ridden in a while,' he said more loudly behind me. 'She senses ability and will do anything you ask of her.'

Mouse was a much smaller chestnut horse, about fifteen hands at most, but sturdily built – an ideal size for me. I walked up slowly towards her, and she wandered forward to meet me halfway, inquisitive and instantly sniffing at my pocket. Her eyes were soft and reminded me of Ember's in some strange way. She nudged me in the stomach and I laughed quietly to myself at her confidence, as no doubt she was expecting me to be carrying some treat for her in there. 'Sorry, Mouse. I have nothing for you.'

The next thing I heard was the sound of heavy footfall and, as I looked back round, Gabe was leading Warrior past the stable towards the main door. I grasped Mouse's reins in my right hand and turned to gently lead her out.

Outside, Gabe let go of Warrior's reins, and headed back towards me, wearing a worn cowboy hat that shaded his eyes. I paid little attention to him as I thought he was going past to close the stable doors. I looked up to see Warrior take a couple of steps forward, turning slightly, then he waited, looking round for Gabe.

I drew the reins loosely back down Mouse's neck and hooked my left foot into the stirrup, grabbing the front of the saddle with both hands. She was tall enough that it would have taken a fair bounce to get up on her but just as I was just about to make my attempt to climb on, I felt Gabe behind me.

He moved in closer and I felt the upper part of his body make light contact with mine. He towered over me and his presence felt like a dark shadow. He stood motionless for a few seconds, his breath brushing at the back of my neck, and then he slowly slid down and took a hold of my right heel.

With effortless movement, he pushed me up and onto Mouse. He held the stirrup while I re-adjusted my foot, before turning back towards Warrior. As I fiddled around getting comfortable, I looked up to see him hook his dusty brown boot into the stirrup, easily pushing himself onto Warrior's tall back.

Gabe led the way and I followed a short distance behind, remembering the way it felt to be on horseback. I was always a natural rider, falling comfortably into the saddle, my body swaying and moving in perfect timing with the stride of the horse. It was an ability I had not gained from my parents. My father hated horses and my mother had no opinion, other than considering them beautiful, strong creatures. I knew I would feel it in my legs and butt in the morning, and for a few days afterwards, but I was also sure Gabe would take me on a pretty steady ride until he knew my level of ability.

We meandered through the groups of people looking around at the animals in the enclosures and on past the office, where Caitlin paused and acknowledged us through the window, smiling. Gabe passed by and raised his hand to his hat, with me following maybe ten feet or so behind. She waved at me and I gave a shy wave back, feeling a little coy about riding out with him.

As we put more distance between ourselves and the buildings, I looked out over the vast panorama before us, which lead into open grassy plains towards the hazy mountain trails. The same wild flowers grew here as in all the open meadows I'd seen in the area, pretty and untouched.

We continued in complete silence until we reached the end of the meadow, where I could see that we were heading towards a winding pathway, which climbed up gradually through the valley between the mountains. While I was gazing up at the height of the range, I heard the increased pace of Warrior's hooves in the loose dirt. Gabe set off at a fast but relaxed trot and I squeezed my knees on Mouse to follow suit.

Without hesitation, Mouse changed her speed, and started taking deep trotting strides to follow on. Gabe rode on ahead, deep in his saddle, and I had to tame Mouse down a little for I could feel the haste in her stride, wanting to be off, needing to run.

I shortened my rein and held a little tighter onto her, so I could dictate our speed. She was chomping at the bit to be off, though, and after a few minutes we were deeper into the valley. I looked back and saw the meadow disappearing out of sight. As I looked back to where I was going, Gabe's head turned slightly, as if to check my position.

I evened the pace on Mouse and started to relax until, without warning, Warrior was off again. He moved into a slow canter and left us behind. I felt Mouse's feet skipping and dancing under me, so I looked ahead, let the reins out a little, and let her go. Mouse needed no more encouragement as she chased down Warrior and we caught up easily, thanks to her fast stride. Gabe's eyes again came round to check I was close behind, losing no speed as he turned his head.

We cantered for a good five minutes before I saw a narrow left turn ahead. I sensed our move beforehand and pulled Mouse back into a fast trot at exactly the same time as Gabe reined in Warrior. As we approached the turn, the dust lifted loosely from the ground into the still air surrounding us.

All I could hear now that the pace had slowed were the horses huffing and blowing through their noses. At first I thought they were regulating themselves after the canter, but I realised what they were doing the minute we turned left through the narrow gap, which was overhanging with rocks, and my eyes caught sight of the vast meadow sprawling out before us.

As soon as we had cleared the tapered, rocky path, the sound of the horses' hooves changed as they moved onto the solid, grassy earth underneath. I braced myself for what was to come and shortened Mouse's reins. Gabe held Warrior easily and circled on him slowly once, giving him the chance to gauge my expression. As Warrior returned to face the meadow, he set off like lightning into a fast gallop, heading straight towards the centre of the meadow and the distant solitary tree that stood there.

I held Mouse back so tightly I could feel the pull of leather under my bare hands. She knew what this place meant. She itched and pulled harder for me to release her to follow. I felt a little nervous, worried that I hadn't ridden this hard in a long time. I leaned forward as she trotted and pushed my weight into the stirrups, before slowly inching the reins out to loosen them in preparation for a canter, then a gallop. Gabe was far ahead already and getting further, a mere silhouette in the sprawling meadow.

As our speed picked up, the wind blew into my face and the loose strands of hair whipped around my forehead, causing me to squint to protect my eyes. Mouse flew after Warrior, focused, chasing. My nerves subsided faster than I'd expected as I let my body relax into the movement, remaining still and balanced above Mouse's long, galloping stride. We closed in on Gabe and Warrior, who looked to have slowed a little.

Mouse did not slow as we closed the gap and when we were about a hundred feet away, well towards the centre of the meadow, I could see Gabe turn in his saddle, watching our fast approach. The slow canter he had adopted moved instantly into another gallop, and he turned around and started to angle Warrior into our path.

As we galloped on, Gabe and Warrior moved in alongside us, keeping pace, both horses focusing ahead. I glanced quickly left and, as I did, Gabe picked up the pace again, urging Warrior into yet another gear. My heart was racing, not from fear, but from adrenaline. As he increased speed, so did I, and I pushed Mouse on hard as we galloped side by side, only a few feet apart, past the tall, dead tree, and on towards the more distant woodland. After a few minutes I started to slow, at exactly the same time Gabe did. I pulled Mouse steadily back and gradually eased her into a fast canter, before we slowed to a trot and, finally, a walk.

'Enjoy that?' Gabe asked, not remotely out of breath.

'Yeah, that was awesome,' I replied, panting and trying to regain my heart rate and breath. 'I'll suffer for it in the morning, though; it's been a long while since I've ridden.'

Gabe looked over and gave me a delightful, laughing smile. 'You ride well.' The look of freedom in his face was perfect and I got a new picture of him, one I preferred much more. His eyes, for once, looked bright and at ease, even though they were still the darkest of browns. I stared at him until he turned away, this new image lingering in my mind.

When I looked back round, we were just reaching the edge of the trees and as we walked the horses in, ducking under the low hanging branches, the air became pleasantly cool in the shadowy darkness. We meandered silently, twisting and turning and heading gradually downhill.

As we descended further, I could hear the noise of water in the distance. The horses' breathing slowly returned to normal and, as we walked, I patted Mouse, feeling the clammy sweat on her long neck.

We ambled around a corner and the sound of water became louder. We headed for the wide, stony stream in front of us. As we reached the water's edge, Gabe stopped and flung his long leg over Warrior's back, jumping to the ground in one fast, easy movement.

He released Warrior to go to the stream and then walked back and took the reins close to Mouse's mouth to hold her steady while I dismounted. I managed it easily and Gabe let her go as soon as I was clear. Mouse went to happily join Warrior at the water's edge, dipping her hot muzzle into the water to cool off.

My legs and butt had started to stiffen already, and I stretched and pulled my legs up and down towards my back to free them off. Gabe smiled at my movements and walked slowly towards a large flat stone, several feet away from the horses, where he sat down.

I stood, pushing my hands into my back and stretching myself out, watching the horses drink. I walked to the water's edge and looked downstream, seeing the water disappear around the bends covered with heavy-set trees. I felt at ease as I wandered back towards the large stone, took a seat and then leaned back onto my arms only a few feet away from Gabe.

Gabe sat forwards, leaning his elbows onto his opened knees with his hands clasped together, forming a ledge to rest his chin on. 'Some place, isn't it?' he asked, his eyes staying firmly on the horses, or beyond them to the water and trees.

'It's beautiful,' I said, looking towards his still profile, then back to the horses again.

We sat there at ease in the silence. 'So, how long have you lived in Manzano?' I asked.

'Just over four years now,' he replied. 'I love it here. The peace and quiet, the seclusion.'

'I can't imagine anyone not falling in love with a place like this,' I said.

'You've come from Boston, very different for you here,' he said, sounding like he knew the place.

'Yeah, I lived there for about eight years. I love Boston, but I think I love it here more. It suits me better, I think.'

'So, how did you come to end up in Manzano?' he asked.

'Well, I'd visited California a few times in the past on vacation, and Liv recommended Manzano to me. I love the warmth, the wildlife and outdoor activities; all of it,' I said, looking into the distant trees and inhaling deeply but quietly. I felt like we were finally both starting to relax in one another's company.

'You know,' he said, as if finding the right words, 'the way I come across, to you, and to other people around here. They see the veterinarian, the quiet, strange man. They don't understand me; they never will. But it's all I can give them.'

I looked towards him, seeing the conflict start behind his eyes again, the torture I'd seen in them already. I wondered what had happened to make him so defensive and distant, so...reclusive.

I stared at him, wondering, trying to find some words myself. 'I got the impression, on a couple of occasions, that you've wanted to say something to me but you hesitate and say nothing. Am I wrong?'

Gabe paused and clenched his jaw hard, his eyes flitting around as he thought. Then, he stopped still, looking ahead of him. 'I think we'd better get the horses back.'

I stood shortly after he did, and watched him walk to the horses, a little angry with myself for bringing it up. Yet it was now clear what the answer was, apparent by his behaviour on being asked outright. There had been, or still was, something he wanted to say or ask. But I knew I wouldn't hear it, not yet, not here.

He took hold of the horses and walked them towards me, letting Warrior go before giving me the rein for Mouse. I walked to Mouse's side, and offered no resistance when he walked up behind me, keeping a gap between our bodies, and lifted me by my heel up onto the saddle. We rode the whole way back in silence. One thing I needed to remember in future conversations with Gabe: restrain my mouth.

By the time we'd trekked back to the shelter, the place was buzzing with people. Gabe dropped his head and meandered through them towards the stables, keeping a low profile under the brim of his hat.

Once we reached the stables, we both jumped off and Gabe took hold of Mouse's reins.

'I'll sort these two out. Your dog will be wondering where you've got to,' he said, smiling lightly, but more hesitantly, now.

'Are you sure?' I asked. 'I don't mind helping.'

'No, it's fine, really. I enjoy this bit. Will I see you Monday?'

'Yeah, I'll be here Monday. And thanks for taking me riding, I really enjoyed it, enjoyed the freedom,' I said, smiling at his watching face.

'My pleasure. We'll do it again sometime,' he said, smiling back. He nodded and turned to take the horses through to the stables.

I wandered back to my car, knowing I was failing miserably in forcing my head to rule.

Chapter 9

The rest of the week passed quickly and, before I knew it, the lodge was almost finished. I had taken a couple of runs with Ember once the stiffness from the ride had eased, and the only shopping I had to do in town was for food, which hadn't taken long.

I had also bought some new clothes at one of the city malls, knowing now I might be heading out with Liv from time to time. Well, by new clothes, I actually mean I had bought some new tops of the going-out variety. Jeans could be dressed up easily.

As Saturday night approached, I spent some time in the yard doing a little work but mainly lolling around on the lounger on the bunkhouse deck, a real sun trap, where I read most of a book, looked through some of my new photos and willed the sun to show me some grace.

I had thought little of Luke, about what he'd asked of me, but I knew inside that I only said what I did to run away from our conversation, to escape hearing him plead with me. I couldn't bear to hear him do that. Someone featured constantly in my thoughts but it was not Luke.

The nights had been peaceful, all of them, since I had reported the incidents. If someone was hanging around, they had long gone since the police had been more visible.

On the Saturday morning, I took Ember for an early morning run and called Liv to check details for the evening. She'd given me her address, along with the basic directions I needed to find her house in town, and we were all set to meet at her place at 6:30 p.m. Maria had, sadly, cancelled due to being ill with a stomach bug. I got myself dressed and made-up, enjoying the routine again. With my hair and face ready, I slipped on the black Grecian strapless top I had just bought and zipped it shut. It fitted nice and snug around my average chest and flowed out longer onto my hips. It suited my shape and I could tell the body I preferred had made a slight comeback, giving the impression I actually had a butt now.

I hadn't eaten since lunch, wanting to save myself for the culinary delights Liv had promised. I felt so hungry I gave in to bag of potato chips to tide me over. With everything I needed in my purse, I kissed the kids goodbye, then ran into the bathroom to remove the husky fur from my lips before heading out the door.

My car smelt much better after a good cleaning session and was now ninety-five percent hair free. I was sure Liv would not care about the other five percent, which would no doubt attach itself to her clothes. I found her place easily; it was just one more street up and across from Abigail's store. As I pulled into the drive, the curtains twitched and I saw a light being turned off, just before she appeared at the front door. She looked far better than I did, wearing a fitted pencil skirt, killer blocky heels and a cream, barely buttoned shirt, which sat snugly tucked into her skirt. Now I felt underdressed.

She had a more feminine shape compared to mine, small, but well balanced. The hips, slim waist, shapely legs and choppy short black hair all fit together well. You could tell she was a city girl.

As she climbed into the passenger seat, she spun her legs in carefully to maintain her modesty. I smiled watching her, awaiting the reaction.

'Well, only you would drive this big old thing,' she said, pretending to be bemused. 'Why can't you just have a small car, like mine?'

'Yeah, because I can really see Ember in that,' I replied, nodding towards her sweet little sporty Mini parked in front of the garage.

'I'm sure he'd fit perfectly,' she countered. 'Now, can we go eat, although not much will fit in the space between my stomach and this waistband.'

I chuckled at her as I turned to watch where I was reversing and swung out onto the small side road. We fell into chatting easily and she filled me in on her week before I told her about mine. I didn't mention riding with Gabe; I didn't need to, as that was her next topic of conversation.

'So, you had fun out riding with Gabe at Caitlin's, then?' she asked, looking towards me, awaiting an instant answer.

'Yeah, it was great to get back out on a horse again. It's been so long,' I replied, keeping my answers basic. 'How did you know about that?'

'I just know,' she said, refusing any further reply. 'You know, you should be careful with him.'

'What do you mean?' I asked.

'Well, he's okay on a working day-to-day basis, in company and all, but he can just be so odd. I think there's a bit of a dangerous edge to him,' she said, looking out of the window.

'Well, he was perfectly fine with me,' I lied, hoping to change the obvious opinion she had. 'Anyway, what do you mean by 'a dangerous edge'?'

'He's come back a few times from the talks he goes off doing, his random little trips, and I've seen funny scars and marks on him. He already has quite a few visible scars on him but they fade to white lines you can hardly see. He also has a strange tattoo thing on his right arm, barely visible under his watch strap, a symbol or something. He could belong to a weird cult. You never know,' she said.

'Now I think your imagination is running wild,' I said, snickering at what she had said, but secretly questioning him just a little more than I already had. 'I think he's just a little reclusive is all.'

'Well, there's just something about him; something I can't place my finger on. All I'm saying is I know you're fragile right now and he is someone who might not be right for you.'

'Look, all we did was ride out. It was nice company for me, some-one else to say I know, apart from you. He was perfectly nice and friendly, and I am in no way interested in anyone, let alone him,' I lied again.

'Okay, sorry. You know by now I speak my mind. Can't help it. I just don't want to see you get hurt.'

'I won't. Now enough, okay?'

'Okay,' she replied, sensing my irritation.

We chatted idly the rest of the way to the restaurant, which was about twenty minutes out of Manzano. When we arrived outside the building that looked like a log cabin, I looked across at her, puzzled.

'Trust me. It's an amazing place,' she said, as we pulled up to park. 'Don't judge a book by its cover.'

And an amazing place it was. The menu caused me over ten minutes of deliberation before I settled on the crab legs with lemon drawn butter and tiger prawns sizzled in garlic. A portion of fries and coleslaw sat alongside and, by the end of the meal, only a handful of fries remained.

'You can sure tuck it away,' Liv laughed, looking at my plate.

She'd opted for the Caesar salad, something I only ate as an accompaniment to a meal, and the broiled lobster, sans butter.

The dessert menu was refused before I'd even had a chance to look through it. There was no way she was going to sit through me eating a dessert while she watched; the buttons of her skirt wouldn't allow any more food to enter. We had soft drinks and let our meal settle before we paid the check and headed out to the car.

'You need lifting in now?' I asked, laughing and watching her re-adjusting herself into her clothes.

'I can manage just fine, thank you,' she said, taking a deep breath and struggling into the passenger seat.

It was only another fifteen minutes to the neighbouring town of Antala, where a lot more bars were spread along the Main Street. Driving through, I thought the popularity of the town showed in the number of people milling around, hopping from one bar to another. Antala had a population dwarfing that of Manzano, having somewhere close to thirty-two thousand residents, or so I'd read in a book I'd bought from Abigail's store.

Liv's directions took us to a parking lot, just off Main Street. I hopped out, slammed the door shut, and waited for her to emerge, moaning as she did about how she'd eaten too much.

'Oh, enough already,' I said 'It'll help you fill that skirt out, provided the buttons and zipper can take the strain,' I laughed.

'Yeah, yeah,' she said, walking round to my side of the car.

It took us five minutes to walk down to the first bar and Liv's personality came to the fore in her excitement, with her whooping and singing as we walked arm in arm towards the sound of the music coming out of the place where we were headed. If I were being honest, Liv's loud and extroverted side scared me a little; it was something I wasn't used to, nor had I ever been like that.

But, differences in personalities sometimes worked well. It had for me for over six years with Luke. And as much as we were like night and day in some ways, Liv and I got on really well and had a lot more in common than I'd anticipated. Despite her brash exterior, she also had a deeper, more understanding and caring side.

As she opened the door to the first bar, the music of No Doubt came flooding out, and Liv automatically danced her way inside with me following a few paces behind so no one would look at me like they were now looking at her. I couldn't bear that kind of attention.

The bar was very full and we squeezed through the crowd to order drinks. I liked the music and relaxed a little as people chatted easily and danced around. A group of about four men standing at the far end of the bar looked over at us and, on seeing their attention, I instantly looked away while Liv danced away, shaking every bit of her body to the music, obviously the source of their interest.

With our drinks in hand, we headed for a quieter space and attempted to chat over the music, shouting at each other and moving closer to hear. Each time the music changed, Liv started a new little dance, thoroughly enjoying herself and knocking the vodka and Coke back at a decent pace. We returned to the bar several times and as I ordered soft drinks Liv's became doubles. I knew she was on a sure-fire route to vomiting and a hangover.

On our fourth round, I asked for a juice and headed off to the restrooms, leaving Liv bopping her way to the bar. When I returned five minutes later, I couldn't see her anywhere. Scanning around the room, I caught sight of her talking animatedly with the group of men who had been ogling us – well, ogling her. She was tipping my juice down her arm while she talked to them and she hadn't even noticed she was doing it. Great, the evening was just about to get worse.

I closed in behind her and relieved her of my drink. She looked back and threw her arm round my neck, kissing my cheek. 'Hey, guys, this is Meg,' she said, introducing me. I smiled nervously and said a pretty soundless 'Hi.'

Although Liv was a little drunk, she seemed to sober up the more we spoke to the men, probably helped by no further visits to the bar. One of the group, Hayden, homed in to chat to me. He was a couple of inches taller than I was and seemed different from the others, a little quieter. I didn't really take offence to him as he seemed like an okay kind of guy.

We talked awhile, keeping the conversation simple. He was reasonably attractive and had a surfer-look about him, with straight, long blond hair and piercing blue eyes. Normally, blonds with blue eyes did nothing for me, but in an environment without alcohol, and at a time when I might be more interested in men, I would probably have still liked him.

All the while we talked, I kept glancing over towards Liv, making assumptions about her behaviour and the way she acted with the men, all of whom were paying her the kind of attention she clearly enjoyed. Hayden, like me, seemed the quieter of the bunch, laughing now and then with his friends but then bringing the conversation back to me. I remained chatty but reserved with him, never giving anything away that I didn't want him to know, and whacked the odd flirting comment away often enough that he soon saw I was not worth all the hard work and was really not interested.

We hung around with them for awhile longer before I managed to whisper in Liv's ear, suggesting that it was time to move on to another bar. Hopefully, she'd get my subtle way of saying 'Let's go' without thinking I was a miserable cow, spoiling her flirty fun.

To my surprise, she agreed and I managed to ease her away from the men, their eyes beckoning us back, while I smiled cautiously and dragged her outside.

When we got to the next bar, I glanced at my watch; it was only just after 9:30 p.m. This place was a little more modern and had a younger crowd but the music was more Liv than me. We had a couple of drinks in there and I relaxed a little when Liv stopped talking about the men in the last place and settled on more idle chat. Her mood was good, and her tipsiness had subsided a little.

We finished our drinks and headed to the restrooms before we left for the last bar of the evening. As we peed and chatted through the thin walls of the cubicle, Liv's sense of humour came out in full flow and she had me laughing so hard, it was a good job we were in the restrooms.

We left arm in arm and headed on a longer walk to the other end of town, to a bar that was set back from the road, and surrounded by a large dusty parking lot. There were a lot of cars parked there and I could hear Nirvana banging out 'Teen Spirit' as we approached.

'You'll like this place,' she said. 'Got that weird rocky element you're into.'

I grinned back at her and we pushed our way through the saloon-style doors into a dark but very chic interior. There were drapes and booths and black leather couches surrounding large round tables. As we made our way towards the bar, I checked out the wide variety of people hanging around, from young college types to couples a whole lot older. It made me relax being in such mixed company, and I loved the atmosphere and music straight away.

We got our drinks and headed over to a table just being vacated. Liv leaned forward towards me and cupped her hand, shouting over the music to me.

'So,' she shouted, 'what do you think of this place, then?'

'It's great. I love it. I would have never believed it would be like this from the outside,' I shouted back.

'Thought you'd like it,' she said, with a smug look on her face. 'Next time, we must get a cab. Then we can both get wasted,' she grinned. 'Maybe leave out the food so we can dance too.'

Well, a drink, yes. Leave the meal out, pretty hard but okay. But dancing? Erm, no. That was never going to happen. I'd have to break it to her gently, but break it I would.

'Okay,' would do for now.

We took it in turns to go to the bar, more often for Liv than for me. We giggled and cracked jokes, and I remembered what it was like to enjoy the single life, relaxing and appreciating the company of a girlfriend, gossiping and talking crap.

Mid-conversation something broke Liv's loud cackle and I only had to look at her face to gauge what had done it. Her flirty exterior had presented itself again and I tried hard not to roll my eyes when I realised who was coming up behind us.

'Hey, guys,' she called, standing to hug most of the group but leaving Hayden out of her show of affection, presumably because she mistakenly thought I was interested in him.

'Hey, Liv, Meg. Great to see you guys,' one of them called and I knew straight away it was the annoying, loud and overconfident one called Adam. He had a bulky build and cropped hair, and he had irritated me from the start. And, to annoy me further, he'd shortened our names as if he'd known us forever.

'Hi,' I replied, trying my best to be friendly and catching Hayden's face staring at me.

'So, may we join you two ladies?' Adam asked. I tensed my face to hide the grimace before it came out.

Liv answered instantly and as I expected. 'Sure, so long as you get us some drinks,' she said, smiling sweetly.

'Not for me, thanks. I'm juiced out,' I said, before he asked what I wanted.

'Well, as Meg's not having one, I'll have a double vodka and Coke to make up for it,' she said, as I sensed the pleasant evening had come to an abrupt end.

Hayden sat opposite me at the end of Liv's couch and I was thankful he wasn't any closer. He had already taken on the face of a loyal puppy dog, his alcohol-reddened eyes sagging and an overly sweet smile on his face, which I could only presume was meant as an attempt at flirting with me. I was glad I was single, although looking at the men on offer in a large town like this, it occurred to me that I probably would have no choice, being as choosy as I was.

This was the part of Liv I didn't care for. Everything else, brilliant. Even with a little booze inside her, it only made her humour sharper. But in this Liv I saw the easily led girl who was flattered by any male attention.

As my concentration waned, I found myself thinking about Gabe. Even though he was a little odd and had mood swings, I had much more in common with him, even considering my reclusive, quiet side. I was suddenly brought back to the present when Liv leapt up, squealing and dancing to a new song that had just started playing.

Three of the men stood up with her, Adam being one of them, and started to dance, closing in around her. It looked and felt smutty, and I gulped as I became wary of the situation. Hayden, probably tired from his attempts at wooing me, was fast asleep on the couch and the other man, Taylor, got up to join in with the dancing.

Liv seemed too drunk to understand their dirty little advances, letting herself go with the music, and none of them paid me any further attention. I'd obviously repelled them all ages ago. I was starting to get pissed off now and was not at all comfortable with the situation. I'd had enough.

I stood up and pushed my way into the centre of the group, taking hold of Liv's arm, and shouting in her ear, 'I'm ready to go now. We need to go, okay?' She looked up at me with her glazed eyes and instantly sensed I was not happy. She stumbled towards her purse as I leant and grabbed it for her, keeping hold of her arm.

'Thanks, guys. See you again,' I said, trying to remain polite yet firmly manoeuvring Liv through the crowds towards the door.

'Hey, come on. Stay a while!' Adam shouted, following us, a little miffed I'd broken up his intimate party.

'I'm driving all the way home and I am really tired right now,' I countered, 'we'll catch you guys again.'

I turned my face away without listening to anymore and Liv twisted round over my shoulder to wave at them, stumbling as she tried to walk.

Once on the street, I took a deep breath, my heart pounding. As we reached the main road, I looked back when I heard the door go but it was just a couple leaving behind us. Liv mumbled incoherently while we walked and my breath became harder from propping her up, but I made haste, closing the distance to the parking lot.

Liv was still laughing to herself at some drunken joke as we turned off Main Street and onto the darker side of the road where the parking lot stood. 'Come on,' I said, as her legs started wobbling. But she continued to giggle to herself.

I stopped for a second to adjust my grip around her waist. As I faced her to transfer both our purses into one hand, I saw three shadows just turning off Main Street further behind us. I gulped nervously and found the necessary strength to drag her with me on the last stretch to the car. I quickly remembered where my car keys were, but was unable to take them out with my hands full.

We turned into the lot and headed through the few cars still parked there towards mine. But before we reached the car, a familiar voice called behind us and I could tell they had closed in on us considerably.

'Hey, come on. You guys can't leave yet,' Adam said, putting his hands up to us in a welcoming gesture.

'Sorry guys, but I'm whacked and we have a long drive home. We're hoping to come back next weekend,' I lied, hoping like hell my face appeared truthful.

'But the party's just got started,' another man said, as all three of them stood about twenty feet away from us, forming the same uncomfortable arc I'd seen in the bar.

'Look, guys, go enjoy your party,' I said, trying to take my keys out at the same time. 'And I'll enjoy it more the next time when we can both drink.'

I tried to see their faces in the dark lot but the dim light from the side road made it difficult.

In the few seconds while I struggled to reach for my keys, still supporting Liv's weight, they were next to us. Adam grabbed the still-giggling Liv and the other two came to my side. Adam's bulky frame overshadowed Liv's tiny one and he started to mess around with his hand in her shirt, trying to unbutton it.

I took a step forward and instantly felt two pairs of strong hands grab hold of my arms. Liv started to come around a little at that point. 'Hey,' she said, her giggle being replaced by a drunken scowl as she tried lamely to move Adam's hand.

I snapped then, losing it completely, taking the man on the right by complete surprise by forcing my loosely held arm back into a high right angle and elbowing him full in the face. He cried out and automatically lifted his hands to his face. I twisted round to the left and threw my right knee up between the legs of the other man, which I had recognised in the shadows as being Taylor.

As I turned back towards Liv, I felt a tight grasp on my hair and someone pulling my head sharply back. My hands fell back automatically waiting for the fall to the ground but his weight was behind me, holding me up by my hair.

'Fucking bitch!' Taylor's furious voice hissed as he hunched up in pain. I managed to twist my head slightly to see Liv's shaking body slung to the ground, one of her shoes a couple of feet away.

'Get the fuck off me!' I screamed, struggling and ignoring the taut, ripping pain in my scalp. A large hand came forward to muffle my mouth but I struggled like a wild animal, my fury and determination taking over, lashing out and giving everything I had, at anything I could. There was another pair of hands on me now, belonging to Taylor, and he slammed my head forwards into the side of my car.

My vision went strange, like a shutter on a camera, taking snapshots of the scene unfolding. Adam pulled me from the ground and turned me to face him. I lifted my hands a little too late, trying to protect my face, and felt a flash of pain as his fist connected with my right cheekbone. At that moment and, mercifully, I heard Liv scream out loud, her sobering mind realising what was happening. I hoped to God her scream would draw the attention of any people nearby.

It did have an effect as they shoved me down against my car, my back grating with the force as I slid down the nuts on the wheels. As a leaving gesture, Adam flung his boot hard into my stomach before all three men ran off in different directions. Liv crawled towards me on her hands and knees, crying, her screams weakening.

'I'm so sorry,' she cried out, putting both her hands onto me. She was shaking violently and tears streamed down her face, along with big black streaks of mascara. Even in the dim street light, she looked awful. God only knows what I looked like.

I could say nothing. My legs were like jelly beneath me, the shock of the attack sinking in. I felt a trickle of fluid fall somewhere from the right side of my face and reached up slowly to wipe it away, seeing easily in the dim light the darkened blood spreading over my fingers.

I sat back against the tire, unable to move, the air taken out of me from the kick in my stomach and the pain quickly setting in. I leaned my head back to see a couple walking briskly into the lot, the man shouting that the police were on their way. As they approached us, they slowed down and continued to reassure us. My breaths were shallow and painful, and I actually felt scared of breathing in case a rib had punctured one of my lungs.

'Oh my God. Are you okay?' the man asked, the woman with him also crouching down to look at me. It was then that everything went black.

The next thing I knew, I was being treated by a paramedic and I felt cold as he checked me over, before placing a warm blanket over me. I was stretchered into a waiting ambulance and it only felt like the sirens were wailing for a matter of minutes before I was being carried into the hospital, squinting at the bright fluorescent lights. I shut my eyes. Everything hurt.

I heard Liv's voice beside me as we moved through the corridor. She was holding tightly onto my left hand, still crying.

'Meg, I am so, so sorry. It's all my fault. I'm so sorry I let this happen to you.'

'I'm fine, honest. Just a little roughed up is all. It's not your fault, Liv,' I said, turning my head slightly towards her to break a simple smile before thinking better of it and returning my throbbing face to its original position.

It wasn't her fault. Yes, she'd gotten too drunk, as many millions of other people did, and, yes, she had started flirting with the group, but she hadn't told them to follow us, to attempt to rape her or to beat the shit out of me. Only they were responsible for that.

The doctor spoke gently and clearly to me, asking me personal questions: where does it hurt? Could I feel him pressing in certain places? He checked my eyes with a light before examining the painful parts, the ones I hadn't seen myself.

The nurses flitted around, getting some kind of drugs ready, as the doctor checked me over more thoroughly. The only real pain I could feel was in my stomach and on my cheekbone, but I knew I'd been subjected to more blows. As I lie there, letting them do what was necessary, I slid my eyes across to the opposite bed, where Liv sat crying her heart out, a nurse tending to a bad graze on her knee.

'You okay, Liv?' I asked, my voice weak.

She looked up at me; mascara smeared everywhere, her eyes full of sadness and regret. 'I'm so sorry, Meg.'

'Look Liv, seriously, I'm fine. Please, don't beat yourself up. You're not to blame,' I said, feeling the tears fill my eyes as I looked at her heartbroken face. 'Anyway, least I roughed up their sorry butts a bit too.'

As I lay my head back, I saw two police officers walk in and speak with the doctor. They went to wait by Liv until the nurse was finished with her and then I saw her go outside with them into the corridor.

'Is this going to take long?' I asked the doctor, who had returned to my bed. 'My dog and cat are at home. They'll need to go out.'

'I think you'll be staying with us for the night, I'm afraid. Your body's received quite a lot of trauma. Your cheekbone isn't broken but the wound will need sutures, and we'll need to X-ray and scan your chest and abdomen to make sure there are no ruptures or fractures in there.

'Oh, great. Anything else?' I asked, sarcastically. 'I'm sorry, but I feel fine. I just want to go home,' I pleaded.

'I can't let you leave tonight. We will monitor you to check no swelling occurs, get you cleaned up and the sutures in place. After a rest tonight, you can leave tomorrow morning, provided everything is okay.'

'Fine,' I replied, lifting my eyes to the ceiling. 'While you're at it, my back really hurts too.' On saying that, he gently tipped me onto my side to check the area close up.

'Some nasty grazing down there too. We'll get that cleaned up and get you on some antibiotics and anti-inflammatory pain relief, okay?'

'Okay, thanks,' I muttered, moving onto my back. Lying with my arms over my chest, I worried about taking care of Ember and Ned.

I looked over a few times towards the place where Liv had gone with the police and waited impatiently for her to return.

I shut my eyes, thinking about the kids, as the nurse started fixing up my face and then my back. As soon as I'd got my shots, I was taken through to get X-rays and scans done. Once I was back in the ward, I closed my eyes, resting, and worrying.

I fell asleep for what must only have been a few minutes before a voice I recognised, one that didn't belong there, woke me from my slumber.

'Hey,' he said. I opened my eyes and saw Gabe crouching by the bed.

'Hey,' I replied, croakily, not understanding what he was doing there.

He looked at my face and I reached up to cover the damage with my hand. My fingers touched my face before they should have, and it was then I realised it was already very swollen and very sore. I slid my fingers over the sutures that held the painful gash together.

The next thing happened very unexpectedly. Tears started to well in the corners of my eyes and then involuntary spilled down my cheeks. I think I was so overwhelmed by the events that had unfolded a couple of hours before, the shock kicking in, and now it was made worse by seeing Gabe next to me.

His eyes were gentler than I'd ever seen them but they still showed pain deep within. My chin started to waver and I tried to clench my teeth together to stop the emotion but, as I clenched, a pale hand, colder than ice, moved over the top of my cheeks and very carefully brushed away the tears.

'So, you had an eventful night,' he said, smiling, the lines at the corner of his eyes creasing.

'You could put it that way,' I said, finally bringing myself under control. His hand hovered gently around the edge of my face, brushing the strands of dampened hair back behind my ear. 'How did you know I was here?' I asked.

'Liv called me. Asked if I could come collect her.' I thought it was strange. Gabe was not one of the people I had thought Liv would call in a situation like this. Maria, yes, but Gabe? Strange.

'Oh,' I replied, puzzled. 'What time is it?'

'Just after 1 a.m. So, what's the extent of the damage?'

'I can go home tomorrow. Just a few cuts and bruises. The X-rays were fine. Is Liv still here?'

Gabe clenched his teeth hard and his eyes lost their soft veneer. 'Yes, she's in the waiting room.'

'Is she okay?' I asked, worried about the state she'd been in.

'She's fine, Meg, but you're not, no thanks to her behaviour.'

'Have you spoken to her?' I asked.

'No,' he replied, 'not yet.'

'So, how do you know it was her fault, and how do you even know what happened? Look, Gabe, it was not her fault. Those creeps followed us from the bar and they knew exactly what they were after. It wasn't her fault at all,' I said, in her defence.

'Fine,' he replied, moving his hand away and pulling a chair up alongside me. 'You want me to see to your dog and cat?' he asked unexpectedly.

'Oh, well, would you mind?' I asked, baffled again. I had a dog, he knew that, but I had never mentioned Ned to him. Maybe Liv had been feeding him more personal information.

'Not at all. I'll go straight after here and let your dog out and feed them both,' he said. 'May I take your key?'

'Sure, thanks. It's in my purse somewhere. It's Ember and Ned, by the way. Ember's the Husky. I live—'

'I know where you live,' he interrupted. 'Liv told me the address. I'll see to them.'

I moved to adjust myself against the pillows and a sharp pain shot through my stomach, causing me to yelp a little.

'Megan?' he said, with an edge of concern in his voice as he stood to hover over me. 'I'll get a nurse.'

'No! Please, Gabe, I'm fine. It's just the bruising. It's because I moved. I'm fine. It'll go away.'

I managed eventually to unfold myself and lean back against the pillow, his eyes cautiously watching my movements. With no questions, he leaned over me, pulled my arms away and slid the bed sheet to my hips, followed by the hospital robe, which he carefully pulled upwards, leaving me decently covered by both. He stayed completely still as he took in the damage, looking over my swollen and already blackened abdomen. His hands started shaking.

'Gabe, it's only bruising. The doctor said the swelling will go down quite quickly with medication and rest.'

He acted like he hadn't heard a word I said to him. 'Where else?'

'What?' I asked, puzzled.

'Where else are you hurt?'

I sighed and gently rolled away from him onto my side, keeping hold of the sheet to cover my butt. I felt his cool hands slowly untie the robe, each time causing a sensitive tingle in my otherwise sore body. As the robe slipped away, his hand was there to keep it in place, saving some of my embarrassment. I felt the robe pull apart and waited as he viewed the injuries.

'Is it bad?' I asked, frustrated not to have seen anything there yet.

'Bad enough,' he replied, before tying me back up. 'The gouge runs the full length of your spine.'

As I turned back round, I saw him holding his head in his hands, leaning on the edge of the bed. 'Gabe, what's the matter?'

'Nothing. I'd better leave now, go to your house,' he said. I sat looking at him just as a nurse came through the doorway.

'Excuse me,' she said sharply, 'How did you get in here?'

'It's okay. He's here to visit me. I know him,' I said, defending his presence.

'That may be so but you are supposed to be resting, and we do not allow visitors through the night, so if you can please leave now,' she said, glaring at him.

Gabe said nothing but I grabbed his arm before he could move. His eyes moved to mine in a flash and I released my hold in complete shock. His eyes were crazed, black, and I didn't recognise the look I saw in them now, as if he had suddenly been possessed. I heard a low noise in his throat, like he was going to say something. Nothing came out, but the grumbling continued.

He turned away, heading for the door. 'I will care for Ember and Ned until you're home. I will be back first thing to collect you,' he said, walking through the door, not even looking back at me.

The night was an uncomfortable one, not only because of the pain but due to an almost total lack of sleep. I thought over the attack again and again, wishing I'd done something differently, been stronger to defend us both. But I was relieved I'd done *something*, and stopped what would have surely happened to Liv if I'd panicked or done nothing. Unlike my injuries, a physical attack on her like the one Adam planned would never have healed.

I wondered about Gabe getting into the lodge, knowing where I lived. How had he known we were at the hospital? It made no sense. I also worried about him a lot after I'd seen his angry face. He'd scared me for the first time. But it wasn't to be the last. I couldn't understand what had infuriated him so much.

I was already awake when the nurse arrived in the morning, opening the blinds to let the light in.

'How are you feeling, honey?' she asked.

'I feel fine, thanks. The sleep has done me the world of good,' I said, completely lying.

'Well, the doctor will be here soon and, all being well, you can go home.'

'Great. Am I okay to use the bathroom?' I asked, desperate to see myself and bursting for a pee.

'Sure, take a left out of here and it's just down the corridor on your left,' she said, as I was already making a silent pained attempt to climb out of bed.

The bathroom light came on automatically as I walked in and I wandered into the cubicle. Once I had finished my never-ending pee, I went to face the mirror. My cheek was purple and swollen like a balloon and, thanks to that, my right eye was smaller, half the size of my left eye. I'd had three sutures holding the skin on my cheekbone together. My scalp hurt from where it had been pulled so tight, much like when I had worn a tightly bound ponytail for far too long.

I lifted my robe to see my abdomen, the bit which hurt the most. The bruising was black and yellowing already, and my naval ring stuck well out on my pot belly. I twisted to try and see my back, pulling the robe away, and saw the long, deep gouge running all the way down my spine. All in all, a variety of injuries, but all ones that would heal quickly, except the wound on my cheek would scar, I was sure.

As I shuffled back to my room, I wondered where Liv had gone. I hadn't seen her since we were brought in and she went to talk with the police. I got back into bed, thinking about getting dressed, but knowing the doctor would probably want to look me over first.

About half an hour later, a flurry of events happened all at the same time. The doctor came in and after several checks gave me the all-clear. But before I had chance to go and dress, the police came through and I had to ready myself for their questions.

While they were asking me about the events of the previous evening – what had happened leading up to the assault, during the assault and for full descriptions of our attackers – Gabe walked through the doors into my room. I stopped and clammed up, a little unsure if I should continue with him there. I'd seen the fury in his face while he looked at my wounds, and didn't want to push him, especially not in front of the police.

The police asked him who he was and, when he replied that he was a friend, they looked at me for my confirmation. I said he was fine to stay and, even though it worried me, I continued in full flow, telling the police the build-up of events. When I reached the point of how they started their attack by grabbing Liv, I looked towards Gabe, trying to gauge his expression and mood. He gave me nothing, staying still, his face ashen-white, his eyes fixed and motionless, listening intently to the conversation.

I gave them every possible detail I could remember; I desperately wanted those guys to pay for what they had done to us. As I moved onto my attack, I saw Gabe look towards the window, distancing himself from the details, I thought. I told them it was Adam who attacked Liv and then threw the first punch at me, followed by the kicks. I only managed to give two other names, one was Taylor, who was present and joined in the attack, and the other was Hayden. I gave them a description of both, in case it would help, but made sure they knew Hayden had nothing to do with the attack.

When the police had completed their very thorough notes, they thanked me for my time and wished me a quick recovery. I was given the contact details of the investigating officers, and was told to call them if I remembered anything else. They promised me they would do everything they could to apprehend those responsible, and with the details I'd given them, along with the defensive punches I had given two of the men, they believed it should not be too hard.

Gabe said nothing through the interview, not a word, and I wondered what was going on inside his head. As the police shook my hand and left, I stood up carefully to go and dress in the restroom.

'How are you feeling today?' he asked.

'A lot better than last night,' I answered, 'although I'm aching more today. Suppose it's the bruising coming out.'

'I brought you some fresh clothes from your house. I hope that's okay,' he said, passing me a bag full of things.

'Oh, thanks, I really don't wanna dress in last night's clothes,' I said, grateful for his kindness yet a little embarrassed thinking he had been through my underwear collection.

'Are Ember and Ned okay?' I asked, looking through the bag.

'Yeah, they're fine. I walked Ember this morning, a long walk in the woods. Ned hasn't eaten and pretty much hid from me upstairs, watching through the stair rail, probably missing you and wondering what a stranger's doing in his house.'

I smiled at his kindness, grabbed my clothes and headed to the restroom, where nobody would hear my winces. I washed my face and wiped the mascara smudges away from under my eyes. My head still hurt, a deep, dull ache which was most prominent at the back, but the wound on my cheek had scabbed over and the tension in my scalp had lessened. I twisted round to try to see my back and was shocked by how deep and long the wound ran, right from under my shoulder blade to the lower part of my spine. That did hurt more now. As I bent down to pull my jeans on, the movement caused the deep, dried graze to crack in several places, stinging and causing me to wince with the pain.

After about ten minutes, I ambled back towards my room, and noticed Gabe talking to the nurse at the desk. I approached them and heard him talking to her about the medication I was taking away.

'Hi, honey,' the nurse said. Her kind face was probably set in place doing this job.

'Hi,' I replied, 'are those my meds?'

'Yes they are. You have some strong pain relief, which must be taken with food, and some antibiotics. Make sure you complete the course and take the pain relief only if you need it, okay?'

'Okay, thanks. What about the sutures?'

'You can call into your local medical centre and they'll take those right out for you in about ten to fourteen days, okay?'

'Okay, thank you for everything you've done,' I said, grateful for the care I had received, even though I was kept against my will. I knew now it was for the best.

'Oh, you're welcome. If you get any further pain in your head, or any eye problems, go to the medical centre as an emergency case, okay?'

'I will.' I signed my discharge forms, checking my insurance details, and turned to grab my bags. Gabe already had a hold of them so I put the medication inside and carrying only my purse followed him outside into the bright morning sun. He walked patiently alongside me, allowing me to take my time, his arm hovering behind my back in prepared support. It was so bright I had to stop to allow my eyes to adjust for a minute; the intense light hurt my head.

Gabe walked ahead when we got to the parking lot and put the bags in the trunk of his Jeep. He then moved around the side and opened the passenger door for me. As I reached the open door, he took hold of my hand and gently helped me as I climbed gingerly into the passenger seat. The bending motion on my back as I sat down hurt like hell and I flinched, trying to ease myself into a comfortable position.

With Gabe in the driver's seat and the engine roaring to life, I looked towards him. 'I need to collect my car from the lot,' I said, dreading going back to a place that would set my nerves on edge.

'No, you don't. I already took it back to your house,' he said, leaning over to clip my seatbelt in place.

'Oh. Thank you,' I said, amazed by him again.

We set off and headed towards town in the busy traffic. As we reached Main Street, my stomach churned. I saw familiar places from the previous horrific evening. We drove past Franklin Road, where the parking lot was, and I looked up in the direction where everything had happened, my eyes filling with tears as I remembered vividly the events of the night. I clenched my teeth hard and kept my face away from Gabe's no doubt concerned eyes. As we reached the far end of town, I looked towards the last bar and noticed a police car was the only one parked outside. They must have already started making enquiries about the group.

My head didn't hurt so much now, especially as my eyes had adjusted and accepted the bright light better, and the scenery heading back towards Manzano calmed me down. We spoke little but we both seemed at ease with the silence. Gabe drove home pretty fast. I was sure he understood that I was desperate to be in the privacy of my own home and back with Ember and Ned.

As we reached the outskirts of Manzano, the place was bustling with Sunday tourists. I was so glad to be back in this familiar, safe place. We continued through town and out towards home. As we pulled into my estate, Gabe slowed down a little.

'Ember will go crazy when he sees you so I was thinking I could hang around for a while, make sure you're settled, if that's okay with you?' he asked.

'That'd be nice. I'd like you to stay a while,' I said, grateful for his company and, for once, not feeling bothered that I needed someone.

We rolled up my drive and Ember's sweet little face appeared at the side window. When we eventually reached the front door, Gabe opened it for me and took hold of Ember to stop him leaping up. He lifted him into his arms with no effort and moved forward to let me through before leaning his back against the door to shut it behind us. Ember wriggled and whined loudly in excitement, desperately trying to free himself, but Gabe had him clamped in place. I walked towards him, letting him lick my face, my pain-free side, and fussed him through his dense fur.

'Hey, baby boy. Have you been good?' I asked stroking him and feeling my energy ebb away quickly. 'Oh, I've missed you.' As I fussed Ember, I looked over and saw Ned sitting in his usual spot on the window sill, but rather than looking towards me, he was watching Gabe intently, his eyes wide and nervous.

Gabe finally let Ember down and he seemed to sense I was not too good. He walked up to me and sniffed me all over, taking in the weird hospital smells. Gabe walked to put the teakettle on and I meandered towards the living room, Ember in tow. As I eased myself down onto the couch, I noticed two bunches of flowers. There was a huge bouquet surrounded by greenery, so large it spilled out from the hearth in abundant colours. On the small table stood a smaller arrangement, a simple mix of hand-picked wildflowers.

'Who are they from?' I asked, pointing to them.

Gabe looked back and answered. 'The one on the hearth is from Liv, and Ember and I collected the others on our walk this morning,' he said, turning back to make drinks.

'They are beautiful, thank you,' I said, pushing the lump down from my throat.

When I was able to talk, I asked him what he was doing, watching him find his way easily around my kitchen.

'Lunch,' was his simple response.

I lay my head back against the soft cushions, with Ember naturally alongside, obviously pleased I was home. I closed my eyes to rest. The sound of someone other than me buzzing around the lodge was soothing and it helped me relax. Before I knew it, I could feel my head gently rolling to the side, and I started to fall asleep.

It seemed like only minutes later when Gabe was lifting me quickly from the couch, holding me easily in his strong arms and looking deep into my eyes. He seemed rushed and I could tell he was trying to tell me something important but with no words. I stared back at him, only inches away, and I noticed suddenly I could feel no pain, nothing at all. I stared into his eyes, trying desperately to decipher what he wanted me to understand.

He suddenly started kissing me, eagerly, and it felt like we were short on time, like it had to happen now because for some reason, and I didn't yet know why, he was leaving me. As he kissed me, my eyes started to close and I could feel my grip on consciousness weakening, my head falling backwards from him. His face started to fade away and I saw his pained yet beautiful eyes fade into darkness.

My eyes opened and I was in exactly the same position on the couch, in front of my flowers, with Ember by my side. The quiet clattering from the kitchen came to an abrupt halt. I took a deep breath and my heart double-thumped deep in my chest as I listened to the silence. I knew I'd been dreaming. I searched through the silence, looking first to the silent clock and then slowly around to the kitchen, where Gabe stood, statue-still, his hands resting on the worktop, looking out of the window into the far distance.

I sat back facing the flowers, their smell suddenly enveloping me, their familiar scent wafting down through my nose. I waited for some movement, something to happen. Nothing else did.

For lunch, we had warm snow crab meat, diced and spread on a small bed of salad with a lime dressing, along with coleslaw and fresh warm bread and butter. I surprised myself by eating it all, washing the last forkful down with orange juice.

'Where on earth did you get the food from and please don't say my fridge!'

'Well, it was your fridge, actually. After I brought it home from the supermarket and put it there,' he said after he'd finished chewing, his eyes lighter now.

I smiled wryly, turning my attention back to my empty plate. 'Why don't you go lie on your bed and rest a while,' he suggested, turning his head towards me as he gathered up the dishes.

'No,' I said, looking out through the window. 'I would really like to go for a walk with Ember. Just a light walk, maybe around the neighbourhood, or a drive to the park,' I said.

'Okay. If you must go, I'll come along with you. Besides, you can't walk Ember alone, not yet.'

'To the park?' I asked.

'Okay,' he replied. With Gabe, things had suddenly become so easy, like we had been comfortable friends for a long time, the nervous awkwardness well in the past.

I walked upstairs slowly to fetch my thick fleece. Although the mid-afternoon sun was warm, I felt a little cold. A few minutes later, I returned downstairs to find Ember and Gabe gone. Ned sat looking out through the opened door but made no attempts to go outside. I grabbed the lodge keys on the way and saw Ember already waiting in the back of the car, his head poking through the middle of the front seats, with Gabe in the driver's seat, stroking his head and waiting patiently for me to join them.

We returned home after our short walk and I felt exhausted. I made a beeline for the couch and eased myself down to rest. I was weak. My injuries hurt even more now and my energy was completely depleted. Yes, it was probably not the best thing to have done, but mentally I felt much, much better for it.

We had talked briefly during our walk but I hadn't dared to ask him about finding my house, or how he knew what would make me eat. I knew these questions would put us ten paces back and likely to make him retreat into himself once again. Instead, we talked about the local area and I asked about the flowers I loved that were everywhere around us. He patiently walked alongside me, pausing when I needed to take a minute to catch my breath, resting next to me on a fallen tree, our arms touching, closer than we'd ever been before. Ember happily obeyed his every command, better than he did for me, which annoyed me but in a cute way.

'I'll stay here this evening, in the bunkhouse,' Gabe said, bringing me back from my fond memories of the afternoon.

'Gabe, that is really kind of you but I'll be fine, honestly. You need to rest too. Besides, I will probably crash the whole night,' I said, trying to persuade him to go home.

'Well, if you sleep through the night, you won't even know I'm here, will you?' he said. Why did he always seem to have an answer for me?

'Fine,' I said. 'I'll get you some bed linen.'

'No need. It's all sorted,' he said, hitting another one back at me. I felt like a redundant host. He made his way to the fire and had it up and running in no time, encouraging me to curl warmly into myself on the couch.

Minutes later, as I drifted in my horrific memories, he passed me a fresh cup of coffee and Ember jumped down onto the floor, allowing Gabe to take a seat next to me.

'What would you like to watch?' he asked.

'I really don't mind,' I said.

Gabe switched the TV on. He stopped when he found a girly film and looked at me. 'This?' he asked.

I shook my head and wrinkled my nose, 'Nah, too chick flicky.'

He smiled wryly and carried on trying to find something else.

'This?' he asked, smirking and awaiting my reply.

'This'll do,' I said, grinning at the screen.

He placed the remote between us on the couch and crossed his right leg horizontally across the other, his long, lean leg stretching out towards me. I tried to watch the movie, forcing my mind onto something other than the attack or, more often, the man sitting alongside me. The situation felt very odd, surreal, yet somehow familiar. I casually turned my head to the left, and scratched the right side of my head, allowing me to take a sneaky peak at him out of the corner of my eye.

He was looking at the TV but in no way appeared to be watching the film. He was looking through the screen, past it, deep in his own thoughts as I was in mine. I wondered what he must be thinking but, whatever it was, his face was straight, his expression getting harsher by the second. His demeanour worried me.

Before I knew it, I was drifting off, the sound of the movie in the background becoming quieter and more distant. Then I woke up and stretched lengthways, sending a stinging spasm down the length of my back. I'd caught the long scab on something, and must have torn some off. 'Ouch!' I yelped. After a few seconds I opened my eyes wide, expecting to be a few minutes further into the movie. Instead, I found myself lying in bed, Ember alongside me and Ned in his usual place on the bedroom couch, lying facing the rails overlooking the family room. I reached carefully across to tap the light on.

I looked across the room, remembering nothing of how I got here. I was still fully dressed. I lay back, eyes shut, listening to the old clock downstairs releasing its familiar deep tick into the silent night. I sat up on the edge of the bed, letting my tired head drop low, trying to wake myself up.

It was just after 3 a.m. I forced enough energy through my body and pushed myself up off the bed, making my way carefully downstairs. As I reached the main room, there was no sign of Gabe. I wandered into the kitchen and pulled the curtain covering the round porthole door window away a little so I could look out towards the bunkhouse. There was a faint light coming from the small side window, dull, but definitely light.

The door was unlocked and I walked outside into the cool, gentle breeze and made my way towards the bunkhouse. As I reached the door, I gently tapped, not wanting to wake him but not wanting to let myself inside unannounced. I waited, but got no response. I tapped a little louder, and waited again. Still nothing. I twisted the doorknob and opened the door a little way, quietly calling his name. There was no sign of him anywhere in the room. Two thick candles flickered on the bedside cabinets but I saw no clothes or food, only some keys lying on the table next to one of the candles.

I shut the door quietly, puzzled, and walked back to the lodge, looking back towards the drive to see if maybe he'd gone home to fetch something, but both cars were parked alongside each other. I shut the door behind me and left it unlocked, leaning back onto it, wondering where he'd gone. I made my way back to bed and struggled to slide my jeans off, dumping them on the floor. I clambered back under the duvet, leaving my vest and panties on, tapped the light off, and turned onto my side, snuggling deep into the quilt so only my face poked out. I lay there deep in thought and listened intently for any sound of him.

I woke to the bright light blazing through the window. As I stretched carefully, I looked over towards where Ember should have been but he was gone. Ned, however, was asleep in exactly the same position facing the rails, refusing to acknowledge a new day had begun. I listened carefully for any sounds which would tip me off as to Ember's whereabouts, or Gabe's for that matter. I couldn't hear anything.

I got up and wrapped my robe around me and headed gingerly downstairs. Everywhere was silent and as I walked into the kitchen Ned suddenly appeared, sliding his way past my ankles and peering around anxiously into every visible room. I had never known that a cat could possess what appeared to be facial expressions. He could look annoyed, upset, worried, and angry. He was such a strange boy, but it made him all the more special to me.

I headed to put the teakettle on and caught sight of a piece of paper placed next to my cell. Underneath one of the handpicked wild flowers was a note. I picked the flower up, seeing my name on the front of the folded sheet.

Have taken Ember for a long walk.
Get some rest, enjoy the sun, read and relax.
Back around noon.
Gabe

I smiled to myself, pleased Ember would be out having fun with someone capable of walking him, and happy to have a little time alone to shower, dress and, as instructed, relax a little and read. After the shower, I looked myself over and felt relieved to see that the swelling, as promised, was reducing and the bruising was yellowing, signs that it would hopefully fade away soon. The scabs down my back still hurt as they healed and I suspected the depth of the injury would leave a scar, as would the gash on my cheek. My abdomen still ached, but only when I tried to use the muscles by stretching or standing up. The bruising was still vibrant there but was at least covered up and out of sight.

With a little makeup and clean hair, I felt much better, and I looked it too. The foundation had worked well to cover most of the bruising on my face, making it almost unnoticeable. I went back into the kitchen and made coffee, then headed for the table and collected my cell to call Anna.

After a half hour's conversation, where I filled her in on the events of Saturday night and made her promise to stay where she was, we got onto lighter subjects, such as her, Cam and the kids, and also Gabe. Anna's silence when I said Gabe had collected me and stayed over to look after me for a few days said it all. 'Oh, that's really nice of him. So, who exactly is Gabe?' she'd asked.

I told her pretty much everything in a nutshell and she sounded genuinely relieved I'd had someone to stay with me. The fact it was a man who was with me – who I kind of forgot to mention I had fallen like crazy for – made her a little uneasy.

Later, after reading some of my book, I placed it beside me and leaned back onto the side of the bunkhouse, closing my eyes and taking in the warmth. I felt content, strangely, and I knew why.

I sat there for a long time until the sound of an engine heading up the hill brought my attention back and I knew at once it was Gabe and Ember returning. I stood too quickly and had to steady myself before heading towards the drive to greet them. Gabe's silver Jeep bounced up onto the drive and I smiled when I saw that Ember had wangled his way into his favourite position up front. He was staring right at me through the windshield, with his content, laughing husky face on full view, and his tongue lolling out about a foot.

They spun round to park alongside my car and Gabe was out of the door in a flash, holding it open for Ember to jump out. Ember flew towards me, swishing his tail crazily, but he didn't try to jump up.

'How you feeling?' Gabe asked, as I continued to fuss Ember.

'Much better, thanks,' I replied honestly. 'The sleep, shower and sun have done me the world of good.'

'That's great,' he said, moving closer and gently taking hold of my face, turning it to the side so he could examine how it looked now. His touch sent shivers down my spine, partly due to his always gentle approach with me and partly due to his cold hand. 'Have you eaten yet?'

'Yeah, I was so hungry. Can I make you some lunch?' I asked.

'No, I ate first thing. I'm fine, thanks.'

We walked alongside each other towards the lodge and, once inside, I filled Ember's dish with fresh water.

The rest of the day passed quickly and we sat watching old movies late into the night, with me nodding to sleep from time to time, while Gabe sat there, seemingly at ease and happy in the contented silence we shared. We chatted idly on and off and I learned more and more about him as the hours passed, about his work, his previous jobs and his interests. But our conversations never got past that, never got into anything deep or too personal. I'd learned when to stop asking questions with Gabe. And he respected what I knew he understood; my need to heal. Not only in my injuries, but also in my mind.

I told him about some of my past: about Boston, Luke, my work and my passion for photography and animals. I even told him how I'd lost both parents almost ten years earlier in a motorcycle accident, something I rarely talked about now for fear of heading into a downward spiral of depression. He listened but never acted shocked or surprised by anything I said. The only thing that saddened me was that however much we laughed, however much we talked and however much he stared at me when he thought I didn't notice, there was always something in his eyes that bothered me. There was torment lying deep beneath the surface of his face, as if he were torn being around me, as if at some time, only I didn't know when, he would tell me something I didn't want to hear, or just go off somewhere one day and I wouldn't see him again. He wouldn't return. But he was here now and I was going to make the most of it.

The next day, we headed towards San Diego, which was a surprise because Gabe wouldn't tell me where we were going. We stopped short and turned off I8 towards an Indian reservation, a few miles into the mountains, which was home to a couple of casinos and a small shopping complex set deep into the trees. It was full of original, quaint stores, dotted along random pathways, offering everything from lamps to books to large carved furniture, all of which were made by people on the reservation.

I adored it and came away with two metalwork spindly lamps, a carved log, which had wolves running around it, and some throws and cushions, all dyed in earthy cream and brown tones. Gabe insisted on carrying everything back to the Jeep except the cushions. We loaded the shopping inside and I got into the car.

'I'll just be a minute,' he said, disappearing back towards the stores. I sat waiting, puzzled, and about five minutes later I saw him walking toward the car with something in his hand.

He got into his seat and handed me a brown paper bag. I opened it to find a small box. Inside was the most amazing and intricately carved pendant, hanging from a dark brown leather thong. It was a piece of rugged dark wood in no particular shape and had a perfectly burned claw mark embedded into the middle. I was lost for words as I sat looking at it.

'Do you like it? I can always change it,' he said after many seconds of silence.

'It's beautiful,' I replied, a tear welling in my eye. 'It's perfect. Thank you,' I said, looking up at him once I knew the unwanted tear had retreated.

'You had me worried then,' he laughed. 'Turn around.'

I twisted myself as best I could and waited. Seconds later, his hands came over my head and the wood lay cool on my chest. He fastened it and moved back. 'There, let's see it then,' he asked.

I turned and looked down at my neck, still a little overwhelmed by his gift. It sat perfectly: not too big, not too small. He waited for me to lift my head but the sudden surge of love I felt inside for him stopped me from making eye contact, scared about what my feelings would urge me to do.

He carefully moved his hand to my chin and I was very aware that there was only a matter of inches between us. I gulped nervously as he slowly lifted my chin, forcing my face up to his so he could see the necklace. I averted my eyes, focusing on his left shoulder as a last-ditch attempt to gain control. 'What is it?' he asked, obviously sensing that I was uncomfortable.

'Nothing,' I lied, my eyes involuntarily flitting to his.

Suddenly, as I looked into his dark eyes, it was as if they changed before mine, as if in that one second he made a decision he wouldn't go back on. Gone was the turmoil and worry, and there in its place were the deepest chocolate colours which were suddenly in the present; no torture, just the most soulful eyes I'd ever seen.

He leaned slowly forward, moving his face to my level and tilted his head slightly. As his mouth gently locked around my top lip, I knew the tiny piece of self-control I had left with him had been wiped out, gone in a second, and what I felt for him now was irreversible. And to make matters worse was the fact that I'd fallen for someone who, for whatever reason, was completely wrong for me.

The kiss became more passionate, more intense and, at one point, rough as he bit hard onto my lip. After a few minutes, I had to prize myself away from him, highly conscious that we were making out big style in a parking lot where people passed by freely. I was just relieved the windows were darkened out so as to offer at least a little privacy. I took deep, uneven breaths, trying to calm down, looking out of the window to concentrate on something else.

After a short silence, I looked towards Gabe, who was sitting relaxed back in his seat, his hands loosely over the steering wheel, grinning. 'What are you grinning at?' I asked, smiling back, overjoyed to see this 'new' face.

'Nothing,' he said, shaking his head. 'How are you feeling, anyway? I didn't hurt you, did I?'

'Erm, no. I feel fine. Really fine, actually,' I said, twisting and pressing my injuries to see if they hurt now. They didn't. 'Hmm,' I muttered, surprised by how good I felt.

'That's good. Can I take you somewhere else now?' he asked, his face excitedly looking towards me. How could I say no?

'Where?' I asked.

'You'll see,' he said, starting the car. 'We need to collect Ember first.'

With my purchases unloaded in the lodge, my camera in my backpack and Ember in the back, we headed West on 78. An hour later and we were weaving through a track towards the ocean. 'Where are we?' I asked.

'It's a little place I found a few years ago. I come here often. You'll love it,' he said. It was a tiny, rugged beach, no more than a quarter of a mile long, with high cliffs that caused none of us any problems getting down, especially Ember. I stood on the empty beach and saw, to the far left where the cliffs were at their highest, a cave.

It was not as hot as it was inland, the light coastal breeze making it nice and cool even though the sun was still glaring. Ember darted about sniffing the driftwood and peeing on everything to mark his territory, while I stood at the water's edge, looking out across the ocean and taking deep breaths of fresh, salty air.

'Come on,' Gabe said, taking hold of my hand and turning to head towards the caves. He whistled Ember who happily ran alongside us. His hand felt slightly warmer, yet still cold against mine. I felt completely at ease as he gripped hold of me, towing me along at times as he stooped to grab a stick to throw for Ember or to skim a stone through the water. He suddenly seemed like a carefree teenager.

Just before we reached the caves, he stopped and took a step out in front, before turning to face me. I looked up at him, my hair sweeping around my face as he looked down at me, his smile fading a little and his lips twitching as if he were about to blurt something out. I waited, and my face started to echo his. I decided in that second, before he managed to say anything, that there was nothing I wanted to hear from him. Not now, anyway. I stretched up onto my tiptoes, shook my head and wrapped my arms around his neck, locking my lips onto his to halt the words.

It worked, and our bodies pressed hard together. He wrapped his arms around my back and held me carefully in place. Minutes later he pulled away, showing me his impish grin again.

He threw his arm around my neck and we headed back to the water's edge. We threw some stones in for Ember to chase but he just became annoyed with himself because he was afraid to go in the water past his paws.

After a while, we went to sit down on a rock and I set my camera up to take a photo of the three of us. Then, I lay back on the sand, enjoying the sun on my face. Gabe fussed over Ember before lying down, then he turned in to face me. I did the same and we just lay looking at each other, saying nothing.

He suddenly pulled me into his arms and I rested my head on his chest, nestling there, taking in his smell. He stroked my hair with his free hand and I felt the most secure I had felt since I was a child, when my mom used to wake me up from the screams of my nightmares and do the same, her slow breathing and loving hand stroking the fear away. A tear rose to the surface as I made the comparison but vanished the second Gabe leaned in and kissed my head.

It was the one perfect day we got together, the only one, and I should have known that fate would step in and spoil things.

The following morning, Gabe had gone home to sort some things out. He also needed to call into work. I decided to put all the bits I'd bought from the reservation where I wanted them, then head into town to do some food shopping. As I dashed round the aisles in the supermarket, I grabbed the local paper and headed to the checkout.

With everything loaded on the conveyor belt and being packed for me at the other side, I glanced at the paper and my heart jumped into my mouth when I saw the cover story. I reached into my purse and switched on my cell, entering the four-digit pin incorrectly twice before I calmed down enough to be able to do it right the final time. I hadn't had it switched on for almost two days, and with no landline in the lodge, I only had my cell for contact.

Sure enough, a bunch of text messages flashed through, along with two voicemails. I checked voicemail and heard the voice of the officer who had questioned me about the attack. He was notifying me that an incident had occurred with the three men who were wanted for our assault and to contact him straight away.

I didn't need to speak to him to know what he urgently needed to talk to me about. I knew they'd caught two of the men who were responsible for assaulting us, but not in the way they'd planned. The paper told me all that.

TWO MEN WANTED IN CONNECTION WITH SERIOUS ASSAULT FOUND DEAD

I felt dizzy reading the headline over and over again and I reached up to touch the sutures on my cheek. The words weren't sinking in as I read and re-read them. 'Two men believed responsible for a serious attack' read one part, 'found dead in their homes' read another. 'Serious injuries' and 'severe blood loss' led them to believe 'the killer had cleaned up all evidence' were other words that sank in.

'Ma'am, are you okay?' the young male cashier asked me, but my eyes were glued to the pages. 'Ma'am?' he asked again.

'Oh, sure. Okay, so, how much is it?' I asked, my voice shaking as I fumbled around in my purse.

'Do you want the paper too, Ma'am?'

'Erm, yeah, sure. How much is the total?'

'It'll be ninety-four thirty-eight,' he replied.

'Oh, okay,' I said, giving him the cash.

'Would you like help loading?' he asked.

'No, I'll be just fine, thanks. Okay, bye then,' I said, heading away feeling light-headed.

I shoved everything in the car and sat there taking deep breaths. I opened the window to get some air and took hold of the paper, pressing it flat from its strangled state where I'd been grasping hold of it all the way out of the store. Sure enough, the photos on the front were of the men I recognised. Taylor Pentecost's and Adam Chandler's faces sent shivers down my spine three-fold. The first was because I was seeing them for the first time since the attack, the second was because they were now dead and the third was because I was pretty sure the man I was in love with had killed them.

I drove home in a trance, completely numb. I carried the groceries inside, not even able to stroke Ember. Ned sat watching, alert as ever, with wide, cautious eyes. I sat on the couch and read the article in full. They wanted to know if anyone had any information to provide. I laughed out loud, becoming almost hysterical at the request. Surely this is what Gabe had wanted to say to me on the beach and why every instinct in my head told me to stay away, except that my stupid heart was telling me differently, even now.

I sat back and my first thought led me to when I'd gone to look for Gabe in the bunkhouse a few nights ago and he wasn't there. My rational side told me that he couldn't have got to Antala on foot and back again, not easily, and I'd seen no signs of anything odd the following morning. It wasn't possible, just coincidental. Gabe was often distant and moody, and, yes, I could tell he had a temper, but killing someone? No, that wasn't him. He couldn't, and yet the fury in his face when I was in the hospital and he saw my wounds for the first time flashed in my mind. 'Shit,' I muttered, and headed to grab my cell.

I found his number and pressed the call button, trembling.

'Meg?' His voice sounded surprised.

'Where are you?' I asked.

'I'm just outside work. Is everything okay?'

'No Gabe, not really. We need to talk. Now.' There was a long pause.

'I'll come over to yours,' he finally said.

'No!' Meet me at the park outside town in ten minutes,' I said, ending the call.

I grabbed my purse and keys and paused, leaning on the counter to steady myself. How on earth was I to broach the subject? *So hey, Gabe, you know those guys that attacked me. Well, I was wondering, did you kill them?* I started to shake again, my focus blurring as I passed the possibilities through my head.

It was the knock at the door that brought me out of my stupor and into panic mode. I jumped out of my skin and looked towards the door. A horrible thought passed through my mind. I knew it wasn't Gabe, even he wasn't that fast. What if it was the police, come to speak to me because they hadn't been able to contact me on my cell, to tell me what had happened, question me? My car was parked right outside. I knew I had to answer the door. I needed to act normal, unsuspecting, but I knew my eyes couldn't lie. 'Fuck,' I muttered, and my heart raced in my chest as the fear kicked in.

I took some deep breaths to calm myself, preparing myself to lie, and walked to the door.

Chapter 10

I stood staring at him, completely shocked. Why was *he* here? He knew not to come.

I remembered his face too well, as if I'd only seen it yesterday. But it had been almost a month now. Words stuck in my throat as I looked over his dark, familiar features, with no longing to touch or hug him. He was like a spirit now, a ghost of my past.

'Luke!' I finally managed to utter.

'Meg,' he said, smiling his famous grin at me. 'I'm sorry to turn up unannounced but Anna told me what happened and I was so worried about you. I had to check you were okay.' I saw his eyes flick to my cheek and quickly back to my eyes again.

It was then that a wave of relief washed over me. Relief that it was not the police standing at my door, only Luke. Luke, I could handle. 'So, you gonna invite me in then or leave me standing here?' he asked, staring past me, looking into the lodge.

'Oh, erm, sorry. Come in,' I said, moving aside to let him pass. As he walked in, Ember rushed to him and made the biggest fuss. Even quiet little Ned walked up in recognition and rubbed through and round his ankles.

'Nice place,' he said, looking around.

'Yeah, I love it,' I said. 'Really suits me and the kids, you know,' I added for his benefit.

He placed his case down next to the couch. A whole suitcase. I really hoped he hadn't planned on staying here. He sat down on the couch as I stood and briefly explained what had happened but that I was totally fine now. I said I needed to go out somewhere but he just kept firing question after question at me. I casually kept glancing at the clock, becoming edgy as almost twenty minutes passed.

'Look, Luke, I have really got to go out. You're welcome to stay here. I won't be long,' I said, looking at the clock again. I heard the rumble of the Jeep's engine before I'd finished the sentence. I turned to walk to the door to go meet him. 'Stay here please, Luke,' I said, turning to look at him.

By the time I got to the door, Gabe had spun round and, with the engine still running, was standing behind the open car door looking at me. I stared back. 'I'll meet you where we said,' I shouted to him. He stood looking at me, a concerned expression on his face, puzzled and bleak again. Luke had walked out behind me and intentionally placed his arm around my shoulder, looking right at Gabe. I should have known he'd do it – jealous and possessive as always.

I shrugged his arm off, annoyed, but Luke had done enough. Gabe looked towards me, pain in his eyes, and he lowered his face to the ground. He swung himself into the car and shut the door. 'Gabe, wait, please.' But he was already setting off. I ran across the path to the drive to try to stop him but I was too slow.

Then, he was gone.

I marched back to the lodge and picked up my cell, pressing the re-dial button. It rang and rang, but he didn't pick up. I sent him a message as fast as I could, trying to explain what he thought he'd seen, as Luke jabbered on in the background. 'Oh Luke, for fuck sake, shut up!' I finished texting and turned to him, infuriated.

'Luke. Why are you here? Are you stupid? Did you not get the message? We're finished, okay? Now, I love you, Luke. I probably always will in some way but there is no more *us* and there never will be again. Have you got that Luke, huh?' I shocked myself by just how hard and blunt I sounded. 'I am with someone else now or I was until you did that. So, if you please, will you piss off back to Boston so I can get on with my life and you can move on with yours.' Luke's face was shocked but a familiar hard edge suddenly developed, the one I remembered most recently.

'Sure, sure. Take care, Meg. I hope you'll be very happy with that freak,' he said, marching past me. 'Although, I doubt it'll work out,' he added, as he grabbed his case and walked out the door and down the pathway towards his car.

Who did he think he was? He didn't even know Gabe! I heard the trunk slam on his hire car, followed by the engine revving loudly and the sound of flying gravel as he flew down the drive. His erratic driving scared the hell out of me. Regardless of what I now felt for Luke, I still worried like crazy in case he had an accident on his way home because of his bad temper. What was it with me and moody men?

I walked back to the kitchen and slumped to the floor, leaning with my back against the unit. I covered my face with my hands and started cussing. 'Shit, shit, shit,' I ranted. Within minutes, I forced myself up and grabbed my cell. I hit redial but it was still the same; it rang and rang until I reached his voicemail.

I continued that way for a couple of hours until I was at breaking point. I searched through my cell for the practice number and hit 'call' before even thinking about what I was going to say.

'Manzano Veterinary Centre. Good morning,' the voice said.

'Hi. Can I speak with Liv, please?' I asked.

'May I ask who's calling?' replied the woman.

'It's Megan Anderson. I'm her friend.'

'Oh Hi, Megan. It's Jen, the receptionist. How are you?' she asked politely.

'I'm fine thanks. Is Liv there today?' I had no time for small talk.

'I'll just go see if she's free, Megan,' Jen said, putting me on hold.

It seemed like forever listening to the irritating, so-called 'soothing mood' music. Then, she picked up the line. 'Meg, it's Liv. You okay?'

'Yeah, fine. Did Gabe come into the practice just now?' I asked, desperate for her answer.

'No, we just took a call from him. Said he won't be in for a few weeks. Some kind of family emergency or something. Is everything okay, Meg? Jen said Gabe sounded weird on the phone.' Liv sounded concerned, anxiety in her voice.

'I'm fine,' I lied, deflated now I knew he had taken off. 'Look, Liv. I'll call soon, okay?' I said, pressing the bridge of my nose tightly between my fingers, the tension pounding in my head. I ended the call without waiting for her reply.

I dropped the phone to the floor and rested my head against the unit. How long I sat there, I had no idea, but it seemed like hours. By the time I stood up, aching and numb in my ass, I felt completely flat. In the space of one morning, I'd alienated Luke completely, probably sending him on a collision course with drink and fighting, and lost Gabe.

Now he'd disappeared to who knows where with the notion in his head that I was with another man. I was on fire.

**

Three long weeks passed and I felt myself slumping into a deeper depression. My calls to Gabe drew a blank. His phone now said: *the number you are calling is not available and you cannot leave a message.* Great, thanks.

I missed him so much, constantly wondering where he was, and if he would be coming back. I decided that if I saw him again, I would not say anything about what I believed had happened to the men who attacked me and Liv, even though I didn't think they deserved to die. I was grieving more for Gabe than I ever had for Luke, and I'd been with him over six years.

The texts a few days earlier from Liv had confirmed that they'd heard nothing from him, except that he'd called in to say that his stay with an ill family member was going to be longer than expected and they should get a temp veterinarian in or replace him if necessary. But William would never replace Gabe so a temp stepped in. Liv once told me how William thought the sun shone out of Gabe's backside, so his job would remain open indefinitely. That gave me a little hope that one day he'd return.

In one of my now usual trancelike days sitting on the couch, I looked over to Ember, who appeared as fed up as I did. I wasn't being fair on him. I hadn't been out for days and the look on his face kick-started me again. I needed to get rid of the tension, change the scenery and pull myself out of this depression. A run was a good idea. I needed to mentally and physically push myself, get some fresh air in my lungs.

I changed into my running gear and made my way out the door. Ember ran ahead to the car, while I juggled with my water, keys and wrist pack containing my cell. I slid my sunglasses on as soon as the engine was running, swung round and down the drive and headed in the direction of my favourite wilderness park, which offered privacy, freedom and wildlife.

As we parked up, the late afternoon sun was shining through the tops of the trees, making its slow descent behind the mountains. There was only one other car in the lot, so I knew it was unlikely that we'd cross anyone's path this late. I only had a few hours until darkness set in but it was plenty of time for a solid long run. I climbed out and attached Ember to his bungee leash, took a long drink of water and made sure everything I wanted was in my wrist pack.

We followed the red route for the first time and set off at a fast walk to stretch my legs. I then moved to a light jog, giving my body time to warm up. After five minutes, I let Ember off his leash, against park regulations, and we set off running. Ember never ran too far ahead and, whenever he was out in front, he kept looking back to check that I was still following.

I ran hard, feeling my heart banging in my chest as I pushed myself to the limit. I managed to clear Gabe and all the recent horrible events out of my head as I ran, taking in the beauty of the surroundings and enjoying the cooler air. The sun shone through the trees and the birds made their last calls of the day. No matter how sad I felt, being out alone in the woodland always made me feel happier, even if it was short-lived. I pushed myself even harder, concentrating on my breathing, feeling the muscles in my legs tighten the more I pushed.

The light started to become brighter as Ember ran to the next corner, most likely turning into a clearing where the trees were less dense. I ran around some rocks, twisting and turning through the trees on the pathway, and just before I reached a large stone at the corner Ember disappeared round the bend. I was completely lost in thought, watching but not concentrating. That's when I heard the loud, snarling growl. The bark that Ember let out was not a good one. It was a ferocious sound I'd heard only twice before, and on both those occasions something had been very wrong.

The first time Ember had barked in this way was about a year and a half ago when Luke and I had been play-fighting and Luke was pretending to thump me in the arm (before he actually did hit me in the face). His protective instinct kicked in and he ran at Luke snarling and barking, which was rare for Ember, stopping a little short of him and warning that if he did not move away from me, he would attack and mean it. Luke stopped instantly, not wanting to stress him out. Afterwards, we both looked at each other, amazed at Ember's response.

The second time was when Luke and I were out walking one evening in a Boston park and a mugger had approached us brandishing a knife. Ember let rip at the hooded man, drawing his teeth back, and lunged to attack. This halted the mugger momentarily, then Luke finished the job by grabbing him in a flash and taking him to the ground with such force I heard something crack. The snarls and action were fast and furious. I just stood there, shocked, not only by the mugging attempt but by my two boys, Ember and Luke, who had saved the day. That's when I found out Luke had taken martial arts lessons to an almost professional level before I'd met him.

With those thoughts flashing through my mind, I raced around the corner and into the object of Ember's fury.

Chapter 11

I skidded to a halt on some loose stones, gasping at what faced me. I stood completely still, my heart thrashing in my chest, my legs weak and trembling and my eyes wide. This was the unexpected encounter that I should have expected. Ember stood facing the towering creature as my protector, yet again, with his teeth bared, snarling and ready to face certain injury – or maybe even death.

He started lunging directly at the creature facing him: a bear. I didn't know too much about bears but I knew they could be ferocious attackers. It was big, but not massive; a female, I thought. She was standing on her hind legs, which made her look even bigger, and her claws were spread wide, facing us, her adversaries.

I stood there completely frozen for what seemed like an eternity but it must only have been seconds. Ember was snarling and lunging back and forth at the bear, warning her. But she stood her ground, becoming more and more agitated by our presence. I knew calling Ember back in this situation would not work. I also thought about walking backwards and then gradually running in the hope that Ember would follow me. But as I slowly backed away, he remained completely focused on the bear. I knew then that running was no good and screaming would not bring anyone to our aid. There was no one around to help us.

Ember took one more lunge towards the bear before I could think straight, then she flung herself forward and struck him on his flank.

He yelped loudly as the blow knocked him to one side. He lowered his head in shock and backed away a little but not far enough, his eyes staying fixed on the bear, the growling lower in his throat. As she drew her claws back into a striking position, I could see Ember's fur lining the claws on her right paw; I quickly glanced to look at him and saw blood oozing through his dense undercoat, making its way to the surface. The wound looked deep.

As she started to approach Ember again, I knew I had to protect him in any way I could. My decision was made in a split second and I threw myself into the path of the striking claws to protect my beloved boy.

I let out the loudest and most aggressive growl I could and followed it by clapping my hands until they stung and burned. I made myself as big as I could, shouting and screaming at her with all the force I had in me. My throat hurt and I had to fight back the urge to cough. I could feel it scratching in my throat. It didn't work. It had the opposite effect, making matters a whole lot worse, and I could tell by the way she lunged forward that I couldn't compete. I wasn't going to stop her.

Her first strike threw me easily to the ground, a trickle of blood appearing instantly on my upper arm. I screamed at her again but it was no use. After once seeing a programme on bear attacks, I suddenly remembered that lying still could help, so I curled up my body, trying to protect myself and act submissive. I saw little of the bear's claws as they came down and slashed into me again, this time striking my waist and arm. I suddenly felt a deep burning pain as she tore into my skin. I thought the attack was going to stop, that it was a warning, and that she'd put me in my place and so would leave. She didn't.

I peeped through the spread fingers covering my face to see if she was moving away, then turned slightly to see Ember standing alongside a large rock in the direction we'd just come from. The next blow caught me on my thigh and with nothing protecting my legs, the searing pain made me move my hand down to cover the wound, where I instantly felt the trickle of blood spilling over my fingers.

I screamed out in pain and looked back at Ember. Tears spilled down my cheeks because I could now see his face, petrified, and knew he was in turmoil wondering how he could help me. He moved forward, then back, then forward again. 'Run Ember! Go!' I screamed at him, desperate for him to listen to me and run away. As the bear's growl neared my face, I could see Ember deciding and thinking. Then he turned and ran, his dense brush of a tail bobbing into the distance.

He was gone and I was alone.

I knew she wasn't going to stop, and I knew I was willingly offering my life to save his, but the way I was feeling about my life right now, I didn't care. If I did get out of this, if someone found me, I was sure to be severely mauled. I kicked both of my legs out hard, refusing to give up the fight, and as my heel sank into some soft part of her, another blow struck my ankle, rendering me defenceless. I went into the submissive posture again, playing dead, in a final attempt to convince her that I wasn't a danger. But as I lie there, receiving blow after blow, I began to give in, my body numbing to the pain. To be faced now with the one thing that had terrified me all my life was easy. The desperate fear of losing loved ones had haunted my life, more so after the death of both my parents, and yet the fact my own time had come was easier to deal with. I had, for whatever reason, accepted it.

The next attack was short and fierce. The bite to my shoulder was the last my body could take; the pain was agonising and excruciating. The last thing I saw as my body slumped open onto the earth was the beautiful, peaceful high swaying trees and the sun shining through the leaves and into my eyes. I heard a distant sound, one I knew, one I needed to hear. It was Ember's pained howl, not too far away but, thankfully, at a safe distance.

The tears fell from my eyes, down my cheeks and into my ears. I let go easily. My eyes started to close, the vision of the sunlight and tree tops fading along with me into a dark, lifeless state. I heard more growls and snarls – she was closing in – but I felt nothing more for a few moments until the sudden stab of her teeth pierced the flesh on my arm. The pain then was unbearable but I had nothing left and just writhed on the ground. The burning sensation and pain started to ease as I gave in. I felt cold and numb, as if my body was becoming immune to the physical blows.

I knew at that exact second I was dying.

Chapter 12

Nothing.
Nothing.
Nothing.
Faint noises.
Louder noises.
Nothing.
Nothing.
Burning eyes.
Light. Faint light, but definitely there.
Then it was all gone again, back into the blackness.
I found myself thinking that this is exactly what people who had had a near-death experience had felt and it was true. I saw the lights, heard the noises and I was dying. I thought about what I was seeing, sensing, feeling.
Wait a minute! Dead people don't think, do they?
Light again, a tingling, burning sensation in my eyelids. Flickering.
I waited.
I didn't feel pain. I felt nothing.
There it was again, burning in my eyes, the light a little brighter this time. Gone.
Nothing.
Blackness. Everything had gone again.
Peace.
Quiet.
Pain free.
Nothing.

'Megan, can you hear me?'

'Megan, if you can hear me, can you squeeze your hand or blink your eyes?'

Nothing.

Crash, crash, crash. Wow, that was loud. What was that?

'Megan, come on, can you squeeze my hand?'

There was a crash again. The light was brighter too, direct, burning. I'd had enough. The light burned. I squeezed my hand with all my might.

'Whoa! Okay, I think she can hear me,' a voice said, startled.

There was nothing then for a while. The sounds became a dull drone, constant, but bearable. I'd gotten used to them; they actually made me feel more at ease. So, was I dead or not? Was this the afterlife or had I hung on by the skin of my teeth and scraped through?

As thoughts meandered through my head, a sudden and vivid flashback hit me and I jolted. The bear's face, Ember's face disappearing around the corner, the pain, the warmth of my blood, the claws and the teeth. All of it condensed into a few seconds and then it was gone.

My eyes opened.

As I stared upwards, I saw nothing. The bright lights high above me all merged into one. I blinked slowly, trying to focus and clear the smog in my vision. It didn't happen. I turned my head to one side and tried again. I could see dark shapes, shadows of what looked like chairs, and tables, flatter on top and longer underneath. Yes, a table or chair. I could see movement in the distance, more shadows. I think they were people, yet I didn't know who they were. Nothing made any sense.

I turned to my other side, finding my body moved easily. In the distance there was what appeared to be a large dark shape sitting statue still on one of the table or chair things. Was it someone? I couldn't tell.

'Is someone there?' I asked, my voice barely audible. There was a long pause. 'It's Gabe, Meg,' the voice replied, and I instantly remembered him. And it all came flooding back.

I said nothing more but remained staring in his direction, trying to make out his face in the dark blur.

The shadow stood slowly and made its way towards where I lay. Although I couldn't see clearly, I knew it was him when I felt the cold, strong hand wrap around mine. 'But you left me,' I said, as something wet trickled from my blind eyes.

'And I'm never going anywhere again, I promise,' he said, stroking the tear from my cheek with his free hand. As he did, more tears followed until I felt his wintry cheek press against mine. 'Shush,' he whispered. 'You're safe now.' But his words didn't stop the pillow getting damp.

I lay there for a long time, his hand in mine, before I drifted off to sleep again.

The next time I woke, my vision, after a few seconds, seemed slightly better. I could see more defined objects, make them out and faces no longer blended into light and dark; I could see where the eyes should be, where the lips were and their movement as someone spoke. This time, the person speaking wasn't Gabe.

'Hi Megan,' the voice said. I instantly recognised it as the one I'd heard when I regained consciousness.

'How do you feel?' he asked.

'Where am I?' I asked, confused.

'You're in the hospital, Megan. Do you remember anything?'

I paused to acknowledge where I was. 'I remember running, the bear, Ember. Where's Ember?' I asked, suddenly panicked, remembering he'd been wounded.

Another voice came into my ear from the other side. 'He's fine, Meg. He's with me.' It was Gabe again.

'But the bear got him. She struck him hard,' I argued.

'Yes, she did, but I found him, waiting by the car, howling. I've fixed him up and he's recovered fine, although he's a little bald on his left side. I'm staying at your house with them.' The relief hit me hard and the tears spilled again, but this time they were tears of relief.

'Seriously, is he really bald?' I asked, chuckling through the tears, imagining how stupid he'd look.

'Just a little. It helps him keep cooler, though,' Gabe said, and I could sense a mixture of feelings in his voice: worry, relief and definitely a little happiness.

'Thank you,' I said, choked. 'For finding him, for looking after them both, for coming back.'

Gabe grabbed my hand again, squeezing it hard in reassurance.

'Now, Megan,' the doctor continued, sensing that now I was relieved, I was able to concentrate on him. 'You have been a *very* lucky girl. Your wounds are healing amazingly well, your scans and X-rays are looking good and you'll just need some time to heal. No broken bones, no long-term damage; it's quite amazing. You will have scars, though, and you lost a lot of blood but, again, you have amazed us all with your recovery from such an attack.'

'When can I go home?' I asked, stupidly.

The doctor gave out a startled laugh. 'Not for awhile, I'm afraid,' he said, and I could hear a smile in his words. 'You're not Wonder Woman, you know. Now, I need you to rest and I've left some cards on the table next to you, which I want you to look at a few times every day. Practice focusing on them, okay? It will strengthen your vision and help your eyesight return. They're pretty self-explanatory; just name the colour and object, okay?'

'Okay. How long was I out for?' I asked, time meaning absolutely nothing to me.

'For three days,' the doctor replied. 'You gave us quite a fright.'

'Three days? That long, huh?'

'Yes, that long Megan. Now I will leave this young man with you but you need to rest, no idle chatting, no pushing yourself. Rest, okay?'

'Okay,' I lied. Like that was going to happen. I watched the doctor's shadow fade away, and turned to the face I could just about recognise as Gabe's. 'Seriously, how bad am I? And be honest, please.'

'You look fine, more than fine. You will have a few scars but they'll heal and be less visible.'

'Okay. Now, pass me the cards. I want to get going. I need to get out of here.'

Gabe didn't argue. Whereas in the past he'd protected me, looked after me, this time he didn't deny my request. It was as if he'd resolved that I would go ahead anyway, with or without his help.

I collected the cards in my hands and named what I saw. 'Green apple, blue car, black cat...' I went through the cards three times, there were about thirty of them in all, and by the time I'd finished, my vision was, amazingly, much improved.

'My turn. Let's make it harder,' Gabe said, taking the cards from my hand.

He shuffled them like lightning; even I could see that. Then he pushed his chair backwards away from me before turning the first card towards me.

'Orange pumpkin...red shoe...black and white husky – I want to go home. I'm fine!' I screeched.

Gabe shook his head, laughing at my impatience. I'd got them all right, again, even from about two feet away. We went on like this for over half an hour. As the cards became clearer, so did Gabe. I had forgotten just how gorgeous he was. His pale, drawn skin, his perfect dark features, his unruly hair. It all flooded back into my memory. Yet, it was as if I was looking at him for the first time and a little gasp slipped out.

He paused and looked back at me, before placing the cards on the table and propping himself on the edge of the bed, leaning over me and grabbing both my hands tightly in his.

'You scared me...again,' he said, his face serious. 'I won't go through this anymore.' He shook his head, adamant.

I stared back at him, scowling, with only inches between us. 'I'm fine, Gabe. Look at me. I promise I won't go try to kick a bear's ass again.' My attempt at lightening his mood failed; the hard lines in his forehead didn't relax. His lips parted, as if he were about to say something, but he pressed them closed again as he decided against it.

He quickly leaned into me and I gasped again. Suddenly, all his captivating features were crystal clear, right down to the deep lines around his eyes that formed when they narrowed with his familiar smile. Without hesitation, I lifted my face to his and kissed him. His kiss was just as I remembered, urgent, passionate.

But there was still a difference in him, in the way he felt to me. I just couldn't put my finger on it. As we moved apart, I held him in place so I could look into his eyes. As I looked up at him, trying to summon up the words I wanted to say, I could almost make out images in his eyes, pictures, as the light moved through them, the depth of their dark-brown colour seemed to go on endlessly. 'Gabe, about Luke, the man you saw me with the day you left...'

'It's okay. I know he's nothing to you now. There's no need to discuss it.' And that was the last time Luke's name was mentioned between us.

I worked hard for the next three days and I felt completely fine by the end of them. The doctor had said my wounds were terrible when I was brought in, but they were healing nicely. I wondered if he had over-exaggerated, because in the mirror they looked minor to me. My eyesight also continued to improve rapidly.

I completed an interview about the incident for the San Diego Herald, the reporter asking question upon question about the attack: Did I feel lucky to survive it? And what was my advice about running in the parks? My reply of 'run faster' didn't go down so well, so instead I kept it plain and simple, advising people to take wildlife spray with them, control their animals (big oops), and stick to main tracks; all of which I'd been advised to do in articles I'd read. Never mind. They described my miraculous recovery and remarked on how I'd beaten the odds to survive such a horrific attack.

By the time the doctor made his daily visit, my annoyance and impatience was obvious.

'Okay, so can I leave today? Please let me leave before I kill someone,' I said the minute he walked into my room.

'Well, I'd prefer to keep you in for a few more days, just to make sure everything is fine before we discharge you,' he said, in his usual over-helpful manner.

'Well, I *am* fine. I feel one hundred percent. I'm eating okay, sleeping well, healing fantastically and, as for my eyesight, I can see the fly on the wall over there,' I said sarcastically, pointing behind him to the far wall.

The doctor looked concerned and naively searched over his shoulder to where I'd pointed. 'Sorry, I was joking about the fly. But, seriously, I'm going stir crazy. I need to go home. And I promise I will continue to rest and take it easy.' I pleaded with him, willing him to agree to my discharge.

'Well, I am against it but if you promise you will take it easy and have someone look after you for a few weeks, I will consent to your release, okay. Happy now?' he said, leaning in towards me. I gave him a huge grin and mouthed a silent 'Thank You.'

When Gabe came in about a half hour later, I had started to pack the few things he'd brought in for me. He eyed my bags and then his eyes moved to me, wondering.

'It's okay. I'm not breaking out,' I said, replying to his unasked question. 'The doctor has agreed to discharge me, under strict orders of course.'

'Oh, that's great news. Are you totally sure?' he asked, looking me up and down.

'Yes. One thousand percent sure! I really do feel great,' I said, taking the few short steps to void the gap between us. 'See,' I said, pulling my vest over my injured shoulder to show him the healing wound there. 'Everywhere else is the same too.' I paused in front of him, wondering what the agitation in his face was about. He looked blankly at my shoulder, and then he moved away, seeming uncomfortable or frustrated by something. 'You'd better finish packing then,' he said, moving to the window and resting his hands on the sill, looking out into the distance.

'I'm on it,' I replied, sensing a change in him. Then I turned to pack the remainder of my things. With all my clothes and personal items in, I looked around and collected the teddy bear Anna had sent me, along with the black and white husky and the tabby cat soft toys that Gabe had bought for me, telling me that Ember and Ned had been out specifically with their weekly allowance to buy them so I would remember them until I got home.

I smiled to myself and placed them carefully on top of my clothes, along with the handful of cards I'd received and zipped the case shut.

After thanking the staff and signing my discharge and insurance forms, I made my way out into the bright, hot sunshine. As I left the shelter of the main entrance overhang, Gabe hovered close, taking hold of my hand in anticipation. My eyes instantly started to burn as the bright light hit them. My vision started to fade and the clouding started again. I blinked constantly, trying to blink out the haze until my focus returned a little. 'The doctor warned me this might happen,' I said, hoping Gabe wouldn't march me back in again. He didn't, but his face showed that he was not happy. He led the way to his car quickly and all I could do was trust his lead as my eyes watered and fogged over. I kept my face pointed to the ground, blinking furiously as the water from my eyes trickled down my cheeks. It felt like I'd peeled a hundred onions.

Gabe helped me into the car, shutting the door quickly behind me and throwing my case into the back. It was a relief to get out of the sun and the darkened windows helped ease my eyes instantly. He started the engine and turned to me, lifting my hidden face up with one hand and holding it there as he inspected my eyes. I still couldn't open them fully and when I did, water trickled out, making me close them again quickly for relief – just like when you stab yourself in the eye with a mascara brush.

'It will improve soon,' he said flatly, turning his attention to reversing the car out.

'It'd better. It's driving me nuts already,' I replied, closing my eyes to offer some relief.

Ten minutes later, the burning started to ease. I was able to open my eyes and relax, and gradually begin to focus on things again. I looked at all the dials on the dashboard and then towards the window, sighing with relief as the trees and open planes in the distance became clear again.

The sign for Manzano approached and I was so pleased to be home. I had only been in the hospital for a week but it felt like forever. Gabe glanced over at me as we entered town and I could feel more tears coming. I looked out of the window as the emotion became too much. I cried tears of joy to be home, along with tears built up from everything that had happened to me: the ordeal with the bear, missing the kids, Gabe returning from wherever he'd gone. I felt overwhelmed and couldn't fight the tears as they spilled out. It was short-lived, though. The surge of emotion passed quickly and I composed myself. Having his hand squeezing mine gave me the reassurance I needed.

The next few days passed in a blur. Ember's face seemed strange, as if he understood everything that had happened to us and was still worried. Ned seemed oblivious at first, looking at me in surprise when I went into the lodge, before he moved cautiously towards me, swished through my legs, sniffed me and then ran off to the window sill, watching our return home with distant interest. It was curious that he seemed to watch Gabe more than me.

I struggled to sleep every night, even with Gabe at my side. Every time I woke, which was often, I remembered having a nightmare but I could never remember what it was about. And each time, Gabe would turn towards me and pull me gently into his strong arms, cradling me, stroking my hair and kissing my forehead until I fell asleep, or dawn broke. It was often the latter. As I dozed back off to sleep, he would hum or quietly sing a song I recognised, but I was so far out of it that I couldn't remember where I knew it from.

As much as my broken sleep woke Gabe, he never tired of me, nor I of him. He never seemed tired or had the need to recover any sleep through the day, but then neither did I. Ember had moved to the floor beside me through the night now and he also woke when I did, a worried shadow falling over his inquisitive face whenever I woke up cold and gasping for breath.

We took Ember on long walks every day and I never once felt afraid of going back into the park or woodland, never once worried about crossing the path of another bear: I had my boys with me for protection.

As I got up just before dawn about a week after leaving the hospital, Gabe and Ember were already gone. I walked downstairs and found them sitting out on the edge of the porch, taking in the peaceful morning. Gabe was leaning forward with his hands resting on his knees and Ember lay alongside him, his neck stretched out and eyes flitting through the garden, watching for any sign of something worth investigating.

I went to sit beside them and Gabe wrapped his arm around my shoulder. I slid my legs over his so I nestled into his chest. I felt so safe, happy and in love.

My vision was almost perfect now, as the doctor had promised, and so it only took a few seconds in the bright light before my eyes relaxed and I could take in the vivid beauty of the morning. I was watching the blue jays flit from tree to tree, my vision absorbing their colours, when Gabe said some words that sent a shiver down my spine.

'I have to go away for a week, for some lectures I arranged months ago, and I can't get out of it.' My heart stopped beating for a few seconds. 'But Anna called first thing this morning and she wants to come and stay with you while I'm away,' he quickly added.

'Where are you going?' I asked, feeling instantly flat and deflated.

'York, England, to give some talks at the university there. It's only for six days.'

'When do you leave?'

'On Monday, from San Diego. Anna's arriving around the same time so you can collect her when you drop me off. That way, you won't be alone and she can drive if necessary.'

'Oh. Did you and Anna arrange this between you then?' I asked, feeling a bit left out of the loop.

'Yes. She wanted to visit anyway and with me going away we agreed it was the best time, until you fully recover.'

I said nothing, taking it all in. I was happy that Anna was coming to stay but devastated that Gabe was leaving again. I sat quietly, mulling it all over. I, naively, thought when he said he would never leave me again he meant it.

'I am coming back. I promise,' he said, leaning into me and kissing my forehead gently.

Something in his words told me that it was all true, that we would never be separated for any length of time from now on, that something had changed between us.

As I curled into his body, my thoughts returned to a dream I'd had the previous night, one I couldn't remember on waking. In the dream, I was dressed in dark, loose clothes and was collecting logs from under a shelter at the side of a small house. I was humming as I worked and carried the wood inside where I placed some of it on a small open fire. As I returned to gather more from outside, I heard some noises in the distance, voices, hastening towards me. I stopped to look in the direction of the approaching sounds and waited, my breathing accelerating. As some faces came into view, I dropped all the wood I had in my hands and screamed, running towards the house. That's when I'd woken up. I can't remember what or who I saw; I only remembered that I was really scared.

'You know, I had the weirdest dream last night,' I said, before relaying the dream to Gabe as he sat holding me and listening. 'That's all I can remember,' I said, when I'd finished the story.

There was a long, silent pause, as if he were mulling over my dream. 'I have to stop by work to sort some things out and go home to get some clothes and stuff,' he said, changing the subject. 'Should I drop you in town to do a little shopping for a few hours?' he asked.

'Sure, that would be great.' I really did need to do some shopping now I knew Anna was coming the day after next.

We sat attached to each other until just after eight, only moving to catch sight and laugh at Ember as he chased the odd lizard or jay that got close enough to entertain him. The whole time I stayed entwined around his body and he often kissed my cheek and my hair, while I fell in love with him all over again. I turned sideways to kiss his strong jaw and to rest my face into his neck. He often seemed oblivious to my stare, lost in his own thoughts, but sometimes he caught me and stared back, grinning, the lines around his eyes creasing as they narrowed, permitting me to see his most breathtaking smile.

The facts were these: I adored this man – everything about him. I adored that when he looked at me, I wanted him to look at me that way forever. And even in his darkest moods, I adored him, only I felt helpless because I never knew what he thought and I knew he would never tell me – not yet anyway. I hoped one day he would trust me enough to tell me why he disappeared sometimes late in the night, why his eyes held such torment and why he looked at me sometimes like he was leaving. I had so many questions. But I truly didn't care who he was. All I knew was that I was deeply in love with him and I could now tell that he was with me.

As I stumbled through my thoughts, he suddenly lifted me in one easy scoop and walked into the lodge. 'Breakfast!' he ordered.

Gabe rarely ate breakfast, usually opting for the fresh juice he made. I normally had a decent appetite and loved the scrambled eggs, bacon and homemade hash browns he made for me. Except today had been the same as every other in the last week; I wasn't very hungry and instead drank coffee and forced some buttered toast down. Inside, I was a little concerned about my lack of appetite but didn't dare mention it to Gabe.

As Gabe messed around with Ember in the yard, I went to the bathroom to ready myself for shopping: showering and dressing, straightening my hair and adding a little makeup. I needed to get back to a relatively normal life now: running, working at the shelter and letting Gabe get back into his beloved work, rather than chaperoning me. As I thought about things while getting ready, I started to get excited that Anna was coming, looking forward to catching up, giggling and chatting idly into the early hours, and telling her about my new life here with Gabe.

We pulled up next to Hearth & Soul so that Gabe could drop me off, and as I leaned in to kiss him, I felt the usual churn that we would be parted, even if only for a few hours. He sensed this, as he always did, and took my face in both his hands, gently pressing his lips to mine. He moved one hand and ran it down the outside of my bare arm and then onto the inside before he slid it under my vest onto my waist. He followed round to the small of my back and a tingling sensation shot through me, my heart rate shooting through the roof. I wanted him to turn the car around and go home right then.

He pulled me into him, kissing me hard and grabbing at my lip with his teeth. Unusually, the urgency of our closeness got the better of him and he bit a little too hard, the edge of his tooth piercing my top lip. He noticed what he'd done instantly and pulled away, examining the break in my skin, before moving closer back into me. We both kept our eyes open and he gently placed his lips around mine, sucking the blood clear with his lips. And in that instant, I knew he wanted to go home too.

A matter of seconds later and he was moving back away from me, sensing the need to stop things right there. We sat looking at each other and his eyes glistened, moving between brown and black in the dim light of the car.

As I clambered out, I felt the blood rush to my head and a spell of dizziness overcame me. I stood for a few seconds to catch my breath. As Gabe pulled away towards the practice, I gathered myself, and turned to head into the store, with no idea what I wanted now other than to be back with him at home.

I wandered around, gathering an array of products to freshen the lodge for Anna's visit. I bought some scented candles and a variety of soaps to place in the bathroom, blowing over fifty bucks on bits and pieces.

As I walked along Main Street towards the supermarket, I glanced over and caught a glimpse of Abigail sitting in a rocking chair on the porch outside her store, her head tilted back, taking in the sun. I decided to go and have a quick chat; I still had plenty of time to kill. I glanced both ways and crossed over, heading to see her.

As I reached Washington Street, I wandered up, looking forward to catching up with her. I hadn't seen her in such a long time. Before I'd even reached the steps, she had stopped rocking and was sitting upright looking at me, straight-faced.

'Hey, Abigail,' I said, keeping my mood light.

'Hi,' she replied, staring at me. 'Long time, no see.'

'Yeah, I was in town, so wanted to drop by. How've you been?'

'Fine, thanks, and you? I heard you had a couple of accidents.'

'Yeah, I'm really good now though, thanks,' I said, wondering how many people in town knew about what had happened.

'You look…unwell,' she said, staring at me, scrutinising my face, my body.

'Oh, well, I feel great,' I replied, taken aback a little.

'You still seeing him, then?' she asked, nodding her head towards the surgery side of town so there was no mistake as to whom she meant.

'If you mean Gabe, the veterinarian, then yes, I am,' I replied, coldly, wondering what problem she had with him.

Abigail started slowly shaking her head. 'Suppose it was on the cards.' Her snicker afterwards was sarcastic.

'Look, Abigail, I have no idea what your problem is with Gabe, but he's a fantastic man. He takes care of me and I'm very happy with him.'

'You have no idea,' she muttered quietly but enough for me to clearly hear. 'Don't say I didn't warn you.'

'What on earth are you talking about, Abigail?' My voice was angry now, annoyed by her opinion of him. She looked away, across the street.

'I'm wasting my time here,' I said, rolling my eyes and shaking my head dismissively. 'I'll see you around,' I said, turning and walking down the steps.

'I'm here if you need me,' she shouted after me. 'Just be careful, Meg,' she warned.

'Oh, whatever, Abigail,' I muttered, storming off towards Main Street.

It all felt so perfect with Gabe, whatever Abigail said.

Chapter 13

As we approached the perimeter of San Diego Airport, I started to get the numb feeling of knowing he was leaving me. I stared out the window towards the terminal as we headed to the parking lot, wondering if the time would pass faster with Anna here. Six whole days without him. I could hardly bear to think about it.

We found a space and I reluctantly climbed out, throwing my purse over my shoulder. Gabe was already at the trunk gathering his small case; he carried very little considering he was lecturing in England for almost a week. As we walked towards the terminal, he grabbed hold of my hand firmly.

Sadness started to fill me the closer it got to him leaving, and when we reached the escalator at the entrance, he suddenly let go of my hand and placed his arm around my neck and over my shoulder, pulling me tightly into his body. I rested my head on his shoulder and bit my lip, fighting to keep myself composed. He'd booked in online so we headed straight to a Starbucks and ordered coffee to pass the half-hour we had before he needed to go through security. Anna's flight was due to arrive only an hour after his left so I thankfully didn't have much time alone. We sat with our drinks and stared at each other.

'What time does the return flight land?' I asked, for the hundredth time.

'6 p.m.'

'And call me when you land in England, okay?'

'I will, I promise.'

I returned to staring at my cardboard cup. 'Make sure you have fun with Anna, okay? Make the most of your time together,' he said lowering his head to make eye contact with me.

'We'll have a great time.' I tried to sound convincing. 'I'm gonna miss you though.'

'I know. I'll miss you too. But I have to go. It will pass in no time, trust me.'

'Uh-huh,' I muttered, looking back at him. I swallowed hard and lost my breath as I stared at him. He reached forward to place his cool hand on mine and, as he did, a light static shock hit me, pushing a weird vision through my mind. It all happened so fast; I got what seemed like a huge amount of information in what could not have been more than a few seconds. As the static struck, I saw his face and then it suddenly drifted backwards so fast that by the time I blinked, he was standing far in the distance in the light at the other end of a dark tunnel, surrounded by trees. His silhouette waited for me through the narrow walkway but I couldn't make out his face any longer, and he looked bigger, much bigger, and wider. He beckoned me forward but I was scared of going to him; something wasn't right. I wasn't sure it was really him and I hesitated. But it *looked* like him.

I pulled my hand away from his and started to shake. My throat was so dry; I started to cough, to choke. Gabe leaned his body towards mine, panic reflected on his face. 'Meg, are you okay?' he asked, as I started attracting people's attention.

I held my hands to my throat and the cough subsided, along with the tremor. I looked up at Gabe, unable to speak. 'Megan?' he said, using my full name, anxious, waiting.

'I think I swallowed my coffee wrong,' I said, having no other answer.

'But you didn't take a drink of your coffee,' he said, questioning my response.

I looked at my watch. 'I think you'd better be heading through security,' I said, trying to change the subject.

He nodded slowly but concern covered his face. He left his hardly touched drink and we headed towards the flight notification board so I could check when Anna's flight would be coming in. We then moved on to security. Once we reached the area where I could go no further, Gabe's face had returned to normal, his eyes soft again. 'Well,' he said, looking down at me, 'I'd better go through.'

'Call me when you get to the hotel, okay? No matter what time it is, call me.'

'I will. Take care of yourself and the boys, and enjoy yourself with Anna. I'll see you in a few days, okay?'

With that, we both effortlessly reached towards each other and I wrapped my arms around his neck so tightly I thought I might hurt him. I stood there for a few minutes, taking in his smell and feeling his strength, before he gently pushed me back and we stared at each other, our faces only inches apart. I awaited the final goodbye. His kiss didn't disappoint, only it didn't last long enough. Then, he pulled away again, staring deep into my eyes, before he turned and headed for the security gate. He didn't look back and part of me was glad.

I watched, possessed, for a good ten minutes as he went through with no problems and out of sight. I felt an instant ache of sadness and lowered my eyes to the ground to control myself. I checked in my purse for nothing so I could hide my face until I was composed enough to make it look to passers-by that I was doing something. I checked my cell before heading towards the arrivals terminal to meet Anna.

Thankfully, her flight was right on time and as I saw her come through the gate, I realised instantly that she was what I needed – my best friend. It had been so long since we'd seen each other and so much had happened, to me anyway. Anna would be here for one day when Gabe returned so I was really looking forward to them meeting formally. Although knowing Anna and her 'say it like it is' personality, I wondered what she'd think when she met him in person.

When she saw me waiting in the arrivals area, she waved frantically and ran towards me. Her two-tone blonde hair was shorter and she was carrying a little extra weight, but she still looked really well. Her face seemed vivacious and happy, and her bright blue eyes sparkled.

Anna was a little shorter than me, about five foot five, so when we reached each other, she had to reach up to get a good grip on our hug.

We giggled and squealed like a couple of schoolgirls when we embraced and checked each other over. 'You look great!' I said, the obvious happiness in her life shining though. It was not surprising. Cam was perfect for her; he was a clever, funny and caring man, and they were like two peas in a pod, tailor-made for each other. Having kids had only strengthened their relationship and they were each other's lives. I loved what they had together, but never envied it. My future had never included children. I was too selfish. I loved my free life, roaming and doing what I liked, when I wanted.

'You look…different,' she replied. 'Mind you, I'm hardly surprised considering what you've been through lately.'

'Well, I feel great, never better,' I said, meaning every word. I felt cheered up already; she was my perfect tonic.

'Come on, then. I'm dying to see your place, the boys and hear all about Gabe,' she said, pushing her arm through mine as we headed towards the exit. 'He has the sexiest voice on the phone,' she added. I just grinned widely.

It was just over an hour's drive home and we never stopped talking. My main topic, as expected, was Gabe, along with the kids, my new home and the volunteer work at the shelter. I loved hearing the news about her boys, Oliver and Jake, who were my godsons, and about her husband, Cam. I was promised disks and envelopes full of photos, and I couldn't wait to see them.

As we arrived in town, I got a proud feeling as Anna raved about how beautiful Manzano was. She loved it and as we headed onto my estate she was even more thrilled to see where I lived. I bounced up the drive and slowed to almost a halt, pointing to Ember peering out through the blinds. Anna laughed and cooed when she saw his face peeking out.

When we got inside, the kids went crazy and Ember's tail nearly fell off in excitement. He followed us around as we did the full tour of the lodge. Anna was suitably impressed with what I'd done with the decorating. I showed her around the yard while we waited for the teakettle to boil, then we sat down to have a chat and look at the photos.

It was so nice to have her company, and now that she was here I realised how much I loved and missed her being around all the time. Later, we settled down on the couch for an evening of talking, with a mindless girly movie playing in the background. She didn't fail in lifting my spirits with her ditzy stories, and my sides were aching by the end of the evening from laughter.

I filled her in on what I'd been doing, other than just having accidents, and painted an honest picture of Gabe so she knew what to expect when she met him. She took it all in, and when I tried to describe him physically to her she raised her eyebrows and grinned. We talked for a few hours while looking through a bunch of her photos before she said she was beat. After a quick shower she headed to bed and was off to sleep in no time.

I went to sit with the kids for awhile longer, thinking about Gabe, and also about Anna, Cam and their children. I started sifting through the photos, taking more time to look at them than earlier. Every photo of them oozed happiness and fun, and I started to feel a little sullen again. As I slowly browsed the pictures, I came across a section she had tucked discreetly in the back of the packet behind the negatives. It showed one of our many nights out, when Luke, myself, Anna and Cam had gone out for a meal. I think she'd thought better of showing them to me and had hidden them so as not to upset me or to bring things to my attention that she knew I was no longer interested in.

I looked through the photos, which were similar to some I had tucked away, and as I flicked to the next one, my heart stopped completely still in my chest. I paused for a few seconds until it gave out a massive thud. There, sitting at a darkened table in the background, was a face I recognised. 'How…" I muttered. But there was no denying it. There was Gabe's face staring right at me. Not at our table in general but directly at me. I lifted my head and my eyes darted around the room, trying to remember how long ago the photos had been taken, and I worked it out to be just over a year ago.

I flicked through the rest of the photos but didn't see him in any others. Remembering the stash I had in the 'not to be viewed' section of my album, I crept upstairs into the spare room and pulled the album out, sitting quietly on the guest bed to go through it. I searched every photo for that one face, and was almost at the end when I saw it again, only this time it was in a crowd at the Boston Zoological Park, where I was feeding a giraffe.

He was glaring right at me. He stood out against the strangers like a sore thumb, his pale face exaggerating his intense dark eyes. The photo was taken by Luke and I worked out that it had been taken two months before the one at the restaurant. I looked through the last few but there were no more with him in them. What the hell was going on? I knew I wouldn't get any answers until he returned but I'd had enough. Enough of the strange events, of his odd ways and mood swings, and acting like he wanted to tell me something. And now, to add insult to injury, here he was in my photos long before I even knew him.

I lay in bed for awhile thinking, trying to work out what time it would be when he rang. Throughout the night, I woke, thought, became stressed and eventually went back to sleep. It was dark when I woke again, gasping, as if I was not getting enough air into my lungs, with sweat streaming down my face and my palms.

I'd dreamt I was in the centre of the large open meadow where we'd gone out riding, standing next to the dead, spindly lightning tree. I was waiting for something, someone, but I didn't know what or who. In the distance, at the edge of the trees, I saw a dark shadow taking form. I knew it was Gabe. He came marching rapidly towards me, not running, but moving fast as if he were. He was wearing a long fitted black leather coat, a black T-shirt and dark blue jeans. His hair was longer and wild around his face, sweeping around his side burns and getting caught in the stubble on his jaw. He was in front of me before I had time to catch my breath.

His face was guarded, angry, and somehow defensive. I stood searching his expression. He stared down at me, and for the first time I saw fear in his dark eyes. He gently pinned me to the tree, his arms wrapped protectively around me, and he started to look around, searching for something. As I examined his face closely, his eyes were jet black and I could hear a low rumbling coming from deep within his throat. He had a long scratch down his cheek but there was no blood, just the deep wound. I tried talking to him to get his attention but it was as if he could not hear me. I started screaming at him but my voice was lost and no words came out. Tears fell down my face and I tried shaking him but all he did was look around, as though he could not hear or see me anymore.

As I rested my head back onto the tree crying and screaming, I felt a strong breeze brush past me, wafting my hair around so it covered my face. I pushed it out of the way and it was no longer Gabe pinning me to the tree but a man I didn't know. He was of medium height and strong build, with dirty-blond shoulder-length hair. He had an older face, a wise face, with a square jaw and a cleft in his chin. I was shocked by the brilliance of his pale green eyes. 'It's the way it has to be,' was all he said as he tilted his head, taking in my face. I heard a growl like that of the bear that had attacked me. It got louder but I couldn't see past the man; he blocked my view intentionally, not allowing me to move. I suddenly felt a thud and a sharp pain shot up through my skull.

The next thing I knew, I felt a burning in my eyes as I opened them to the bright morning light. I could hear someone singing downstairs: Anna. I shot out of bed, annoyed when I saw the time; it was just after nine. I wandered downstairs as casually as I possibly could. Anna greeted me as she and Ember danced around the kitchen making breakfast. 'Are you always this annoyingly happy in the morning?' I said, moodily.

'Well, I slept a whole night with no kids waking me or climbing into bed with me, and I have almost a week of it now. Anyway, since when were you so miserable in the morning?'

'I always have been. It's just that annoyingly happy people don't notice,' I replied, poking my tongue out at her playfully as I collected my cell from the worktop and switched it on.

I went to gather my running things as my cell started up. When I was dressed to go, I wandered into the kitchen. 'Where are you going?' Anna asked, looking at my clothing.

'Running,' I replied. 'You eat, relax, I won't be long.'

Anna shook her head and then I heard the familiar howl from my phone. I picked it up and flipped the lid. I was notified that I had one message.

Tuesday August 12. 7:43 a.m. Sender: Gabe
Hey. I'm here safely, England's cold and wet – you wouldn't like it! I'll call you when I get chance, I have a busy schedule. Oh, and Meg. Love you.

I beamed from ear to ear as I read his words, and re-read it three times before I shut the lid. Now I was happy.

My uplifted mood didn't get past Anna. 'Gabe, I take it?'

'Yup. Okay, I'm off running, will only be an hour tops. See you soon,' I said, marching to the door with my phone, car keys, water and Ember.

When Ember and I reached the local park, I jumped out, invigorated. I let Ember off his leash but ordered him to stay close, which, amazingly, he obeyed. Since the attack, he never left my side, always insisting on staying next to me. We set off at a decent pace and by the time we reached an open wooded area about a mile into the run, I was hitting a brisk pace. I noticed this more because Ember usually slowed to trot just in front of me but now he was running to keep up. We were not doing too bad considering the length of time since our last run. I ran hard and found I was not even losing my breath, my body pushing me on. Amazing what one text message could do.

My thoughts turned to Gabe and the photos as I started on a slightly downward slope through winding trees. As my mind wandered, the trees passed by quickly and the air brushed my cheeks. I didn't pay much attention to where I was going; I just ran. Ember's tongue was lolling now, his pace only just keeping up with mine. I found I didn't want to stop running and I pushed myself harder still, going back up the slope at the other side of the wooded valley.

By the time I looped back towards the car, Ember was actually slowing behind me. 'Come on old boy,' I said to him, looking back at his face and grinning. I set off at a sprint when I saw the parking lot in the far distance and Ember gave a last spurt to keep up with me. Once I reached the car, I was barely out of breath, and as I opened the back for Ember, who jumped in and drank a whole dish full of water, I glanced at the pedometer on my wrist. It read just over nine miles, even though I had only been out running for just under an hour. 'That can't be right,' I muttered. I must not have zeroed it before we started.

When we got home, I showered, dressed and sat with Anna outside while I drank some water with a coffee chaser, which I wished I had skipped as my stomach churned from drinking it so quickly after running.

'So, what would you like to do today?' I asked her, ready to have some fun.

'Well, I was kinda hoping to check out the town and then maybe we could go for dinner tonight,' she replied.

'Sounds great. Well, get your ass dressed and we'll get going,' I said.

We planned an early dinner at the restaurant Liv had taken me to on the way to Antala. Then, we could get back home early to relax and catch up some more.

It was late afternoon by the time we were done shopping, and, after a quick coffee, we each hit the shower and started getting ready to go out. With Kings of Leon blasting out on the stereo, it felt so good to have fun like we used to. Anna spent ages on her cell to Cam and the boys as I finished getting ready, and I shouted out snippets I wanted to add to the conversation from the bathroom.

Once inside the restaurant, we were directed to a booth and the waitress took our drinks order. The poor girl ended up coming back three times to ask if we were ready because every time we started to look through the menu, we'd end up chatting again.

'You guys ready now?' she asked, looking a little fed up with waiting for us.

'Sure, I'll have the filet mignon, rare, with fries and a side of coleslaw, please,' I requested.

'Erm, can I have the grilled tuna steak with jacket potato and coleslaw, please,' Anna asked.

'Sure thing. Any more drinks?'

'Yeah, the same again, thanks.'

When the meals arrived, we ate and chatted throughout. Anna was too full for dessert, and I'd just managed to eat my steak and a few fries. We thanked the waitress for the meals, paid the bill and headed out to my car. The light was fading and we were both ready to get back, change and relax into another evening of catching up.

The next few days passed quickly, which I was pleased about in one way. Our trip to San Diego was a huge success and we spent more than we should have on clothes, DVDs, CDs and other unnecessary things. Anna also bought another suitcase to take all her new purchases back home. Cam would surely ban her from another visit once he saw how much she'd spent, but actually they were comfortable financially thanks to a healthy family business in I.T. and so they never went short on anything.

Gabe had called me in the evening on Wednesday, which I worked out to be the middle of the night in the UK. We chatted for awhile but his voice seemed reserved, hesitant and a little preoccupied. I didn't want to bring the photos up on the phone, for the fear of sending him off into a mood, so I bit my tongue and kept quiet. He said his lectures were going well, and he confirmed times again for picking him up on Sunday. I couldn't wait. I filled him in very briefly on what Anna and I had been up to and then all too soon he was gone again, leaving me in a slightly deflated stupor. I missed him terribly.

For Friday, Anna and I had planned an easy day, chilling out in the yard, popping into town and walking Ember. By late morning we had returned with food and made a huge buffet lunch, before heading out into the garden with a glass of rosé to take in some sun.

After lunch we took Ember for a walk in the park. Later, when Anna returned from her shower, I fell into fits of hysterics at her lobster impression. Way too much sun in one day for her pale complexion and she had the strap lines to prove it. I, on the other hand, looked unchanged: a creamy white with no more than an extra dozen freckles to make me look slightly tanned. The factor twenty five lotion had worked a little too well.

'You know, California does suit you, Meg,' she said suddenly whilst watching a film that evening. 'Not that I don't totally miss you like crazy and also worry about you.'

'Worry, why?' I asked, pretty sure I knew where she was heading.

'It's just, how many incidents have you had here, including one which could have easily ended your life. Then there's Gabe, who, I have to say, sounds gorgeous and intelligent and like he can be funny on occasion, but he also sounds very intense and moody. How well do you actually know him?'

And there it was, my overly concerned best friend starting her over protective attack on me, the one I'd fully expected.

'Oh Anna, come on. Accidents are exactly that – accidents. I was in the wrong place at the wrong time with the bear. As for Gabe, well, yeah, he can be a little distant and unpredictable, but he is truly wonderful to me: caring, protective and very funny when you get to know him. He adores the kids, and me even more, and takes care of us all. He can be a little intense, but he also intrigues me. You'll see when you meet him.' I paused, waiting, but she didn't say anything at first. 'You know, me and Luke, it'll never happen again. You do know that, right?'

'Yeah, I know that now. I just don't want you taking another fall. It'll break you. I love you too much to see you go through hell again. And, you've changed, Meg. I can't put my finger on it. I don't mean purely physically but in your personality too. Your temper is shorter right now and the only reason I see for that is, well, being here, being with Gabe.'

'Well, maybe this *is* me, maybe I am now who I always should have been and being with Luke suppressed all that. And as for the temper, I don't see that at all.'

Anna paused again, contemplating if she should carry on, I suspected. Especially as she thought my fuse was short. 'So, who's Isaac?' she asked.

'Who?' I asked, puzzled.

'When you *do* sleep, which I have to say doesn't seem to be a great deal, you talk a lot and you mention him, only I figured he was someone you knew here, a friend or something.'

'I have no idea who he is! How often have I mentioned him?' I asked.

'You talk about Isaac a lot and you laugh when you mention him. It's always the same conversation.'

I actually felt queasy hearing her describe it. I had never known anyone with that name, either here or in Boston.

'It just doesn't seem very healthy to me, like you're never truly resting, so much going on in your mind. And you keep coming out with words I've never heard of, but you're always talking to Gabe or this Isaac when you do it.'

I sat trying to think who they were, why I would talk about them in my sleep, but it didn't make any sense.

'Anyway, mini-lecture over. I'm sorry, Meg, but I love you so much, and I worry about you.'

'I know you do, but, seriously, Anna, I'm really happy,' I said, trying to curb her concern.

'Okay, well, just be careful, take your time and be sure of things.' She leaned over and grabbed a hold of me, hugging me tightly for a few seconds.

By the time it got to Sunday morning, I was bouncing off the walls. I'd managed to get two hours sleep or so the night before, but that was all. I took myself and Ember out running to burn off as much energy as I could to ensure I could remain as calm as possible throughout the day. It had no effect; I was completely excited one minute and apprehensive the next. Gabe's flight would be in at six so I had the whole day to kill until we could set off to collect him. I was also a little worried about how Anna would react to him and hoped they would hit it off.

My run was as good, if not better, than the last. I took the red route and pushed myself up and over rugged terrain, sometimes involving climbing over rocks, which I managed with ease. Ember played catch-up for most of the run, his tongue lolling left then right in his panting mouth. I took one bad stumble but bounced right up again off my hands without breaking pace or damaging myself too much, thankfully, and only had a couple of light grazes to show for it.

I had no idea how Gabe would behave towards me when he came walking through the doors of the arrivals lounge. I really wasn't sure if he'd be the same man I'd left almost a week ago or the quiet, tormented one. I didn't care, not in the slightest. I was just desperate to see his face, and the minute Anna left I would be free to throw at him my many unanswered questions.

We set off for the airport about an hour earlier than we needed to, which was Anna's idea. I'd seen the look on her face, the one which was a cross between worry and amusement. She'd had enough of me dancing around the lodge, hyper, and talking so fast she couldn't keep track of our conversations. In my mind, I was wondering how I was going to approach the subject of the Boston photos with Gabe, worrying it would send him over the edge again. But I had a right to know, to get some answers. He'd held out on me for too long, now. Enough was enough.

It took us less time than normal to reach the outskirts of San Diego, and as I didn't want to look like a completely obsessed nut, I decided to take Anna to the huge Borders store to browse through some books and have a coffee. This went down well and I was sure it removed some of the loved-up lunatic label she'd bestowed on me.

It was just after five when we left, both armed with a couple of books and a maple pecan pastry to keep us sustained. The sugar rush and coffee did nothing to ease my excitement as I drove a little too fast into the airport perimeter. We parked in the lot and headed to arrivals with fifteen minutes to go. Anna went to the restroom while I checked the information screen to see if his flight was on time. It had already landed. My heart skipped double beats and I started looking towards the exit for passengers.

'It's already landed,' I said to Anna as she returned, my voice almost reaching soprano level.

'Great. Look, I'm gonna have a browse round the stores for awhile, let you two catch up without me. Call me on your cell when you're ready to leave, okay?'

The last thing I wanted was for Anna to feel uncomfortable around us. But I was also very appreciative as I needed to see him alone first to assess his mood and catch up privately for a few minutes before he met Anna in person.

'Okay, thanks,' I said, kissing her on the cheek. 'I'll call you soon.'

With that, Anna disappeared off towards the retail section and I headed nervously towards the arrivals waiting area.

I stood waiting anxiously next to a pillar, amongst a couple of dozen other people whose faces looked far more relaxed than mine did. I tried to look casual, leaning against the pillar and bending my knees, yet felt as if I wanted to run around the whole room squealing at the top of my voice to get rid of my nervous energy. I examined every face that came through the gates and, with each one, the intensity built further. I knew he had a small case to collect so, knowing my luck, and just to rile me up further, it would have to be the last to reach the carousel, or even worse, be lost.

As I passed inconsequential thoughts around my head, peering blankly at the arriving faces, I caught sight of a tall, dark silhouette moving slowly behind the fogged glass of the final security and declaration section.

He was here.

Gabe appeared around the corner, his case dangling from his arm and his passport in hand. I waited for him to start searching around to find me so I could walk towards him or raise my hand, but I didn't need to. He found me straight away; his hooded, dark eyes met mine instantly and his face looked exactly as I had kept it, tightly locked in my mind.

He walked directly towards me, the weathered lines under his eyes creasing as a subtle grin fell on his lips. I knew as soon as I saw his reaction that he was pleased to see me. The tension and apprehension started to dissolve instantly but, still, I wanted to run and throw myself at him, and never let go again. Cool was the way, though, and so I tensed every muscle in my body and willed myself to stay put until he reached me.

I dug my hands deep into the front pockets of my jeans, my purse dangling from my shoulder. I couldn't help the huge grin that took over my face and he reacted to it well. I knew then that he would be a delight for Anna to meet in his present mood.

He stopped in front of me and stared down, looking me over in an approving manner before fixing his eyes on mine. 'Hey,' he said, his deep, reserved voice melting my last ounce of discipline.

'Hey,' I replied, my voice breaking at the end. I stretched up onto my tiptoes and tentatively pressed my lips on his. He responded to my unspoken demand by placing his case on the floor and taking hold of my face in both hands. 'I missed you,' I said quietly as our lips parted.

'I know,' he said smugly, leaning in to whisper in my ear. 'I can feel it in your kiss.'

I swallowed and chewed on my lip trying to catch the shy smile that crept onto my mouth, feeling a little embarrassed. 'You have no idea what I want to do with you right now, but as we have company heading our way in about thirty seconds, and we won't be by ourselves for another day, it'll have to wait,' he said. The quiet, low tones of his voice and the statement itself sent shivers down my spine and I looked sideways up to his face, grinning. He grinned back then his eyes glanced away over my shoulder.

'Fine, one more day it is,' I whispered back, struggling to string an understandable sentence together.

I turned to see the familiar face of Anna, smiling but wary as she watched on from a distance. She mouthed to me, asking if it was okay for her to approach. I waved her over and she confidently walked towards us. *Here goes* I thought.

I looked back at Gabe one more time and we grinned at each other, before he moved his arm around my waist and stood alongside me, looking towards the face of my best friend.

By the time Anna reached us, I was grinning like a Cheshire cat and she suddenly looked embarrassed. 'Anna, Gabe...Gabe, Anna,' I said, introducing them casually with my hand. I didn't take my eyes off her, desperately intrigued to see what her face would give away about what she thought of him. Judging by the way her demeanour suddenly became coy and appreciative, her smile wide and appraising, I needn't have worried.

'Hey, it's great to meet you…eventually,' she said, putting her hand delicately out to shake his. As she did, her eyes seemed to assess his face more closely and I knew she was taking in his, for want of a better word, 'different' appearance. She was still, however, more than a little mesmerised, unable to move her eyes away from his.

'And it's great to finally meet you, Anna. Megan has told me much about you. It's a pleasure,' he said, returning the handshake.

Then she let go, grinned at him and then at me. 'So, did you have a good trip?' she asked, still beaming like a teenager.

'I did, thank you. Have you enjoyed your time in Manzano, or did you both spend so much time talking that you never got out anywhere?'

'Hey,' I added, playfully tapping his chest with my free hand and narrowing my eyes at him.

'Yeah, believe it or not, we actually did lots of fun things together and I believe my husband will be taking the bank cards off me for future visits!'

'Oh, that's good,' he said, smiling, relaxed. Phew.

We set off towards the car, Gabe's arm tightly around my waist, and we chatted about his trip to England and what Anna and I had done over the last week.

Once we were back at the Jeep, Anna stood at the rear door, insisting silently that she would be sitting in the back, allowing us to sit together. I went to the driver's side and Gabe looked at me, surprised, since he had expected to drive.

'I'll drive back so you can relax after your long flight. It's fine,' I said, unlocking the doors and climbing in before he could challenge the decision. We all climbed in and, once through the exit and onto the freeway, we settled in for the hour-long trip home. It surprised me again just how relaxed Gabe was in the front seat, holding the high rail above the door, his elbow on the side rest. As he stared out of the window, taking in the familiar scenery, his free hand was resting on my right leg as I drove. If only it had been an automatic, I would have been free to grip his hand tightly the whole way home.

Anna spent most of the time probing Gabe with inquisitive questions, sometimes making me cringe at her directness. On occasion, I slid my eyes over to him when she asked a truly shocking one, such as something about his past, his marital status and the like. Yet in some respects I was grateful that she was asking the questions I so desperately wanted to ask, but couldn't for fear of sending him packing.

He answered her easily, quickly, like he was expecting her close examination, and he never once appeared to become irritated by her, his eyes staying open and friendly. I looked over at him a couple of times with an apologetic face, but he just smiled wryly, as if her questions were the least of his concerns. I looked back to concentrate on the road but I could see out of the corner of my eye that his eyes stayed on me. He started to trace his thumb over the top of my thigh, and even with the lightness of his touch, I felt goosebumps rise on my arms. With a racing heartbeat, I reached down into the holder for my can of soda to interrupt my not very wholesome thoughts.

After half an hour of investigation, Anna sat more quietly in the back. I knew she was processing the answers Gabe had given to her million and one questions for later discussion with me in private. He had told her that he had been married very briefly once but that his wife had died suddenly. He didn't go into details but it shocked and saddened me, and gave me some understanding as to why he sometimes distanced himself from me and spoke very little of his past.

He'd had no long-term relationships to speak of since his wife had died, and he'd lived around the world. Born to a wealthy family in rural France, his father was a bigwig in law, while his mother cared for Gabe and his younger sister, Madeleine. They lived just outside of Paris, although he didn't say much about his parents or mention if he ever saw them. He had travelled through Europe, staying short-term in Italy and Bulgaria, and longer in England where he still had many friends. For the past ten years, he had been a legal resident in the States, living and working on occasion in Canada, and had accepted short term positions in Seattle and New York. But for the past four years, he had been in California. He still travelled the world, though, lecturing in veterinary medicine at many universities.

Listening to his answers had intrigued me, hearing little bits of information I'd been desperate to know. As we headed slowly into Manzano, I was still somewhat lost in my own thoughts. When we arrived home, Anna made a dash with my keys, mumbling something about needing the bathroom. Gabe and I walked to the back of the car to get his case.

When I looked up at him, I could see that he was distant, deep in thought, but staring deeply into my face. I looked at him, asking no questions, and then, suddenly, the sadness in his face disappeared, changing back into a gentle smile as if he'd pushed whatever bothered him to the back of his mind.

He took a deep breath and exhaled in a sigh as he gently raised the back of his hand to my cheek, sliding it down to the underside of my chin. His hands were cool, and I lifted my hand to take his and closed my eyes as I moved it to my lips. As I opened my eyes, kissing his hand, I asked him simply, quietly, 'what is it, Gabe?'

'Nothing. Nothing is wrong,' he replied. He released his hand from mine and playfully tapped the tip of his index finger on the end of my nose before putting on what can only be described as a strained smile. 'Come on, let's go get something to eat,' he said, managing to bring some life into his words. 'Make the most of Anna's last day.' He leaned to kiss my forehead.

Back in the lodge, Gabe spent a good ten minutes playing with Ember, who went completely crazy the second he walked through the door. He knelt on the floor and Ember voluntarily rolled over, belly up and legs in the air, demanding a longer rub. Ned watched on from a distance. He still didn't seem too keen on Gabe, which wasn't really surprising since he'd never been too comfortable around strangers.

Anna was in the kitchen watching Gabe and Ember, and laughing at Ember's behaviour. 'Should I start dinner? I'm so hungry,' she said, turning to the fridge.

'Sure,' I replied, leaving Gabe and Ember to it and joining her to retrieve the seafood and accompaniments we had bought in town that morning. We pottered around the kitchen laughing and chatting. Shortly afterwards, Gabe went to sort through a few things in the bunkhouse, where he planned to stay that night.

Anna couldn't wait for him to leave, knowing that she only had about ten minutes of question and answer time. Still, it was long enough for her to give me her full and honest verdict. She started the minute the door closed behind him.

'Oh my God,' she exclaimed, grabbing my arms.

'So, what do you think?' I asked, hoping for a good response.

'He is gorgeous, Meg, such a gentleman. He's so sweet and old fashioned, and he adores you completely,' she said. 'It's like he's absorbed by your every move and he's always watching you.'

'So, is that a thumbs-up and no more worrying about me?' I asked, when I could get a word in edgewise.

'Yeah, I really like him. He seems a bit intense at times, as if there's more going on beneath the surface than he'll ever let on to me, but I guess that's how he is. I wish I were single…' She went quiet, lost in perverse thought, no doubt. 'He's so spellbinding,' she said afterwards.

'Hey!' I said, slapping her arm. She moved away in anticipation. 'You can't go saying things like that, *Mrs* Whiteledge. Remember your husband!' I chuckled as she acted all coy and fanned herself down.

I started to lay the table, and we giggled and chatted like teens, watching cautiously through the window for Gabe to make his way back. I got a bottle of wine from the fridge and it was open before it hit the table. Anna poured three large glasses. I grabbed mine, chugging a few mouthfuls straight away.

When Gabe returned, his mood seemed a lot lighter. I hoped he'd pulled himself together while he unpacked, especially because we had company for the evening.

We all sat down to dinner, talking freely. Gabe ate most of his meal but apologised for leaving some of it, explaining that he was feeling the effects of the journey a little now.

We moved to the living room after dinner, leaving the dishes to soak in the sink. We chatted for a while longer and I could see that Gabe was mesmerised by the way Anna and I were with each other, our bond so close. By ten we were all exhausted and Anna made her excuses first, heading upstairs and smiling endearingly at Gabe as she said her goodnights.

Gabe got up immediately after her and tugged me from the couch with him to the front door. 'Time I caught up on some rest too,' he said, drawing me tightly into his body, his hands grabbing mine and locking them around my back with his. This was not the sort of position to be standing in if it was sleep he wanted, his body pressed hard against mine, his heady, earthy smell swirling around my nose.

I gulped hard. 'Sure,' I muttered, my chest visibly heaving against his. 'Sleep.'

His smile was suddenly wide and tempting, just like the one he'd shown me at the airport when we'd made our intimate promise for the following night. He pulled my head towards his quickly and into a kiss far more intense than I was expecting. My response was a little stunned and apprehensive. I knew this was going to be one of those occasions when I would be unable to control myself so I put the brakes on early, halting the kiss right there, pulling back and out of his spell. I couldn't bear the frustration.

He looked at me a little surprised and frowned. 'Okay, so this isn't a great idea,' I said, trying to calm my breathing down, placing my hands over his, which were now attached to the sides of my face. He looked into my eyes and I noticed for the first time a long, pale white scar which ran horizontally just under his right eye. It blended into the weathered lines embedded in his skin. His eyes burned into mine, as if it was him who was unable to let me go this time. But he broke off the stare seconds later and his eyes softened. He released my face and kissed my forehead. 'I forgot how much I missed you,' he said, with an impish grin. 'I'll see you in the morning.'

With that, he turned, still grinning, and walked into the dark of the night to the bunkhouse.

I shut the door and turned around to lean back on it, trying to bring my pulsing body and wandering mind back to earth. After a minute or so, I pushed myself off the door and made my way into the bathroom to get ready for bed.

Anna was already soundly asleep by the time I crept in next to her and I pulled the covers back carefully trying not to wake her. She shifted a little when my weight sank into the mattress but dropped off again instantly.

I lay thinking about Gabe for what seemed like hours, about him lying alone outside and the fact that there was only about fifty feet between us. Yet I had to wait to be with him even though patience was *not* one of my virtues. As my hormones calmed down, I fell into much needed sleep.

I was somehow strangely conscious that I was dreaming, especially when I saw Gabe dressed in a pale shirt and dark trousers, looking like someone from an old movie that played in joined-up, jumpy pieces.

His normally unruly hair was shorter and pushed back behind his ears, and he was smiling at something, holding his hand out. His skin was warm-looking and dark golden brown, but it was his deep green eyes that shocked me the most. They were mesmerising. I was desperate to see what held his attention.

There before him stood a petite and beautiful Native American woman, with full lips and black hair hanging almost to her waist. He beckoned her towards him and she moved to him easily, taking hold of his hands. I was dreaming of Gabe and who my brain imagined was his wife. My mind had been so full of her since Anna had boldly asked him about his past and my unconscious state created the mental picture. I wanted the dream to continue but it ended there, just as something she wore glinted in the late afternoon sun.

I gasped loudly, waking myself and Anna in the process. Everything else was completely still.

'You okay, Meg?' she asked, her croaky voice barely a whisper.

My breath was choppy, my heart rate erratic when I answered. 'Yeah, I was just dreaming,' I said, turning my head to face her. She paused, looking towards me for a moment.

'Sure you're okay?' she asked.

'Yeah, honestly. Go back to sleep,' I said, lowering my head to rest on the pillow so I faced the darkness of the ceiling.

I tried to recapture all the images I'd seen in the dream but they were already starting to fade. I lay there, knowing that my sleep for the night was over, and looked towards the clock next to my bed. I was in for the long haul; it was only just after 2 a.m.

When I was fully awake, which didn't take long, I started thinking about Gabe again. With Anna sleeping soundly next to me, I carefully pulled the covers away and snuck out of bed. I crept down the first few stairs which led to the side window, the only one overlooking the bunkhouse. I looked out into the darkness and saw the faintest flickering of light through the curtains. He was still awake. I really felt like I needed to be with him, just to talk and be close.

As I looked for signs of movement inside, the wind picked up, tunnelling through the branches. I was sure I saw a tall shadow moving through the distant trees towards the lodge. It moved so fast, I had to keep refocusing to see it. It took just a few seconds to move from the far end of the yard to the side of the lodge. By the time I blinked again, it had disappeared.

I went down the rest of the stairs and over to the back door, wearing only my vest and shorts. As I opened the door, I felt a cool breeze that was pleasurable against my skin.

I walked tentatively towards the door of the bunkhouse and could hear the creaking of the floorboards as Gabe moved around inside. I paused for a moment, wondering how I would announce my unexpected visit and, as I thought about it, the creaking inside stopped. Had he heard me? I didn't want to appear to be creeping around, watching him, so I rapped gently on the door.

'It's open,' he said, as if expecting me.

As I opened the door, a smell I didn't recognise wafted out. It was a mixture of burning candles and something metallic, but not unpleasant. Gabe was sitting on the edge of the bed, leaning forwards onto his knees, wearing only his jeans.

'Oh, erm, sorry to disturb you. Were you just going to bed?' I asked, feeling a little embarrassed. I felt my cheeks flush seeing him sitting there semi-naked. Maybe being here wasn't such a good idea. It certainly wouldn't help me on the getting-to-sleep front.

'No, it's fine. I've slept a little anyway. I was just getting up, actually.'

'Getting up?' I asked. 'It's only just after two.'

'Jetlag,' he said quickly. 'Anyway, since you're here, come sit with me. I have a gift for you.'

I relaxed a little at the invitation and moved slowly towards him to sit on the bed, keeping a safe distance between us. 'You shouldn't have got me anything,' I said, trying desperately not to stare at his chest. He seemed to notice my attempts to avert my eyes and my rigid body; he grinned sheepishly, the smile reaching all the way to his eyes. No, I definitely should not have come here.

He turned and leaned forward towards the bedside table to retrieve a small box, which sat next to the candle. As he moved, the muscles in his back were defined further and I could see a long scratch down his back, which extended to his slender waist. It looked fresh. I gulped and exhaled quietly, wondering where on earth he got the mark from.

With the small box dwarfed in his hand, he turned back around, lifting his knee up and across so his body faced me completely. One one thousand, two one thousand I counted, trying but failing in an attempt to keep my cool. I tried desperately to focus on the small midnight blue box tied up with string, which he was holding out towards me. As I studied the box, he tensed his other arm and leaned across to rest on it. In one swift movement, he'd bridged the nice, safe gap I'd kept between us.

I looked up at him and smiled. 'You really shouldn't have gotten me anything,' I said, feeling a little uncomfortable about taking it from him. He just smiled at me, his eyes refusing to move from mine. He pushed the box towards me and I reluctantly took it from him.

I examined it for a few seconds, biting on my lower lip, and then tentatively pulled the ends of the string. When they came free, I looked at him and smiled, shaking my head. Inside was the most beautiful antique silver locket, hanging on the finest of chains. It was so heavy I knew it must have been solid silver. I forced myself to breathe normally when I felt an overwhelming, heady feeling. I looked up at him to see that his eyes were still on mine, only this time the grin had been replaced with an intense expression. His eyes glistened and he clenched and unclenched his jaw as he watched me.

I looked back at the locket and felt goosebumps cover my arms. I slid the edge of my finger into the indentation at the side and carefully opened it. What I saw inside made my heart skip and I held the open locket, staring at the initials engraved within.

GL   MA

I could do nothing but stare. 'It's beautiful,' I eventually whispered, smiling up at him.

He gently placed his hand under my chin, raising my eyes to his. My breathing instantly started to quicken and I tried hard to hold back.

The blackness in his eyes had all but gone, replaced instead by the warm chocolate colour I adored so much. He slowly leaned towards me, the seconds seeming to take forever to pass, until his mouth reached the side of my face where he brushed my cheek lightly with his lips.

He lingered there, his cold breath tickling my skin. I couldn't move and my eyes closed in anticipation, knowing there was nothing I could do to stop him. I was completely under his spell and had no complaint about it.

He slowly moved his lips further down and gently bit my tensed jaw, before sliding them onto my neck. His lips moved faster, more eagerly and the loose strands of his hair danced around on my skin, causing a delightful sensation that pushed me past the point of no return. I ached for this moment to last forever, yet at the same time felt I was about to explode. I lowered my mouth to kiss the top of his head and slipped the pendant into my left hand, freeing my right hand to reach around his tense, solid back. I grazed the icy surface with my finger tips, starting at the nape of his neck, reaching down over the raised scar on his lower back and following all the way down to the loose gap at the back of his jeans.

He took the pendant from my weak grasp and effortlessly slid behind me onto both his knees until his frame towered behind mine. I felt like I was on the edge of a precipice, about to drop off any second. As his dark shadow moved over my head, the sparkle of the silver shone before the cold, flat surface of the locket reached my chest. The length of the pendant dropped as he fastened the clasp, and I felt an odd burning sensation as it rested on me.

I lowered my head, looking at the simply etched jewel lying on my bare skin, and knew it was something I would treasure for the rest of my life. As I examined it, I felt Gabe's body press firmly behind me, before his lips were on me again, rubbing sideways along the length of my neck. He carefully slid the straps of my vest from my shoulders, and pulled my hair up into his hand and out of the way, before kissing around my neck.

I twisted round, forcing him to lean backwards and bent my legs, placing them over his and sitting back onto his knees. It shocked me to see how sunken yet muscular his torso looked. He ran his hands from my shoulders down the length of my arms.

I linked my fingers around the back of his neck, staring into his face. He leaned in and with one hand forced my face to his, kissing me hard before his other hand wrapped around my neck. He flipped me round onto the bed in one easy move and his body hovered above mine, his arms locked as he held his weight easily. He slowly lowered himself onto me and moved to slide my vest off. All my inhibitions fell away. It felt easy being with him, natural, as if this wasn't our first time.

He was everything I imagined and more. At times his strength became overpowering, and it was as if he had to remind himself to be careful.

The following hour passed slowly, wordlessly, and afterwards we just lay facing each other, the sheets placed loosely over us, the candle burning lower on the bedside table. I closed my eyes, hoping to sleep for a little while, but I fought against it, not wanting to miss a minute of this time with him. I turned over in the hope that not seeing his face might help me sleep, but as I did he wrapped his arms around my waist and pulled me back into the crevice of his body. Bang went the sleep.

We spent the rest of the night like this, neither of us wanting it to end. Every time his scent wafted around me, it aroused me and, with no complaints on either side, we consummated our relationship again and again.

But the night had to end, and as the sun started to creep up over the distant mountains, Gabe picked me up easily and slid me to sit in-between his legs, using the sheets as a shawl wrapped around us.

He turned round to face the window, leaning to pull the thin curtain back, which allowed the early morning light to cover us. I placed my head back onto his shoulder and we just sat, watching another day begin.

Chapter 14

It was just after six-thirty when I crept as silently as possible back into the lodge. I looked around for any sign of life but saw only Ember as he lifted his head up over the back of the couch and stared at me, as if to accuse me. I crept over to him and kissed his head.

I made my way to the shower, the water invigorating me. It was Anna's last day, and we planned to go into town and have a nice long, leisurely breakfast before heading to the airport. Her flight left at two, so we had plenty of time.

I readied myself quietly, wrapping my wet hair in a towel and rubbing the mist from the mirror. I jumped and let out a high-pitched short scream when I saw something flit past the door of the bathroom. I turned quickly and walked to the door, poking my head around the corner, expecting to see Gabe or Anna out there. As I scanned the room I saw only Ember, lying in the same position, his head twisted round on the back of the couch, looking towards me. I waited and listened but still saw and heard nothing. I went back into the bathroom and grabbed some face cream from the cabinet, squeezing a good dollop onto my hands and rubbing it into my face.

As I stared closely into the mirror, I heard Ember's low, deep-throated grumbles. Someone was there. I headed back out, nervous and jumpy. Anna was only upstairs and Gabe was outside, so it was irrational to feel as worried as I did. As I followed Ember's stare, I heard some trees cracking outside and the wind whistling past the back door. I turned my head round to follow the noise but it passed quickly towards the back of the lodge and then became distant. I went to look through the porthole window, out towards the bunkhouse, but again saw nothing.

I went back to finish getting ready, rubbing in the last bits of cream. I stared at my reflection and noticed for the first time that the past few weeks of little sleep were catching up with me. My eyes were flat and much darker, and the deep shadows beneath stood out to highlight the fact.

I put on my makeup and brushed my hair through, leaving it loose to dry naturally, since I didn't want to wake Anna with the dryer. I wrapped myself in my robe and headed towards the stairs to fetch some fresh clothes. As I crept to the top, I could see that Anna was still sleeping. I had just reached the door to the spare room when I heard her.

'Where did you sneak off to last night, then?' she asked, not sounding very asleep.

I let out a little gasp as she spoke. 'You made me jump. Did you sleep well?' I asked, trying to change the subject.

'*I* slept fine. You do much sleeping?' she asked, knowing full well where I'd been. She twisted over to look at me, grinning.

'Oh, be quiet,' I hissed at her, embarrassed.

'So, what's that dangling around your neck?' She pointed to the pendant.

I went to sit next to her on the bed, grinning from ear to ear. 'Gabe gave it to me,' I said, placing my hand underneath it to show her more closely. 'Isn't it gorgeous?'

'It's so heavy. Are there cute photos of you guys inside?'

I rolled my eyes and slid my finger into the side and opened it carefully, showing her the initials. 'No, but he got this done.'

'That is one *serious* gift,' she said, examining the inside of the pendant closer. 'So, I guess it's official then.'

I shrugged and acted nonchalant, but my wide grin was the only reply she needed.

We chatted for awhile as we got dressed then headed to the kitchen to make coffee, just as there was a light knock at the door.

When I opened it, Gabe, who was looking over his shoulder, turned his attention to me and leaned down to give me a gentle kiss, if a little short. 'Morning,' he said, grinning. 'Did you sleep well?' he asked, maintaining the charade.

'No point. She knows,' I said.

'Oh. Morning, Anna. I trust you slept well?' Gabe asked, as polite as ever.

'I did, thank you, and you?' she asked, smiling angelically, subduing her grin.

'I rested well, thanks,' he replied. Ember trotted towards him, interrupting any further probing or insinuations from Anna.

We sat outside on the porch to drink our coffee, me wearing my sunglasses so the bright light couldn't play havoc with my eyes. Gabe seemed a little distant. Whether he was allowing Anna and me time to chat on her last day, or was just tired, I didn't know. He got up several times and followed Ember as he wandered around the yard, throwing him sticks and looking around with his cup in hand.

As we finished up, Anna went to pack her things and I wandered off to look for Gabe. I found him leaning on the railing of the bunkhouse decking, with Ember alongside, both staring through the trees. I must have surprised him when I placed my hand gently on his lower back, as he swung around at such speed that I barely saw him move. I jumped as he grabbed my arm in a vice-like lock, his eyes black.

'Sorry,' I said quickly, surprised that his grip didn't actually hurt even though the colour of my skin went even paler as the circulation was cut off.

He released my arm immediately, recognition coming into his face. 'Gabe, are you okay?' I asked.

'I'm fine. You just took me by surprise is all,' he said, his dark eyes becoming lighter.

'Sure doesn't seem like nothing,' I said, rubbing at my arm, relieving the circulation. 'You seem to be on edge this morning.'

'I'm fine. Is Anna ready to go yet?' he asked, dangling his arm around my shoulder and towing me towards the lodge. Ember obediently followed behind as Gabe called for him.

'She won't be long,' I said, looking up at him, willing him to give me *something*. He didn't. But I knew something was wrong, that something had suddenly changed.

He guided me into the lodge and closed the door behind us, peering through the door window for a second longer than necessary. Had there been someone prowling around the lodge earlier when I was in the bathroom? He sure was acting like there had been. Goosebumps shimmied down my arms and spine.

I gathered some things into my purse as we waited for Anna. Gabe paced around the lodge, trying to make idle chat with me, but when I spoke it was as if he heard nothing that I was saying. As he started on again, I paused and leaned against the kitchen counter, staring at him. He didn't even notice me. He just continued to pace and mumble.

'So, I think I will leave you two to have breakfast together. I need to go grab some things from my house. I'll pick you up when you're ready. You got your cell? Ring me when you've finished. Where are you going for breakfast again?' he asked.

I stared back at his distant eyes, unable to reply. I drew a breath and exhaled loudly; he didn't even seem to hear. 'Anthony's, Gabe. We're going to Anthony's.'

'Oh, right,' he said. 'What time's Anna's flight?'

'She flies at two. You know that.'

Anna came downstairs, oblivious to our weird discussion. In truth, he'd spoken more in a few minutes than he sometimes did in as many hours, so I knew something was very wrong.

As we reached town, I tried to make small talk with Anna. I didn't want her to know something was wrong; it would only bring up more concern and lectures. 'Cam and the boys will be so desperate to see you,' I said, looking over my shoulder and forcing a smile.

'I know, I dread to think what state the house will be in,' she said, shaking her head.

Gabe pulled up outside Anthony's and came around to open the doors before we had chance to get them ourselves.

'Okay, I'll see you in a while. Ring me when you're ready to leave,' he said. I just stood there, bewildered, and didn't even move as his lips pressed against my cheek. 'See you soon, Anna,' he said, disappearing back into the Jeep. He took off way too fast.

We walked inside and were led straight to a small booth in the busy diner. We ordered coffee and breakfast, but I knew my suddenly nervous stomach would be unable to hold much food.

'So, why's Gabe not eating with us?' Anna asked, as I'd expected her to.

'He wanted to give us some time on our own on your last day, and he has to collect some things from his house,' I said, covering for him.

'Ah, that's nice. Is he okay? He seems a little distracted.'

'Yeah, he gets like this from time to time. I just leave him be and he gets over it, you know,' I said, looking towards the passing waitress and taking my eyes from Anna's watchful ones. I was never good at keeping eye contact, especially when I was lying or uncomfortable about the conversation. She picked up on this right away.

'Don't you get fed up of his moods? I mean, don't get me wrong, I actually *really* like the guy but it seems like hard work for you at times. You're always walking on eggshells.'

I thought about what I was going to say. Yes, his moods were cause for concern, but he had gotten much better since I'd been home from the hospital. Besides, he never, *ever* took his temper or bad mood out on me. He always just distanced himself, took himself off out of the equation for a while. How could I explain this to her?

'This will sound odd but, in a way, I do know where I stand with him. I know him well enough to read the signs now, to know when his mood is changing, and I know how to be with him then. I just don't know enough about him yet to understand why it happens. But, I will. I promise you. And I'm happier than ever. It's like in some way he makes me feel complete, like we are meant to be together. Fate, I suppose.'

'Well, I know you, and I know how you work,' she said, leaning to take my hands. 'I also know what you went through with Luke and the most important thing is that you deserve, have earned, happiness with someone. I just hope he's the one who can bring it to you.'

That was exactly the thing – I *did* know what she meant. What I also knew was that after the last episode this morning, especially after such an intense night, the minute we returned from dropping Anna off I was going to approach him, challenge him about the many questions which were swimming around in my head, causing me to fret. The photos, his night-time outings, the men in Antala. There were things I *had* to know and I would get my answers this time.

I called Gabe as we were finishing our juice, renewed strength in my voice. His voice still sounded edgy, but I supposed I had sounded a little rude and direct myself.

We paid the bill and wandered out into the bright sun, putting on our sunglasses to fend off the punishing glare. I saw Gabe's Jeep come around the corner. He drove past a short way to swing round in the next intersection and as he pulled to a stop next to us, he jumped out of the driver's side to come open the doors. I beat him to it. As fast as he was, I'd already opened Anna's back door. As I climbed in, I briefly saw his pained expression but made no eye contact.

When we were both in, he jumped back into the driver's seat, refusing to belt up as he always did. He looked over at me, his eyes a little more relaxed. 'Good breakfast?' he asked, attempting a smile.

'Yeah, we really enjoyed it,' I said, looking at him once before I looked out through the windshield.

I could tell he noticed the change in me instantly. I felt bad; I had Anna in the back, looking out of the window and obviously feeling a little uncomfortable, pretending she wasn't there. I doubted he was anticipating the explosion which would follow in a few hours.

We drove pretty silently to the airport and the odd comment Gabe made was stilted and awkward. He sat with his elbow on the door rest, rubbing his mouth, obviously mulling over whatever was bothering him. I tilted my head back onto the head rest, planning in my head what I was going to say, how I would broach the subjects that were bothering me. The way Gabe drove, we made the airport in about forty minutes. Fast, even for him.

'You know, you guys should get yourselves away when you've dropped me off, no point hanging around,' Anna said, making me jump as her voice interrupted the silence. 'And when you can, head up to Boston to stay with us.'

'Gabe can park in the long-stay and I'll wait with you until you're through security,' I said without turning around. 'I'll let you know some dates in a few weeks.'

'You know, I was planning on getting a few magazines and calling Cam. I'll be on the phone to him for ages. There's no need for you to stay,' she said. I knew there was no point arguing.

'If you're sure, Anna. Can you pull in the short-stay then, please,' I said to Gabe without looking at him.

'Sure,' he replied, dangling his arms over the steering wheel.

We bounced up into the parking lot and found a space. The light was dull so I took my glasses off and then unclipped my seatbelt. Gabe was out and taking Anna's case out of the trunk in a flash.

'You okay?' she asked, quietly.

'Yeah, I'll be fine,' I said, looking around at her worried face and smiling. 'Trust me.'

Gabe opened her door and Anna climbed out, collecting her case. I was already out before he had chance to open mine. He looked at me again, worry showing in his face. I took hold of Anna's case and waited for them to say goodbye.

'I'll carry this,' he said, trying to take the case.

'I got it. We can manage fine,' I retorted, pulling the case back from his hand. I wasn't sure how he'd react but he let the case go and stepped towards Anna.

'Anna, it was truly lovely to meet you. I hope to see you again soon and look forward to meeting your family,' he said, leaning down to kiss her gently on the cheek.

'It was nice to meet you too, Gabe,' she said, smiling up at him. 'Thank you for driving me. I've had a great time.'

'Won't be long,' I said, turning quickly to walk towards the entrance. I saw him hover outside the car as we walked off but made no attempt to look back.

With Anna checked in, we walked away from the desk. We looked at each other for a few seconds, neither of us knowing how to start.

'I'm worried for you,' she said, her eyebrows pulling together, her eyes a little tearful.

'Oh Anna,' I said, grabbing her for a huge hug. 'I'll be fine, always am,' I whispered in her ear. 'We'll sort this out. I'm holding the trump card and if it's not right, I'll just walk away, I promise.'

'Just think about yourself. Make yourself happy. And call me tomorrow or as soon as you can, okay,' she said, her voice breaking at the end.

'I will,' I promised, a huge, unstrained smile on my face. 'Seriously, I'll take no prisoners. It's my way or the highway. And call or text me when you get home, or I'll be worrying.'

'Okay,' she said. We hugged a while longer.

'Right,' she said. 'Now get going, so I can call my husband up and talk gooey to him to soften him up before he sees how much I've spent.'

'Give everyone a huge kiss from me.' I set off towards the exit, waving, with tears welling up in my eyes. I was going to miss my best friend and, for some reason, I knew I wouldn't see her again for awhile.

When I reached the car, Gabe was sitting with the window open. I saw his dark gaze in the wing mirror as I walked back. I clenched my jaw hard, anticipating what was about to come. I slid my glasses on to hide my eyes and opened the door to climb in.

'Okay?' he asked.

'Yeah,' I replied, his question forcing more tears into my eyes, my emotions running high.

We drove the rest of the way home in silence and as we pulled up onto the drive, I saw Ember appear at the window. My stomach started fluttering, the tension building up inside and ready to come bursting out. Getting answers was something I wanted, but would they be the right answers or would they end my happily ever after.

I didn't feel optimistic.

I darted out of the car the second the wheels came to a standstill, and marched up the path, opening the door, and feeling terrible that Ember got only the slightest brush from my hand. I stood leaning onto the back of the couch, shaking and fit to explode, and waited for Gabe to follow me in so the onslaught of questions could begin.

I waited.

I started to get impatient, my temper flaring at what was keeping him. I was ready for this now.

I heard the Jeep's engine start and ran to the door, just in time to see Gabe spin the car around flinging loose stones into the air. I raced at full speed down the path and cut the corner onto the dirt to reach the top of the drive, just as he bounced down the rise at the bottom, screeching around the corner and away.

I stormed back inside, cussing, screeching through my teeth. How dare he slink off like that? I grabbed my cell and car keys and marched out of the lodge again, slamming the door behind me. I jumped in my car and roared the engine into life. I knew roughly where he lived – that was a start. He'd probably go home, thinking he was safe because I'd never been there, and he wouldn't expect me to find him, but I would try.

I drove a little too eagerly into town, breaking the speed limit by a good ten miles per hour. I slowed as I came to the junction at the bottom of the road leading up to the estate where he lived. Liv had told me in one of our chats that he lived at the top end of town, the exclusive end, in a secluded and private wooded estate.

I slammed my gear shift into second to get some pull up the steep hill and kept driving, looking across the side streets, searching for something to be obvious, but nothing was. I hit the gas again, reaching the peak of the hill, where the road descended a little before levelling out into winding bends.

It was a beautiful part of town that I'd never visited before. In front of me were small, discreet turnings, leading into dense woodland at both sides. I slowly took the first left turn, driving around winding corners, passing randomly placed and mansion-like wooden houses.

Down some of the drives, I could only make out small details of a house, a window or the peak of a roof, the rest hidden by trees.

How on earth would I find his house? Then, as soon as I said it, I knew how. I reversed a little too fast back to the first house I'd passed and looked across to a mailbox which sat there, telling me the family name was 'Gordon'. Further along, the next box was labelled 'Dr Albertson'. I paused, swerving to the other side to find more names, all of which held no interest to me. I only hoped no one saw me and wondered what I was doing.

This was definitely the money side of town; I could only dream of living in one of these houses. I gradually followed the road back around, checking every mailbox I passed, and ended up back at the main road. I would do this in every street until I found his name. I took the next turn and did the same, the road looping back to the main street, and again onto the next. I came up blank and then I ran out of roads, so I did a U-turn and started on the other side, heading back towards town.

I made a left and pulled up alongside the first mailbox, checking the name. I slowly zigzagged across to the other side. Nothing. As I approached the curve in the road that took me back around towards the main street, I came to a halt in front of the farthest property on the corner. I pulled up at the bottom of a tree-laden drive but was unable to see the house. Just to the left stood a black and silver mailbox, with the name I had been looking for, 'Letenierre'.

This was it. I'd found his house. I was still ranting inside, shaking about the fact that he'd just driven off. He must have known exactly what was coming. So, now what should I do? If I parked on the roadside, I'd attract attention to myself and my car. If I were his girlfriend – which I was beginning to doubt – I would just drive on down to the house. But would that look forward? Would that piss him off?

'Oh, to hell with it,' I muttered, swinging onto the gravel drive. It was longer than I thought, with dense trees on both sides. I must have driven a hundred yards before the house came into view. I raised my eyebrows and my jaw dropped a little as I slowly pulled to a stop in front of the vast, dark wooden house. It was two-story, simple and understated. To the right and slightly set back was a wide garage, which matched the house, and would have easily accommodated several cars.

I scanned along the front for any sign of his car but saw nothing. Maybe he hadn't come home yet. Maybe he was already parked up in the garage. I tapped on the top of the steering wheel, wondering what to do. I knew I should turn around and go home. In theory, that was the best option. But I knew I wasn't going to do that. Maybe I should just wait in the car until he showed up. I was pretty sure he wouldn't head back to mine, not now. Or maybe I should go take a look around, have a little snoop now I was here. No, I couldn't do that; it would be so wrong, so…intrusive.

As I opened the door, I listened for any sound of a vehicle approaching but all I heard were birds, the light breeze through the trees and the very distant engine noise of a car passing on the main road to town. I left the keys hanging in the ignition and gently placed my feet on the ground, the gravel crunching underfoot. I looked around, wondering if he was watching my sneaky approach.

I shut the car door quietly with both hands, allowing it to close to but not completely click shut. I turned and walked cautiously towards the front door, which sat perfectly in the centre of the house. The windows were small, cottage-like, heavily leaded and dotted every few feet across the front at each side of the door. I scanned around, looking up towards the second floor.

With no one around, I slowly walked up to the huge front door and rapped lightly. I stood back, waiting, pretty sure that no one would answer.

I knocked again, louder this time, and then side-stepped to the first of the windows, peering through and into the darkened room. The bright reflection of the sun prevented me from seeing much inside but I could make out slightly different colours on every wall. As I squinted and moved my head to find the best angle, I could see the walls were lined with books. I glanced further around the room and made out a small, dark table with only a lamp sitting on it, the metal stem shining back at me in the light.

I stepped back and looked sideways towards a path. Maybe I shouldn't have – I know I shouldn't have – but I decided to go around the back in case he hadn't heard me. I seemed quite good at talking myself into things I really shouldn't be doing, but my temper was running the show now.

Looking for an obvious route to take, I turned to the left, heading away from the garage. As I crunched my way along the gravel, I stepped up some old paving stones and onto the grass. As I came alongside the house I looked over into a vast garden, sprawling out to the distant trees. The garden was beautifully kept, with a short lawn and, strangely, no flowers, only trees and shrubs. They stood everywhere, surrounding the whole perimeter of the house.

I continued around the side, surprised by how far back it went, and when I reached the corner, I peered around, looking for any sign of movement. I listened for any noises, noises which would send me running back to the car, but heard nothing. I slowly walked up to a large paved area, the stones spreading out in a fan shape forming steps that led down from the elevated position of the house onto the back lawn.

I felt a mixture of emotions – surprise at the beauty of the house and gardens and fear at what I was doing. My heart raced and my senses were on high alert. I walked up to the French doors and peered in, looking in onto another huge room, basic and simple but still refined. It was easy to see into this room because my eyes were shaded from the sun and there were no reflections to impede my view.

It looked like a family room, only ten times more luxurious than a standard one and with furnishings that I could never afford. There were two large black leather couches facing each other just in from the side walls, and a low glass table in the centre, with a tall bronze statue of a rearing horse placed in the middle.

As I looked around, I saw a door at each side of the room and high on the walls hung two huge paintings. I couldn't tell what they depicted; the colours were too dark. I leaned in closer, pressing my body close to the French door to get a better look.

I heard a slight click and the door opened a tiny fraction. I really shouldn't have been thinking what I was but before I allowed my common sense to kick in, my hand reached up and gently pushed at the door, causing it to swing wide open. I peered around, looking and listening, and stepped forward into the house.

Standing there and looking around the large room, I could smell him. The earthy, natural smell he carried. Every sound made me jump: the woodpecker tapping in the tree outside, then the deep chime of a clock somewhere else in the house. The sensible part of me told me what I was doing was very wrong, unforgivable, but the more intrigued part forced me further into the house.

I knew I would have to look around quickly and walked over to the paintings first. They were both oil paintings, heavy in colour and dark. One showed a house, an amazing country house, with pillars and stairs leading up to the front door. The grounds surrounding the house were palatial, with vast lawns and shaped trees. The sky was painted in dark reds and blues, making the scene storm-like, and as I scanned the beautiful house my eyes fell on one window where a face could just be made out. Not in detail, though, it was just a porcelain face staring out of the window.

I felt goosebumps along my spine as I was drawn into the painting, intrigued by its vast size. The sight of a tiny face in one of the windows of the house seemed, well, odd. Like an afterthought.

I looked out of the French doors, which I had left open in case I needed a quick exit, then turned to examine the other painting. This one was altogether different although it was dark, as before, and it appeared to be painted in oils. It showed a simple wooden house in the forest with a log pile stacked up at the right of it. The house was in some kind of clearing with trees surrounding it, but there was no door, no way in. It looked similar to the painting in the bunkhouse. And then I saw it again. As in the other painting, there was a small, barely noticeable face at the window but this face was different, darker, and harder to see in the wooded setting.

As I thought about the paintings, wondering why he'd bought them, I looked towards the bottom and my mouth dropped open. The same signature sat in the same position in this painting as it did in the two hanging in my bunkhouse.

I dashed back to the other painting and stared in disbelief as I noticed the same scrawled signature on this one, too. I looked closer, unable to make out the name.

Γαβριελ Λετενιερρε 1852

Unlike the paintings in the bunkhouse, this painting held a date, 1852. I darted back to the other painting to see if it too had a date.

Γαβριελ Λετενιερρε 1910

It did, but it was much later. Also, the colours in this painting were noticeably warmer, the surroundings more natural. It had to depict another place.

I pondered them, my eyes unblinking, trying to make the link to those at my bunkhouse. But nothing fit and it was all becoming very confusing. I looked up towards the two doors, deciding where to go next. My well-behaved side told me to leave as I'd seen more than enough already, but my bad self told me that if Gabe wasn't going to give me the answers I needed, I would find them myself. The bad side won outright.

I walked through the door on the right and into a long hallway with more doors leading off. I stopped myself mid-stride and tried to be rational. What was I looking for? I needed to decide where to look for whatever it was I was searching for, and quickly. I wouldn't be able to stay here much longer. He was bound to come home before too long. Where else would he go?

I opened each door I passed, looking into the rooms, which were all simply decorated, dark, sparsely furnished and offering nothing much to look at. As I approached the last door on the left, I opened it and found myself in the doorway of a library, the room I'd seen from outside. I went in and walked cautiously to the window, looking for any sign of Gabe outside. It all looked the same and, thankfully, I was still alone.

I looked around the room, and my attention was drawn to the mass of books covering every wall from top to bottom except the window wall. I glanced across book after book on veterinary medicine, some modern, most of them old, noticing that all of the spines on every book were in pristine condition, hardly used. I glanced to the shelf above to find an array of antique books with wide spines, displaying deep colours and heavy lettering.

My eyes locked onto one book which caught my eye, one that looked not as perfect and new as the others. I stretched up to the tips of my toes and reached to pull it down. I almost dropped it but managed to re-balance myself, keeping a tight grasp on the heavy book. The cover was brown with black lettering on the front, reading 'Notre Dame De Paris'. I opened the cover and saw a handwritten inscription, beautifully written in black ink.

Aiyana,
I will go with thee
And be thy guide
In thy most need
Go by thy side
Endlessly
Gabe

A lump formed in my throat as I read the beautiful, personal inscription. Aiyana must have been his wife, and she was most obviously loved and treasured. I flicked through the next couple of pages looking for a date. It was a first edition, published in 1831. As I loosely held the book, I saw the corner of something poking out from one of the later pages. I held the book up so the pages loosened, and as I did three small, thick pieces of card fell onto the floor.

I picked each one up and turned them over, knowing I'd found something I probably shouldn't have. I was holding three photographs in my hands. The first one depicted a group of Native Americans, old and young, standing and sitting casually around a wooden cabin. I turned it over and saw the date 1910, written in faded handwriting. The quality of the image was poor, but the photograph itself was in perfect condition, being only a little creased at the edges.

As I looked into the faces of the men and women, my eyes were drawn to a tall white man and a petite dark-skinned woman standing at the back of the group on the porch of the house. The man stood behind her, both his hands resting on her narrow shoulders. The hat he wore and the shadow from the top of the house covered the upper part of his face. The woman he stood with wore a simple dress, and her straight, black hair hung neatly over her shoulders and down to her waist.

I could see she was a native woman, a very beautiful one. It reminded me of a family gathering. It was then that I noticed something so obvious, something that my subconscious must have been looking for, which up until now I wouldn't have seen. For even though his eyes were hidden, I recognised every part of the face from the nose down. It must have been Gabe's grandfather – or some other relative – they looked so alike.

I squinted to look more closely, before sliding the photograph to the back of the pile and looking at the next one. This one was of the same man, wearing the same low-tilted hat, standing in an open meadow. He wore loose, working trousers and his shirt was dense, a heavy weave.

He had a small native-looking boy on his shoulders, who was laughing and facing towards the camera. And that's when I saw it; the smile I recognised, even though the eyes were almost hidden. The resemblance was uncanny. There was no question about it; he had to be related to Gabe. When I'd found out about the French links, I'd wondered if he had actually meant French-Canadian.

I moved on to the last photograph, my heart skipping beats again. The same man was crouched down looking towards a little boy, who had what looked like two wolf pups in his arms. The boy, who looked barely two years old, was smiling at the cubs and had one of his tiny fingers placed on one of the pups' noses. The native woman was crouched between them, looking at the little boy. Everyone was smiling.

As I replaced the photos, I worried that they might have been left in a specific place and that he would notice that they'd been moved. There was nothing I could do about that. I just had to put them back in a page, all together, and put the book back where I'd found it. I was thankful that I'd paid enough attention to remember its location, helped by the small gap left in-between two books, and I slid it back in.

I had no idea how long I'd been in the house. It can't have been more than ten minutes or so, but there was one room I still wanted to see. I walked out of the library and down the hallway into the first room with the paintings and through the other door. I was relieved to find the staircase that I'd been looking for. I made my way up the winding metal steps, then into a wide hall, where three doors led off.

I opened the first door and looked into a bathroom I'd only ever seen in high-quality interior design magazines. The floor was black slate and the furnishings were all old-fashioned, the bathtub and the sink resembling those from a period house at the turn of the twentieth century. There were no trinkets or bathing products lining the slate unit under the small mirror. It seemed like a bathroom in a fancy hotel, all clean and empty and ready for use.

I shut the door behind me and opened the next one which was much further along. As soon as the door opened, I knew it was the room I was looking for.

It must have been half the length of the whole house, with two long leaded windows at the front, and the same at the back, overlooking the garden and letting a subtle amount of light in. To the left stood the largest bed I'd ever seen. It was low to the floor and, as I noisily made my way across the wooden floor, I saw that the headboard was actually a long piece of carved driftwood, stained as dark as the floors, and attached by thinner matching wood to the bed.

There was a bedside cabinet perfectly placed at each side, a thick candle in a black holder placed centrally on each one. The only other addition was a thick book lying on one of the tables. I walked over and picked it up, being more careful now to check where it was placed so I could return it to its exact position. I tried to open it but it was locked, a solid metal clasp wrapped right round it and clicked shut. 'Damn it,' I muttered.

I bent down and pulled at the drawer of the cabinet which, to my surprise, slid open easily. There were a few things placed inside, nothing obvious. I lifted out a small jewellery box, similar to the one Gabe had given me with my pendant in, and when I opened it I saw a tiny, worn thin gold band inside. Then I found another photograph. This one was more modern and when I turned it over to look, I couldn't believe what I was seeing.

It was a photo of me, taken on a hike that Luke and I had taken when we were on vacation in Montana a couple of years ago, our last holiday together. It was one of Luke's favourites and so I knew Gabe must have stolen it from the lodge.

I placed everything carefully back in the drawer and closed it, before running to the door and shutting it loudly behind me. I ran down the stairs and stood trying to get my bearings to re-trace my steps to where I'd come in. I found the main room and slipped out of the French doors, shutting them carefully behind me. I paused for a second to catch my breath, before walking speedily to my car.

The car door was in the same position I'd left it in, pushed to but not shut. I jumped in, turned the keys in the ignition and the engine roared to life. I saw my cell on the passenger seat and flicked it open. I had one new text message.

Monday August 18. 4:02 p.m. Sender: Gabe
I'm sorry I left like that. I needed to think. There are things you need to know. I will come back to your place at 5. Gabe

I looked at my watch; it was quarter-to-five. 'Shit,' I cursed, slipping the car into reverse and carefully turning on the loose gravel. He could not know I'd been here – I had to be sure not to leave any evidence. What if his neighbours told him they'd seen a strange car and described it to him? What if he knew exactly where the photos had been placed in the book and he knew someone had been inside? 'Shit, shit, shit,' I muttered, heading down the drive and onto the road.

I broke all the speed limits and got back to the lodge with five minutes to spare. I walked through the door, my breathing uneven and my heart racing. I went to the sink and leaned there, trying to compose myself and remove the guilty look from my face. I grabbed a glass of water and drank it quickly, hoping to take the edge off my dry, choking mouth.

I fussed Ember briefly to stop him from following me for a fuss so Gabe wouldn't notice from his behaviour that I'd just come back in. 'Go lie down, Ember,' I said, rushing off to the bathroom. I wet my face and quickly applied a slick of mascara, then brushed my teeth.

I'd just got back into the living room when I heard the Jeep heading up the drive. It came to a halt and I waited for him to come in, not knowing what to expect but feeling apprehensive and nervous, not to mention guilty for snooping.

I didn't hear him come in; I only heard the slight squeak of the door which announced his arrival. Then, it was totally silent. Ember jumped off the couch to greet Gabe. I closed my eyes and took a deep breath, before my first words spilled out.

'Why did you disappear like that?' I asked, my voice sounding louder than normal in the silent room.

I stood up and walked to the back of the couch, leaning back onto it for support, and looked directly at him. His eyes were pained and dark, flitting around as he thought, probably about how best to answer. I waited as patiently as I could but only stayed quiet for about ten seconds before my impatience got the better of me. 'I have photos of you watching me in Boston, long before I met you. I notice some nights you have disappeared to God-knows-where but you never tell me anything. What's going on, Gabe?'

Now it was his turn to struggle. I could see he was contemplating something, worry etched into his face, but then he looked at me and the expression I saw was unrecognisable. He took a step towards me, closing the distance. I held my nerve, thinking about Anna's concern and staying true to the confrontation that was about to start. Enough

Elizabeth Stokes

was enough, and I wanted to go no further with him until I had some answers.

I clenched my jaw constantly, rapidly. 'What the fuck's going on, Gabe?' I shouted. However bad the things were that he wanted to tell me, whatever was wrong, at least I could make my own informed decisions about our relationship if I knew the truth.

He took another slow step forward without taking his eyes off me and paused next to Ember, only ten or so feet away from me. What was coming was not good; I could see that in his face and sense it in my trembling body. For the first time ever, I suddenly felt scared of the blackness of his eyes. He sighed deeply. 'You need to see something first, to realise,' he said, numb, no tone to his deep voice.

I frowned as he slowly bent down next to Ember. He stroked his dense fur and whispered into his ear. 'I'm truly sorry, my friend.' I looked at Ember's trusting face and then back to Gabe's, confused.

Before I had time to think about anything else, everything changed. Gabe quickly wrapped his arm tightly around Ember's neck and lifted him easily off the ground, holding him firmly in his arms. Ember let out a distressed grumbling noise, trying desperately to squirm out of Gabe's arms.

'Gabe…what are you doing?' I shouted, lurching one step forward towards him. I started to tremble uncontrollably. Gabe looked directly at me and his grip tightened at my advance, his eyes jet-black and his lips parting slightly as a low grumble came from deep in his throat. 'Gabe,' I screamed, holding my position as I looked on. 'Why are you doing this? What did I do wrong?'

'I think you know what I am capable of, Meg. You know there is a lot more to me than meets the eye.' His deep voice was harsh, shouting back at me. 'One tiny little twist and I'll break his neck, I swear to God.' He reapplied his tight grip around Ember's neck and I saw nothing but anger in his face.

I stood motionless, the shock hitting me hard, and was at a complete loss as to what I should do. What could I say to diffuse the situation, to get Ember out of his grip? 'What are you gonna do now, Meg? You think you can stop me? You think you can save him?' he roared, before suddenly bellowing with laughter. Ember looked confused. Of the many faces I'd seen in Gabe, I had never seen this one. This was a man I didn't know at all. How had I not seen how evil he was? Was I so gullible, so naive and so hurt that I didn't see something like this coming?

I looked at his grinning face and back to Ember's. In that split second, I knew I would do whatever I could to save my boy. And yet, I knew it wouldn't be enough. How could I take him on and win? My anger grew as I looked into Ember's eyes again and I felt a shooting pain stabbing at me, in my neck, then my arms, then down the whole length of my body.

My head shook the most, shuddering as my temper flipped into outright fury. I looked down at my slow writhing body. I seemed to be swaying, almost dancing.

I looked back up unable to comprehend what was happening, and focused my eyes on them both. But there was something else, I was seeing through them, past them, and the colours in the room were becoming brighter, more vivid. I saw no wavering in his face and subconsciously I started gauging the distance between us and how quickly I could reach him. What would I do when I got to him? How would I free Ember? I didn't know yet; I only knew I would try.

The shaking remained steady, but I just stood there, staring, assessing. Seeing me look on silently seemed to infuriate Gabe even more and he re-adjusted Ember into one arm, taking a sideways step. 'I know,' he screamed mockingly, his voice so deep, so rough. It jolted me back to the situation. 'Let's go find Ned. Let him join our party.'

'No!' I screamed, and without hesitation I lunged towards him. I was in the air, my mouth opening, a deep growl spilling out.

Gabe tossed Ember towards the couch but I didn't see what happened to him, I was so focused on stopping this monster. I landed in front of him, almost touching his body, and crouched down, snarling. He mirrored my position, jumping gracefully back to create a small distance between us. Then I stopped and stood up, my mouth closing slowly and shock crossing my face. What on earth had just happened to me; how had I just done that?

I could not make sense of what was happening and shuddered and swayed from side to side, my body trembling in contorting spasms. Without warning, Gabe suddenly whipped past me, landing a hard blow to my left shoulder as he passed. I hardly saw him move and felt the blow before my eyes caught his movement. I was thinking too much and Gabe was already one step ahead of me, making the first strike to knock me off balance.

I stood for a second and looked down at my bleeding shoulder. It was the weirdest thing. I knew I was me; I knew where I was and what was happening, but there was a surreal edge to everything, as if I were outside my body, watching it all unfold from above.

As soon as the bleeding started, I watched in amazement as it came to a halt, as if my skin were sucking all the blood back into the wound, leaving behind only the smallest amount of dried matter in the long, deep gouge. It wasn't possible. I turned around to face him and I felt like a complete stranger. The juddering in my body had stopped, and the colours all around me were vibrant and crystal clear. I gasped and as I did felt two tiny pricks on the inside of my bottom lip.

Again, without warning, Gabe launched himself into the air and over my head, landing behind me on the kitchen counter in a low crouch. I whipped my head around, following his every move with no motion blur, and crouched on the floor in front of him. In that precise second, I saw something change in his eyes, sorrow and regret briefly filling them, but just as soon as I saw it they changed back to black.

I saw the next move coming and as he pushed hard from the counter, I summoned all my energy, shut my eyes, and forced my strength out with my arms. I didn't feel myself touch him, no cold, hard skin, and no pain in my hands as they made contact with him, but I must have struck him a full-on defensive blow as, when I looked, he was skidding past me on the floor. It all happened so fast. The sound of cracking bones was real enough, though. I'd injured him.

I flung my body over his, pinning him to the floor. The deepest growl came from my mouth, and my eyes caught a quick flash of movement from the stairway. Ember sat at a safe distance, watching our fight, but without fear this time, as if he somehow knew I was capable of at least matching Gabe's strength. It was my second mistake, but also my last. As my concentration broke, I saw the flash of Gabe's hand and felt the instant crack on my face.

It knocked me off balance to the side, but I spun round fast and regained my position over him, throwing my hand to his neck and holding it in an iron grip. He, for some reason, remained still, as if accepting my assault. I felt my face contort but had no idea what I looked like. My mouth opened like I was gasping. I threw all my strength into what I had left.

I forced his chin up and his head sideways and, without pausing, I pushed my mouth to his neck, growling deeply, and sunk my teeth into him. With my teeth in place, I paused.

Then it hit me. The complete and utter realisation passed through every part of me. He had never intended to hurt me, and I'd always known as much. With the strength he had, he could've easily stopped me, probably even killed me in a second if he'd wanted. I slowly moved my face back from his neck, my mouth closing. I looked down at him as he lay still, waiting for some kind of response. But guilt and sadness covered the whole of his face. I knew right then why he was not fighting back – this is what he'd been trying to show me.

'What's happened to me?' I whispered, pitifully, tears welling in my eyes. I slid back onto his legs and my body weakened and slumped.

Gabe gently lifted me and it was as if I had no bones holding me together. He scooped me up as he stood and pulled me into him. 'I'm so, so sorry,' he said, pulling my head towards his face, pressing his lips to my forehead and holding them there. 'I had to make you see. Ember was the only way,' he said softly, pulling away from me a little. 'I knew it was the only way to make you understand.'

I looked up to his face and knew I was about to hear all the answers I'd long been waiting for.

'What am I?'

Chapter 15

Gabe walked over and placed me carefully on the couch. 'What I am about to show you, what is now part of you also, please don't be afraid of it,' he said, leaning to kiss my forehead before he knelt in front of me.

'I would never hurt you or Ember. But I knew using Ember would force your temper and allow the dormant changes to begin. I love you so much – I have for a long time. What I've done to you, though, I shouldn't have allowed myself to do. I did it to save your life. For my own selfish reasons, I could not let you die. I need you to see me, see who I am, and what you, in some small way – although I don't know how much yet – have become.'

I stared into his face. 'Don't be afraid,' he repeated, his voice soft. I looked into his eyes as they changed from dark brown to black in front of me. I couldn't believe it was possible for them to become any darker. I held my gasp in, but my mouth opened in surprise. He then opened his mouth slightly and my tear-filled eyes drifted down to his parted lips. His face remained gentle as his canine teeth descended, growing in front of me into sharp points. I couldn't hold the gasp in this time but it was not because I feared him.

He looked at my face, concerned, his teeth shrinking back to normal. He stood slowly, I imagined so he wouldn't scare me, and walked backwards into the kitchen, his eyes on me all the time. He took something from the cupboard and paused where he stood. Then, he cautiously walked back to where I sat and bent before me. I gulped loudly.

He lifted his hand to my eye level and opened it, showing me the porcelain egg cup balanced on his hand. I looked down at it, then to his eyes, waiting. My face gave him nothing; it had nothing left to give. He started to squeeze his hand, softly and without effort as it closed around the solid piece. The cracking and grating sound lasted only a second before I saw a small amount of dust falling through his fingers.

He slowly opened his hand, forcing the remains to spill out through the gaps in his fingers and onto the floor. Under the dust and the shards of porcelain lay several deep cuts to his hand and his fingers. 'No blood,' I said, cocking my head to one side as I looked at his injuries. Only dark purple marks remained where bloody wounds should have been. I stared in disbelief as the deep gouges closed in an instant, and the purple wounds in his skin returned to alabaster-white in front of my eyes, with only the faintest, almost invisible, white scar remaining. I frowned as I searched his hand for the marks.

Gabe traced his finger across my forehead, holding it there, closing his eyes. 'So, am I the same as you now?' I asked, my voice subdued. I stared into his face, waiting for his eyes to open, for him to acknowledge what I already knew was true.

He opened his eyes and I could tell then that every word he would utter from that moment on would be the truth. 'I had to find you,' he said, lowering his eyes from mine. I couldn't quite comprehend why my feelings for him were not changing, why I wasn't mortified by what I was slowly beginning to understand.

I slid my hand under his chin, lifting his face until his eyes met mine again. 'I don't care what you are, don't you see?' I said, pressing my lips to his. I moved away, looking at him. 'I love you whatever you are. But I am a little scared of what I've become,' I said.

He stared into my face before he lifted his hands and wiped a rebel tear from under my eye. 'You are not exactly like me, no,' he said, his voice solemn, carefully preparing his words. 'You are what is known as a night timer. You are part human, part immortal, although I don't know yet how much of each species you possess.'

I sat dumbstruck as I waited for him to tell me more. 'When I found you in the forest, being attacked and literally grasping onto life by your fingernails, I had to make a decision. Did I leave fate to decide, or did I intervene against the rules and save you? I decided easily on the latter – as selfish as that may have been on my part – but I couldn't lose you. I made the decision not from the heart I no longer have but from the soul that will always remain within me. I couldn't bear to let you leave me.'

I just stared at him. It was all too much to take in, to believe, yet my own eyes had seen the truth. 'I don't think I understand,' I muttered. 'I'm tired. I need to sleep.' And I did. I needed to rest my brain, my failing mind, in the hope that when I awoke I would understand more.

Gabe scooped me into his arms and I noticed that his smell was much stronger than before – the sweetest scent in the world – a heady mixture of everything in life I adored. 'Don't leave me, though,' I whispered, my voice barely audible.

'You silly, beloved girl, I will never leave your side again. I have no reason to now,' he said, leaning in to kiss me deeply, as if through his lips alone, I would believe his every word – and I did. His kiss lingered and, suddenly, every inch of my body started to react to his touch. I pulled away quickly.

'But, I need to know more,' I said, finding the last ounce of breath and energy I had left.

'I will tell you everything, but not now. Wait until tomorrow, when your body and mind are able to take it.' As soon as the last word left his mouth, he carried me towards the stairs, nestling me deep into his chest, with Ember following loyally behind.

As Gabe reached the bed, he laid me down gently underneath the already-turned quilt and covered me over. He sat alongside me and Ember approached, to my relief, without showing any concern towards Gabe, his eyes only on me. It was as if he seemed to understand he had a part to play in the whole 'finding out' thing. He placed his front paws on the bed and inched towards me, licking my face. I ran my hands through his neck, deep into the fur, and used all my strength to lean forward and kiss him.

As soon as I had, he turned and walked to the foot of the couch where Ned was lying, his eyes wide and watchful.

I looked back up towards Gabe, who never took his eyes off me. As my blinking slowed with the weariness setting in, he went around to the other side of the bed and quietly lay down beside me. He reached across and pulled me around and into his chest, cradling me. I lay with my face semi-buried, as he reached out and wiped away the tears from my jaw with his thumb. With the final comforter in place, I started to doze as his protective hand brushed tenderly through my hair. It was the most soothing feeling in the world.

I remembered nothing else. I woke up, dazed and confused, the reality laying in wait for the first few seconds of oblivion to pass. When it did, I looked towards the vacant space next to me.

I squinted towards the stairs and then, miraculously, it was like having someone switch my vision on again. The illuminated numbers on the clock told me I had slept for over five hours, and it was pitch black outside.

I slid out from under the covers and walked to the top of the railing overlooking the living room. Gabe sat in the dull amber reflection of the burning fire, his hands still and his head resting on the back of the couch, Ember at his side.

I didn't think he'd heard me, but the second I took a step towards the stairs he looked up and smiled.

'What are you doing up?' he asked, his voice low and subdued.

I made my way down the stairs towards him. 'I've had the sleep I need. Is what I am the reason I sleep less?' I asked, starting the onslaught of questions straight away.

As I reached the bottom of the stairs, he looked back down into his lap, and answered me quietly. 'Yes. I have noticed your sleep patterns changing gradually. Sometimes you sleep a few hours, tonight you slept for over five.'

'Why is that? Should I sleep a lot, or not at all? How much does someone…something like me need?' I asked, sitting down next to him and tucking my knees up under my arms as I turned sideways to face him.

He looked across at me and smiled, his eyes deep brown, the lines under them looking heavier than usual. 'Firstly, you are someone, *not* something. And secondly, I don't know the answer to that. I have only met one other night timer throughout my existence, many years ago, and never found out anything much about him because I had no need to.'

I rested my head onto his shoulder, knowing he would answer anything I asked now. 'Do you only sleep for a short time?'

'No, I don't sleep at all. The existence of a vampire is not something that can change or vary; there are certain elements of our make-up that are necessary, fact, and they are the same for all my kind. For example, we do not need to sleep, as such, we just rest. I can stay motionless for hours on end, having no need to blink or breathe, my thoughts sending me into a, well, I suppose a trance, which in essence feels like what sleep would to you. We are built to remain strong, prepared, and alert.

'I don't need food in the sense you do; I only need blood to survive and stay strong. And unlike the myths surrounding my kind, I can eat. I could eat ten meals a day easily and it would cause me no problems, only food is of no use to me, my body doesn't need the nutrition that you get from it. I get all that from drinking.' He gently stroked the back of his hand down my cheek, looking into my bewildered yet fascinated eyes. I was mesmerised, desperate to know much more, anything he could tell me, both about himself and his kind and also about what was now my kind – a night timer. He continued. 'I can run forever. I have no need for a strong heart – I haven't had one for many years. And the lungs inside my body need no oxygen, so I will never tire.'

'What...who do you, erm, you know, drink from?' I fumbled, getting all tongue-tied.

'Ah, the scary bit,' he said, grinning impishly before his smile faded. 'Sadly, that is one of the facts I have to live with, something all vampires must do. I have a unique way of dealing with this part, several methods, really.'

'Several methods?' I asked, feeling my face involuntarily grimacing.

'Okay, are you sure you want to hear this?' he asked.

'I'm sure,' I said, as if I were a child now, listening intently to the scary story about to unfold, my eyes wide.

'I do drink human blood. But I have ways of, how can I put it, selecting who I choose. I only take those who do not deserve to live, who have done cruel or evil things or who are about to do those things. I also use animals to satisfy my thirst, the ones which live in high populations that natural predators, such as wolves, would take out if they walked the earth in larger numbers. I also have my own improvised version of getting what I need, to acquire what is necessary, and I use this as often as I can. I use blood donors from the practice, buy it in, store it for when the need arises, like when I'm in a position where I'm unable to hunt and feel the desperate need to drink.'

My face must have been a picture. I had no idea what it showed, but Gabe looked down at me, worry showing in his face. 'Are you okay?' he asked, turning sideways to look at me properly. I thought I'd been taking it in quite well. Obviously not. I nodded my head quickly a few times, probably a bit too fast, fooling no one. 'I'm fine, honestly,' I said, a little too high-pitched. Gabe looked at me for a few seconds.

'So, do I need to drink it?' I asked, not wanting to think of me and drinking blood in the same sentence.

'You will but, again, I don't know to what degree you'll need it. From the research I've done on your behalf recently, I expect you will manage quite well with easier methods. Kidney and liver along with any slightly cooked meat should be ideal, and possibly donor blood. Again, I'm not sure what your body will need yet. You may just go through phases of needing blood.'

I thought back to any changes in my diet, to the food I'd bought, and remembered eating rare steaks on recent occasions. I'd always balked at the idea of meat showing any sign of blood, the thought of it turned my stomach. I swallowed back the bile as my brain pictured my future diet. 'Maybe we should have left diet alone for awhile,' he said.

'I'm fine now. It's just a bit of a shock is all,' I said, trying to smile convincingly.

We both sat quietly for a few minutes. 'For what I have done to you…I'm truly sorry,' he said solemnly, his voice almost breaking at the end. 'I came back, unable to stay away from you any longer, to fight for your heart. But I ended up fighting against a much stronger opponent. When you weren't at home, I guessed where you'd be. I heard the bear and Ember's protective barks. I raced to find you and when I saw the bear attacking you, I didn't hesitate. I knew what I had to do – the only thing that would save you.

'I took her head on, finishing her quickly. But you were fading fast. There was no time so I made the only decision I could. I injected enough venom into your veins to keep you alive, to keep the blood inside you pumping through your body. But your wounds were so bad, I knew I needed to get you to the hospital. When I got you to the parking lot, a couple came to offer help. They phoned ahead to the hospital for me and I raced there with you.'

'Didn't the doctors detect the venom in my blood?' I asked.

'They would only notice your bloods were not quite right when you were first admitted, this would be expected after such an attack when the victim is shocked and has blood loss. After the venom had spread more, I easily managed to switch some blood results and so yours appeared normal. After that, no one knew anything. I am so sorry, Meg.'

I tried to find the words, words to soothe his pain, to make things easier for him. 'Gabe, what you did…I understand you did it to save my life and, for that, I am eternally grateful. How can I not be? I am here with you, and Ember and Ned, and I'm happy.' I sat staring at him and leaned my head sideways against the back of the couch.

'And when I say eternally grateful, just so I know, how long is eternally for me. Does what I am lengthen my lifespan or will it have no effect on it?'

'I don't know, exactly. From my research and what I knew of the other night timer, you'll probably live for two to three hundred years.'

'And you will live forever?' I asked, knowing his response.

'Yes.'

I sensed my loss right there. I would only have him for as long as I existed; he would out-live, or should I say, out-exist me. And then he would find another and I would be only a distant memory for him. Whatever Gabe sensed, he knew I was upset by this and leaned over to scoop me up onto his knee. I should have been ecstatic at my extended life span, but I wasn't.

I nestled my head into his chest, hiding my face. He forced my chin up and I tried to avoid his eyes as mine welled at the thought that he would, some day, go on without me.

I was expecting him to hug me tight, to talk me out of the worry I felt, but he didn't. He placed his whole hand along my jaw and held my face close to his. 'What upsets you the most right now?' he asked.

'That one day I'll die and you won't. You'll carry on,' I answered honestly.

'Whatever happens, we'll always be together. You must trust me on that,' he said, but it made no sense unless he planned, one day, to make me exactly like him. I could always hope. Then, he pushed his lips on mine. I couldn't get enough air through my nose – the intensity of his closeness was overwhelming. I opened my mouth a little to catch the air I needed. Gabe cocked his head slightly, keeping his eyes firmly locked on mine, before he lowered his mouth to mine again.

I felt the deep quiver in my stomach that lay dormant until he was this close to me. My heart fluttered as though a butterfly was trapped in my chest. He moved me around until I was sitting with my legs bent over his, facing him. He traced my bottom lip with his.

My ragged breath came out audibly and he grinned under the kiss, placing his hands under my vest onto my bare back and pulling me impossibly tight into him. I slid my thighs tightly around him, gripping him there with my new strength, while I put my hands on each side of his face and kissed his lips, his chin, making my way slowly along his jaw and up to his ear, where I whispered, 'I know I still have a heart, and it's all yours.'

I had no more questions to ask that night – they could wait. I felt normal again, practically human. I lay facing him in bed, looking over the perfect pale body beside me as he leaned upon the pillow, his hand gently stroking my shoulder. The quilt covered him just below his waist, drawing my eyes to his defined abdomen. I managed to push my unwholesome thoughts aside, and fell asleep.

I woke up naturally. It was still dark outside. I turned over to check Gabe was still there, that I was not dreaming, and smiled as I saw him in exactly the same position, staring back at me, the moonlight shadowing his face, glistening in his eyes.

'So still,' I said. 'Have I caught you snoozing?'

'No,' he said, grinning back. 'No snoozing tonight for me.' His eyes had the 'look' in them that I now recognised. I liked this look, a *lot*. The butterflies started another fluttering session and I turned over to him, roughly pulling him down the pillow so he lay flat, and then I practiced at being 'human' with him again.

'What time is it?' Gabe asked, as we lay entwined together after-wards.

I leaned away from him and looked over at the bedside cabinet for the clock. It wasn't there. 'Oh,' I said, puzzled, stretching further over and looking on the floor amongst the scattered pillows and trailing sheet for my clock. The second of our 'sessions' had got a little, shall we say, heated, and with two extra-human strengths involved, things had gone flying around the room. I grinned to myself and retrieved the clock from the floor.

'Just after three-thirty,' I replied, twisting my head back and getting comfortable on his chest again.

'Good, I think it's time. Get dressed,' he said, twisting quickly from underneath me and onto the side of the bed, reaching for his jeans.

'Erm, why are we getting up in the middle of the night?' I asked, frowning and still admiring his naked back.

He turned back to me, leaning over onto the bed, and grabbed the back of my head so he could kiss me in a way that really should be illegal. He stopped abruptly. 'Get up and into your running gear,' he said, grinning. He walked towards the top of the stairs, putting on his shirt but leaving it unbuttoned. Ember, as he always seemed to be now, was by his side as they headed down.

I lay for a minute, wondering. What kind of freak was I? I mean, I loved a vampire for God's sake. And I was, to whatever degree, a mutant vampire myself. My whole life was completely changed from this day on, and what was I doing? Grinning my face off. I was grinning because, first of all, I loved this particular vampire *very* much. And, secondly, I was a new person. I was fast and strong, and I had a kick-ass body to boot. Apart from my complete love for Gabe, the next best thing was the fact that I would possibly live for up to three hundred years.

Ever since I was a young child, the thought of death had petrified me and had thrown me into horrible screaming nightmares. Yet here I was, smiling like a complete maniac. I couldn't think of one bad thing about it. And that had to make me abnormal, didn't it?

I jumped out of bed and wrapped my robe around me before I danced downstairs and got into my running gear. I had no idea what was going on, but I felt invigorated and excited.

We left the lodge and I was surprised at how warm the night was. As we stepped off the porch deck, my eyes felt perfect: no stinging, no squinting, no burning. They enjoyed the darkness and everything seemed much easier to see. But I hadn't really noticed this change in my vision before; it was as if by knowing all the facts now, the whole truth, that all my senses were suddenly tuned in.

'Gabe, what are we doing out here?' I asked, keeping my voice to a whisper in case the neighbours heard us.

'We're…testing you,' he said, grabbing my hand and pulling me towards the trees.

'Testing what part of me, exactly?'

'You'll see,' he said, before he let go of my hand and disappeared silently into the dark.

'Gabe?' I stood where he left me and waited for a response. 'Gabe. Where are you?'

'Here,' came the whisper. 'Run to my voice, as fast as you can.'

'Okay. Erm, why?' I asked, worried about doing such a, well, stupid thing.

'I want to test your speed, your reactions. Just run to my voice, as fast as you dare, and try to avoid hitting anything.'

'Right,' I muttered to myself. 'I'm not sure that's a good idea,' I whispered back.

'Ah, come on, chicken. Just do it already,' he whispered back, his voice coming from a slightly different direction.

'Okay,' I said, shaking my head in disbelief. I took a deep breath and tried to focus on the first few trees, looking for the gaps. I ran forward and gave the first tree a glancing blow, which set me off stride into a wobble and over onto my side.

'Ouch!' I squeaked, feeling the numb blow to my butt and the scrape along my arm. My reaction was instinctively human, not because it actually hurt at all.

I heard a muffled chuckle in the distance and it pissed me off. 'Oh, you shut it Gabe. This is stupid,' I whispered louder through my teeth as I stood up and brushed myself off. I took a few breaths and let my eyes focus on the darkness, on shadows more than the trees. 'Right,' I said to myself, leaning forward and ready to set off again.

I shot forward and focused only on the shadows this time. I danced a little clumsily but far more accurately through the first few trees, listening as he called my voice.

'Here, Meg. I'm over here.' His voice sounded like a rasping whisper, and my body started to sway more than jolt around the obstacles. I concentrated hard and went from a jog into a faster run.

'Ouch, shit, oh!' I blurted out, a little too loudly as I hit something solid. But it was not a tree this time. I was sitting on my ass again, this time at Gabe's feet.

'Shush,' he muttered, chuckling. 'I said run to me, not into me. Are you alright?' he asked, pulling me up to my feet.

'Oh, I'm fine,' I shot back sharply, brushing myself down again. 'Not sure how much vampire is in me, Gabe, but I don't think it's a lot.'

'Ah, come on. It's your first time. You just have to practice, see how many of our instincts you have in there.' He chuckled again and it infuriated me. It was obviously highly entertaining for him, watching me hit trees and solid vampires.

'Okay, I'm sorry I laughed. Look, I'll run ahead of you this time and you follow behind. Follow my sounds, my scent, if you can, see how you go,' he said, taking off without waiting for my decision.

I tilted my head up to the sky and took a deep breath. 'What the hell,' I muttered, looking back into the direction he'd disappeared in. I stood up, took a few more breaths, and let my eyes focus on the shadows again.

I bent down, ready to go, then lurched forward and ran at full speed, heading between the trees. I couldn't hear Gabe at first but he must have been waiting for me further ahead.

Suddenly, I heard a faint crunching up ahead and I tried to focus my eyes in the direction of the sound that was slightly to my left. I changed course quickly and kept up the pace, following the noise but seeing nothing. As the sound got closer, I could smell him, that earthy, sweet scent. Now I had two things to track.

I ran faster, focusing only on the sounds and his smell, and then the realisation hit me. I wasn't even thinking about the trees I was dodging or the raised roots I was jumping over. I was completely focused on only sounds and smells.

On a couple of occasions, I miscalculated the trees, and branches struck my face both times. I felt a brief trickle of blood, but as soon as I noticed the heat and the tickling sensation, it stopped.

I pressed on and felt that my body was not just leaning to pass the obstacles, it was now twisting sideways, passing through narrow gaps, my instincts telling me to duck the split second I reached a low tree allowing me to clear it.

I was suddenly aware that the noises were coming from further away, his smell fading. I slowed down, trying to pick up the sounds better, and just as I did my head snapped across and I turned sharply to the right.

I halted instantly, flinging my palms out in a blocking manoeuvre. A black shape hit my hands, jolting me hard backwards, before it veered around me and grabbed me from behind to break my fall.

'Told you that you could do it,' the voice said in the dark, and I could hear the approval running through his deep voice. His lips were suddenly running along the side of my neck. I breathed easily, my heart rate even. I hadn't even broken into a sweat.

'Now,' he said, 'I want you to try something else. I want you to run towards me, and when you sense where I am, I want you to grab me.'

'Do I have to do another test?' I asked. My mind was consumed by the lips brushing my neck, and I was not remotely interested in his so-called 'training'. But, in spite of my reluctance, he let go of his grip and silently vanished, only his dark shadow barely visible as he disappeared into the blackness in front of me.

I sighed in defeat and stood, trying to focus again on the sounds, inhaling deeply in an attempt to catch his scent. I saw a gap in the trees and heard some faint sounds becoming louder. I could tell he was closing in on me, and I threw myself forward to the noise and leapt into the air, almost floating a few feet above the ground. Before I knew it I'd landed, and the noise had rushed past me.

I turned and re-gauged his position. I ran forward, sensing a slight difference in his movement, which was now away to the right. I leapt again and threw myself slightly higher, skimming underneath his super-fast shadow. This time, he had moved above me by a good two feet, thwacking my head as he passed, and had landed much further away in the trees.

'Oh, come on,' I heard him bellow, laughing again, the restricted hush in his voice becoming louder. 'Try harder.'

'I'll give you come on,' I said, infuriated by his mocking tone. But, like before, it worked. The key to my newfound ability seemed to be me losing my temper. In the lodge, when he'd first shown me what I was, he used Ember as bait. Now, he had me running through the trees and leaping into the air to tackle him. As my temper flared, so my ability improved.

I took some deep breaths, lowered my head and lifted my eyes like an animal to assess the shadows, the obstacles. I ran faster than ever, towards the crackling sounds in the earth, and as I let my ears and eyes do the work, I launched into the air, pushing my left foot harder to change direction, and headed into the path of Gabe.

Instinctively, I reached my hands out, locking them from the elbows. I had to reach up a bit higher to grab hold of his upper arms, but I did it. I got him. I was just about to whoop it up, thrilled I'd been able to do it, when he pushed me down to the ground, landing on me and pinning me in the dirt.

I struggled to get out of his grip, my temper close to boiling point, but I couldn't budge him – not more than an inch, anyway. He was just too strong for me. My human weakness showed easily against his full immortal strength and I gave up the fight.

He loosened his grip on me and rolled over onto his side. 'That was pretty good,' he said, brushing my flailing hair away from my face.

'I couldn't fight you off, though,' I said, annoyed by not being able to win. With my competitive nature, winning was the ultimate goal in everything I did, and now even more so.

'Oh Meg. Did you really think you could?' he asked, leaning in to gently kiss my cheek. 'It's not possible, even if you were ninety percent vampire, it still wouldn't be enough against my strength.'

I felt inferior, a little useless as the truth sank in: I could never be stronger than him. But, I would be stronger than pretty much any other human. That thought helped the disappointment subside. 'Come on,' he said, pulling me to my feet.

'Aw Gabe. I don't want to do any more tonight,' I said, dragging my heels.

'Don't worry. We're done for tonight,' he said, towing me along behind him. 'Let's go home.' We turned around and set off at a fast run.

I kept pace with him easily, although I was pretty sure he was running slowly to accommodate me. We ran side by side, all the way through the dark trees on the winding route home.

Chapter 16

I woke easily, naturally, stretching out as the bright morning sun shone through the tall window. I looked towards where Gabe should be and opened my eyes gingerly, squinting to keep the light out. I heard the clatter of plates downstairs and smiled, knowing he was close by. I lay for a few minutes thinking over the events of the past day and night.

With only a sheet wrapped around my body, I caught sight of dried blood on my arms, along with a few new bruises on my thigh. But nothing hurt at all.

When I got downstairs, Gabe was busy in the kitchen and Ember was on the couch. I looked for the missing link, Ned, and saw him sitting by the back door, watching Gabe moving around.

'What you up to?' I asked, walking up behind him as he busied himself. There were bags all over the counter.

'Making you breakfast,' he said, walking up to me with a large carving knife in his hand. He manoeuvred me forcefully back against the kitchen wall, stepping wide so he didn't stand on the trailing sheet, or my feet, and pressed his body against mine, lowering his head to kiss me. My eyes glanced at the knife in his hand, as he pinned it and me up against the wall.

When he finally released me from his intense body lock, he headed back to the counter. 'I'm preparing a little food that'll build your strength.'

'Oh, you're not going to make me eat raw, dead things are you?' I asked, feeling my guts churn a little at the thought.

'No, I'm making you a selection of chopped cooked meats and some eggs, so don't worry,' he said, turning to dice some meat.

'Cooked meats?' I asked apprehensively, walking towards him at the worktop and peering round his arm.

'Well, *slightly* cooked diced beef and kidney with scrambled eggs and potatoes,' he said, chopping away at the meat.

'Eeew,' I said, pulling the worst face. 'I can't eat that, I'll throw up.'

'You'll see,' he said, grinning at my reaction and taking the bloody concoction to the frying pan.

Within a few minutes, he was serving it onto two plates. A huge pile of diced red stuff, eggs and potatoes. 'You having some?' I asked, surprised that he was eating with me.

'I can eat Meg, remember?'

We sat at the table together and, to my surprise, the food smelled really good. I picked up one small cube on the edge of my fork and put it into the front of my mouth, nibbling on it carefully. But, as I tentatively chewed, I was surprised to find that it tasted really good. The taste was almost sweet, the texture noticeably tender. I hardly touched the eggs until I'd cleared all the meat and potato.

I cast a glance over to Gabe's face, to see him grinning while eating his food. 'Don't you go laughing at me,' I said, whipping my hand at him and punching him hard on his arm. I looked towards my hand, still amazed by the natural speed and quick reaction I now had.

I took a long swig of the fresh juice next to my plate and looked towards Gabe's glass. Both juices were the same colour, and in the second I swallowed the first mouthful, I realised I was not only eating the almost raw meat he'd cooked but was drinking an unknown substance – the very same one he had drank regularly when he was here.

I choked up, coughing loudly as I tried to stop swallowing, but the fluid was already down my throat. My eyes started watering as I coughed, covering my mouth as the excess fluid spilled into my hand. 'Oh no. Oh my God. What's in this?' I spat out.

'Nutrients, Meg,' he said, watching from his chair in shock at my ridiculous reaction.

'What nutrients, Gabe?' I threw out more audibly.

'Just drink it,' he said, shaking his head.

'No, I won't. Not until you tell me what's in it.'

'Okay. First, you'll feel much, much better once you've drunk it. Second, you'll be a lot stronger with it inside you and, third, it is from an unknown donor so all I know is it's blood,' he said, in a matter-of-fact way. 'It's mixed with some juice, though,' he added, as if that made it a whole lot better.

I balked again, a thick lump in my throat.

'I'm sorry I find it so amusing. It's just, you grimace so much,' he said.

'Okay, I'll try. But maybe from now on we should call it, say, cherry juice. Would that be okay?' I asked, nodding to myself at this hopefully effective new way of getting myself to drink the vile fluid.

Gabe hid his face slightly to stifle his laughter. I whacked him again, but it only served to make him laugh out loud. 'I'm sorry,' he whispered, in hysterics. This was all at my expense, but I saw then something I hadn't seen before: Gabe laughing like a real human being, enjoying the things – eating, drinking – that people enjoyed every day. The laughter echoing in the room was magical, perfect, and I started to laugh with him.

'Anyway,' he said, 'on a different subject, don't forget you're meeting Liv for lunch and shopping today.'

'Oh, crap,' I muttered. 'Shit. I should cancel.' I'd completely forgotten we'd arranged the get-together weeks ago.

'No you don't. You've had this arranged for a long time and I think it will do you good to get out and about with a friend, a normal, human one, anyway,' he said, finishing his drink. 'Besides, I think it will be better for us if you continue doing normal things.'

I sighed deeply and stood up from the table, taking the plates with me to the sink. 'Okay, I'll go. What are you going to do?' I asked.

'I'm going to go see William today, to sort out working hours,' he said.

Gabe had taken time off as annual vacation to be with me since I came home from the hospital and this would be coming to an end after this week. I wasn't looking forward to it. I would miss not having him around all the time, miss our new adventures of discovery, and miss our new favourite pastime.

I text Liv to check that we were still on and, with her confirmation, readied myself for a girly day out.

Gabe offered to walk Ember for me before he went into the practice, so all that was left was for me to do was change, grab my purse and head out the door.

He dropped me off at Liv's, who wasn't yet aware of just how far our relationship had developed. We pulled up outside her drive and I shuffled around, checking I had everything in my purse. 'I'll see you when I get back,' I said, looking towards Gabe, whose hands leaned casually over the steering wheel.

'No problem,' he said, smiling a little too nicely at me.

'Don't you go looking at me like that right now,' I said, calming my double heartbeats and scowling playfully at him. 'You need anything?' I asked, shaking my head at his teasing.

'Well, I could do with some skimpy underwear and maybe a crash helmet and some shin pads. Oh, I forgot, that's *your* shopping list,' he grinned impishly. 'Nothing for me, then, thanks.'

I took a deep breath, stifling my wide grin. 'Okay, then,' I said, leaning towards him. He met me halfway, grabbing my head and planting a huge kiss on my lips.

I came up for air a few seconds later, gasping and a little flushed in the face. This vampire just got better and better at the whole intimacy thing. I looked into his eyes for a few seconds, taking in how deep and sparkling they were.

'I'm definitely going now,' I said, twisting and opening the door, and hopping lightly out of the car. As I turned towards Liv's house, I saw the curtain twitch back into place. This was going to take some explaining.

As I was just about to rap on the door, I heard Gabe's Jeep roar off. Before I had chance to knock, the door swung open and Liv's beaming face met mine. She had her purse and keys in her hand and she darted to her car, smiling.

As we both climbed into her little Mini, she looked at me. 'Okay, so you gotta tell me *everything*,' she said, completely hyper.

We headed off towards San Diego and I had little chance to ask any questions of my own since I spent almost the whole hour answering hers. I gave information I felt happy about but naturally, omitted quite a lot. A little too much of *that* information would have sent us and her little Mini flying off the road.

We parked in downtown San Diego and Liv wanted to head straight for lunch. Lunch, oh crap. I could just imagine the waitress's face when I ordered. '*Oh, hello. May I please order half a live coyote and a pint of human blood?* Maybe not. No, I would keep it light; a salad would work.

As I ate a steak salad, washed down with Coke, the conversation had thankfully taken a different turn, and Gabe was now no longer the main subject of the day.

'So, come on,' I said, teasing her, 'Who's the latest man victim?'

'Okay, he's called Josh and he's, like, six years younger than me. He works in Hollister and, I swear, he has got to be on their next ad campaign,' she said, completely excited. 'He is soooooo gorgeous!'

We chatted more about both of our new men, keeping it simple, before we paid the bill and headed out to shop.

Our trip was quite a success and I really enjoyed her company. I'd missed her recently. She didn't mention the accident much, which was something I was grateful for. I bought a few things: clothes, a new perfume I'd tested, and some expensive underwear.

All the way back to Manzano, we laughed and giggled like school girls. But, as much as I enjoyed the day, I couldn't wait to get back to Gabe now, and so I was secretly urging the journey to pass quickly.

As we headed up the drive, I saw the familiar flicker of moving blinds as Ember peered out at us. Gabe's car was gone, so he must still have been at the practice.

'Okay, so call me and we'll arrange a night out,' she said, hugging me tightly.

'I will. Looking forward to it already!' I said, hugging her back.

I headed into the lodge, threw my keys and purse on the counter, and dropped my shopping bags on the couch. I fussed the kids and went to put the teakettle on. As I grabbed some milk from the fridge, I saw the 'cherry juice' on the shelf. As much as I wouldn't admit it in front of Gabe, I really wanted a glass. He'd been right: since breakfast, I really had felt better, stronger.

I put the milk back and took a tall glass from the cupboard instead, filling it with 'cherry juice'. As I sat on the couch, with Ember squished in-between me and the shopping bags, I had a naughty idea. I removed the skimpiest set of underwear from one of the bags and walked into the kitchen, grabbing some scissors from the drawer and cutting the tags off. I grinned as I made my way out to the bunkhouse, the place where I plotted to get my way later.

I walked in and straight towards the bed, looking over some of Gabe's things lying around the room. I searched for a good hiding place, where he could find them later. I threw back the sheet and grinned as I placed the bra underneath, the black strap poking out suggestively. I went to lift the pillow, to place the panties so they would be poking out. But, as I lifted it, I saw the edge of something dark sticking out from underneath.

I lifted the pillow a bit higher and saw a heavily packed envelope lying in-between the two pillows. I paused while looking at it, as déjà vu kicked in from my previous snooping attempts. Only, this time, I hadn't been snooping...although I was about to.

I picked up the envelope; it looked expensive and old. I turned it over to the flap side and pulled out a small handful of photographs, some of them so thick and tattered that I could instantly tell they were old. There was also a letter inside but this looked much more modern and recent, and it was in almost perfect condition. I opened the thick folded sheet and saw written in beautiful black script a half-page letter with a signature at the bottom. But I couldn't read or understand it, since it was written in French. I could pick out a few words, enough to identify the language, but I couldn't understand any of the big words that might have given me a clue to what the letter was about.

I put the letter down and turned the photographs over, looking straight into the face of a well-dressed tall man, his trousers and long coat fitting closely and very obviously well tailored. The black top hat he wore sat regally on his head and his whole body held a military pose. He stood behind an ageing woman, who was also very well dressed. She wore a dark, tight-fitting, full-length dress, the buttons fastened all the way high up on her slim neck. Her hair was pulled back into a taut braid. The man's arm was placed caringly on her shoulder.

As I looked over the photo, fascinated by it, I was drawn to a shining object which hung around her neck. I looked more closely, my new eyes picking up far more details than my old ones, and gasped when I saw what sat there: she was wearing my pendant. My *exact* pendant. I turned the photo over to see the date, 1850.

Maybe my pendant was more special than I'd ever realised, a family heirloom. The man in the photo looked surprisingly like Gabe, the genes in his family obviously strong. The only real difference between the two faces was that the man in the picture looked younger, not so weathered, and had more colour, particularly in the cheeks.

I flicked to the next photo. It was another one like the Native American ones I'd seen at his house. It was a close-up and this time the native woman looked relaxed, her beautiful white smile reaching all the way to her big, brown eyes, her black straight hair framing her dark skin. The same man stood beside her, without a hat this time, his huge arm hanging loosely over her petite shoulder, as she hung onto his hand with hers.

The man looked older than in the previous pictures and the sepia colours of the photo emphasised the weathered lines in his face. No shadows or lighting masked the pale face looking back at me now. They both smiled towards the camera. It was so natural, so easy to look at them – they were both so beautiful, so perfect. I turned the photograph over and saw a similar date to the other photos I'd seen at his house, 1909.

I tried to understand why he would bring these photos here and hide them. As I stared at the last one, thinking, I saw something shining that made me move closer to look. In the depths of her loosely buttoned shirt hung the same pendant as in the previous photo, the one which now hung around my neck.

I kept getting strange sensations in my stomach, weird flashes, as if by looking at the photo, I was able to understand what they'd be talking about, their life, their family, what they went on to do.

I suddenly felt light-headed, dizzy, so I sat on the edge of the bed taking deep breaths and closed my eyes, waiting for the spell to pass.

As the eerie judders in my body subsided, I concentrated on my breathing, on bringing myself back to the room. Behind my closed eyes, the faces in each of the photos flashed before me but, in particular, the man's face – the same face as Gabe's, only somehow different. So similar and yet so unfamiliar.

Then the first woman's face came into my head: impeccably dressed, older, maybe a family member, the man's hand proudly resting on her shoulder.

But the native woman struck me the most, though. Her face was alive, as if she were actually there in front of my closed eyes. She was so small and slight. Her raven hair looked heavy, long and shiny, framing her round face, the sepia photograph highlighting the stark contrast in her dark complexion and his pale one.

I then heard the sound of a familiar engine drawing close. I opened my eyes and looked up, as if waking from a vivid dream, the picture still clear in my head and refusing to fade.

I heard the engine cut off and the car door shut. The crunch of his boots became louder as he neared the lodge and he stopped where the pathway cut off towards the bunkhouse. I paused, listening, as he moved closer.

I left the underwear where it was; at least then he'd know why I was in his room in the first place. He pushed the door open slowly and stood looking at me as I sat on the bed with the photos still in my hand.

'Hi,' he said, pulling his brows together as he moved towards me.

'Hi,' I muttered, my voice quiet, subdued. 'Gabe, I need to know something.'

He walked to sit beside me on the bed. As he sat down, he carefully took the photographs from my hand and slowly looked over them. He took a deep breath, his face saddened. He closed his eyes, and as I looked towards him his jaw started to clench. 'The man in the photos is the same man you are sitting next to now,' he said.

It suddenly all started to make sense. I knew he was a vampire, of course, but what I didn't know was how *long* he'd been one. How had I not made the link immediately? I mean, vampires don't age, right? So why were there slight differences in the photos I'd seen, and not just in the clothes he wore but in his face.

As if sensing my questions, Gabe carried on. He lifted one of the photos, and leaned in towards me, the black and white image facing us. I looked down into it as he pointed to the woman. 'This was my mother, Amelia,' he said, running his finger over her face. 'I belonged to a powerful law family in France. I was born in Paris in 1814 and became renowned in my field, fighting for justice against the evils of the rich and powerful and serving the common French people. My full name is Gabrielle Emile Letenierre and at thirty-eight years of age, my human life ended.

'There were a group of powerful, evil men who did not like my father and myself for what we were doing to protect the vulnerable. They were wealthy, greedy men who wanted to put a stop to me and to my father. On the night of a gathering my father had arranged, large numbers of their henchmen came to my parents' house – they knew we would all be there – and fought with us, with our loyal guests, killing many.

'Both my father and mother were killed and I swore to avenge them. The day after, I left home with only one intention – to find these men and kill them. I gave up the life I knew, turning into a recluse and dressing like a pauper. My fury and hatred ran deep. I wandered the streets of Paris, not knowing where to go or what I should do, trying to figure out how to find them.

'I slept in dark alleys in the seedier parts of Paris, stole food and cheap wine and, to an extent, started to lose my mind. One night, in anger, I picked a fight with the wrong man, someone who had done no more than try to help me to my feet and offer me a hot meal and a warm place for the night. He saw through my desperation and perceived an inner strength inside me, something unique that I could not see for myself. Instead of providing an easy meal for him, he took me somewhere that even now I don't recognise. All I remember was the darkness and a few others like him skulking around in the shadows and watching from dark corners.

'I was too far gone, desperate to die, wanting to join my family, but they offered me something that years afterwards, I was very glad I accepted, and am especially glad now,' he said, looking towards my numb, shocked face before he smiled and gently kissed my forehead.

'At the time, I didn't want it, didn't want to live day by day thinking about all that I had lost, but the opportunity to live on, in some form, anyway, was one that I later came to appreciate.'

My hands were weakly placed on my legs, and I could see the immense pain and torture in his face. It was plain to see he did have a heart and a soul, only not in the biological sense.

I stroked the back of his bowed head. I knew he had more to say but was holding it in. 'The Indian girl,' I said, encouraging him to tell me more.

'Aiyana,' he said quietly, looking away from me, switching photos carefully and smiling down into the face of the beautiful Native American. 'When I came to America in 1902, I got work with other nomadic men in Montana, breaking wild horses. It enabled me to maintain my free-living lifestyle and feed as I needed from the animals in the wild, without anyone knowing what I was. I was very good at wrangling, the best in Montana. That's where I learned to ride so well and where I fell in love with mustangs: their wild, free spirit.

'The only problem I had was with the white man. They were taking too many of the wild horses and leaving too few for the Native Americans. I worked for a fair man, fair for those times, anyway, and he was one of the few who would work with the Indians. We established boundaries with them, encouraging a peaceful co-existence, which the Indians didn't trust at first but which, over time, worked well. I felt more and more drawn to them; drawn to their peace, their pure and natural way of life and to their ability as a tribe. I, after many long years, felt almost human again around them.

'As we don't sleep, as such, my resting times enabled me to spend more and more time close to the Indians, thriving in their simple, honest companionship. The hatred I'd carried in France subsided and my new life in America seemed perfect. And then, one day, as I was gathering more horses, I came across a new Cherokee camp. It was a small group and at first they were wary until I spoke to them in their native tongue and introduced myself.

'I sat and talked with them, instantly at ease in their company, and that was when I first met Aiyana. She walked out to the campfire and looked straight at me. She was only twenty-four years old, and so beautiful. Where my heart once was, the hole in my chest began to fill. I fell instantly in love with her: her compassion, her free spirit, her beauty, and, as I spent more free time with the tribe, our bond grew.

'She was everything to me, and always will be. Her people did not care about differences in our culture or our skin. They saw happiness in her and, eventually, a son in me. The tribe travelled to North Carolina and we married in a simple native ceremony in 1909. We had our first child in 1910, named 'ayo-ne-gev wa-ya.' It means white wolf in English.

'I lived in complete peace with my wife and our son, and we set up a more permanent home at the edge of the camp. I built a small, simple house in the woodland on the edge of the Smokey Mountains with the money I had saved. On our son's second birthday, I took him out on one of our horses, deep into the forest, to fish. We hadn't been gone too long but as we neared home I heard screams in the distance, my finely tuned hearing picking it up from miles away. I galloped as fast as I could with our son crying and cradled in one arm in front of me. I left him hidden in a safe place a little way from home, not knowing what I would find. I ran as fast as I could to the house to find my wife's burned, mutilated body in front of the porch. The struggle she'd put up was evident.'

I felt an involuntary gasp come flying from the pit of my stomach as he talked, picturing the scene so clearly, the tears welling in my eyes.

I began to shake violently inside but forced it to stop, knowing he did not need to comfort or worry about me right now. 'What happened to your son?' I asked.

'The tribe found me kneeling in the dirt cradling Aiyana's lifeless body. They'd also heard the screaming from their camp nearby. The rage inside me had shown my teeth, my black eyes, everything that gave away what I truly was. Not even Aiyana had known; I had kept my true self so well hidden, even from her. They saw me – a monster to them – holding her dead body, and their legends and beliefs gave them their answer. They saw what I was and believed that I had done this to her.

'They retreated in fear and, after a while, I went to find our son in the place where I'd carefully hidden him. But he was gone. They had tracked his cries and found him easily. They took him from me, fearing for his life. And I understood why. How, after seeing what they had, could they not believe I did this to her? They were only seeking to protect him. I tracked them back to the camp, but I knew I had to leave our son with them. I also knew that one day they would tell him what they believed his father had done and he would grow up hating me. There were other killings after that, for which I was surely blamed, but I later discovered that a band of white men had been travelling through the camps, killing any unprotected Indians they found.'

I couldn't stop the tears from spilling down my face and I started to sob uncontrollably. I felt so bad to be crying when he was the one who had to carry all this pain, over however many years. But my body continued to tremble, the images vivid in my head, as if I were watching the scenes unfolding in front of me. The stabbing pain in my chest became stronger, forcing the uneven breaths out.

He placed his arm around me. 'It's alright, Meg,' he told me, smiling. I was more than a little surprised at how he seemed to cope so well. How he could tell me about all the death, all the lost love, and not be screaming and furious and ready to kill again?

I jumped up, still shaking, and felt a sharp prick on my bottom lip. I lifted my finger and wiped away a small drop of blood, then moved my hand to my mouth, and gasped as I felt two tiny yet razor-sharp teeth in place of my canines. My eyes were seeing the room in clips now, like someone was pressing the shutter on a camera constantly, showing me something new each time.

I ran to the door, the shaking becoming worse, and looked back at him once. He looked troubled but still managed to offer me a small smile. I flung open the door and ran out towards the trees, into the darkness. I had to get away from him, try to understand why I was feeling this uncontrollable and overwhelming grief and sense of loss.

I ran deep into the trees, not knowing where I was going or how far. I needed to run to clear my head. Clear the images of his mother's face, and Aiyana's – both dead. His face – the same, yet so different. His lost son. The death, the sadness – all of it playing so clearly like a movie inside my head. I felt as though I was having a breakdown. I saw more than what he'd told me, as if I were making the story up as I went along, my subconscious moving scenes forward.

I hadn't even noticed how fast I was running, but my speed was incredible, the trees flashing past me. I was not even concerned about them, my new mind and body becoming fluent in this environment. I ran away from the few lights dotted around the housing estate, faster and faster, with no idea as to whether he was following me or not. I hoped not.

After awhile the images, thankfully, started to fade, moving slowly to the back of my mind. I became aware only of the present and of the complete darkness, of the shapes of mountains in the distance, and of the sounds of animals scuttling in fear from my scent and rapid approach. They had no reason to fear me, though.

I knew when I was nearing a road because I could hear the occasional car way off in the distance. So I avoided that direction. I didn't hear anyone following so I knew, for now, I was alone. As my head cleared more, I tried to become aware of where I was, of how far I had run. I saw a gap in the thicket of the trees coming up and slowed, feeling cautious.

The trees thinned out as I started to move uphill and I heard water running freely from behind me somewhere. I stepped slowly and carefully out to the top of a ridge and into a clearing. As my eyes focused, I saw the mountains in the distance and looked up to the dark sky, the stars shining brightly.

I tentatively walked forward, with only the merest hint of being out of breath. My eyes flitted left and right, looking for danger and trying to help me establish where I was, but I still didn't know. I'd just been drawn to run in this direction. As I took a few more steps forward, I caught sight of a dark shape on lower ground in the distance, something big, something solitary.

I focused on the dark shadow and I suddenly realised then where I was, where I had, for some reason, run to. I was in the open meadow where Gabe and I had come riding, where we had raced against each other on Warrior and Mouse, past the lightning tree, where I was now headed.

I picked up speed and ran towards the dark shape of the tree, its spindly arms spreading wide as if welcoming me. I stopped short and stood looking up at it. A strange sense of peace started to fill me and I walked the last few steps to the trunk. I turned and sat down, leaning back against the cold wood, the dead branches above me forming a protective canopy.

As I retraced the events of the evening, my mind felt cluttered. I rested my head back and closed my eyes. My ears enabled me to hear, my nose to smell, so my eyes could rest for awhile. But, as much as I thought things through, I still felt something was amiss, something was as yet untold. I just needed to rest for awhile first.

My head rested easily on the thick trunk as the cool air swirled around my face and I must have dropped off into a light sleep. I heard faint crunching sounds on the earth and I flicked my eyes open to find I was moving, passing under the dark, dense trees again. But there was no sound coming from whatever carried me. Then I inhaled deeply and I knew he'd found me.

I automatically wrapped my arms around his neck and gripped tightly, closing my eyes. When we got home, I was still unwilling to release my grip. I clung to him tightly as he put me gently on my bed. He easily disentangled himself from the iron grasp I thought I held and took his hand in mine as he climbed over me to his side of the bed. He stayed with me all night, until dawn broke. Only then I could see that the bed was covered in dirt and dust, and pieces of tree.

He tentatively slid himself down the bed to my level, and leaned onto his elbow, resting his head on his hand. He kissed my cheek and waited for my response. I smiled at him, sending relief shooting through his pained eyes. He smiled back at me, my favourite smile, and the lines around his eyes creased heavily at the corners.

The following morning, we sat on the porch and drank our special juice.

'When are you heading back to work?' I asked, not having had the chance the day before.

'Monday,' Gabe said, staring into the trees.

'Well, I think we need to go shopping today, stock up on food. Maybe take Ember out for a long walk later?' I asked.

'That sounds good. I need to call into the practice sometime to collect rotas and see what work I have on for next week.'

'No problem. We can stop by there and then go shopping,' I said, pleased to have our day a bit more mapped out and feeling things were returning to normal.

We climbed into the Jeep to go to town just before noon, the intense sun baking everything in sight. I was so thankful for the dark sunglasses. I needed to get some things in town so Gabe planned to drop me off while he went into work to arrange his working hours and collect some things he needed.

I knew I wouldn't be long so, as he pulled up at the sidewalk, I hopped out at the first store I needed. 'I'll see you at the practice in about twenty minutes,' I said, and slammed the door shut.

I ran into Hearth & Soul, rushing to buy some soaps and shampoos and more scents. The earthy smell was sometimes a little overwhelming inside the lodge, especially combined with the metallic smell from our 'juice,' and even though I knew it was hardly noticeable, I still thought it was a good idea to cover it up to avoid any possible questions from the few people who visited.

With my bags in hand, I headed over the street towards the pharmacy with my contraceptive prescription. I absent-mindedly fished through my purse for the piece of paper and, as I stepped onto the sidewalk, walked head on into a passer-by. The impact caused me to stumble backwards. A leather-covered arm reached out and gently grabbed hold of mine to steady me. Once I regained my balance, I looked up at the person to thank him or her.

I stuttered out a feeble 'thank you' as I faced a far too gorgeous man towering in front of me. He was not the usual resident or tourist-type I was now used to seeing around Manzano but more the alternative L.A. city-type. His layered black hair sat just above his shoulders and I could see chunks of bright red showing on the longer strands underneath. He had the largest, most piercing blue eyes, very round and youthful, almost feminine. 'I'm so sorry,' I said, looking up at him as he continued to hold onto my arm. 'I wasn't watching where I was going,' I added. Obviously.

'No problem, Miss,' he said, flashing a wide white smile. 'Are you okay?' He was looking deep into my sunglasses, as if he could easily see my eyes through the dark screens.

'Erm, yeah. I'm good, thanks. Sorry about that,' I replied, still a little tongue-tied.

'Well, take care now,' he said, turning and walking towards another man waiting further up the sidewalk. I casually watched them walk away but he didn't look back; he only nodded once to the other fair-haired man. I brought myself back down, shaking my head to clear the image of his face. He must have been melting in the long, worn black leather coat he wore, however good he looked in it.

While I waited in the pharmacy, I wandered around the store and thought about using contraception while dating a vampire. I wondered if I had a need for it. Could a vampire impregnate a night timer? It was not a subject I expected to find well covered on the internet.

'Anderson,' the voice called out. I turned to retrieve my packet, probably surprising the man as I approached with the wry smile I still had on my face.

I walked out of the store and back across the road towards the practice. I suddenly heard someone call my name. I barely recognised the panicked voice as I looked over my shoulder and up the side road.

Abigail was standing on the sidewalk halfway down the street, her face white, just staring at me.

'Hey, Abigail,' I said, puzzled by her nervous expression. Please, not another crazy Abigail episode.

'Meg, here,' she said, beckoning me towards her with her hand. She looked out of breath, shaken.

Apprehensively, I walked towards her. Her eyes were wide and flitting around anxiously, looking down the street, over the road, behind her. I frowned, puzzled by her odd behaviour.

'Hey, Abigail. Are you okay?' I asked, becoming concerned.

She reached forward and grabbed both my arms. 'Meg, please, listen to me,' she said, checking to make sure no one was close enough to overhear. 'You have to go now! Get out of Manzano. Leave the state.' Her voice was urgent.

'Oh, come on, Abigail. What are you talking about? Is this about Gabe again?' I asked, remembering her words of warning the last time we spoke.

She looked into my eyes and whatever she saw silenced her for a second. 'Meg, I tried to warn you. I tried to help you to see. My first warning you didn't listen to,' she said, looking deep into my eyes. 'I can see that but, please, listen to my second,' she said, squeezing my arms. 'Turn around, go home, get your things and leave,' she said, pleading. 'Please, Meg.'

'Abigail, I'm not going anywhere. I'm fine. You have nothing to worry about, trust me,' I said, knowing she was worrying about Gabe but also aware that she had no idea that I knew everything about what he was. Her warnings meant something, even though how much she would actually 'see' was a mystery to me.

'Gabe is the least of your worries now,' she said, releasing me from her harsh grip, dropping her hands in defeat and shaking her head. 'If you take one more step in his direction, the wheels are in motion,' she continued, trying to make me listen. 'You really do need to get away from here, Meg. Your life depends on it.'

I stood examining her face and for a moment, I almost listened. But then I thought of Gabe and the life here we were developing together. I couldn't leave. I wouldn't. 'Abigail, thank you for your concern but I have to go now,' I said, backing away from her.

She shook her head again and looked far away, through my face. 'You silly girl,' she said, turning slowly and walking back towards her store. I watched as she climbed the stairs to the porch and opened the door, pausing briefly in the doorway before walking inside.

I walked a little more slowly to the other side of town, puzzling over what Abigail had said and trying to clear it from my mind before I met Gabe. He would sense something was wrong and probably not be too pleased with her interfering.

I looked up towards where his Jeep was parked and, after taking a few more steps, I clearly made out the top of Gabe's head. He was standing by the side of his car. I smiled, knowing that he was finished with work and waiting for me. After a few more steps, I saw the head of another man who was standing in front of him. He was tall, but not as tall as Gabe, and he had shorter, blond hair. I paused in my stride and peered towards them, not wanting to interrupt.

I figured he was maybe a client, but something about their manner told me otherwise. I stepped back out of sight, into the porch of the DIY store, and looked on. Gabe looked slightly down at the other man, who stood only a couple of feet in front of him, his face growing angrier, his jaw clenching constantly. Something wasn't right.

As the blond man spoke, Gabe turned and looked over the top of his Jeep, just as I ducked back, not wanting him to see me spying. I waited a few seconds before I peered back over to them.

As I looked towards them, Gabe was opening the driver's door and was about to get in. The blond man stepped forward and grabbed hold of his arm. Whoever he was, that was not a good move. I gasped, only just staying put, but prepared myself to run and diffuse the situation if it got out of hand. I saw Gabe whip his head around, and I heard the deep growling sound coming from low in his chest. Whatever was happening between them was bad. Very bad. I was torn between running to his side, to help in whatever way I could or staying put. Deep inside, something was telling me to stay where I was, not to go near, that my presence would make things worse.

I saw Gabe's sharp teeth slightly bared as his mouth parted, the glint of the sun shining onto them as he faced the stranger. It seemed that things were about to get a whole lot worse until the blond man released Gabe's arm and raised his hands in an apologetic gesture, looking tentatively around as if he was concerned about passers-by. He spoke again but Gabe remained quiet, attempting to avoid any further eye contact. They stood quietly for a few moments, then Gabe nodded his head once. The blond man walked around to the other side of the Jeep and climbed in.

As he came around to the side of the car nearest to me, I saw his light green eyes and pale white skin and I knew instinctively that he was a vampire. I started shaking inside, the now familiar juddering taking over my body, but I was here, in town, and too many people were around. I had to be very careful.

I cautiously slid back into the doorway when the Jeep roared to life, trying to keep myself out of sight. Gabe reversed out fast and turned in my direction. I pressed my shaking body deep into the doorway as he drove past. Suddenly, and without warning, I heard his voice in my head. *'Go home, pack, and leave. I'll find you,'* it said. He made no attempt to look in my direction but I was sure it was his voice, warning me, as Abigail had done only five minutes earlier.

I watched them drive past and peered around the doorway to see him turn onto Washington Street, leading to his house.

I stood in complete shock, trying desperately to fathom what I should do. How could I just leave, leave him in whatever trouble he was facing and just go? I was stronger now, much stronger, and I could help him in whatever way he needed – I knew I could. Surely one and a half vampires were enough to face one lone immortal? I started to think about his voice in my head. How had I heard him? It had never happened before.

I closed my eyes and tried to feel what my instincts were telling me. After a few moments, I knew what I was going to do and, right or wrong, I decided on my course of action. My first stop was his house since I expected them to go there.

I walked out of the doorway and back around the corner onto Washington Street. I now knew it would eventually lead to Gabe's house so I walked as fast as I humanly could, trying to look calm, normal.

As I passed by Abigail's store on the other side of the road, I caught a glimpse of her face in the window but I didn't acknowledge her. I looked away.

I headed off the road into the trees alongside and looked around, checking that I was pretty much out of sight. I dropped my bags and set off running. As I ran, I tried to think through what I was going to do when I got there. Should I watch from a distance and see what happened? Or, should I just go in and make up the numbers, acting as normally as possible and serving as a witness.

Within a few minutes, the big, expensive houses started to come into sight. I reached the main road, slowing as I crossed over to the woods on the other side of the street, before picking up pace and finding my way to the end of Gabe's street, deep in the thick-set trees.

I saw the pointed arch of his house come into sight first and slowed down, trying to listen as I closed the last few yards to the perimeter of the property. I couldn't see any sign of movement and my acute hearing could pick up no voices. I ran crouching low through the trees to the side of the house to see if his car was there.

Still deeply hidden in the trees I looked out and felt numb to see the driveway empty. I snuck to the edge of the garage and threw myself to the ground, peering through the small gap under the door. It was empty except for a set of two wheels – his motorcycle.

I stood up and headed towards the back of the house, unconcerned now about being seen. No one appeared to be there to see me anyway. I ran around and opened the French doors. I had to find something, a clue about this blond man, about where they had gone, about why he was here now. 'The library,' I muttered, and marched down the long hallway to the now familiar door. There had to be something about his friends or visitors or vampire lore, if that's what it was called. Something that would help.

I marched in and went straight to the desk. Without thinking – I could answer for my actions later – I took a firm grip on the handle and yanked it open. The locked drawer gave no resistance to my strength and opened easily.

I searched through the drawer, my eyes scanning quickly, but I found nothing. I pulled at the handle on the next drawer down. It too came free with no trouble. There were little books and trinkets and other old-looking items neatly placed inside, but still I found nothing relevant. 'Damn it,' I whispered, panic setting in as I rummaged through the bottom drawer. This came away easily, but not through strength. It was already unlocked.

What I hoped to find, I had no idea. Anything that would give me a clue, any clue. As I pulled some photos out of the way, a few fell out onto the floor and I quickly bent to retrieve them.

I held a similar group of photos in my hand to the ones I'd already seen: photos of Gabe's mother, Amelia, and ones of Aiyana and Gabe together all those years ago. He looked at her in the same way he looked at me. I flicked briefly through them, staring into their faces for too long and at Aiyana's face in particular. I studied her body, her whole form, all the time thinking and worrying about Gabe. And then, I dropped them all. Every single one of them now lay scattered at my knees.

I was breathless, gasping for air, and grabbed onto the edge of the desk, freezing shivers spreading through the whole length of my body. I became crippled by what had been there all along. I'd seen it, but not really *seen* it. It had been sitting dormant in my mind, waiting for the right time to show itself. It had been there in my dreams, in the woman I studied in the photographs, and in Gabe's face as he looked at her in the past and at me in the present.

I forced myself back onto my feet and stroked my hand across the top of my left arm. Then, as difficult as it was, I pushed my thoughts to the back of my mind.

I turned and ran through the house, my mind close to exploding, my body vibrating. As I bounced out through the French doors, I ran harder than ever, knowing what I needed to do.

I wasted no time heading towards town, opting to take the best route home, through the areas which would allow me the most discretion, with fewer people to spot me. My course took me to the eastern side of Manzano, towards the open planes that had less cover. I slowed when I heard traffic, forcing myself to jog, to look more normal.

I hardly paused to check for passing cars and ran straight across the road, hearing someone honk at me as I reached the other side. I idly wondered how my body would deal with that. Would it kill me to be hit by a car? Or would I stand up and walk away from it? As I reached Manzano Elementary School, I picked my stride up even more until I was completely out of town.

With no one to see me, I knocked it up into high gear. I rounded the corner, the road to the lodge in sight, and checked around again. I turned a sharp left, ducking into the trees, which would keep me pretty much under cover until I reached home.

As I saw the lodge coming into sight through the trees, I stopped dead and crouched low, watching, listening for any sign that Gabe might be there. Everything looked normal, with only my car on the drive. I sprinted for the door and rummaged through my purse for the keys. I unlocked the door and ran inside, slamming it behind me.

As I went to put my purse on the kitchen counter, something came into my peripheral vision and I snapped my head around to look.

I stood, motionless, holding the gasp in as I saw someone sitting on the couch. His arms were stretched out at both sides, casually strewn over the back rest. It was the same man I'd bumped into in town.

As I looked at him, I was making instant snap assessments. Ember was my first thought. Where was he? Who was this man? And what the hell was he doing here? How had he gotten in? Ned. Where was Ned? I kept eye contact, summoning up some courage. I was so close to the edge I knew I only needed the slightest push to topple me.

I tried to keep my voice calm as I spoke. 'Who are you?' I asked, keeping an even tone, attempting to disguise the panic in my voice.

He took a deep breath in and exhaled loudly. 'Ah Meg. Welcome home,' he said, the smile on his face not matching the coldness in his eyes. He looked me up and down, nodding in some sort of weird approval.

My eyes flitted around quickly, taking the room in, trying desperately to decide how to react, to keep the kids safe – wherever they were. I didn't ask him about them in case they had somehow known to hide; if they were safe, my bringing them into conversation would only put them in danger.

I asked again, taking a bold step forward, trying to make myself taller. 'Who are you?' I demanded, raising my eyebrows, waiting for an answer. 'And how the hell did you get in here?'

He flexed his neck from side to side, slowly, keeping his eyes on me, and the dull cracking of bones rang loud in my ears.

'I'm…the messenger. I bring tidings of, well, bad news, actually,' he said, laughing at his own comment. His smile started to make me feel even more uneasy as he casually ran one of his hands through the blackness of his hair, letting it fall loosely over the glaring red underneath. He let his hand lay where it landed on the cushion of the couch.

At that moment, I could see what lay behind his eyes. I knew that beneath the piercing, astonishing blue was pure evil. I also knew that he had something to do with Gabe and what had happened in town. And I knew in the flash I got of Gabe's worried eyes that something was horribly wrong, and that my decision to go to his house instead of packing and leaving there and then had led me to this. Whatever this was.

Act dumb, my brain said, the human side trying to protect my immortal self. 'I don't follow,' I said, concerned by the silence in the lodge.

As I stared into his face, I felt numb, the feeling of being in a trance returning. My breathing deepened, my body softened. He smiled again. 'Mmm,' he murmured, parting his lips and cocking his head, 'I can see why he wants you, why he did it.' He stood slowly, jolting me out of the trance. I blinked rapidly, clearing my head.

Why was I feeling an overwhelming attraction towards this man? This vampire who had broken into my property. I'd felt the same for a split second when I'd bumped into him in town. The sudden attraction, the deep thudding in my chest as the butterflies re-awakened. I pushed the feelings back, made them stay dormant. He was *making* me feel this way; it was not something I chose.

He turned slowly and looked around the lodge before he walked over to the window and pushed the hanging blinds out of the way, peering into the yard. With his back turned, I scanned the room quickly, searching for the kids.

I stopped still when he turned back. He leaned casually against the sill, his arms pressed wide against it, holding his weight as his long leather coat hung open. All I saw was black, except for the vivid deep red streaks in his hair. And his eyes, those eyes again. His complexion was exactly the same as Gabe's: pale, drawn, with a hint of dark shading under his transfixing eyes. He was also lean, as Gabe was, his tall body sunken in the middle with hard muscle layering the top, enlarging his frame, highlighting his inhuman strength.

But maybe he hadn't bargained on me, on what I was, on my new strength, my determination.

'I think you'd better leave…now,' I said, lifting my head defiantly.

'Oh, don't worry. We're *both* leaving shortly,' he said, pushing himself from the sill and taking a careful stride towards me.

'You're the only one who's leaving,' I said, making a mental picture in my head of the room, of what weapons I had nearby. 'Oh, I've had enough,' I blurted out, feeling the vibrations within my body becoming stronger. 'Get the fuck out of my home!' I screamed, a deep rumbling building in my throat.

'Oh, Meg. I really don't think you're following me,' he said, smiling. I knew he was trying even harder to get me to look at his face, into those eyes again. But I let my eyes haze over as I stared at him and concentrated on what was going on within me.

He took another tentative step forwards, closing the gap to only a few feet. And that was it. I threw myself towards the TV cabinet, landing precisely alongside it, about four feet away from him. I grabbed a heavy glass wolf figurine off the top but when I turned to face him, he'd gone. I re-focused and spun around to see him standing in the kitchen.

I crouched low, holding the figurine in my right hand, getting the best grip on it.

He threw his head back, letting out a deep, throaty laugh. Then he looked right at me. The laughter was gone, his face harsh. 'Well, now I *know* Mr Letenierre has been a naughty boy. Your actions – or, shall I say, abilities – are the only proof I needed.' When he lowered his head, his eyes had turned from a piercing blue into jet black and I knew then it was all about to begin.

Chapter 17

I adjusted my position so that I kept him in sight of me in front of the window. At least if I missed him, I would hopefully make enough noise to draw attention to my situation by smashing the glass. He crouched low and I saw the glint of sharp white points emerging from under his top lip.

He quickly advanced a step, but I held my nerve, swaying from side to side, ready to react. I wanted him closer; I couldn't attack just yet. With a sly grin, he took another bold step forward, goading me, and I flung my right hand forward, throwing the heavy glass weight towards him with all my strength. My aim was perfect as I caught sight of the sharp top part of the wolf's ears heading directly towards his face.

He whipped his head sideways to avoid the impact and caught the figurine perfectly in his hand. The heavy blow didn't even force his hand back a fraction. I saw the shards of glass breaking off as it hit, dropping to the floor. 'Tut, tut, tut,' he muttered, waving a single finger from side to side as if chastising a naughty child. Before I could think, he launched himself at me and my body instinctively moved completely sideways, my right side almost lying on the floor, my feet perfectly in balance facing forward.

I slammed my hands to the floor to take the impact, and pushed myself hard back to my feet to spin around to where he had passed overhead. The only strike he got in was on my arm, the sharp gash of what felt like a razor slicing through my flesh. I glanced towards what I wanted to use as my next weapon, and faced him again, my hand ready to make the move. 'Oh, Meg. Why don't we try to keep this as nice as possible? Now, let's go find your boyfriend.'

'I'm thinking no, actually,' I calmly said. As I spoke, I felt the wet drops on my bottom lip where my own sharp teeth had cut into the soft skin.

He took a deep breath, his face becoming irritated. 'Fine. We'll do this your way. I've had enough of these fucking games,' he said, marching unconcerned towards me.

Within the blink of an eye, it had all happened. I reached for Ember's leash, grabbed the handle, and swung it at full speed like a whip into his face. Again and again I swung it around, keeping as much momentum as I could manage, the metal clasp lashing hard into his face. But it didn't cause him to falter; he just kept coming. He didn't even blink as he threw himself into the air towards me and wrapped his hand around my neck, taking me down to the ground.

The thud as I hit the floor and the sharp crack in the top of my arm stopped me dead. I knew I didn't stand a chance against him. There was still too much of me that was mortal to defeat the immortal that faced me now. I lay on my side with sharp, shooting pains running up my arm as his solid weight crushed me.

He pinned my arms to the ground and straddled me, holding me completely still. Only then did I see the damage that I'd managed to inflict. There were four deep gashes to his face, with the slight drip of dark red welling at the surface but refusing to spill. His black eyes were different from Gabe's; they were much harder and completely soulless – just empty vessels. I stared into those lifeless eyes and knew there was no point fighting against him. I would lose. If I were going to die now, soon, I'd want to see Gabe, be with him.

When I looked up at his face, he smiled widely. The wounds I'd inflicted healed before my eyes, leaving only faint white scars in less than a minute. He bent down, hovering over me, and I turned my face away, avoiding contact with those eyes. With my face twisted away as far as possible, he inhaled deeply and then licked the full length from my jaw to my temple. The cold wet of his tongue felt like ice, as if it had formed a frozen layer all the way up my face.

I shut my eyes and grimaced. He moved closer, his lips touching the edge of my ear. 'Now, if I didn't already have plans for you, instructions, I could be tempted myself…or, at the very least, drink you dry,' he said, as the shuddering inside me made a comeback.

I clenched my jaw hard, keeping my face away from his. I didn't want any part of me reciprocating his sick games. He leaned over and grabbed Ember's leash off the floor and slid upright, yanking me up to my feet with him. The shooting pain in my arm sent waves of agony through me but I didn't let him see it. He looked towards my eyes, smiling, as he bound my wrists with the leash. I kept my stare down, over to the side of his arm, my face hard, unrepentant. He wrapped the leash through and around my wrists tightly, locking them there, the click of the clasp ensuring it stayed put.

'Okay, I think we're done,' he said, looking around. 'Now, let's go find Monsieur Letenierre, shall we?'

He led me towards the door. With his eyes averted, I glanced around, tears welling in my eyes. I couldn't let them spill now. I just needed to know if Ember and Ned were okay. The pain of not seeing their faces was unbearable. But there was only silence throughout the lodge and I was sure this psycho had killed them. Where else could they be? It broke my heart more and more with each step he took me away from the lodge. If only I could just see their faces and know they were unharmed.

As we passed the first few trees, he took a slightly shorter step and twisted underneath me, pushing his head easily through the loop where the leash tied my wrists together. Then, he stood up into a half crouch so I dangled around his neck and onto his back.

He ran so smoothly that I hardly even moved on his back, my body making only slight swaying motions as he blurred through the trees. The dull throb in my upper arm became worse the longer I was suspended there. I was unable to fight anymore. When we were deep into the trees, he ran faster, my legs struggling to lay straight behind him. I relaxed them and let them fall around the leather coat wrapping his slim waist so that he was piggy-backing me. As much as I abhorred him, I felt too weak to struggle.

With my eyes closed, feeling his solid, lithe body, his easy move-ment, the wind brushing his hair into my face, I could so easily have imagined being on Gabe's back. But I needed to remember that I wasn't.

As the early evening sun shone high through the leaves of the trees, I saw only shadows and light flickering through my closed lids. I felt my body become heavy as I thought back over the past months and how my life had come to this.

I thought of Luke, of how I had given it all away because of his one mistake. I'd heard the complete remorse in his voice on the phone, and so nearly changed my mind and went back to him in Boston.

I'd intended to start a simple new life with Ember and Ned: the peace, the simplicity, the solitary existence. It had all disappeared the second I laid eyes on Gabe. I knew now, in the far depths of my mind, what I think I'd known all along. That Gabe was wrong for me in so many ways, yet right for me in many others. But so far, the wrong had far outweighed the right, just like Abigail had been warning me all along.

The one image that stuck in my mind was the day we'd taken Ember to the small cove outside of San Diego, the tiny rugged beach with hidden caves and high dunes. I remembered the absolute privacy – just the three of us – and the trust I'd placed in him. As I'd messed around in the pools surrounding the large rocks, looking for life as the tide moved away, Gabe rested on a rock behind me with Ember sitting between his legs. He'd leaned down to him, rubbing his hands deep into the fur of his neck, smiling easily towards me.

His eyes in that one second, that one memory, were perfect. No sadness, no torture, just deep, chocolate-brown eyes with nothing behind them but happiness and love. I'd never forget the eyes that watched me that day and I couldn't forget them now.

The feeling of him grabbing onto both my legs jolted me from my thoughts. I lifted my face from where it rested on his shoulder and looked forward, hearing the distant sound of water. A wide river I didn't recognise ran fast through the middle of the trees, and he didn't slow as he ran towards it. His head looked quickly from left to right, assessing something.

He slinked across to the right, heading towards a slightly narrower stretch of water and, without hesitation, flung us both into the air, travelling straight and only inches from the top of the rapids. His agile feet landed without breaking stride and he carried on into the trees on the other side.

I tried again to change the course of what was coming. I leaned forward, my face next to his, and twisted my lips so they were touching his cheek next to his ear. 'Please, don't do this,' I whispered, the begging clear in my voice.

He let out a deep, throaty laugh. I'd had no effect on him; my pleading hadn't worked and my words had not even broken his stride. I tried a new approach, still whispering in his ear. 'What exactly have *I* done wrong?' I challenged.

The moment I said it, he crouched until he almost reached the ground, my legs hitting the earth alongside him, and he ducked his head under the loop so I came free, dropping to the ground as he stepped out in front of me.

He turned to look back at my body lying bound in the dirt. I waited for whatever he was about to say.

'Meg, Meg, Meg. You see, *you* haven't done anything wrong, but your boyfriend has. A halfling like you, well, you are simply not allowed to exist, I'm afraid. It threatens all the…pedigrees, if you like, in these lands. If you follow my drift. You are a risk to us all and we can't allow you to live,' he said, twisting his head in a fake sympathetic pose. 'You're paying the price for his mistake, Meg. Now, do you still love him?'

'But, how do I threaten *you*…the others? I mean, it's not like I'm going to say anything, draw attention to myself, am I?'

'The law is the law, human or otherwise. And I am here to enforce it, follow my instructions. This is what I do, what I was made for, and I'm one of the best,' he said, proudly explaining himself and taking pleasure in his role, his smile widening slowly. 'So, you see, you have done nothing wrong per se. You're just paying the price.'

I looked up at him as he spoke and his eyes caught mine directly, intentionally. The instant they fixed on me, I was stuck, glued to them, as if hypnotised. I lay there on the earth, my eyes hazing over, my breathing becoming heavy again. With his eyes fixed on mine, he walked slowly towards me, careful not to break the stare.

My eyes followed his as he crouched onto the ground in front of me. He placed his hands on each side of my face. As the daze continued, a deeper part of me dredged up other thoughts: Ember, Ned and Gabe; home, the beach. I was grasping at anything to get him out of my head. He pulled me to my knees in front of him and moved his face towards mine, making sure he didn't break eye contact until the last second.

'I never did taste the blood of a halfling,' he said, his deep voice penetrating my ears. The sound of it was harmonic, deep and enticing. Just before his eyes broke their hold over mine, I saw them change from blue to jet black and, a second later, the skin on my neck was broken, pierced by two sharp points.

There was no pain and, as much as I didn't want it to, it felt nice. The touch of his teeth penetrating my skin made me want to twist my head further to the side, allowing him better access so he could enter deeper into my flesh and make the feeling more intense, more intimate. I exhaled loudly and quickly opened my eyes. I turned towards him, forcing his teeth to disengage, and looked into his face.

'Get...the fuck...off me,' I whispered, staring straight into his eyes. They changed back to blue and his face became puzzled as he wondered how I was able to break his spell. He smiled at me, knowing I would not give in any more. His smile then faded and he jumped up, pulling me up to stand with him.

'You taste like shit, anyway,' he snarled, his face mocking.

He dragged me roughly along this time and I looked up at the darkening sky as I stumbled into more dense trees. He held my weight effortlessly to stop me from stalling him and made more haste to wherever we were headed. I saw light ahead in the distance and a low grumble emerged from his throat.

His body was becoming defensive and I could sense that something bad was imminent. His eyes flashed from black to blue and back to black again. I stumbled to the top of the slope and suddenly realised exactly where I was.

He stopped just as we reached the peak of the slope and looked straight ahead of him. As he stared into the distance, he pulled me closer and wrapped his arm around my neck, covering my mouth with his hand.

I could see the lightning tree clearly in the distance, the fading sun highlighting it from behind. As I searched to see what he was looking for, looking at, I saw two tall dark shadows behind the tree to the left, standing completely still several feet apart. With the rumbling still in his throat, he dragged me over the mound of earth and onto the open plane.

He marched forward with a grin on his face, his eyes still flicking between blue and black, and grumbling like a dog about to attack. As we approached the shadows in the distance, I scanned ahead, looking at the figures, their faces still too far away to make out, even with my sharp eyes.

A little further on, I could make the shapes out more clearly, their profiles changing as they tracked our approach. Suddenly, one of the figures started to crouch, ready to move, but the other one reacted more swiftly, halting the manoeuvre in its tracks and holding the shadowy figure back. I heard a low whisper ringing in my ears as one of them spoke. 'Wait,' the voice demanded.

When we were no more than fifty feet from the tree, my captor came to a halt and wrapped his arm around my shoulder, putting his hand around my neck and digging his nails into the skin to tighten his grasp on me.

I heard another growl, one that I recognised. I could just make out his features, even in the failing light. I could see that his eyes were black. I stared towards him, looking for some sign, listening for his voice in my head, to tell me what to do. But he gave me nothing. I knew my strength – however much immortality it contained – was nothing against the monster that stood beside me. Whatever happened next, I knew I would not be of any use to Gabe.

'Let her go,' Gabe said, and the familiarity of his deep, rumbling voice sounded like heaven, my heaven. As he spoke, I looked towards the other man, still holding onto Gabe's arm, his blond hair breezing gently around his chiselled face. He stared back at me, silently.

He had deep wrinkles in his forehead, a weathered look like Gabe's, but with pale piercing green eyes. 'You know they can't allow this,' he said, his voice possessing the same deep tones as Gabe's, only his accent was different and difficult to place.

'Let her go, Ethan,' Gabe repeated, keeping his eyes on the vampire holding me.

Ethan let out a deep menacing laugh, as if to throw Gabe's words back into his face and refuse his request as absurd. He retorted with a single word. 'No.'

Gabe turned to the blond man. 'I will not go through this again,' he said, shaking his head as he spoke only to him. 'Nathaniel, you've known me a long time and in my one-hundred and fifty-eight years, I have only breached one rule, only once, and for a good reason. You know this.'

'My friend, even in ten-thousand years, one breach in our law is one too many,' he said. There appeared to be a flicker of emotion, of pity, as he spoke.

'Yet, I have done all that they have asked,' Gabe responded. 'I have been a guard of the council, something *they* requested of me, not something I chose to do, and I didn't take on the role lightly. I would have most certainly been happier travelling and existing alone, obeying no rules, and hurting no one. Not only do I abide by their laws but I have always ensured that others of our kind do as well. Can I not be allowed to save the life of one person, especially as you know why I did—'

'Innocent or not,' he interrupted, 'she cannot be allowed to exist. Her very being threatens our existence. She is not immortal and, as such, she is not as pure as we are. She can ail, she can be found out and she can raise suspicions about us,' he said, finding another answer for Gabe. It didn't seem to be going well.

Gabe shook his head, sensing that his words were falling on deaf ears. He had not even come close to changing Nathaniel's mind. I looked towards him, the trembling in my body still there but lying dormant now, waiting for when it would be needed.

'Nathaniel, I ask one thing of you, only one,' Gabe pleaded. 'Let me go to the council and ask them myself, state my case. It is their decision to make, not yours. They should deal directly with me and not use you or your assassin over there as the messenger. We've been friends for a long time and I never thought it would come to this, that you would turn against me,' Gabe said, shaking his head.

'I'm not against you, Gabe. I have no other choice. I was the one they chose to sort this. I do not carry this task out lightly, easily. I only act under instruction—'

A deep, snarling growl came from Gabe's throat, halting Nathaniel's words. 'I will not lose her for a second time,' he shouted. 'I adhered to the laws the last time, against what better human judgement remained within me, and I lost her. Never again,' he said, turning his face from Nathaniel and looking straight towards my puzzled face.

'Explain,' Nathaniel said simply.

Gabe shook his head, seeming angry at himself for what he'd just said. Then he looked backwards towards the darkening sky. After a few seconds, he lowered his head and turned his eyes to mine. I was waiting, as the others were. Waiting, but not understanding. The look he gave me went straight into my heart, deep into me, and I felt something new, something strange. The shaking within me increased, not because of anger this time but due to something I didn't yet understand.

The vampire beside me tightened his grip, digging his nails deeper into the tender skin of my neck, as if he were anticipating something, an attack. I hardly felt the cutting sensation, only the pressure of his nails. I stared towards Gabe, blood trickling slowly down my neck onto my bare shoulder.

Gabe did nothing. He stared back at me, remaining very still. My eyes were searching his, through them, and I was seeing deeper inside than ever before. *'Don't be afraid,'* his voice said in my head, yet his lips didn't move at all. *'Please, understand,'* he pleaded. My eyes became fixed on his, the trance taking over, images appearing, darting through my mind. They flitted around in a random order that made no sense to me and I had no time to decipher them. The more I relaxed, the more the images started coming together to make pictures, scenes. *'Understand,'* the voice whispered, before the images stopped flitting around and it was suddenly as if a movie that was being fast-forwarded had started to play in normal speed again.

The big house, the pendant, Gabe's face, his mother, all the blood...
Warm, sweltering heat, something heavy and moving in my arms, a feather placed onto my skin, tickling me, Gabe's face laughing above mine, long black hair hanging on my shoulders...
Native music, fire, dancing with him, dancing with the child in my arms...
Lying naked under a thick blanket, the wooden house, crackling logs in the fireplace, his hand running down my arm...
Pain, stabbing, blood trickling through my fingers, looking into fading faces, burning...
The noises, my people, fear and hatred in their eyes, being bound, burning, my screams...Aiyana...
The black and red hair hanging close beside me, the nails pressing into my throat, the blond man before me, vampires, Gabe's face, the lightning tree...

I suddenly understood, as he'd asked me to. I pulled away from his eyes as if being sucked back by an incredibly powerful wind, making me retreat into my own body. And then I came round, still hanging by my throat in the vampire's grip.

Aiyana.
Meg.
Me.

In that one cohesive moment, I felt awake again – and alive – so alive that my whole body vibrated violently before stopping suddenly and falling completely still. My abrupt dead weight caught my captor off guard and I slid through his sharp nails, out of his grasp, and down onto to the ground. He left me there, crouching slightly in front to face Gabe.

I heard Gabe's voice again, not as close as it had been before but instead distant, as if I were dreaming. He looked at me, and only me, as he spoke.

'I found Aiyana in 1909. She was a Cherokee Indian, living in North Carolina. I happily gave up everything for her, this human, pledging never to turn her into a vampire, never to hurt her or her tribe, only to love and live in happiness together, staying true to the laws of my people. We married later that year and our son, ayo-ne-gev wa-ya, who we came to call Isaac, was amazingly and unexpectedly born the following year. How he was born to us, I never knew. I didn't think it possible. He was two-years-old when she was murdered.

'She was bound, stabbed several times and set alight, left for me to find outside our house. When I returned, I saw the smoke and left Isaac safely hidden to go and see what was happening. I found her dying and began screaming and growling in fury. I had my chance there and then, to inject her with my venom, to try and save her so that we could still be together, but I stuck to their damn laws and my life ended again.

'Her people came, hearing the screams and seeing the smoke as I had done, and they saw me hovering over her dead body. My anger had brought out my black eyes and my teeth – and both of us were covered in blood. They believed I had killed her. So, they tracked and found Isaac from his cries and took him away. I approached the tribe when I was calmer, after several days, but they had hidden him from me. I was banished from ever going near him again. For years, I hid in the shadows, watching him grow. I heard them tell their stories; stories they believed to be true, about how his father was evil, one of the un-dead, and how he had killed his mother, taken her blood, her life. He believed the lies as he grew and by the time he was six years old, I knew his life would never include me because of the hatred burning so deeply inside him. And so I left.'

I heard the story as he told it but I was unable to truly absorb it. My vivid dreams made more sense to me now and I realised that they were not just dreams but visions of the past life I had lived, all those years ago.

Nathaniel looked towards the trees, slowly nodding his head. 'If this is true, Gabe, how do I believe it? How do you prove it?'

I lifted my weak eyes upwards from my slumped body to see Gabe taking some items from his back pocket and passing them to Nathaniel. He pointed to something in one of the photos and I knew then what I needed to do.

Nathaniel looked towards me. 'Ethan, look at her left arm,' he called. I hadn't realised I was rubbing over the mark with my fingers as I sat slumped on the ground.

Ethan slid down to me baring his teeth, his eyes glancing towards Gabe in defiance, and grabbed my left arm aggressively. 'Is there anything there?' Nathaniel asked.

'A dark brown diamond shape with a droplet beneath,' he replied reluctantly, dropping my arm and re-establishing his crouch.

I looked up again to see Nathaniel nodding to himself. He appeared deep in thought, debating, wondering. Gabe stood silently, waiting, but his eyes were still black and unsure.

Trying to strengthen his case, Gabe continued, 'I never sought her out here. I've lived around these parts for over four years. She moved here of her own accord, I had no bearing on her decision. I only did what I did to save her life and I only injected enough venom to save her from dying. I wasn't sure what that would do to her but I did not anticipate changing her.'

As Gabe finished talking to Nathaniel, who was beginning to look as if he might sway in his decision, a thunderous laugh erupted from Ethan. 'Oh, come on. Rules are rules, Nathaniel, and there are no excuses for breaking them, regardless of his so-called story. I mean, your girlfriend should be dead. It's meant to be, my friend. That's fate for you. Mortality's a bitch, ain't it?' he mocked.

I heard a deep rumble from Gabe and his eyes were completely focused on Ethan now. Then Nathaniel spoke. 'Gabe, I understand your loss, and the reasons behind what you have done, but I must make my decisions based on the laws of our kind and the facts placed before me.' He raised his hand to Gabe's arm, grasping it but saying nothing more.

Gabe nodded slowly in defeat. 'Then allow me to take my case to the council,' he said, still slowly nodding.

'As a leading guard of the council, I know you have served us well and will continue to do so. But I have the full authority of the council and my decision stands. If we allow you this one indiscretion, where do we draw the line? We would be making a rod for all our backs with this.'

Gabe bowed his head. The long silence was eerie. The wind in the distant trees started to pick up, the sky losing its hold on the last remnants of sun as it began to drop below the horizon. He flashed a quick glance in my direction. I stayed crumpled on the ground but the shuddering inside started to build again. In my head, I heard his voice: '*I will save you, I will stop them. Do what you can to protect yourself.*'

And so it began, in this vast meadow, next to the lightning tree from my dreams. We would either win or lose. Live or die. There was no in-between. I, saved by the man I loved, was facing certain death. I could feel it. And the fear building up within me was not for myself but because I didn't want this to be the last time I saw his face. I wasn't ready to leave him.

There was no fear in Gabe's eyes. No fear that the vampire assassin beside me could wipe me out in a split second and he could do nothing to stop him. And Nathaniel knew Gabe would fight hard, right to the bitter end.

The wind became stronger and my hair started to whip around my face, stinging as it struck my eyes. Ethan looked up and around, and started whooping. 'So it begins,' he said, dragging me from the ground by my neck and holding me in his steel grip, obviously pleased that he could finally do what he'd come here for. I looked up at him as he spoke and saw his teeth had changed into sharp points, his eyes black.

I tried to gauge what I could do, how I could make my escape. I looked back towards Gabe, I remembered his words, '*Do what you can to protect yourself.'* I repeated it again and again in my head, closing my eyes. The shuddering became more violent and I felt my own teeth growing. My body was preparing itself as were theirs. My eyes flashed open and I saw Nathaniel backing off towards the trees.

I could tell by the remorse in his face that, although he'd made the final decision, he wanted no part in the fight. He would not do battle against his friend. It also made me realise by the easy way in which Nathaniel retreated that Ethan was a one-man band when it came to the crunch: he needed no other immortal to help him fight.

When Nathaniel had fallen a good eighty feet back from Gabe, he looked towards Ethan and gave one solemn nod in his direction, permitting the fight to begin. Gabe's head shot up, his eyes glaring from beneath his heavy brows, and he looked straight into Ethan's face. His teeth seemed longer and sharper than ever and, as his lips curled back over them, a deep snarl spilled out of his mouth like a wild animal. Ethan smiled at him confidently and twisted his head from side to side, the bones in his neck cracking again.

'Don't worry. I'll make it quick for her,' he said, smiling at Gabe while stroking my hair as if petting a weak little puppy. Gabe took a deep breath and his chest filled out as he inhaled. His eyes rolled back as his head moved up, the growling aimed at the darkening sky.

I watched and waited, the shaking growing stronger within me, and I felt my own breaths deepening, filling my lungs, making my head dizzy. The failing light in the meadow flashed from a dark, dull grey to the most vivid of dark blues. It was suddenly so dark that I momentarily looked up in surprise.

As his growl rolled on, he slowly returned his eyes to Ethan, looking like a completely different person. I could see it was his face, his skin, his eyes, but above all that was a mask – a mask of something unreal, something even darker than Gabe himself.

Heavy rumbles of thunder rolled in the sky and lightning began to flicker randomly behind the clouds, flashing in every direction but towards the earth.

Gabe's face reflected blues in the white of his ashen skin, the veins more prominent beneath the almost transparent surface. As I looked on, the breaths pounded through me, stronger and harder, as if my lungs would soon explode.

With only fifty feet between us, Ethan looked at Gabe and smiled as he tightened his grip around my neck. Then his smile vanished. He yanked me from the ground so I was almost dangling from his hand and dug his nails hard into my neck. I barely felt the pain; the air rushing in and out of me was so violent it resembled a tornado building inside, desperate to find its way out. The angrier I got, the more it built.

They both stood staring at each other, neither of them making a move, and I glanced over to see Nathaniel's dark silhouette in the distant trees, where he was watching, checking that the deed would be done.

Ethan slowly twisted his head towards me, his teeth bared, and I flinched, knowing he would strike at any second. Gabe glanced back, yet he didn't look worried or scared. It was as if he were gauging something, planning.

A roar spilled out of Ethan's mouth and his head whipped towards my neck. I heard the rips as his teeth penetrated my skin, the tissue giving way like butter penetrated by a hot skewer. Then I felt the heat as his venom started to pump into me. I tried to pull away but he was too strong and I looked back to where Gabe was standing, knowing he could not stop him. I closed my eyes.

Within a second, there was a deafening crack from the sky and a white flash of lightening shone through my eyelids. It seemed so close I shuddered. In that same moment, the teeth that had sunk into me were gone. I opened my eyes wide to see Ethan lying ten feet away on the ground.

The lightning had hit his left shoulder, throwing him aside, but not far enough to halt his attack on me. He stood up, preparing to strike again. Smoke rose through the charred leather covering his shoulder and the acrid smell of burning flesh reached my nose, sticking in my throat. There was still too much distance between them for Gabe to be able to reach him before he attacked me again.

I shuddered and inhaled deeply, my body automatically taking over my actions. I watched him break into another smile and step towards me. As I watched Ethan, I could see Gabe set off towards us out of the corner of my eye, but to me, it was all in slow motion.

Ethan had almost reached me as I forced all my anger out. 'No,' I said, almost silently. I was completely calm. A sudden heat raged through my whole body, bubbling to the surface. An explosion had been triggered off inside, causing a fierce heat that flowed through my skin and out onto the surface.

I looked down and could see a pale blue aura as the heat swirled over my body.

I didn't dare move. I just stood still, watching the flames. I looked towards Ethan just as he reached me. His jaw clenched hard, his face was agitated, and he raised his hand towards my throat to take hold of me again. I flinched, anticipating the pain as he grabbed me, but nothing happened. I watched as his hand pushed into the flames that were now licking around me. He drew away quickly, shaking his hand frantically and patting it onto his coat to extinguish the flames.

The shock on his face as he examined the charred remains of his hand was evident. There was surprise in his black eyes at hitting something impassable, a barrier of fire that even he could not penetrate.

I looked at him, safe in the sudden realisation that he could not breach my defence, and moved forward until my face was almost touching his. He glared at me, raging, his teeth ready, and I did the one thing I would have never expected. I smiled at him so smugly that the one word he spat at me in fury echoed through the wind. 'Bitch!' he roared.

In the few seconds it took for the whole event to take place, Gabe had time to make his approach. As I looked on at Ethan, still smiling at him, Gabe's body struck him hard from my right, knocking them both into the trunk of the lightning tree. My focus lapsed as I saw Gabe strike him, but I knew that I was the weak one, the vulnerable one, so I quickly summoned up my anger again, bringing the heat back to surround me once more. I was desperate to help Gabe, but it was his fight now.

I watched as Gabe pinned Ethan to the tree, their teeth lashing at each other. I saw several rips on Ethan's face from the safety of my protective firewall and my heart started fluttering. I was worried and wanted to go and help Gabe. It took every last inch of effort I had to hold on to this urge, to keep my feet grounded. Every time I panicked watching their fight unfold, the flames started to ebb, leaving my face and shoulders open to attack as the cold air rushed to the exposed parts of my body.

I concentrated and willed the flame back up, lifting it high to cover the whole of me again, and looked back towards them, watching helplessly. Ethan lifted both his legs up to his chest and he struck a blow that forced Gabe away so hard that he flew through the air, crashing to the ground. Ethan gave me a fleeting glance, checking to see if he could approach, and seeing that I was still protected, turned towards Gabe again.

They ran hard at each other and I saw for the first time the long gash running down the side of Gabe's face, from under his left eye to his jaw. They hit each other in mid-air with such force I shuddered and lost my power altogether. But I knew Gabe would not let him go now.

They grabbed and lashed out at each other and I heard a loud crack as Ethan slammed Gabe down to the earth. Gabe span around on one arm, pushing himself clear of Ethan, and pushed back to his feet. He threw his leg high and planted his heavy boot deep into Ethan's face, pushing him back within feet of the tree. As Ethan tried to lift himself up, Gabe threw himself over him, his knee pinning Ethan by his neck.

As much as I knew he deserved to die and I wanted him to die, it was horrific to see such hate and violence unfold before me. With Ethan almost touching the tree, Gabe jumped back off him and whipped his right hand across Ethan's throat, causing a deep red gash to form, blood oozing out of his neck and spilling over onto his body.

With Ethan wounded and gripping his throat as he tried to stand, Gabe leapt high into the lightning tree and snapped off a thick branch before leaping off again, directly above Ethan, and planting the sharp edge of the branch straight into his chest. He pushed and twisted it, his pure strength forcing it through into the earth, as Ethan's body jerked with each turn of the branch. A high-pitched squeal came from his mouth, spilling out into the air. Gabe didn't stop until the twitching ceased.

I started to heave as I witnessed this hideous brutality, bile rising up into my mouth. I tried hard to hold myself together but as the acidic fluid came rising through my throat, I dropped to the ground and threw up violently.

After a few seconds on my hands and knees, I looked up to see Gabe mumbling something in a language I couldn't understand as he looked up to the sky. It began to change back to greys and blacks again. The dark clouds moved so rapidly it was as if they were being fast-forwarded, the last rumbles of thunder moving away.

I turned my head towards the trees and saw the same silhouette standing there, in the same position, watching the gruesome events unfold. Was Nathaniel himself about to spring a second attack on us? I looked on, my eyes filling with tears, my body completely weak, but he just stood, staring.

The sudden and unexpected crack of thunder that followed made me jump and a sharp bolt of lightning struck the ground. When I followed its course, I saw it had hit Ethan's body, setting him instantly alight. The flames shot upwards, burning dark red, as if following the same course back to the sky.

Suddenly, there were two arms wrapped tightly around my waist and I jumped in fear before realising Gabe had taken a hold of me. His face still held the same terrifying blackness; it was a face that petrified me. I screwed my eyes up tight, shutting him out, not wanting to see him like this. But the frightening numbness began to fade when I felt his hand tenderly touch my face.

I opened my eyes, tears flowing down my cheeks, and forced myself to look into the face I still loved. His chocolate eyes were there, his sharp teeth were gone and the blue veins had retreated deep beneath the surface of his skin. I stared at him in shock – there were no words – I just flung my arms around his neck, pulling him tightly into me.

He kissed my hair, my cheek and then wrapped one of his arms around my head, pulling me tightly into his chest.

I pulled my head free, kissing his cheek, his lips, his chin, and turning his face sideways to look at the long scar running down the length of his face, so close to his left eye. I looked into the fading purple wound; the deep gash that Ethan's nail had inflicted, and ran my finger carefully down it, feeling a tingling sensation as I did. Gabe closed his eyes and bowed his head towards me.

He leaned slightly to his side and reached into his back pocket. With my left hand still firmly in his, he raised his right hand and slid a piece of cold metal onto my third finger. Only then did I remember who I was, who I had once been – his wife in another life. I looked down at the thin gold band which fit perfectly on my wedding finger, still overwhelmingly shocked at the realisation of our past.

I could feel the same deep heat emanating from the ring through to my finger, just as I had felt with the pendant. I stood looking at the ring and saw Gabe glance over towards the trees. I followed his gaze and saw the distant shadow nodding towards Gabe before slowly backing off into the trees.

'Will he attack?' I asked, not relishing a new fight with Nathaniel.

Gabe paused, watching him move into the distance, and then turned back to me. 'No. But he will tell the council of the outcome. He will have to, and others will come looking for us.'

In the quiet stillness that followed, we pressed our heads together. But the moment was abruptly interrupted as Gabe's eyes flashed back to the trees. He stood, teeth slightly bared, and my heart shuddered at what he was seeing. Had Nathaniel changed his mind? Had we misread his retreat? I slowly and tentatively looked in the same direction. My eyes caught sight of a shadow moving from the cover of the tree line to the left; it was heading towards the receding shadow of Nathaniel.

'Are there more of them?' I asked, my heart pounding in my chest.

'No,' he said, taking a sidestep, trying to see more clearly.

'Then, what is that?' I asked, just as he placed his finger onto my lips to silence me.

'Stay quiet,' he whispered, crouching low.

I lowered myself to the ground too as I followed his stare, the juddering within me beginning again as my body went into defensive mode. I saw a small dark shape growing larger each time it passed another tree. It was barely a few feet from Nathaniel when I saw him turn to face the shadow before him. He crouched low, preparing to attack or defend, I didn't know which. Whatever it was, it was much bigger than our vampire enemy. And then it made contact, growls and snarls coming from not one but two throats now.

I gasped and grabbed onto Gabe's arm, tucking myself into his side, watching the scene unfold. Gabe placed his arm around my neck, making me feel secure and safe. 'What *is* that?' I whispered.

'We need to go, now,' he said, a sense of urgency to his voice. 'Are you able to run?' he asked, looking at my frail body beside him.

'Yeah, I'll be fine,' I said, lying, but not wanting to hinder him with my weakness.

We set off through the meadow and, at first, pure adrenaline and fear pushed me forward. But I'd only managed to run a few hundred feet before my body slowed and I started to trail behind Gabe. I tried hard to catch up but it was impossible. Gabe dropped back until he was just in front of me, then he slid his hand back and took hold of my arm before he hauled me up onto his back and set off even faster into the trees.

He ran fast but stealthily as I hung on tightly around his neck, more grateful for the ride than he could ever imagine. The wind had dropped completely and the air was still as we ran along the winding track at the edge of the forest. I nervously glanced back over my shoulder into the eerie silence that fell behind us, and the last thing I saw, standing at the edge of the meadow, was a stationary black shadow with two dark, shining eyes watching us as we ran out of sight.

Chapter 18

I held my head low to Gabe's back as he ran, having no idea where we were. After about five minutes, I lifted my head slightly and was relieved to see the twinkling lights of Manzano in the distance. I recognised the scents as we reached the track leading up the hill towards the lodge. My first thoughts as we neared home were of Ember and Ned. I was terrified of finding the lodge empty.

As we reached the yard, Gabe stopped and gently lowered me from his back. I stood, petrified, looking towards the lodge, unable to move forward.

'I couldn't see Ember or Ned,' I burst out. 'When I got home, he was inside and I never saw them.'

Gabe gently took my hand and pulled me towards the lodge, taking slow, cautious steps. When we reached the unlocked door, he pushed it open and gripped onto my hand keeping me close behind him, protected.

We edged our way inside and walked through to the living room. The silence told me all I needed to know. There was no Ember, or Ned. Tears welled in my eyes as I feared the worst.

'Ember!' Gabe called, looking around the room.

'Ember! Ned!' I shouted, my voice breaking as I called their names.

Gabe paused, waiting for one of them to react. They didn't. 'Okay, you go look upstairs, I'll check down here,' he said, releasing his hard grip on my hand.

I shot upstairs, my lack of energy forgotten, and looked around the two rooms. Nothing. I looked under the one place where Ember had never gone, the bed, in case for some reason he'd suddenly decided that it was a good place to hide and wait it out. Still nothing.

I ran back downstairs and looked towards Gabe. He shook his head. 'Let's check outside, in case they got out,' he said, but I knew it was going to be a wasted effort. Regardless of my intuition, we both searched every inch of land on the property, Gabe grasping onto my hand again. We called and called but they were a no-show.

Gabe turned to me, his face grave, his eyes pained. 'Meg, I am so, so sorry, but we need to leave,' he said, anticipating my reaction.

'No, no. I can't leave them behind. I need to know where they are. I won't leave,' I said, shaking my head, tears spilling down my cheeks.

'Meg, I don't know who may come our way, how many or how soon. But I do know that there is something else out there stalking us now and it will continue to do so. I know what we have to do. I know where we have to go. There are answers we need. We have to leave.'

'Leave?' I asked, my voice raising pitch.

'I need to speak with some people, sort some things out, or this will never be over,' he said, stroking the side of my face.

'But what about Ember, and Ned? We can't just leave them. What if they come back, what if they just ran out when he opened the door and they come back to an empty house? I can't leave them, Gabe.'

'We will come back when we have some answers. We'll leave your key hidden somewhere and ask Caitlin to come look for them, or Liv.'

'No, I'll stay. You go, get your answers, and then come back,' I said, going for the solution I wanted. But I knew there was no way he would allow that.

'Meg, if you know anything about me, you know I'm not leaving you here, never in a million years. We'll contact Liv en-route. I know she'll stop by a few times each day and let people at work know they're missing, put posters up. She'll do anything. But you are not staying here,' he said, his voice steadfast.

I knew there was no way, no matter how hard I fought, that Gabe would give in and let me stay. I stood for a minute, listening to my body, my gut instincts. Inside, something told me that they were somehow still alive. As much as I wanted to stay and find them, I also knew Gabe would be true to his word and that Liv would keep looking for them until she, hopefully, found them.

'Okay, but promise me you'll ring Caitlin, in case she hears something, or they get taken into the shelter. And if they're found, make her promise that she'll hold onto them whatever state they're in. You promise me,' I said, looking into his eyes.

'You know I promise you that. You know how I feel about them too. Now, go pack, enough for a few weeks in case it's necessary,' he said, dragging me back towards the lodge. 'I'll take you in your car to Liv's. You tell her that someone broke in and that Ember and Ned are out loose somewhere. Tell her you have an emergency with Anna in Boston, nothing more, give nothing away,' he said, instructing me as we headed into the kitchen.

'Now, get your stuff. I'll get some things from the bunkhouse, then I'll drop you at Liv's. I'll go home, get my things and fetch my car, then I'll come get you and we'll leave right away,' he said, everything planned out in his head.

I grabbed my case from the spare room and loaded it with clothes and a couple of pairs of comfortable boots. I grabbed my backpack and filled it with toiletries, money, my cell charger and photos of the kids. With everything packed in ten minutes, I ran back to the kitchen, looking around for anything I might have missed. I heard the roar from my car a few minutes later and then Gabe was standing in the doorway, waiting to go.

'Ready,' I said, clutching my bags.

Gabe looked around and his eyes were heavy, tortured again. 'Meg, I have caused this and I am so sorry. I never intended—'

I interrupted him mid-sentence, dropping my bags and pressing my fingers to his lips. 'Gabe, this is not your fault. I don't want to hear it. But, believe me, I have a lot of questions and I need answers,' I said, before I moved my fingers away.

He nodded lightly and picked up the bags. I grabbed my keys from the counter and walked back to the door where he waited for me. I looked back around the lodge and took a deep breath. I had no idea when I would be back home and what lie ahead waiting for us. It felt like I'd had two limbs ripped from me, limbs in the form of Ember and Ned. I hid the key and we drove away.

Gabe sped into town, paying no attention to the speed limit. We pulled up onto Liv's drive and as I looked towards the door I saw the curtain twitch revealing the bright light from inside.

I looked back at Gabe and took another deep breath, preparing my lies in my head. 'I'll be back for you in twenty minutes. Be ready,' he said, leaning down and pressing his lips hard on my forehead.

He took hold of my left hand and slid the thin gold band from my third finger. 'Best not encourage any other questions just now,' he said, placing it into the top pocket of my jacket and patting it closed. I looked down at my pocket and took another deep breath.

I swung my purse over my shoulder and got out of the car, turning when I heard Liv open the door. I walked towards her, forcing the best smile I could manage onto my face. I heard the engine roar and looked back over my shoulder to see the tail lights of my car disappearing back onto the main road to Gabe's house.

'Hey, Meg,' Liv said, looking me up and down. 'Oh! Is everything okay?'

'Hey, Liv,' I said, realising why she was looking so shocked. I was covered in dirt and pieces of tree. I'd also forgotten about what was suddenly the main focus of her attention. There was no hiding the deep cuts on my neck as I walked into the porch light. Liv's eyes nearly popped out of her head.

'It's a long story,' I said, walking past her into the house. 'I have to go to Boston,' I said, heading into her living room and feeling her stare following me. 'There's been a bit of a crisis with Anna and I need to go sort some things out.' I looked back at Liv, who said nothing; she just stared in disbelief at the state I was in.

'Sorry about this,' I said, moving my hand up and down my body, highlighting the mess. 'Someone broke into the lodge, and Ember and Ned have gone missing. We've been searching everywhere for them, but there's no sign. Gabe's taking me to Boston. Please, please, can you go to the lodge a couple of times a day, look for the boys, report them as missing at work and with Caitlin?' I asked.

'Sure, Meg. Do you know who broke in?' she asked, her mouth gasping open. She was barely able to speak. 'Have you called the police?'

'We have no idea. Nothing was taken. That I can tell, anyway.'

'Meg, please promise me you've not gotten yourself into something bad? Gabe, I mean, nothing bad because of Gabe?' she asked with sincere concern on her pretty face.

'Oh Liv, don't be silly,' I said, shaking my head and trying to brush off her very accurate reading of the situation as lightly as possible. 'I told you I thought someone was prowling around, right? Well, I think it's the same person. I just don't know who. Anyway,' I said, opening my purse and taking out my favourite photos of the kids, 'take these into work. Please don't lose them. Gabe said you'd be able to copy them and put them up on the board for people to see?'

'Sure, sure,' she said, taking the photos from me. 'No problem.'

'You have both our cell numbers. We should only be a week or so, tops, but call if you get any news about the boys or if you need me for anything. Same with Gabe, okay?'

'Okay,' she said, nodding slowly. But she knew I was hiding the truth from her. I could tell by the look on her face.

'Anyway, Gabe's just gone to grab a few things from his place so put the teakettle on. I'm desperate for coffee,' I said, forcing a smile. 'Is it okay if I go clean up a little?' I asked. I had to get away from her for a few minutes. Being here alone with a normal, human person made me feel like I wanted to spill everything, let it all blurt out. I was so close to breaking point, my mind teetering on the edge. I felt like I was about to explode.

'Go for it. You know where everything is,' she said, heading off into the kitchen.

After a few moments bending over the bathroom sink, hyperventilating, I managed to wash my face and remove some of the debris from my clothes and hair. I borrowed some concealer and started to smear it over my neck. I used half a stick as I pressed it deep into the wounds to fill the gouges. When I returned to the kitchen, Liv was sitting with two large mugs of coffee at the table.

'Better?' she asked, but the concern still showed on her face.

'Much, thanks,' I replied. I told her Anna was having a marital crisis and that there was a problem with Luke and the house. I was such a liar. A bad liar.

I tried to convince her that the frantic searching in the trees for Ember and Ned had caused the wounds to my neck, but I don't think she bought it for a second.

I had only just finished my coffee when I heard the rumble of Gabe's Jeep outside. Liv looked to the door then back to me to satisfy herself that I was actually happy that Gabe was here. I jumped up and walked a little too fast to let him in, relieved I finally had back-up with me. 'I'll get it,' I called, beating her to the door.

I spoke in whispers as we stood in the doorway. 'She suspects something, but I've said nothing except that I have some issues with the ex, and also need to see Anna. She knows what to do about Ember and Ned,' I said to Gabe, noticing that apart from the long deep scratch down his face, he looked perfectly clean and tidy. 'She'll ask about that,' I said, moving my eyes tentatively towards his wound. I told her mine are from searching for the kids in the dark.'

I looked around to see Liv's face peering at us suspiciously. 'You coming back in or what?' she called.

Gabe followed me in. 'Hey, Liv,' he said as he wandered into the kitchen.

Liv's mouth dropped open when she saw Gabe, her eyes wide and focusing instantly onto the very obvious scar. 'What the fuck...' she said, standing and leaning forward towards him.

'It's nothing, Liv, just war wounds from searching for Ember and Ned,' he said, not seeming to care what she believed.

'Oh, okay, whatever. Look you guys. I really don't know what's going on and I don't wanna know either. I just know that branches didn't cause those marks on you two. Shit. Just promise me you are both okay and nothing bad is going on,' she said.

'Liv, please, just look for Ember and Ned, keep searching and let us know if you find them, whatever the situation,' Gabe said. Well, I knew right away what 'whatever the situation' meant – if they were dead or not. 'Everything is fine with us, I promise you,' he continued, and the genuine look on his face must have convinced her somewhat. Her stern expression began to fade.

'Okay. I promise I'll look for them,' she said, nodding.

'Meg, I really think we should get moving, try to get some miles behind us while it's quiet,' Gabe said, taking my hand in his.

'Okay,' I said lifting my purse from the table. We headed to the door with Liv following closely behind. Gabe opened it and I started to tearfully follow him outside. It had gone so wrong. I seemed to be losing everything. I felt strong emotion welling up inside me and had to fight hard to hold myself together.

I turned to Liv. 'Please, Liv, do everything you can to find the boys,' I said, my voice breaking at the last word. 'Keep me updated, okay?'

Liv leaned forward and pulled me into her, wrapping her arms around me so tightly that my tears flowed freely. Gabe released my hand and I returned the hug, holding her tightly back, snuffling into her shoulder. 'Thank you,' I said, my voice muffled in her shirt. 'I'm sorry.'

Liv released her hold and Gabe wrapped his arm tightly around my waist, kissing my cheek. 'It'll be okay,' he whispered.

'Just make sure you both take care, okay, and come back as soon as you can,' Liv said, her own voice breaking. I smiled back at her and turned to walk to the car.

I looked back at Liv as Gabe climbed in and started the engine. As we pulled away, she waved slowly, blew me a kiss and then went back inside, the light from her warm, safe house disappearing with her.

Tears flooded my eyes with the knowledge that I was about to leave my beloved kids behind and that soon I would be hundreds, maybe thousands of miles away from them. Gabe broke the silence. 'I'll just stop and get some cash,' he said swinging out of Liv's road and onto Washington Street, heading towards town. I nodded solemnly, staring out of the window into the dark.

I was still staring into the darkness when he spoke a short time later. 'What's she doing?' he muttered, slowing the Jeep. I looked out of the windshield at the person standing in the middle of the road. My eyes quickly picked up a face I recognised. It was Abigail, waving us down with both hands. As we both focused on her strange behaviour, a shadow moved swiftly from the right, straight into the road beside her.

I instantly recognised the two bright-white eyebrows highlighted in the headlights. 'Ember!' I gasped in complete shock. I opened the door and hit the ground running before Gabe even had the chance to come to a stop. I ran at full speed into the waiting shadows. Immortally fast in the watching eyes of Abigail, but I didn't care.

Ember let out a single howl and then his tail began circling in what passed for a wag as he trotted towards me. For the first time ever, he jumped as he reached me and I caught him in my arms, his weight meaning nothing to me. Tears came flooding out again, tears of joy this time, and Abigail's relieved look told a story of its own.

'I thought I'd missed you guys,' she said, walking breathlessly towards me.

'Abigail...how?' I asked, struggling for words.

'When I told you to leave, I'd already seen what was coming. I knew you would go looking for him,' she said nodding towards Gabe. 'And I knew that very soon the strange man I had visions of would be coming for you at your house. When you set off the wrong way, I drove to your house to wait for you,' she said.

'Oh, Abigail, you really put yourself in danger,' I told her, feeling sick at the thought of what Ethan would have done to a stranger interfering with his plans.

'I couldn't just stay here,' she continued, 'I knew that time was short. I had to try and help.' All the threat and warning went from her face as Gabe walked up beside me. He grabbed hold of Ember and ran his fingers deep into the dense fur on his neck.

'I broke in the back door. I'm so sorry but I didn't know what was happening or how I could help. Then I saw your dog in the room. I had to get him out of there. I knew what that creature would do if he got to him before you or Gabe did. I had to get him out,' she said in a frantic voice, as if she were re-living the horror of events.

I grabbed hold of her in a tight hug. 'Oh Abigail, I don't care if you pulled the whole damn lodge down to save them.' I paused on the word 'them'. 'Ned! Did you get Ned?' I asked, panic returning.

'Ned?' she asked, puzzled. I knew looking at her face she'd not got him.

'My cat, Ned. He was in the lodge too,' I said. She had no idea who I was talking about.

'Oh, honey, I'm so sorry. I didn't see your cat. I didn't even see him in my visions,' she said.

'Well, maybe he got out when you opened the door. Maybe he's in the yard somewhere,' I said, trying to revive my joy of at least having Ember back with me.

'Maybe,' she said, but I knew now her visions had never included Ned. 'I'll keep an eye out for him, sweetie, I promise,' she said, trying to ease the tension on my face. 'Now, you both need to go. You can't stay right now. It's not safe,' she said, her ability allowing her more insight into the situation than we would have believed possible.

I bent to rub Ember, my tension passing to him, which brought him to my side. 'Gabe, can you put Ember in the car?' I asked.

Gabe stood and looked at Abigail, both their faces reserved but calm as they stared at one another. 'Thank you,' he said to her, nodding in gratitude. Abigail just nodded, saying nothing.

Gabe walked to the car and opened the back where Ember jumped in to ensure we didn't leave him behind. I turned to Abigail. 'I'm so sorry I didn't listen, Abigail, but I needed to find him. I have to be with him. He's everything to me.'

'I know. I see that now. But I can't yet see why, knowing what he is,' she said. 'Just be careful. I want you to come home.'

'We'll be fine. We'll be back soon,' I said.

The way Abigail stepped away from me and stared into my face, lingering on it, made me feel odd. 'Just try,' she said, crossing her arms over each other. 'Use your senses, Meg, and...watch carefully.'

I nodded, having no idea what she meant. My energy was ebbing away quickly as I strolled back to the car to climb in. Ember was already hovering between the seats, his head poking through, keeping as close as possible to us. I put my seatbelt on and turned to fuss him. We drove off slowly, past Abigail, who had returned to the sidewalk.

We turned left onto Main Street to head out of town, but before we did so, Gabe pulled up outside the bank to get some cash from the ATM. When we reached the edge of town, he stepped on the gas. I looked around again, watching the lights of Manzano fading away, and felt numb as we rolled past the last few houses on the edge of town. I was really going to miss my new home and longed to be back before we'd even left.

'So, where exactly are we heading?' I asked, turning to face him.

'North Carolina,' he said. 'We'll get some answers there.'

I had no idea what answers we needed or what lie ahead of us. But I trusted him and his reasons. How could I not?

We had a long journey ahead of the three of us, that was for sure.

But it should have been four.

Chapter 19

I returned to staring out of the window into the black nothingness. I had no energy left to ask anything else right now. I was completely exhausted and my mind was shutting down fast, unable to take any more. Gabe called Liv to tell her we'd found Ember, but that we still needed her to look for Ned.

We pulled into a gas station to fill up before we hit the interstate. When Gabe went in to pay, he grabbed a couple of bottles of water and some food for Ember. I filled his dish and sat in the back with him as Gabe filled the tank. Refreshed, Ember lay down quietly, seeming to sense the long road trip ahead of us.

Thankfully, having a driver who didn't need to sleep, we could make good time on the road. As we swung onto Interstate ten, I reclined my seat and slid my body further down, the warm air from the heater softening my cold, worn-out body and moulding me into position. Tiredness took over, making my eyes heavy. I tipped my head sideways on the head rest and looked out of the window, catching sight of lights from houses in the distance.

As I began to tire, the day's memories flashing through my mind, I felt Gabe's hand coming to rest on my thigh. With my temperature running a little warmer than his, and the heater blasting out onto me, his cold hand penetrated the denim on my leg and I felt a cold shiver run through my body.

Sensing I was cold, Gabe moved his hand away, but without looking, and before he could move it far, I grabbed it and put it back in place, wrapping my fingers tightly around his. As lost and messed up as I felt, I needed the contact from him; it made me feel less alone. I needed someone with me who understood, who knew everything, even though in my own head I felt lost, my mind confused.

With the dark shadows and distant lights blending into one indiscernible mass, my eyes gradually shut completely. The last thought I had before I lost consciousness was of Ned and the tears surfaced again, running slowly down my cheeks and onto my chin. I didn't have the energy to wipe them away. I knew I'd lost my boy. My dear, sweet Ned. Somewhere deep inside I knew I wouldn't see him again. He was gone, and I would never know what happened to him.

I was completely unaware of how I went from utter grief to deep sleep, but I was glad I could. The next thing I knew, I started to rouse, hearing a change in the sound of the engine, the speed decreasing as Gabe slowed down. Everything was hazy and unclear. I don't think I actually woke up; I just came around enough to know we were pulling in somewhere that was bright. I flinched and squinted, waiting for my eyes to adapt and accept the change in the light.

I turned my head sleepily towards the windshield and looked down to see that I'd been covered with a long, leather coat. I felt instantly safe encased in his smell, filling my nostrils as I moved around.

I blinked slowly, catching a glimpse of where we were. I saw an illuminated sign offering accommodation, the dotted lights outside the rooms and then the brighter lights of an office. Gabe pulled to a stop and turned off the engine. The silence after the hours of droning seemed odd, uncomfortable. Gabe leaned towards me and stroked the side of my face. 'Back in a minute,' he said quietly, moving away from me as he climbed out of the car.

I watched sleepily as he headed into the office and then glanced back at the clock. It was just after midnight and I had no idea where we were. I twisted my head round to check on Ember, who had the same sleepy interest in his eyes. He was sitting up, looking through the rear window, checking where Gabe had gone.

I turned back and rested my head against the head rest. The engine cracked as it cooled down, making its own sleepy sounds. After a few minutes, I turned back to see Gabe coming out of the office, tucking his wallet into the back pocket of his jeans. A cold chill shot into me as he opened the door and I shivered into his coat.

'Where are we?' I asked as he started the Jeep and slipped it into reverse.

'Yuma,' he said, checking over his shoulder before pulling out and around to the left. We headed around back where Gabe searched for our room number. He pulled up outside number eighteen and switched the engine off.

I unclipped my seatbelt, leaned forward and stretched out my aching back. As I was about to lean back, Gabe held his coat behind me for my arms to slip inside. I slid it on and opened the door to climb out. Ember jumped out eagerly, heading into some small bushes to relieve himself. Gabe grabbed our bags in one hand and I slammed the tailgate shut.

We headed inside where Gabe put the bags down and switched the lamp on. I wandered straight to the bed, sitting wearily on the springy mattress, my legs dangling off the side. My head felt as if it had been separated from my body as I sat half asleep on the edge.

I heard the faucet running in the bathroom, the sound of water falling into metal and then the sound of a tongue lapping in the dish.

I knew I didn't have it in me to go and shower or even brush my teeth. Instead, I opted to make a poor attempt at stripping down to my underwear before sliding the covers back and falling heavily onto the soft sheet underneath. I watched as Gabe sat on the other side of the bed, leaning forward to rest onto his knees. I reached over and placed my hand on the base of his back.

He slid around and leaned in to face me in one fluid movement, and I saw a new look in his eyes. The dark circles under his eyes were more prominent in the dimly lit room and he seemed weaker. 'You need food,' I said, lifting my hand and running my finger along the shadow under his eye. 'You look worn out.'

'I'm not leaving you,' he said, wrapping his fingers around my hand and lowering our hands to the bed.

'Gabe, what use are you in this state?' I asked, shaking my head the more I looked at his gaunt face and dull eyes. 'Please, go. Get what you need. I'll be asleep in minutes so I won't even notice you're gone,' I said, trying to persuade him.

He stayed silent for a while, looking into my face to see if I meant it. What he saw there must have persuaded him. 'We passed a wooded area a few miles back. I'll only be gone an hour at the most,' he said, leaning over me and kissing my forehead. I knew at that moment that he was desperate to feed; he would never have left me otherwise.

'Then please go,' I said, sliding down further under the sheets, trying to encourage him to go immediately.

'Okay,' he agreed. His voice was weary and so deep I could hardly hear it. 'I'll be back soon,' he said, lifting himself from the bed and switching the lamp off which instantly relieved my eyes. I watched as he took off his pale blue shirt and laid it over one of the cases. Within seconds he was back in his earlier, darker clothes of a black fitted T-shirt and black jeans. I had started to notice weeks earlier that he almost always went out to hunt in black, so he could blend into the dark and keep his activities as discreet as possible.

'I'll lock the door and take the key,' he said, moving fast towards the exit. I nodded and watched his dark shadow as he slipped away into the night.

I spent a few minutes thinking about Ned again, before falling deeply into sleep which bordered on total oblivion.

Some part of me must have been aware of them in the room; something made me wake when my body wasn't ready. I opened my eyes quickly and gasped when I saw them both, one sitting in each of the chairs next to the small coffee table at the foot of the bed. I stared at their faces in turn, in total disbelief.

Ethan's face was covered in deep cuts and there was thick blood staining his neck and arms. His skin was smoke-blackened. But his smile was the same – sardonic and evil. His arms dangled loosely over the sides of the chair, his smile widening when he saw the recognition on my face. 'It can't be,' I muttered. 'You're not real.'

I turned to look at the other man, a Native American. He sat only a few feet away from Ethan in the other chair. His expression was a mixture of confusion, worry and disbelief, but there was also kindness.

His thick black hair was tied in a braid and hung over his shoulder, touching the collar of his buckskin jacket, which was decorated in red and dark-brown patterns. The light from the lamp highlighted the dull metal charms hanging from a long, heavy leather thong around his neck.

I slowly pushed myself up against the headboard and waited for something to happen. The Indian's lips twitched at the edges as he looked towards me, as if he were silently mumbling something. He turned his head to face Ethan and started to utter some words I didn't understand, his voice becoming louder and louder.

'Gi-ga dala-nusi,' he said, pointing to Ethan. As he said it, he rubbed his fingers together, and let out a puffing sound through his lips, blowing air towards the vampire sitting next to him.

As he continued to puff air at him, repeating the words, Ethan's smile vanished and he started to writhe about in the chair, his face contorting. I stretched my neck up to see better just as thousands of little dust motes rose, swirling around in the air and racing in circles. They hung in the air for a few seconds before gathering together and racing towards the door, disappearing under the crack at the bottom and into the dark night.

I gulped and looked back at the old man. He was now smiling at me. 'U-was-vee tasi-se-do' he said, nodding in a resigned, understanding way towards me.

The dull light flickering on the charms took my eyes away from his. Their intricate designs captivated me, held my gaze. Then I wondered idly who had turned the lamp on? I felt sleepy again, my breathing becoming deeper and heavier.

When I woke up my breathing was the only audible noise in the silent dark room. I turned my head from the pillow and looked at the empty chairs in front of me. I checked the bedside clock. It was just after 1:30 a.m. Gabe was still out hunting.

I sank back onto the pillow, my eyes wide as I recalled the vivid dream. My mixed-up mind had blended a whole host of weird thoughts together, making its own obscure picture from them all. I heard Ember's paws twitching, scratching the duvet and, as I listened to his quiet whimpers. I fell back to sleep straight away.

It felt like a long time until my sensitive nose caught a metallic scent wafting through the room. Before I had time to process the smell, and with my eyes still closed, I felt the bed indent on the other side.

I came around enough to realise it was Gabe. I felt his naked, cold body press down the length of my own. His arm ran under mine and fell across my chest, coming to rest on my shoulder. The cold ran through me briefly before my body adapted and I pushed myself as deeply as possible into the curve of his body.

It was still dark outside and silent. 'Better?' I asked, my voice raspy and barely audible.

'Much,' he said, taking in a deep breath and exhaling the earthy, metallic scent. It swirled around my face, making my own mouth feel dry and thirsty. I swallowed a few times and he noticed. 'Tomorrow, you must eat something,' he said, re-adjusting his grip around my body, leaving me no chance to move even an inch. 'And I'm not talking McDonalds, either.'

I smiled at his comment but the smile passed as a serious realisation dawned. He knew I needed blood.

The intimate urges stimulated by the closeness of his body subsided and, once again, I fell soundly asleep.

It was just before six when I awoke, the darkness losing its fight against the light and the birds waking to a new day.

I felt alert, fresh and sharp and turned to face Gabe. I studied his face. The dark shadows under his eyes had completely gone. I slid up next to him and rested my head on his chest, wrapping my arms tightly around his neck.

In response, he slid his arm around my waist and gently ran his cold fingers up and down the full length of my back, tracing the long scar there. My breathing intensified and I bit onto my bottom lip. I felt his hair brush down the side of my face and onto my neck as he kissed my shoulder. I ran my fingers roughly through his hair and pushed his head harder into my body. He started to work his way around my neck and then he paused to linger on the front where the scratch marks lay deep into my skin.

I gently pulled his face up to meet mine and smiled, pressing my lips onto his and letting them move and work naturally, in their rightful place. The urges surged in both of us and ten minutes later we both lay entwined around each other. My breath took only seconds to return to normal; Gabe's never changed. No one could ever call this passionate, caring, loving and soulful man a monster.

As I lay thinking about getting up, the usual thoughts passed through my mind, Ned being my main concern. I slid my hand over and grabbed my cell. I had no missed calls or messages so I sent a text to Liv, asking if she'd been to the lodge to look for Ned yet. I sent another one to ask Abigail if she'd been up there or seen anything. I then got up quickly, before I had chance to start feeling miserable again.

As I walked around the bed towards the bathroom, something sharp stuck in the heel of my left foot, causing me to wince slightly and hobble forward to take the weight off. 'Ouch, damn it,' I cussed, sitting on the edge of the bed to examine the injury. I pulled out a sharp piece of metal and saw the gouge in my heel. Had I been fully mortal, the pain would have been excruciating. I looked down at the small piece of metal in my hand in disbelief. It was an amulet, perfectly shaped like a wolf's head and made of pewter or silver, I guessed.

I stood examining the ornament between my fingers, my dream coming back to me. 'What is it?' Gabe asked.

I relayed my dream about the Indian and Ethan to him, telling him everything that had happened and that I'd seen a variety of amulets hanging around the Indian's neck, like the one in my hand now. 'This was one of them, I'm sure,' I said, as he came to my side. He took the charm and examined it, all the time his face showing little more than puzzlement. 'It was on the floor exactly in front of where he sat in my dream,' I said.

Gabe remained quiet but a dark fury covered his brown eyes, turning them almost black. His expression alerted me to the fact that something else was happening, that there was something more to this innocent-looking piece of metal lying in his hand.

'We'll be leaving the minute you're ready,' he said, taking the charm and turning to get dressed. He shoved it deep into his front jeans pocket and looked back at me. 'Come on. Get ready,' he said, a little too sharply.

I took a quick shower, dressed in clean clothes and boots, and returned from the bathroom ready to go.

Gabe had packed some food in preparation before we'd left Manzano but as much as the pastries, fruit and juice filled a smaller, necessary hole, there was a much larger, more needy one growing that I now felt desperate to satisfy. I didn't have time to worry about it now, though. I let him in on nothing as he packed the cases and loaded them into the car. I walked Ember around the lot and into the small brush-lined edges. Gabe's eyes following us constantly wherever we moved, flitting around the bushes.

We were on the road minutes later, speeding towards the interstate on-ramp only a couple of miles away.

I tried to think of a logical way to ask my first question and even though there were ones of more interest to me, I started with the photographs. 'Why were you in the photos in Boston? In the restaurant? At the zoo?' I asked, my voice even, my mind fresh, waiting for the first of many answers. 'I saw you in photos that Anna took,' I added, not that I expected him to lie.

Gabe stayed silent for a moment, his right hand placed loosely on the steering wheel, his left rubbing over his mouth. He looked as if he were trying to work out how best to start.

His voice was as steady as mine as he replied. 'I found you in Boston only a week before I saw you in the restaurant,' he said, looking out the window as he recollected the past.

'I had been searching for you for many years with no success. My tracking abilities are good, but in a land so vast I knew I was in for a long search. I never knew exactly where or when you'd come back and with your scent fading by a tiny amount each day, by the time I found you it was only faintly embedded inside my mind, hanging on by a thread. If I'd lost your scent, the only way I would have found you was by your birthmark, and it would have meant searching the upper left arm of every woman in the U.S. – a difficult task.'

I turned my face to him, amazed and also intrigued by his obsession with finding me.

'I had chosen to work as a veterinary lecturer for only one reason: it enabled me to travel the country often. With each stop I made, I worked during the day and searched for your scent through the night. By chance, I visited an old colleague in Boston to finalise a lecture I was doing with him at the local university and when I walked into his practice, the scent I'd been searching for caught me by surprise, sending me into complete shock. I had to leave immediately. I made a sudden excuse, saying I had an urgent matter to attend to. Then I hid, waiting for you to leave the practice. You walked around the corner and got into your car and I just stared, mesmerised by how you looked.

'It had taken all those years to find you but your scent came flooding back as if it had never faded from my soul, not even in the ninety-eight years since I'd lost you. I followed you home but as I gazed through your window I saw you kiss another man – Luke.'

Up until now, I had no idea what he had gone through to find me: the pain, the sadness, the anger he'd experienced, and I knew then that was why I'd seen the torment in his eyes so often when we first met in Manzano. He had been searching for me for so long, chasing his dream of finding me, yet every day his chances seemed to be slipping away. I couldn't take my eyes off him as he continued to tell me about his search.

'I left that night, telling myself that I no longer had a right to pursue you or to approach you, and that I should leave you in peace, in the life you now had that no longer included me. I hunted fiercely in the days that followed and even took out a number of the criminal fraternity to try and ease my anger, but the pain of letting you go wouldn't go away. I felt broken at the very thought of never seeing you again. So, I told myself that by watching you, happy in your life, might be enough for me to leave you alone, to confirm that I had no place with you. That was how I came to be in the photos in the restaurant. I was watching you with Luke and your friends.

'You all laughed so much, seemed so happy, and I could see the love you held for each other that night and the many nights that followed. I kept tracking you, listening to the conversations you had with others, most of which included him. One day, I followed you to the zoo and saw you interacting with the animals, much as you had when you were Aiyana. You smiled as he draped his arms around your neck, making you laugh and kissing you with as much adoration and love as I once did. When I saw you return his kiss, I felt it. I felt it with all the passion I had all those years ago, only this time, I felt it not in my lips but in the stabbing of my absent heart.'

'Pull over,' I said, tears flowing uncontrollably down my cheeks. 'Gabe, pull over.' My voice was choked from the tears and uncontrollable emotions I felt. He looked at me confused, as if he expected me to get out of the car and run far away from him, overwhelmed by all the strange, surreal events that had recently taken place. About a mile down the road, he pulled off at the next junction and up onto the shoulder, leaning forward against the steering wheel. 'Get out,' I said, opening my door and rushing around to his side of the car.

He climbed out slowly and the force with which I took hold of him pushed him back into the door, slamming it shut. I wrapped my hands over his shoulders and tightly around his neck and pressed my mouth to his as hard as I could. He responded tentatively at first, but then we clung to each other so tightly that I never wanted him to let go of me again.

I looked up into his eyes. 'Gabe, I was once deeply in love with another man, in love with him because, back then, I had no idea you even existed; someone who I could love a million times more. The second I found you, I fell far too deeply in love with you, possibly much more than I did ninety eight-years ago. But, in the end, it was me that found you again, not the other way around. Some twist of fate sent me to the place where *you* were.'

We stood looking at each other for a few minutes, both of us numb, unable to say a word. Gabe's face softened and I saw the torture ebbing from his eyes. He had truly believed that it was all in his hands, that it was his decision alone to search for and find me. Yet I knew inside that it worked both ways. I had been the one to find him in the end. Fate had intervened, and fate had brought us together again.

He stroked the side of my cheek and his lips stretched into a soft smile. In those few words I had exorcised all the terrible demons he had lived with, believing he was the one forcing *me* to change *my* life, feeling like he'd given me no choice but to be with him. He knew now that I had more strength within me, more than he could ever know.

He pulled me tightly to his chest and kissed my hair. We stayed like that for a while until I saw the white eyebrows I loved pressed against the window in an inpatient scowl. 'Erm, I think we'd better move on,' I said, nodding towards Ember's face.

We looked back at each other chuckling. It was disgusting how much I loved him. How much he was in every breath I took. I looked into his mysterious, handsome face for a few more seconds before planting a huge kiss on his lips.

As we climbed back in the car, Gabe grabbed a hold of the dense fur on Ember's neck, teasingly growling at him as he kissed his head. 'Speaking of strength,' he said, as we turned to head back towards the road, 'in the meadow, how did you do that? How did you protect yourself?' It was nice that the questions were not all one-sided.

'Honestly, I have no idea,' I said, thinking back to the furnace encapsulating me. 'I just know I was so angry and so terrified of losing you, I felt so much stronger and determined. It can only have come from that.'

Gabe looked thoughtful for a few minutes and then broke the silence. 'I believe you have a special ability, not only from what you are now but also from who you were all those years ago. It has to do with the basic elements the Cherokee believe in: Earth, wind, rain and fire. And along with the fury of the lightning, you harnessed fire within you and projected it out to protect yourself.'

I pondered his words as I sat and leaned my head against the window, looking out into the far reaching desert and early morning sunshine of Arizona. 'Maybe you're right,' I replied. My eyes felt the usual burn in the dazzling light so I shut them tightly and asked my next question.

'The amulet in the room, someone was in there with me, weren't they?'

'Yes,' he said.

'Who was it? Do you know?' I asked.

'I don't know who it was exactly, but we'll find out when we get to Ravensfork. All I know is that there are many more answers we need, still so much that I don't understand. The charm was of Indian origin, one worn by Cherokee elders. I've seen them before, many years ago, and so have you.'

'Is there some meaning in that charm?' I asked, urging him for more details, even though I wasn't sure how much more he could give me.

'I don't know. Maybe. Wolves feature heavily in their legends and beliefs but so do many other creatures. It was probably just left so that you knew, and I knew, that he'd been inside with you, that he was still on our trail.'

'What happened to Nathaniel in the meadow, has it got something to do with where we're going?' I pressed.

'Whatever we saw, it took Nathaniel's life, and took it easily. It must have been a strong creature to do that. Nathaniel was a member of the council, as I am, or was, and they are highly respected and skilled fighters.' Gabe paused, anticipating my next question, then continued before I had chance to ask.

'Whatever killed Nathaniel was not a vampire. Their kind are known as shape shifters; some call them skin walkers. They are human beings who have the ability to transform, to change into any other living form they choose for whatever purpose they serve. Many choose the form of a wolf or a bear, something ferocious and strong. They live much longer than humans though, normally around three hundred years. Some believe they use powerful elements of witchcraft to enable them to change.

'When Aiyana…when you and I lived in the mountains in North Carolina, I saw them on occasion, changing from the form of an

Indian warrior to that of a beast, which enabled them to hunt, to track and kill their enemy, or to hide and outrun immediate danger. But I haven't seen any in a long, long time and, generally, they are peaceful. They are defenders rather than attackers, unless they're pushed. It seems odd, too much of a coincidence that one should show up, at that exact time, in that place, and kill a vampire, given the links between you and me. That is why we must get answers from the Cherokee. Now more than ever.'

I tried to take it all in. First vampires, then what I now was – a night timer, and now these shape-shifting creatures. Even though Gabe had fed it to me in bite-size chunks, my brain was already saturated, trying to work it all out, trying to make sense of it all. I hated the unknown and feared it even more.

'But, why kill Nathaniel?' I asked.

'I don't know. I suspect it was an act of protection towards you, not towards me, so somehow you are the key in all this. It's all revolving around you now.'

I turned my head towards him the second I heard the word. 'Protection? From who? Or what?'

'Maybe they were protecting you, believing you to be human and anticipating Nathaniel's reaction because I'd killed Ethan. But through every one of their senses, their smell, sight and sound, they would have known, even from that distance, that I was also a vampire, the same as Nathaniel, and that I was with you, a human. That would have puzzled them, I'm sure, and I suspect that is why they are following us now, watching and waiting, not understanding why I haven't killed you, trying to piece together the jigsaw.'

I turned my head back and scanned the desert landscape around us, looking for the slightest movement as if it would show itself to me right then.

'Will they try to kill you?' I asked, concern obvious in my tone.

'They may, yes. They haven't tried yet because they can't quite understand why you choose to be with me, I suspect, why you're not afraid. They surely don't know that you are only part human, but your scent must be new and strange to them and they are learning what they can before they make their decisions.'

I tried and failed to process it all. In mid-thought, I heard the familiar sound of my howling text tone, notifying me of a new message. I hurriedly grabbed my cell and clicked the 'View Message' button.

Wednesday September 2. 11:25 a.m. Sender: Liv
Been to the house, I'm sorry, no sign of Ned. Will keep checking daily and have put notices up. I'll speak to Caitlin as soon as I get the chance. Please be careful, both of you. Liv xx

I flicked the phone shut and shoved it back in my purse. The numb depression started to descend again. It didn't take much to start, not when it came to Ned or Ember. I sighed heavily and Gabe slid his hand over to take mine. I looked out of the window, letting my tear-filled eyes close, until my heavy, slow breathing took over and I dropped off to sleep.

It was strange how much sleep I was getting over the last few days. I normally had between two and four hours, but I slept on and off all morning in the car. Maybe it was my body's reaction to everything that was happening. Maybe my mind was trying to process all the new information while I slept.

I woke again in the late afternoon, with one more question that had suddenly popped into my semi-conscious brain. 'What was my name? My real Cherokee name?'

'Your name was 'U-was-vee tasi-se-do,' he said, fluently and precisely. 'But your English name was Aiyana.'

'What did you just say?' I asked sharply, shooting a glance towards him.

'U-was-vee tasi-se-do.' He looked towards my shocked expression. 'It means lone rabbit,' he said, looking at me, then the road, and back at me again. 'Meg, what is it?'

'That's what the Indian man said in the room last night.' My chest tightened.

'He said your Cherokee name? What else did he say?' Gabe's expression changed, becoming puzzled.

'I don't remember. I can't recall his words. I didn't understand them. I only recognised that one because you said it and I remembered.'

Gabe's eyes narrowed as he turned them back to the road and he stayed silent for a few minutes. 'For him to say that, to say your true name, it means that he knows exactly who you are. And they must know that we are going to them.'

I said nothing more, and neither did Gabe for a long while. When we reached the Texas border, we pulled off the freeway and into a rest stop to take Ember for a walk. I was unable to bring myself to move, so Gabe took him. Minutes later, they were back and we pressed on again, heading towards the next freeway.

As the winding two-lane blacktop meandered through some dense, high trees, the low, late-afternoon sun only managed to shine through now and again, making me feel cold. I zipped my fleece up to my chin and slumped further into my seat, tilting my head on the headrest so I could stare out of the side window again.

I seemed to have permanent creases in my forehead now and had to make a conscious effort to relax the muscles in my face. I felt my body starting to drift off again, my eyes taking the forest view less and less. I let my sleepy but still sharp eyes wander further into the passing trees, seeing through the thick trunks and dense leaves to those much further back.

I suddenly caught sight of something, a dark shadow, moving through the trees. It was almost completely hidden in the depths of the dark forest, running parallel with us, coming into and then out of view. I strained to see it but when it did come into sight I could make it out more clearly. Its head turned every so often in our direction as it moved, as if it were tracking us. Whatever it was, it looked big, even from this far away, and its movement was fluid, effortless. I was sure it was a wolf since it was too fast and agile to be a bear.

Gabe must have seen my body stiffen and my face press closer to the window. 'What is it?' he asked.

'I don't know,' I whispered, trying to keep my eyes focused on the animal as it moved through the trees, 'but it keeps glancing over towards the road at us. I think it's a wolf.'

Gabe ducked his head lower to see past me through the window. 'We need to go faster,' he said, dropping down a gear and pushing his foot flat to the floor.

The sudden increase in speed pushed me back into the seat. Gabe weaved in and out of the cars in front of us, encouraging the odd honk and finger gesture as we passed by. Thankfully, Gabe's erratic, aggressive style of driving never bothered me and I always felt comfortable in his care, mobile or not.

The exit for the interstate was coming up and Gabe kept up the speed as we hit the on-ramp, taking the bend on almost two wheels. Within a couple of miles of getting onto the interstate, I saw a sign for Fort Worth and Dallas; we had just over two hundred miles to go until our next stop. I glanced back towards the disappearing trees as they gave way to more populated suburbs and relaxed a little knowing we could pull away and lose whatever it was that followed us.

We drove at a steadier pace to the north of Odessa and into the suburbs of a small, rural town. I knew Gabe had already spotted the woodland we passed a few miles from the hotel, as I had.

Gabe checked us in at a small motel and we pulled round to our room at the side. As he carried our bags in, I took Ember onto the borders of the parking lot, making sure I stayed in sight of the room, as instructed.

With Ember relieved after his walk around the motel grounds, I took him inside the country-style room, where he drank a full bowl of fresh water before lying down to cool off.

Gabe switched on the air conditioning and the cool breeze slowly wafted its way through the room. I grabbed a handful of toiletries and headed for the shower to wash away the silt and grime from the long day of travelling.

With the shower running, I undressed and stood in front of the mirror. I looked at myself, intrigued, searching for any hint of my ancestry that had carried through to the body I had now. The dark-brown eyes and black hair of my past self had been replaced in this life with dark-green eyes and chocolate-brown hair. My frame was not small this time, petite and feminine as Aiyana's was, but taller, athletic and boy-like.

My skin was a pale, creamy white and so bore no resemblance to the olive tones of Aiyana's skin. The only thing that seemed to have passed onto me ninety-eight years later was my birthmark, my unique birthmark – the one we both carried.

Then I examined the fading nail marks in my neck left by Ethan. The wounds were healing well but, as they did, they were leaving behind almost pure white lines, which were pretty obvious even with my pale skin tone. I twisted my neck from side to side to see them properly. I couldn't even hope that they would blend in to look like creases in my neck since they were the wrong shape.

I stepped into the shower and let the water run down my hair and face, and all the way down to my feet, washing the sticky grime away with it.

With my body covered in foam, I closed my eyes and leaned forward onto the tiled wall, locking my arm to hold me there and letting the water soothe my tired body. I opened my eyes and wiped the water from my face when, through the shower curtain, I saw a shadow on the other side moving slowly towards me.

I watched the shadow approach until it stopped a couple of feet away from the curtain. Then I heard the heavy thuds as his clothes hit the floor. The many human inhibitions I'd had in the past had all but gone now, and I felt much more confident with Gabe.

He slid the curtain back, appraising me. I was raised higher in the bathtub and our eyes were almost on the same level now. I reached out and slid my wet hand into his hair, running it down the length of his face to his chin. 'Hmmm,' he muttered, moving his eyes upwards to mine.

He climbed into the tub, forcing me to move backwards, towering over me. I liked that he did. In this strange new world I now lived in, with these supernatural events happening, I felt guilty about what I was now thinking. Did it make me completely unnatural, a freak, that all I wanted to do was be with Gabe, in spite of all the disasters happening in my life?

Before I could think any more about it, Gabe changed his slow, caressing and tender pace and grabbed my face with both hands, gripping me in place as he leaned in to kiss me. I lifted my hands and ran them down his cold, wet arms, feeling the dense mass of rock-like muscle beneath my fingers. Before I knew it, the air was pushed out of my lungs as I was pinned against the wall. I swiftly and effortlessly pulled up my legs and wrapped them around his waist, his tight grip on my wet skin held me firmly in place. The water flowed over us, spilling around our faces, the heat of it biting against the cold of our skin.

A broken soap holder and a shower curtain with fewer rings later, we were pressed against each other – me catching my breath and quivering, Gabe standing with his forehead pressed against mine as he tenderly moved to kiss my nose, my cheek, my jaw. I recovered quickly, taking us right back to the present. 'I'm so hungry,' I said, looking into his eyes so he couldn't mistake what I craved. I felt disgusted with myself for having an unnatural desire to drink from one of the things I loved most in this world, an animal.

'We'll go out after dark, take the Jeep and park up in the woodland. I'll get something for you,' he said in an easy voice, trying to calm me. *He'd* try to get me some food. That meant *I* would not have to do it. That sounded good to me. I took a deep breath, relief spilling into my eyes. At least I wouldn't have to do the killing.

We both dried off and dressed appropriately for our next task – dinner. I gave Ember some food, which he ate in seconds, and we lay on the bed, the air conditioning drying our hair as it circulated.

We mindlessly watched the limited TV channels we had to pass the time. The light faded quickly with the orange tones of the long, hot day blending to blues and greys, finally settling on the grey-blacks which would remain for many hours ahead of us.

I waited nervously for the right time to come. 'What do I do?' I asked, keeping my eyes on the TV.

'Don't worry,' he said, stroking the hair away from my face, which was buried deep into his chest. 'You just need to shadow me as best you can and I'll catch us something.'

'But, what will you catch? I really, *really* don't want to drink the blood of an animal – I think I'd rather have some horrible, bad person than a cute, innocent deer or whatever,' I said, frowning at the idea of it.

'Okay, here's the thing,' he said, 'there are millions of deer in the U.S. You will only be taking one or two of them, using them for your needs only, not killing them for sport or cruelly killing them for fun. It's for sustenance. You eat beef, right? And chicken?' he said, trying to help me become rational about it. I nodded slowly. 'They give their life for you. It is no different this way.' He was right, of course. The only difference was that I ate meat which did not remotely resemble a creature, but the deer, wild cat or bear would look cute and real. Mind you, 'cute' didn't really cut it anymore with bears.

'Well, yeah, but my meat is never *that* fresh off the bone,' I said, grimacing.

Gabe gave out a low, muffled laugh, trying hard not to offend me or trivialise my concerns. 'Look, Meg. When I became what I am, when I had the need, which was every two or three days, I killed people and, fair enough, the people I chose, that I still choose now, are the less desirable types that I would travel many miles to find, people who I knew about, had information on – targets, if you like—'

'Targets?' I interrupted. 'What, like you're a vampire hit man with lists?' I asked, my voice high-pitched.

He pressed his finger gently against my lips to silence me. 'The council and other local vampires acquire information about certain individuals, people who this world would be far better off without. That way, we feed, rid the world of creatures worse than ourselves and the rest of the time we live off animals or donors,' he said, talking so blandly and openly about it, I cringed.

I thought about what he said for a few minutes until I had processed it enough to ask more. 'So, if I take what I need, say, we share dinner tonight, how often will I need to do this?'

Gabe pulled me even tighter into him. 'Until I can establish your exact needs, I don't know, but *I* need to hunt or drink every few days and as you are only half of what I am I suspect only a couple of times, maybe three, on the whole trip. We'll buy some fresh meat: kidneys and such, to help you out when we can,' he said. He was such a sweet, thoughtful vampire.

I felt a little relieved that I would probably only have to go through this a few times and then never again, if I had any say about it. But, I still had the first hunt to get through. And it was just about time to begin.

We headed out in the Jeep, as any couple would who were going out for an evening meal, only our restaurant had a natural, woody feel to it. We pulled into a parking lot next to the woodland but saw a car parked with two silhouettes entwined inside. We both snickered and drove on.

Gabe drove us around the perimeter of the woodland until we saw a small locked gate, which led down a track. He pulled in front of it and cut the headlights. I sat looking into the darkness, my eyes adapting quickly and easily to the surroundings. Even though I was much stronger than before, and sitting alongside a vampire who was much tougher than anything we would meet in the woods, I still held some human remnants of fear of the dark. Gabe got out to encourage me to follow him, which I did, albeit a little unwillingly.

We walked to the gate and looked down the long track ahead of us. Gabe cocked his head, listening and looking for signs of anyone else around. 'Come on,' he said. He hopped over the gate and I reluctantly followed behind, watching him as he instinctively dropped lower, his body preparing to track something from the slightest scent. I stayed as I was and rolled my eyes, absolutely dreading having to chase dinner.

After a few minutes of moving swiftly and silently down the track, his head shot around to the left, and towards a dense thicket of trees. He stopped and turned his head again, inhaling deeply. 'Follow the best you can. If you lose me, search for my scent. You'll find me,' he whispered. I was so pleased he hadn't looked around or he would have seen exactly how wide and petrified my eyes were.

Gabe set off before I could even utter a word, darting through the trees, weaving around and over obstacles easily until he was out of sight. I took a deep breath and clenched my jaw hard. I heard crunching all around me now that I was alone. Small animals were scampering out of our path and insects crawled through the undergrowth, all of which were easy for me to hear. I squirmed and, believing it was better to follow Gabe, I darted after him. The more I ran, the more my instincts took over and, along with what Gabe had taught me, it all fell into place. I subconsciously started to lower my body, without missing an agile, silent step, and even as I threw myself over fallen trees and raised roots, my feet landed almost silently.

Gabe must have been well ahead now. I inhaled deeply and tried to identify all the scents around me. At first, I recognised nothing – just wood and heat – but then the faintest of smells filtered through my nostrils. I had no idea what it was but my body turned quickly to the right and latched onto the scent. Every twenty or so steps I inhaled, and adjusted my course accordingly.

I ran faster, the smell filling my nose, and then caught another scent, a familiar one, blending in with the new one. My body felt like a torpedo locking onto a target. I felt the slow, juddering vibrations building inside me again, increasing quickly until they filled my whole body. I closed my eyes, letting my other senses do the work. When I opened them again, it was as if I were looking through night-vision goggles without colour, the blackness of the night around me now seeming more like dusk.

I could see every tree and every small mammal darting for cover. It was as if a haze had been lifted from my eyes and a flashlight switched on, enabling me to see everything much more clearly. My body twisted and turned as I hunted down my prey and the once cute, fluffy animal I was dreading catching had suddenly become my primary target – whatever it was. I felt a wave of guilt and shock wash over me as I realised that I had more immortal instincts inside me than I'd believed.

The smell was strong now and it felt hot in my nostrils, suffusing every part of me. I was closing in fast. I'd almost caught up with the hapless creature I was hunting. I swerved sharply to the left, turning my head to catch sight of a large mule deer darting through the trees about thirty yards in front of me. I bent lower and switched up a gear, racing so quickly that the branches of the trees around me lashed at my face. I had no idea where Gabe was. If he was tracking something else, or assisting and watching me, I actually didn't care; I was totally focused on my own target.

The deer ducked and dived, trying to outrun me, but I stayed my course, twisting and turning to follow its route. I was far more agile and much faster than the animal in this environment. As I closed the distance between us, thirty feet, then twenty, I launched myself into the air, forcing myself forward and staying low. With a level of accuracy I could not have imagined, I landed on top of the deer, forcing it to the ground. I heard the snap of one of its legs as it buckled beneath my weight.

The deer was dead almost as soon as I pierced the skin and hit the jugular. It fell limp and had no chance to even struggle. This was something I was glad about, or would be later, and even though I had a need to do this, I was not making the poor creature suffer. I had been fast and accurate – it was all over.

I wasted no time in doing what I needed to, sinking my teeth deeper into its neck. My instincts had taken over now, telling me where to aim. It felt very odd but also very pleasant, a relief. The blood was warm, satisfying, and as I sucked the fluid through my teeth I felt its heat coursing through me, rushing through my veins until my entire body was filled with the warming sensation.

I felt an instant relief. I lifted my head up from the limp body beneath me, wiping the drops of blood from the sides of my mouth with the back of my hand, and looked right into Gabe's face. He was leaning back against the tree in front of me with his arms folded across his chest.

I stared at him, feeling a little embarrassed. All the spiel I'd given him about not being able to kill a living thing seemed like a load of crap now. But it had been true, only now I knew that my instincts and hunger were far stronger than my love of all things furry. Still, as good as I felt, the guilt started to return as I looked back down at the lifeless corpse below me. 'What have I done?' I mumbled, staring down at the creature drained of blood.

Gabe walked over and knelt down beside me, placing his arm reassuringly on my shoulder. 'You did what you needed to, that's all. You wasted no time, made it quick, and now it's all over.' I looked across at him scowling. 'Come on. Let's get back,' he said, sliding his arm beneath my elbow and lifting me to my feet. 'Follow me,' he said, releasing his grip and heading off into the trees.

I looked back at the deer lying in the earth. 'I'm so sorry,' I whispered, and I bent to stroke its head before turning to chase after Gabe.

Chapter 20

Back at the motel and in the light of the room I could see the evidence of what I had done. Remnants of dried blood smeared my face, a spattering of scarlet on my vest, and the brown and green staining of the woodland on my jeans. Nice. It would be quite interesting to explain *this* to someone. 'Yuk,' I muttered to myself, 'I need another shower.'

I headed into the bathroom and stripped down repulsed as I peeled the blood-soiled clothing away. Ten minutes later and lots of scrubbing saw me back to my clean self. I dried off and looked into the mirror, instantly noticing the brightness of my eyes. They were still my eyes, still dark green, but they sparkled as if a light behind the lens was shining through.

I'd fed, yes, on the blood I'd needed but why then did I not feel very strong? I'd felt an instant relief as I drank the deer dry but, apart from that, I'd felt no different then or now. I'd even eaten normal food earlier in the day.

'Has Ember been out?' I asked when I got back into the main room.

'Yes, he's all done,' Gabe replied.

'Thanks,' I muttered and climbed on the bed, looking blankly towards the TV.

I lay thinking about my first hunt and why I felt no different. Maybe blood was no different than any other food to me, maybe anything I ate would have the same effect. Maybe it was psychological: I thought I needed blood because of what I now was – half human, half vampire.

Gabe lay on his side and leaned on his elbow facing me. 'You won't feel much of a change right now, I think,' he said, obviously sensing my worries as he always seemed able to do. 'For me it's quite instant because I'm pure vampire. For you, being half human, I believe it will be more gradual, that it will make you feel stronger as a whole,' he said, stroking the back of his hand tenderly down my cheek.

I thought about what he'd said for a few minutes. 'I just hope I haven't killed that poor animal for no reason. I hope it was worth it,' I said.

'I'm sure in time you'll feel better. Now, get some rest. We have a long day tomorrow,' he said, sliding down into the bed and pulling me with him so I lie nestled into his chest.

I was thankful for one thing; I did actually feel tired. Surely proof that the blood had been of no benefit. I lie mindlessly watching an old Clint Eastwood movie on TCM, Gabe as still as a rock beside me. I didn't even have the rhythmic beat of his heart to comfort me, only the constant, steady breaths he took, which did relax me a little.

I ran through the scene of hunting the deer again and again, and kept lingering on the crack of its limb as I'd landed on it from above. It was a reasonably big deer, and it would enjoy no more life because of me. The cracking of bone rang through my head again and again. I felt like shit.

The next thing I knew, I woke up lying on my side, facing the curtained window in the motel room. My eyes flashed wide open and I looked at the clock. I'd slept over six hours. The bright Texas sun was pushing its way around the edges of the curtain, and I knew right away we had a long, sweltering day ahead of us.

I twisted over to see the other side of the bed empty. I sat up, looking around the floor for Ember. They were both gone. I jumped out of bed and pulled back the curtains, squinting again at the bright light, to see that the Jeep had gone, too. They must be on a walk. Travelling all day was no fun for Ember but at least he was with me. That reminded me...Ned.

It was only 6:20 a.m., so I dressed quickly in the cleanest clothes I had remaining and packed my things, ready to go. I grabbed my cell and switched it on, then gathered the toiletries from the bathroom while I waited for the phone to find a signal and relay any messages I had. After a couple of minutes, the familiar howl told me there was one.

I ran into the bedroom and grabbed my cell, hoping for some good news about Ned.

Thursday September 3. 7:36 p.m. Sender: Liv
Been to the house again, put food and water down, no sign of him. I'll try twice a day until you're home. I'm sure he'll show up. Liv xx

I shut the phone feeling anxious and upset again, thoughts of Ned flooding back to haunt me. But as I hurriedly gathered our remaining things together, I noticed I was feeling stronger today and more energetic. I was raring to go, to get to Ravensfork as fast as we could. The sooner we got there and did whatever it was we needed to do, the sooner we'd be home.

Just as I was packing the last few things, I heard the Jeep pull up outside. Gabe walked through the door and looked at me a little surprised.

'Oh, you're up…and ready,' he said, taking in the packed cases at the bottom of the bed.

'Yep, the sooner we get going, the sooner we'll get there,' I said, fussing Ember as he came puffing and panting towards me. 'Good walk?' I asked.

'Yeah, we headed to the woods. There was nobody there so he had great fun chasing and trying to find me. I think he's pissed I can outrun him,' Gabe said, patting Ember's back and smiling.

I grinned at the thought of Ember searching for him, and felt pleased at how Gabe had relaxed in our company. So much so that I saw a young boy in him at times, taking great pleasure in everyday things like fussing the dog. To me, he was human; I saw him as only that and not as a monster. Just another being and one I loved very much.

What I also found strange was how I had never once flinched when I'd discovered he was a vampire. Inside, I had known for a long time he was different and so when it was confirmed to me, I felt more relief than anything. I was pleased the secret was out. We were soulmates and maybe because of our shared past, however distant, I had no fear of him. I knew that he would never harm a hair on my head.

With the heat building, we loaded the cases into the Jeep and Ember jumped in the back, settling down ready for the next leg of our trip. As we headed back towards Odessa and onto the interstate, the air conditioning was a blessing for Ember and for me.

I had my eyes carefully shaded under my sunglasses to avoid the bright, burning sun; Gabe even had his eyes covered. As I searched around, looking for any sign of our tracker, I noticed Gabe doing the exact same thing. Neither of us saw anything. I felt so alert, so sharp, as Gabe had said I would. And I felt some relief that the life I'd taken had not been in vain.

The day's drive went fast and soon the sun began to disappear. Apart from Ember's short toilet breaks, and a stop for some food and water, we rolled on, covering as much ground as we could. 'Why don't we drive through the night?' I said to Gabe as the roads cleared of more and more cars the later it became.

'Are you sure? What about your sleep?' Gabe asked.

'I slept so much last night, I feel really awake. Besides, Ember is sleeping well in the back and if I need to doze, I will,' I replied, looking over towards him. 'Are you okay to drive through?' I asked, worrying about my non-sleeper.

Gabe looked back at me and smiled wryly. 'I think I can manage it,' he grinned. Of course he could.

So, that was that. We were making good time and instead of stopping at Mt Pleasant as we'd planned, we carried on through. In the quiet darkness of the night we travelled ever faster, always going over a hundred, and only slowing in built-up areas.

We chatted on and off and each time I received an answer to one of my questions, I spent time processing each piece of information in my head, assembling the bigger picture of my past.

Gabe relayed the story in depth about how my people had believed that he had turned Aiyana into something inhumane, something evil, and I felt sad for Gabe that they had assumed so much, knowing him as well as they obviously did. How could they think him capable of doing something like that to someone he loved so much, especially as they had a young son? He had shown nothing but respect for their beliefs and for the people themselves. I knew that much, so how could they think of him in such an evil way…

'So, how did I come to be me, in this body?' I asked. 'How does that work?'

'The Cherokee believe that you don't actually die. You just move on. Your spirit transfers into the body of another. They believe that it travels through the ether, searching, until it finds the place it should be, a being that fits the soul's purpose, has a future mapped out that fits it best. Although it can take a long time to find.'

I took in what he was saying, wondering. 'So, if I died in 1912, is it like my spirit searched and found me as an adult or before I was born or when?' I asked, not understanding at all how it worked. It was so hard to believe.

Gabe was thoughtful for a while. 'Well, I know you're Aiyana. Your birthmark, your scent, your memories and dreams tell me so. And maybe, I'm not positive, but I believe your spirit searched for someone who fit the criteria, someone who was likely to be reunited with me someday. Do you ever remember yourself feeling different, changing almost?'

I thought long and hard but I couldn't remember anything like what he had mentioned, no obvious change, nothing unusual. 'No,' I replied.

And then I asked about our son. Which one of us did he resemble? What he was like? I worked out he would be ninety-nine years old now, if he were still alive, and I felt the sadness that any parent must feel when a child has died before them. I didn't feel the emotional or the maternal instincts of a parent, just a sense of loss that I was once a mother and had a child who grew up without knowing me, believing his father to be something he wasn't and hating him for it.

'He looked very much like you,' Gabe said, recalling him as if he was sitting alongside us in the car. 'He had more Indian than white in him. Big, brown eyes, jet-black hair, but he had my smile and my temper.'

I smiled at the thought, trying desperately to picture his face, and only remembering what I had seen in those few faded photographs.

'He adored animals and would often rough it with the wolf cubs and orphans you helped. You were forever telling him to come inside, that the animals would be there in the morning. But you could never chastise him properly; his impish grin always got him off the hook.' I could see the love in Gabe's face as he talked about our son and how much he'd missed the life he should have had with him. I leaned over and cuddled into his side as he drove, desperate to be close to him, to be together as we both went through our past.

Then, I dropped off to sleep.

I woke as soon as the memory showed itself. 'I remember when,' I said, looking towards Gabe in the darkness and seeing only a dull sparkle in his eyes as he stared back.

'You remember what?' he asked, puzzled as to which of our recent conversations I was referring to.

'When something changed,' I said, panic edging in my voice. 'When I started feeling different. When the dreams and nightmares started. It was when I was seven, just after I'd lost my grandpa. I remember having the same frightening dreams all the way back then, only as a child I didn't understand them. Not like I do now; now the picture is a whole lot clearer. I remember waking from a dream late one night. I felt calm and happy but as if I'd been woken for a reason.

'I remember creeping out of bed and going to sit on the cushion on my window sill, a place where I often sat looking out into the world, lost in my imagination. We lived in Portland then. I remember it was raining and I opened my window when I saw something moving in the distance among the trees. I felt shivers spreading down my back as

I sat in my pyjamas. I could feel the cold breeze, the spots of rain hitting my face and arms…' I paused, trying to recall all the feelings I had back then, twenty-one years ago.

'I saw some eyes watching me, not moving but just staring up at me. Even though I was scared of the dark, I leaned further out of my window trying to see what it was. But the eyes started to back off, and the wind picked up suddenly and whipped around me, unbalancing me. I tumbled out of my window, which was thankfully on the ground floor, and hit the earth hard. I was there, all night, until my parents found me asleep outside in the morning with not a mark or injury on me.' I shook my head as I vividly recalled everything that had happened.

'I was taken to the hospital as a precaution by my over-protective mom, but they found nothing wrong. My parents were worried because in the weeks that followed, I spoke very little. But I felt fine. I kept telling them that. After awhile, they stopped asking if I was okay. To them, I looked the same and behaved almost the same, except I was quieter, more of a loner. My mom once said to me, "You're a special little girl, Megan, lost in your own make-believe world, happy to be all alone." What would she think of me now,' I wondered. Special, no, but unique, yes.

Gabe nodded to himself, taking it all in. 'That could've been when the spirit found you,' he said. 'You were quite a loner as Aiyana too. That's why they named you lone rabbit.'

We travelled on in silence, eventually crossing the border into Arkansas many hours later, and then started the long haul towards Tennessee. By the time I woke again, we had been driving for almost twenty-nine hours straight, give or take the stops for gas and to let Ember relieve himself. But, unlike me, Gabe looked as fresh as when we'd started our journey.

I stretched out, easing my aching back and groaning in satisfaction as my spine found relief in being moved into another position. I pulled the handle to put the seat back up from the recline position and turned to Gabe.

'The paintings in your house, the same artist painted the ones in the bunkhouse. When I first moved in, there was only one person in the painting with the dog, but later there were two people. Do you know anything about that?' I asked, knowing inside that he did.

After another pause, he began to fill in the gaps. 'I knew I'd picked up on your scent in my house! I painted all those pictures. In your bunkhouse, I wanted to show you, to jog your memory, to see if by planting the faintest seeds from your previous life, it would help you remember. I couldn't just come and tell you and, back then, I was undecided. I was fighting very hard to stick to the rules, to keep my distance from you. I added the second person because I wanted it to be myself walking with you around that lake, with Ember. I was desperate for some recognition of your past to start coming back to you because, if it had, then I would have had my excuse to get closer to you.' Gabe paused for a few seconds.

'The signature?' As far as I could make out, it did not say Gabe Letenierre.

'That is my signature but it's in an old French script that's been used for hundreds of years; it's one I learned when I studied law. It also gave me anonymity. I couldn't make it easy for you to put the pieces together. That would have meant I was giving you too much help when you needed to use your own free will.'

I paused again, thinking back and trying to visualise all four paintings in my head. I couldn't manage it; my mind was cluttered with too much junk.

'And you came into the lodge, several times, wandered around my land. Why did you do that, were you just watching me?' I asked.

'Apart from borrowing your keys, I never came into the house again.' Gabe turned to me: 'I only came in once. When had someone else been in?' he asked, and I realised then that he was not the only person who had been prowling around.

I searched back through my memories. 'Ember acted strange one night, rolling about on his back and being submissive, but I couldn't see anyone in the lodge. And, again, the morning Anna left to go home

I saw a shadow outside the bathroom door, but when I searched I didn't see anyone other than the kids and me.'

I thought a bit harder, and managed to recall more events. 'When I looked out of the window late one night, I saw a shadow in the trees with the wind swirling around it. I ran out, shouting towards it, but saw nothing out there.'

Gabe was thoughtful for a long time while I looked at him in scared disbelief. 'So, if it wasn't you, then who the hell was it?'

'I don't know. All I can think of is that maybe the shifters were watching you long before I knew they were. The more you ask, the more questions I have, too. For some reason the Cherokee were watching you long before I came on the scene. They were maybe preparing to intervene if we became close, protecting you. But I don't understand their reasons why.'

So, it seemed that every question I asked not only led me onto more questions but also twisted the plot for Gabe, too. My brain was starting to shut down again.

The next question was a much harder one to ask. I knew the answer, of course I did, but I still needed to ask, to have it confirmed by his own mouth.

'Did you kill the men in Antala?' There, it was out and there was no going back.

He responded quickly, as if he had been waiting for me to ask him for a long time. 'Yes, I killed two of them and badly maimed the other one,' he said, with not a whiff of remorse in his voice.

I gulped. What did I say to that? But I didn't have to say anything; he continued on without any prompting.

'Do you remember what I told you about how my kind receives information, facts that help us decide whom we rid this world of?'

'Yes.'

'Well, we needed to rid the world of two of those men. I found out that you and Liv were not the first women they attacked. The main aggressor, Taylor, attacked again afterwards but this time it was a much more physical and intimate attack. She was a nineteen-year-old student and he raped and assaulted her badly. He acted alone with her but he and another of the men had already attacked two girls before. They would continue to do so unless they were stopped. I'm not ashamed that I ended their lives, and I would anticipate the other man will consider his future actions much more carefully from now on.'

I understood now exactly why he had killed them. My assault had obviously been the catalyst that had thrown him into a rage but it was their sick acts which, in the end, had been the reason for their demise. Gabe was acting purely as an immortal vigilante, ridding the world of the bad.

We planned to stop in a few hours, have some real rest and go and get some 'human' food this time. My body felt the need for it now. Gabe put the radio onto a station playing some melodic country music. It was relaxing and I took hold of his hand while I looked out into the fading afternoon, partly searching for any signs that we were being followed again.

We stopped off at an inconsequential small town and pulled into a quiet-looking motel. Gabe took Ember for a long stroll while I text Liv and showered. The office clerk, a very hospitable southern woman, had given us directions for a good local restaurant so we headed out, leaving Ember to relax in the room.

My head ached from a combination of being overloaded with information, stress and worry about Ned, and the unknown that we were heading into. I couldn't put my finger on it but I felt uneasy about the fact that we would soon be in the place where I'd lived all those years ago and our detective work, whatever that was, would need to begin. I wasn't even sure about the answers we, or rather Gabe, was seeking.

My nagging head soon relaxed in the quiet of the restaurant. Once I'd eaten a much-needed meal and had a couple of drinks, I felt better. Gabe ate too, and I found it ironic knowing that he would have no benefit from the twenty dollar meal he was putting away.

I fell asleep almost instantly that night. The comfort of the soft bed, the cool sheets and the even cooler arms tightly wrapped around me all helped me relax until I dropped off.

But even in my deep sleep, I could feel my body vibrating, telling me something. I was standing in the middle of a clearing, surrounded by trees, and I was slowly rotating. On each turn I made I saw another picture. The first scene showed Gabe talking to a couple of Native Americans. They chatted, standing close together, and there was no animosity, no hatred in their faces.

On the second rotation I saw our old house, the house I had lived in as Aiyana, with Gabe and our son. I saw inside the house, the three small, basic rooms. When I turned again, I tried to keep my head in the same position, not wanting to lose sight of the place that was ours, simple but peaceful. But when I lost sight of it and let my head face forward again, I saw Ned walking slowly into the trees. His eyes were so green and wide. His tail swished from side to side as he stared back at me and I felt the tears fall. 'Ned, please stay with me! Ned!' I shouted. But he turned and walked off into the trees, his eyes darting about, watching all the invisible things he saw floating in the air.

I made another full circle and twisted my head around to see if Ned was still there, but I was suddenly faced with the Indian who had been in our room. Even with age, he had a beautiful face. His long, black hair hung around his shoulders and, as I watched, the lines on his face decreased, became finer. But he was scowling at me, disbelief on his face. He shook his head slowly.

'Argh!' I shouted, jolting myself out of the dream. My breathing was rapid and my heart was banging in my chest. Gabe's arms came from nowhere and wrapped around me, drawing me into him. It took a few minutes to calm myself down.

'What is it?' his quiet, deep voice asked in the darkness.

'Another dream. There were Indians, and our old house in the woods, and you were talking to some strange men. And Ned was there but he just kept walking away. He wouldn't come back to me.'

I felt his hand move over me as he started to stroke my hair. 'The dreams will stop soon,' he said. 'When we know more, they'll start to fade.'

'Something doesn't feel right, Gabe,' I said, out of the blue. 'I don't know what it is but I'm scared of where we're going, what we're going to find out.'

He kept stroking my hair but said nothing to ease my worries. That worried me even more.

I knew then that he was apprehensive about where we were going too.

Chapter 21

The trip today seemed shorter. We got through Tennessee and into Gatlinburg by nightfall, and it only felt as though we had been driving for a few hours, so lost in thought as I was. Time just seemed to pass more quickly.

We holed up in a larger motel in the bustling tourist town and dropped in at the local store for some food for myself and Ember. Gabe picked up a map of the Smokey Mountains and we headed back to our room for a quiet night. I knew we had to talk about where we would be going tomorrow.

I picked at some snacks, the butterflies in my stomach preventing me from being able to eat much. As Gabe sat at the table idly looking at the map, I traced my finger along the inside of his wrist, following the pattern of the tattoo there. 'What does this mean?' I asked. The symbol was dark brown and intricate.

'Members of the council have the tattoos done. Each design is completely unique to each member of the guard. Anyone who questions who we are within the vampire fraternity can tell where we're from and what rank we hold. Only council members have them. It serves as proof of who we are and any non-council vampire must, or at least should, take orders from us.'

'So, you're quite powerful, then, in your world?' I was completely in awe.

'I was. But I doubt that I am now, thanks to recent events,' he grinned. 'I'll be regarded as a dangerous rebel in their eyes now. Stripped of all my control, an outlaw. The English and their rigid laws; they never give an inch.'

'The English. What do they have to do with it?'

'The council is based in York, England. They rule with an iron fist. That was where I went when Anna came. I had to meet with them. They had found out about you from another vampire, who had seen the newspaper article about how you had miraculously survived the bear attack, and had told them of a vampire's possible involvement. It wasn't hard for them to figure out who it could have been and so they contacted both Sebastian and myself immediately, as we are the two council guards for the state of California.

'So, I decided it was best to go to England in person to state my case and give them the reasons behind why I did it, why I infected you. In all honesty, they debated the issues fairly and were in great conflict with each other about what I had done and what the consequences should be. Whatever people believe about vampires, we were all human once and so I believed they would allow this one indiscretion, especially as you were not a pure vampire.'

'So, there are guards of the council and there are knights, and there are other vampires who must live by their rules. How many, all together?' I needed details.

'There are eight knights in all, who rule the immortal world. They are fair men, or so I once believed; they just adhere rigidly to their rules, which, in general, is a good thing. Five of them are English, another is French, another is Italian, the last one is from this country. Henry was the first knight and is the eldest. He is now four hundred and eighteen-years-old. The others are younger, the youngest being two hundred and eighty.'

'And council guards like you, how many of them?'

'Forty-two across the world. Fifteen are here in the U.S., two are in Canada and the rest are scattered across other countries. We are selected for our abilities, for the ease with which we fit into the human community and for our talent to be discreet and fair. But they also select us based on our skills and strength as fighters, expecting us to uphold their laws and lead all the nomadic vampires.'

'*All* the vampires? My God, how many are out there?' I asked.

'I don't know exactly how many worldwide but in the US alone I believe there are about one hundred and fifty that I know of.'

'A hundred and fifty! Don't they ever slip-up and kill innocent people?'

Gabe laughed and took hold of my hands. 'Just films, tales, and myths. What we are is a far cry from all those scary stories. Vampires need blood to exist, yes, but there are very few who stray and take out an innocent human. We are simply another type of being. Humans eat food. Plants need water. Cows eat grass. We need blood. We are just another species, albeit a very strong one.

'The council exists so that we don't have vampires randomly hunting humans. I was selected because I am a fierce fighter; I can easily take out one or two normal strength vampires in a few moves. I was also chosen because of my unwavering compassion, something that carried over from my mortal days, and because the council respected my ability to help people who had been wronged. I also have a special ability, something they weren't aware of when I was chosen. It's something I only needed to show when Ethan attacked. From my days with the Cherokee tribe, I learned a lot about their beliefs and legends. Your people believe in the ability to harness the elements – rain, wind, fire and earth. I learned to summon some of these elements when I was placed in difficult situations, to complement my existing strengths. And so, with Ethan, I was able to call upon the lightning to assist me, to incapacitate him long enough so I could attack. I wasn't sure how well it would work, if my strength would overcome him.'

'So, he was not a council member?'

'No. He was a nomadic vampire, difficult to control but a lethal fighter. He didn't possess the discipline to be a guard but his strength and power still made him useful to the council. He feared nothing. They used him in cases when there was no other option, and there are none who have fought him and won. I am the only one, helped of course by you.'

I sat, taking it all in, clutching his hand, staring at him, but not truly seeing him. 'I can die easily, can't I?' I asked.

'Yes.' I could tell he didn't like the question. 'You have a heart, lungs and blood. I only injected sufficient venom inside you to ensure your survival, nothing more.'

'So how, then, can I live so long?'

'Because the venom circulating within your bloodstream is slowing the ageing process it will keep you younger for a lot longer. You *will* age, but much more slowly than a human. Unless you are mortally wounded, you should live in excess of two hundred years.'

'So why do the council want rid of me so badly? It's not as if I'm a threat to them.'

'But they *believe* you are. They see only that you are capable of giving away the secret of our existence. Say, for example, that you needed a blood test; the results would baffle doctors and instigate unwanted investigations. They will not allow anything to threaten our survival. We have existed this long and this peacefully by being discreet. You are nothing but a loose cannon to them.'

I released his hand and stood to walk to the bed. 'They'll always hunt us then, won't they?'

'Yes, I believe so. Unless I can convince them that you are not a threat and change their decision.'

'So, why don't you change me completely? There are obviously hundreds of vampires in this world. What harm would one more cause?'

Gabe inhaled deeply and looked towards me. The torture I hadn't seen in several days had resurfaced in his eyes. He stood and walked towards me, and I knew he was about to say something I didn't want to hear.

'I can't change you,' he said solemnly.

'Why not?' I demanded. A solitary tear fell onto my cheek.

'If I could, I would. When I infected you, I did it only to save your life. I was going against all their rules, my rules, but I didn't want you to die. By infecting you with a small amount of venom – enough for you to continue living – I saved your life. But if I do it again, inject more to change you completely, it would fight against the venom already inside you; venom that's already mutated with your own human blood, and it would most likely kill you.'

'So, why are we doing all this? Why have we come here to see these people? Why are we not in England, persuading the council to let us live in peace together?'

'Vampires are not the only ones tracking us. We are being followed by the shifters and I need to understand why. This baffles me even more. Once I know the reason and can get them off our backs, we can then hit the Council head on. I *will* make them change their minds; believe me when I promise you that.'

I turned and wrapped my arms around him, kissing him hard, my tears spilling onto his shirt. 'We must,' I whispered. 'We have to.'

We headed out of Gatlinburg before eight the following morning, hoping to miss the bulk of the tourist traffic heading into the mountains. As soon as we arrived at the north entrance, Ember was up at the window, staring wide-eyed towards the trees, believing the long trip he had endured was all going to be worth it because he was now at the most amazing dog park in the world. I flicked the button to roll down his window, smiling as he stuck his nose out, sniffing frantically at the fresh, pine-scented air.

We spoke little as we headed deeper into the winding mountain roads. I was in awe of the park's beauty, the blue haze hanging high in the distant trees forming a light-coloured curtain of mist. We were heading for Cherokee first. We planned to go to the local library to look up some old papers there.

We parked in one of the quieter parking lots so we could take Ember for a long walk, as we'd be leaving him at the lodgings later. Gabe had thought ahead and booked us three nights at a hotel outside of Waynesville, as he'd anticipated that a lot of places would be booked up with tourists. He got us one of the two remaining rooms in a luxury lodge.

Gabe, as he kept reminding me when I tried to insist on paying for things, was certainly not short of money. He had invested wisely over the years, owned two properties and had cash in many different savings accounts. I was still waiting for my share from the house to come through from Luke, which I'd been informed would be just over thirty-eight thousand dollars – a huge sum for me – but still not enough to support me indefinitely.

With Ember shattered after over an hour's hike, he settled down in the back of the Jeep and watched out of the window until he could no longer keep his eyes open. I tried to relax, to see if this place would suddenly seem familiar to me, if something would suddenly click. But it didn't.

By late morning we reached the south entrance and the town of Cherokee. As we drove into the centre, I was surprised by how unremarkable it looked. It was a mass of tourist stores, motels and restaurants. It upset me. I had naively thought it would be a quaint, old-fashioned town.

We parked and headed straight for breakfast. The sky was overcast but the sun was expected to push through by the afternoon so I knew in the darkened car, Ember would be okay for an hour or so.

I felt hungry now and ordered pancakes, bacon, eggs, juice and coffee. Gabe just stuck to coffee. 'So, what are we going to the library for?' I asked while waiting for my food to arrive.

'There will be some records in the papers there so I'm gonna look through the microfiche and try to locate the whereabouts of the tribes people, look for family names that are familiar to me and find out where the descendants are now.'

'Okay. Then what?'

'Then we'll rest up and head out early tomorrow morning to see if we can meet with them. I guess that because they have been tracking us, they will be expecting us anyway.'

I nodded slowly. 'Well, while you're in the library I'm gonna wander off and have a look at some book stores, see if I can find something on the Cherokee. Educate myself a little.'

My food arrived and Gabe politely thanked the waitress, smiling at her. She smiled back until her cheeks were flushed and then turned to leave us to our meal. 'Well, don't go far, okay? And keep your cell switched on so that I can contact you,' he said as I tipped cherries and cream onto my pancakes.

'Okay,' I replied, slyly eyeballing the waitress who was looking back doe-eyed towards Gabe. She just wouldn't stop so I turned my head towards her fully and waited until she saw me. When she finally looked at me, embarrassed at being caught, I wrinkled my brow and threw her an evil glare.

'Oh, come on my little tiger, play nice,' he said, mocking my jealousy as the girl walked off. 'Placate your hunger with what's on your plate, not the pretty waitress.'

'Well, I always did tell you I prefer animals to people and I *am* rather hungry,' I replied sarcastically. 'Anyway, pretty is she?'

He laughed, reached over and grabbed my head roughly. He pulled me to him and traced his lips from top to bottom all the way around mine, before locking them in place. After a minute, he released them so he could bite gently on my jaw. 'Behave yourself,' he whispered in my ear.

Naughtily, I looked over at the waitress, who was staring at us with her mouth open and eyes wide. I rubbed my lips together, savoring his taste for her benefit, and winked. She turned quickly and scurried out back. I snickered to myself and Gabe rolled his eyes. We were not served by the same waitress when we paid the bill; in fact, we didn't see her for the rest of our meal.

The library was only a couple of blocks away so I left Gabe on the corner and headed over to the stores across the road. Gabe was going to ring me when he had gotten the information he needed, and then I would meet him on the library steps.

I found a book store easily; there were a few on the same stretch of road. The first one had some interesting books, but didn't specialise in the local references I was looking for. I crossed over the road to a more charming Native American gift and book store. There were the token native wind chimes and wolf ornaments in the window, which reminded me a little of Abigail's store.

I went in, and found a huge book section. I sighed with satisfaction when I found shelves full of books on the area and the mountain range. There were many on the Cherokee, the 'trail of tears', and there were also some tourist guides of reservations and tribes. They spanned way back hundreds of years and, thankfully, up to modern day.

I grabbed two guides and two books and hurried to the counter to pay. 'Is there a pet store close by?' I asked the lady behind the counter.

'Sure, if you head out, take a right and then right again onto Winston, head to the end of the block and you'll find one just there.'

'Great, thanks so much,' I said, and turned for the door.

I followed her directions, spotting the sign for the pet store before I was halfway down the street. The sun was starting to break through the clouds and it would warm up soon. I decided that once I'd grabbed some dog food and treats, I would go back to the library, get the keys from Gabe and sit in the car with Ember, with the windows down. I was so eager to look through the books, it made sense.

I was almost at the store entrance when I saw a cat come around the corner. I stopped dead mid-stride and gasped out loud, causing a couple walking behind me to step wide to get past me, casting annoyed glances as they passed. I gulped and felt instantly ridiculous. It couldn't be him; it wasn't possible. Yet it had the same eyes, same markings, even the same wide-legged walk. It stared right back at me. I tentatively took a step forward. 'Ned?' I called in a hushed voice. The cat stopped in front of me, cocked its head, and stared right back at me. 'Ned. Here, Ned,' I called. The cat's eyes seemed to soften.

I took one more step, closing the gap carefully, and looked hard at him. I was sure it was him. But, then he lowered his eyes and turned, strolling into the open doorway of the pet store.

I ran after him and stood in the doorway, looking into the store. I frantically looked around, searching for where he had gone. There were birds in cages and small rodents in tanks below. 'Can I help?' the girl behind the counter asked.

I walked towards each of the three aisles and looked down them. 'A cat. Do you have a cat living here?' I asked.

'Erm, no, we don't have a cat. But the birds, rats and hamsters are for sale,' she said. Of course she wouldn't understand.

'No, I'm not interested in buying a pet. A cat, a tall tabby cat just walked right through your door,' I said, edging my way further down the aisles, looking this way and that.

'Well, I'm sorry, Ma'am but I didn't see any cat come through the door and I was standing right here.'

There was no sign of the cat anywhere. The cat that, if it wasn't Ned, was one hell of a double. I looked at the girl, who stared at me like I was some kind of lunatic. 'I'm sorry,' I explained, 'I lost my cat recently and I was sure I saw him outside and that he came in here. My mistake.'

'Oh, I'm sorry,' she said, and her expression softened. 'Would you like me to put a card on the board for you in case anyone comes across him?'

What could I say to that? *Sure, yeah, why not? He is a neutered male tabby, a little odd and watches invisible things floating in the air. Answers to the name of Ned and went missing from Manzano, Southern California. He just happened to stray over three thousand miles to Cherokee.* 'No that's fine, thanks. I doubt I'll find him now,' I answered. And I knew it was true.

I wandered mindlessly over to the dog treats and grabbed a few days' supply for Ember. I paid and headed out, initially struggling to find the library again, my tearful thoughts still with Ned. When I eventually got there, I found Gabe inside, intently reading through old newspaper articles. 'Hey,' I said, touching him on the shoulder.

'Hey,' he said, looking round in surprise. 'You finished already?' he asked. He looked up to my eyes and saw the tears welling up. 'Meg? Oh God, Meg, what is it?'

I told him what had happened and he stood up to hug me tightly. 'Oh Meg. It's probably just your imagination, seeing a similar cat and wanting it to be him.'

'I know, and I feel very silly now. I know rationally that it can't be him. But, you know, he looked just like Ned.'

'Come on, I can come back tomorrow. Let's get out of here,' he said, gathering his notes together.

'No, Gabe. Finish what you need to do. We can't afford any more delays now,' I said, summoning some inner strength. 'I'm heading back to the car to sit with Ember and read through some books so take your time, find out what you can and I'll be there when you're done.'

'Okay, if you're sure. He was still worried, stroking my face, my pain hurting him.

'I'm sure. I'll see you in awhile,' I said. He gave me the car keys and I kissed him quickly before leaving.

Ember was thrilled to see me. I took him for a walk around the lot then put him back in the car, with a huge dog chew to pacify him. I hopped into the passenger seat and took my books out. I went straight to the guides, searching for the reservation. It was, as Gabe had said, in Ravensfork on the outskirts of the park. There were five hundred and twelve native Cherokee living there, according to their last census, with their own school system and council. Many of them worked as crafts people, generating a healthy income by supplying all the local towns with native merchandise: jewelry, flutes, chimes, hand-carved figurines and so on. They also had a visitor centre, with a gift store and educational centre. It was all very modern.

I flicked through the guides, looking at the faces, recognising nothing. I don't know what I expected to find. I think I wanted to feel an overwhelming urge towards the people, *my* people, something inside me which would suddenly switch on like a neon sign saying 'Welcome home!' But nothing clicked. Nothing felt remotely familiar. I carried on studying the books, flicking through the pages, looking at the photos. There were some images of the reservation showing how it looked now and some taken many years ago. I pulled out the last book from the bag and turned to the sepia photographs inside. I flicked through the pages and, as I did, I caught sight of something familiar.

I desperately turned the pages back, looking for the image that had caught my attention. I eventually found it and smiled. Ninety-nine percent of me believed that what Gabe had told me about my native ancestry was true. But there was a part of me that needed further proof. And here it was. The photo showed a long wooden building, with a sign stating that it was the Cherokee General Store. In front of the building, standing on and in front of the porch outside, was a crowd of native people, smiling.

I looked at the writing beneath.

'Cherokee tribespeople gather in front of the first general store, which started trading at the Ravensfork reservation, March 17, 1912'.

I looked back at the picture and smiled. To the far left of the photo stood a tall white man, wearing a hat which covered his eyes. He had his arm loosely hanging around the neck of a petite native woman, who held on tightly to a small boy. A shiver went down my spine. It was all true. Now, I knew it for sure. He wore the same hat as in the photo back home. The boy looked exactly the same and the woman, Aiyana, had her jet-black braided hair hanging prettily over each shoulder. I smiled to myself. Now that I'd seen this one photo, in a published book, I felt the feelings I had wanted to feel, had longed to believe. The feeling of belonging, of being someone else, of my history. I grabbed my purse and unzipped the inside pocket, grabbing the item I sought.

The shadow moving in from the sidewalk drew my attention back. As Gabe opened the door, I looked up to him, my husband, with tears falling down my face. He climbed in and reached for me. 'Ned?' he asked.

'No, look.' I pushed the book towards him, pointing at the three faces. He nodded and looked back at me. 'I feel it now,' I said, elated by the feelings returning inside.

He smiled and drew me into him. I slid my hand up and ran it down his face. He felt it then, my soft fingers caressing his face and the catch of the metal. He took hold of my hand, looking at my wedding finger. 'Because you didn't wear it, I thought you'd decided differently,' he said, kissing my finger.

'It's where it belongs, right? Where it should have always been. Listen, I want us to do something,' I said, wrapping my hands around his neck. 'I want us to get married again, in the names we now have, make it permanent,' I said, hoping I was not making a fool of myself in asking.

His smile, which covered the whole of his face, gave me my answer. As he grinned, the deep, weathered lines around his eyes creased tightly, 'I thought you'd never ask,' he said, forcing his lips onto mine.

'You think we can do it while we're here?' I asked when I managed to pull myself away.

'Well, I think we need to get the lay of the land first but if it's at all possible, then why not?'

I became all squeaky and high-pitched again. 'It would feel so right to do it here, in the place we married all those years ago.'

'If I can arrange it, I will,' he said, still smiling, more now at my hyper-excitement.

Whatever happened, I planned to be Mrs Letenierre again.

Before we left to go home.

Chapter 22

We eventually arrived in Waynesville by mid-afternoon and found our way to 'The Smoking Bear' hotel resort. As I expected, it was stunning. It was set a few miles from the park but the dense trees surrounding the accommodation made us feel like we were already there.

Once we were checked in, with our key in hand, we drove up the winding road until we found our lodge on the far northwest corner of the complex. It was the farthest lodge, set deep within the trees. Perfect. 'Hey, you wanna go hunting tonight?' I asked, a little tongue-in-cheek, but meaning every word. I was hungry…again. And I wanted to eat alfresco.

'I thought you were against killing anything cute and furry?' he asked, raising his eyebrows in surprise.

'Well, I still am. But Mr Hungry is beating Mr Fluffy right now.'

'Fair enough,' he replied, shaking his head.

The lodge inside was amazing, and even though it was a little on the expensive side I was glad we were staying in a cozy, private cabin with a real fire and a diner on our doorstep. With everything inside, we took Ember around the wooded grounds, planning where we would head after nightfall. Bears were out of the question: as angry and aggressive as they were, people still made cute teddies based on the things, for goodness sake.

When we retired to our lodge for the night, Gabe gathered all his notes, all written in beautiful script and some in Cherokee writing, he told me later. He was doodling on the edge of the paper when I approached him from behind. 'Whatcha doin?' I asked, peering over his shoulder.

'Nothing much. Doodling your name, thinking, trying to work things out.'

'Is that my name in Cherokee?' I asked, pointing to a pretty-looking word at the edge of the paper.

'Yup.'

'So, what happens tomorrow? Are we going to see some people?' I asked. Now was the time I needed to know our plan. I was ready now.

'We'll drive to Ravensfork. I know they'll be expecting us so I am heading right to the council building. Whoever is there will be someone big, one of the elders for sure.' Gabe's voice sounded serious, as if from now on he didn't really know what the outcome here would be for us.

'And then what?' His tension was passing onto me.

'Then, we wait to see who will hear our case and when – if – they will hold a meeting with us.'

I nodded and took a deep breath in. 'They'll want to know about the past and you have to convince them that you didn't kill me, don't you?'

'Yes.'

'And what about me? They'll know what I am now, won't they?'

'I believe so, yes.'

'So not only do you need to persuade them that (a) you didn't kill me back in 1912, you also have to tell them why (b) you part-changed me into a night timer and (c) why they should call off their hunt.'

'In a nutshell, yes.'

I didn't need to know anymore. Our work was cut out for us and it didn't end here. Once we had, hopefully, convinced the Cherokee to leave us in peace and to believe that Gabe had acted in my best interest on both occasions, we then needed to plan what we would do with the vampire council. I believed already that it was going to be a much harder job to convince them to let me live and not to punish or even kill Gabe for what he had done.

I sighed heavily and wrapped my arms over Gabe's shoulders, linking my hands together on his chest and resting my chin next to his cheek. I stood like that for a few minutes, as Gabe continued to doodle my name in black ink next to his notes.

I kissed his cheek, inhaling his scent deeply into my lungs. 'I love you,' I whispered, closing my eyes as I said the words.

He twisted round and scooped me up, placing me onto his knee. We must have sat entwined in each other for about an hour, neither of us uttering a word, both lost in thought about what we were about to face.

As the sky darkened over, Gabe lit the fire and I changed into my more comfortable dark clothes. Ember must have thought it was his birthday as he munched on another chew, content to lie on the thick fake-fur rug in front of the hearth.

I sent Liv a message to get an update but my heart felt flat. I knew what her reply would be. After nightfall, when all the other residents were either safely tucked up in their fancy lodges or at the on-site restaurant, I headed out to the main room where Gabe, also dressed in black, waited on the couch, rubbing his fingers thoughtfully across his lips as he stared into the fire.

'Ready,' I said, pulling him back to the present.

We snuck out the back door and checked for people milling around before we made our way into the thick of the trees. It was already pitch-black, the stars bright in the sky and the air much fresher, much cooler than the last place I'd hunted in Texas.

Once we were well clear of the lights and buildings, we set off at a fast run. 'You ready?' he asked, staying a few paces ahead of me. Gabe always spoke out loud to me and unless danger was close I never heard his voice in my head. We both preferred it that way. 'Sure,' I replied. We ran for awhile, and I shadowed Gabe as he weaved in and around, catching scents and following them, only to slow and start afresh. We did that a few times, until he stopped and turned to me. 'I just keep getting bears,' he said, looking at me for my reaction.

'No bears!' I muttered, keeping my voice low. We ran and leapt over the large tree roots easily. I enjoyed my newfound speed, strength and ability a little too much as I leapt around as high as I could. I saw Gabe look round at me and roll his eyes, laughing to himself, so I launched onto his back and tightened my grip around his neck. 'You forget this is all still new to me. Let me have my fun, bat boy.'

He easily peeled me from his back and tossed me into the air behind him, where my nimble feet found their way back to the ground. After a few more minutes of running, he caught the scent of something and, from the way he reacted, I knew it was fair game. The hunt was on.

We ran flat out, ducking and jumping, forcing our way through the trees, the branches and vines catching our faces as we pushed on. Gabe suddenly whipped around to the right and I struggled to follow, losing some pace against him. I'd totally lost sight of him and had resigned myself to following his scent when I smelled something vaguely familiar. In the distance, I heard Gabe's voice. 'Sorry,' it echoed.

A few seconds later, I knew why he'd apologised. He was pinned in a death lock with a massive black bear. It had to be male – it was huge! My human instinct kicked in and I stopped instantly, flinching, remembering the last time I was face-to-face with a bear. It was lashing its claws out at Gabe but with every swipe he maneuvered himself out the way easily. I felt unable to do anything and I didn't want to interfere with Gabe's attack, fearing I could get us both hurt due to my lack of experience. Nor did I actually want to eat the poor thing, either. But, needs must.

The bear's speed couldn't match Gabe's and, with its last swing, it missed and lowered its front paws towards the ground, preparing to lift itself onto its hind legs again. This gave Gabe the space and angle he needed. He launched himself into the side of the bear and slammed it into the ground. He quickly and effortlessly sank his teeth into its neck, pushing its head away to penetrate deeper into the thick skin, hitting the jugular with precision. He beckoned me forward and I reluctantly walked over to the struggling animal. As much as I didn't like it, I wanted its suffering to be over, and as quickly as possible. Gabe drank his fill fast and the bear started to fade. He moved away to allow me space to move in. As soon as I actually smelled the blood, my nonhuman instincts took over again. I took what I needed, which wasn't a lot, and moved away, averting my eyes from the remains. I didn't want to see it lying there.

Gabe joined me straight away. 'You okay?' he asked, sensing my disgust at myself at what I'd done…again.

'No,' I replied. 'Look at what we did, what *I'm* doing. And I have no control over it. How can I be okay?' Gabe lowered his head, allowing me time to calm down. 'So,' I said, finally. 'If someone finds this bear and examines it, will they see it's been bitten, had its blood drained?'

'No. The marks we leave heal over almost instantly because of the venom and our teeth are so sharp, they pierce skin like needles, incising the flesh almost invisibly. You've seen the scar on your arm, where I bit you, and how almost undetectable the two marks are there.'

I nodded. The marks on my wrist were indeed almost invisible. They were more noticeable if I was cold or if my skin was wet, when they wrinkled a little around the edges. But unless I really looked for any length of time at them, they went unnoticed.

When we got back to the lodge, I showered and cleaned the red staining from my skin, scrubbing harshly to remove every last speck. I dressed in my sweats and a T-shirt and returned to the main room where Gabe had switched the TV on and was stoking up the fire, adding more logs to build the heat up again.

Ember was completely flat out on the couch so I sat on the floor, resting my back on a pillow in front of him. Gabe joined me and flicked through the channels, looking for a film or documentary to pass some time. I felt exhausted. The long days had caught up with me and I struggled after ten minutes to keep my eyes open.

'Why don't you go to bed?' he asked, noticing my head jolt as I dropped off again.

I got onto my hands and knees and crawled with my cushion to the rug, facing the fire, the softness of the fibers molding into my body. Within minutes I had no thoughts left in my head and I dozed into oblivion.

I woke a short time later and felt a familiar body pressed behind me. The lights and TV were all switched off, leaving only the fire gently lighting the room, crackling and flickering oranges and yellows. I turned around and looked into watching eyes. I didn't look into them for long, though, since I was back to sleep almost instantly.

I woke a little after seven feeling jumpy and on edge, anticipating today's trip to Ravensfork. Gabe took Ember for a long walk into the trees – we would be leaving him in the lodge while we were out – which gave me time for my human tasks, such as showering and attempting to eat breakfast.

I managed a cup of coffee but nothing more. I felt full from the previous night's 'meal' and my energy levels were high, which didn't help as I anxiously shook my leg, tapped my feet and bit my nails.

With Ember locked safely indoors, we set off for Ravensfork and, some fifteen miles later, took a right towards Balsam Mountain, entering the park through a quieter route towards our final destination.

I looked out at the varying colours in the trees – the deep greens turning to lighter shades on the leaves – and the low-lying mists hovering idly in the distant mountains. I tried to recognise something, anything, but it all felt so new, as if my eyes had never seen these parts before.

We entered Ravensfork on the west side and it looked like a very insignificant place. The houses were normal, the few people milling around the streets looked normal and there were more white faces than native ones. A sure sign that the history of this place was disappearing, which saddened me. I wanted to see the jet-black hair and the tanned skin, I wanted to feel my ancestry and I wanted to feel a sense of belonging. I was starting to become deflated.

Gabe, on the other hand, seemed to make his way around with ease, as if he'd never left the place. He turned right off the main street, which housed a few tourist stores along with the everyday ones, and headed slowly through the thinning buildings until we came to a wide dirt entrance on the left, where we bounced over the uneven terrain into a dusty parking lot.

My heart thumped once hard in my chest. Gabe looked at me, sensing that I would recognise and feel some sense of belonging here. We rolled up in front of the Cherokee General Store, which not only held the same name but looked exactly the same, give or take the several paint jobs it had obviously been given over the years. We came to a stop and I sat looking up onto the porch and across the length of the building. Thump, it happened again. I got out of the car immediately and stood staring at it, the store and council building in one.

I tried hard to recall the photo, the one in which I had stood with Gabe and my son, almost a century ago. I remembered where I had been standing in the photograph, the exact spot, and I walked up to the wooden railing, shuffling the loose earth with my boot. I bent down and grabbed the dust and stones, scooping it up into my hand and running it through my fingers, allowing it to spill back into its rightful place. It was the first time I felt something. It was not this miraculous feeling of being home that I had expected, nothing came tumbling back. It was more a feeling of relief, of finally being here and of hope that I would get some sort of closure.

I stood up and turned to the car. Gabe was standing in the doorway of the driver's side, leaning on the roof, patiently waiting for me. I walked back to him and the feelings it roused just looking into his face meant more to me than being back in Ravensfork. He slammed the door shut and walked slowly to my side, wrapping his arm around my waist. 'Now what?' I asked.

'Now, we try to sort this out,' he said as we strolled towards the building. His arm was tense around me, more protective than loving, and I could feel the apprehension running through his body. I squeezed him tightly and stretched up to kiss his cheek.

We cautiously stepped onto the creaky wooden stairs and focused on the swing doors in front of us. When we reached the top, I heard a low creak, wood on wood, and a shadow appeared to my left in my peripheral vision. A cold shiver went down my back. Gabe froze next to me, without even looking in the direction of the noise, and waited, tensing even more.

I looked to the left and straight into the face of an old Indian man, who wore a cowboy hat low over his eyes. Smoke billowed around him as he puffed on a pipe. 'So, you're finally here,' he said, his voice gruff, low and quiet.

Neither Gabe nor I said anything. I looked at him, Gabe tensed even more, and we both waited.

'You're a brave man to return to this place, under the umbrella of such hatred. So I sit and wonder, what reason would you have to come back?' He paused to draw on his pipe. There was a long silence, until he spoke again.

'They will meet you when the stars come out, in the brightest place to see them.'

Gabe nodded slowly. 'We'll be there,' he said. Then he turned around to lead me back down the steps.

I said nothing. Instead, I twisted my head over my right shoulder and looked back at the man. His wise old eyes came up from under his hat and he stared right at me, sucking on his pipe, smoke swirling around his face.

I waited until we were in the car and Gabe swung a wide circle to head out of the lot, back onto the road. 'Who was he?' I asked.

'He is one of the elders, one of their oldest. He's their peace keeper.' Gabe's words came fast, as if he were trying to answer my question, but his mind was preoccupied with what we would face next.

'When the stars come out. Is that at nightfall tonight?' I asked, too desperate for answers to care if I disturbed his train of thought.

'Yes.'

'I take it you know where they shine the brightest?'

'Yes. We have to meet them at our old house.' His voice was solemn.

'Will they try to kill you?' I was panicking now.

'No, not immediately. They will hear me out. Hear *us* out. They will honor that much.'

'And then?' I was starting to shake.

He sighed. 'And then they will either believe us or not.'

'And if they don't?' I didn't really want to hear the answer to this one.

Gabe took a deep breath. 'We'll have to cross that bridge if we come to it.' I knew I wouldn't like his answer.

I didn't like the sound of it. There was so much at stake. There might be lots of them compared to only two of us. And from what I understood, there would be Indians and shape shifters and who knows what else from the mythical world. 'Maybe we should stay away. Head to the council in England first?' I hedged, hoping he might be thinking the same.

'No.' His voice was firm. 'They need to know I didn't kill you, and see who you are now. That's the only way they'll leave us in peace, believing that I only made you what you are to save your life.'

I knew I wasn't going to change his mind. And I had no idea how he planned to get them to believe that he hadn't killed me all those years ago.

We drove the rest of the way back to the lodge in silence. I knew Gabe needed to think, to plan for all outcomes, and I was a bag of nerves, aware that we needed a strong case. When we got back, Gabe went inside and hardly even touched Ember. I knew it was serious. I took him for a walk around the grounds, trying my best to calm myself down and think rationally. When I returned, Gabe was leaning against the window sill staring out into the trees.

He didn't say another word to me until late afternoon.

By then, whatever he had been working over in his head must have been pretty much sorted out. I sat on the couch with my knees bent into my chest and my arms wrapped tightly around them, trying to imagine our old house, where it was and what would be waiting there for us. I didn't notice Gabe walk up behind me until I felt his arms wrap around my shoulders. He kissed the top of my head. 'Sorry,' he whispered. 'I needed to work things through. I didn't mean to shut you out.'

'It's okay,' I said, wrapping my hands around his tightly and leaning my head onto his arm. 'What time will we leave?'

'About six.' I nodded in acknowledgement. We had a couple of hours until then. Gabe came to sit by me on the couch and I stretched out my legs, laying my head in his lap as Ember lolled on the floor in front of us. It was almost perfect. This beautiful place, the peace and quiet, my soulmate beside me and my favorite boy lying at our feet. Almost perfect, but there was one thing missing, and he left a massive aching hole in my heart.

Surprisingly, we chatted easily. Gabe had a plan mapped out in his head and he wanted us to have our time together with no concerns. He talked about how quickly we could arrange our wedding, which was to be the most simple of ceremonies, where we could once again offer our vows and make it official, our second time around. We would get this night out of the way, *make* them believe us, and spend a few days in peace until we could, hopefully, re-marry.

Then we would return home and plan how to state our case to the council. I had a feeling Gabe was already ahead of me on this, too. I ran my finger idly over his tattoo, tracing the pattern on his skin.

'So, if I got pregnant before and you were a vampire then, does that mean it may happen again?' I asked. I had thought of the repro-duction issue only once, the day I collected my contraception from the pharmacy. But now I wondered again.

'I suppose it could…although, I'm not sure if it would, now that you're a night timer. But, if you'd like to try for a baby Letenierre, that would make me very happy,' he said, grinning widely.

'Really?' I asked. Seeing the look on his face, I could tell he was sold on the idea immediately.

'Sure. How amazing would that be?'

'Mmmm. And that would be an interesting conversation we would have to have when he or she was older. "So, this is all about the birds and the bees and when you get even older, I'll tell you all about how your dad's a vampire and mom's a night timer." Can you imagine if that came out at school?'

We both snickered at the thought and Gabe pressed his lips to my head. 'I love you so much,' he whispered.

'Not nearly as much as I love you,' I replied.

We lie there until the light faded and we could only just see one another. 'I think it's time,' he said.

I got changed and checked I had my cell in my purse, sliding on my jacket while Gabe took Ember for his last stroll of the day. It was getting really cold outside. Gabe had dressed in his usual dark clothes and put on his long, black leather coat.

When they came back, I gave Ember his dinner and a fresh bowl of water and headed to the door. 'Won't be long, baby,' I said as I walked out. Gabe stood holding the door open and just as I reached it, I heard the familiar woo-woo's of Ember's howl. He trotted up behind me and cocked his head. 'Sorry, baby, you've gotta stay here. We won't be long.' The next sound shocked me. He let out a deep bark, which again led into his husky howl. 'Hey, it's okay. We won't be long,' I said, bending down onto my knees in front of him. I stroked his face and ran my fingers through the dense fur on his neck. 'I promise we'll be back soon.' I bent down and kissed the top of his head. I smiled as I looked into his amber eyes and let my fingers run over his ear before I stood up.

As I walked out, I looked back at him. He must, understandably, have sensed the tension in both Gabe and me and wanted to be in on the act – be with us. He sat in front of the door and watched us leave. I knew once he'd heard the engine fade, he would probably head back to his dinner.

We pulled out and around the front of the lodge, and I smiled when I saw Ember's sweet little face appeared at the window, watching our departure, just as he did back home.

It only took us fifteen minutes to reach the park turn off for Ravensfork. The last of the sunlight was falling low behind the trees. I fiddled nervously with the wedding band, which now sat firmly in place on my finger, and looked into the ever-increasing trees, the light becoming darker the further into the park we travelled.

We drove through Ravensfork, where signs of daytime life were coming to an end. In its place were house lights and silence. About two miles further on, Gabe took a left down a narrow lane, which led through overhanging trees, and the first signs of life started to make themselves known. Rabbits dashed into the hedges on seeing our approach and I saw a larger shadow scuttle across the road with eyes reflecting in our headlights – probably a raccoon or a skunk.

About a mile further on, we took a sharp right and started to bounce down a dirt track, the large stones popping and flying out under our heavy tires. I looked harder now, knowing we couldn't be too far away, trying to recognise something. I put the window down and listened, smelling the cold, woody air. I could hear a distant whooshing of water, getting louder as we approached it, and when I looked back out front the headlights lit up a rickety old bridge.

'I doubt anything will appear familiar to you,' Gabe said.

As always, he knew what I was thinking, knew that I was trying to make sense of it all, trying to see something familiar. We drove slowly over the narrow bridge, hearing the thud, thud, thud as the wheels hit the planks of thick wood underneath. The track wound around to the left and then straight on again. Gabe slowed even more and he started looking out through all the windows. I could tell he was wary, getting ready, just in case.

We crept forward until I could just make out some faint lights, over to the right in front of us. 'Is that it?' I asked.

'Yes,' he replied, still looking around, watching and waiting. We turned to the right and pulled into a wider space, an area set out as a parking lot, where two other cars were already parked. There was an old blue truck and a modern silver station wagon. Gabe swung the car around and parked it at the edge of the lot, facing the way we'd just come from: the exit. I looked at him and the nerves really started to kick in.

'In case we need a quick get away?' I asked. But he just looked at me, with ever-knowing eyes.

'Wait here,' he said, as he climbed out of the Jeep. He left the keys in the ignition. I did what I was told, I had to. I was heading into all this blind.

He walked all the way around the Jeep, and I could see he was sniffing the air and his sharp eyes were surveying the trees as far back as he could, checking it was safe, checking to see what hostile territory we might be entering. He opened my door. 'Come on,' he said, taking my hand as I tentatively climbed out of the car.

When I was clear of the door, he closed it to and wrapped his arm around my waist, holding me tight to his side. We walked past the unfamiliar cars and towards a gap in-between the trees, where a path took us closer towards the lights of the house.

Gabe's head moved slowly now but his eyes were flitting, surveying, looking left and right, and towards the house. I did the same and was grateful that my vision was capable of seeing much more and much further than a mere humans. We continued to walk slowly into the wide open space surrounding the house. The windows were high and small, preventing us from seeing anyone inside, but the door was open, waiting for us to pass through.

I heard a crack behind me to my left and swung my head around, gasping in panic. I saw nothing at first and then a pair of eyes, reflecting the oranges of the house lights, peered back at me. It was a raccoon. It watched us and I remembered then what Gabe had told me. *They have the ability to change themselves into any other creature, something which suits the ability they need.* Gabe hung onto me as I watched it back off behind more trees. It walked past a thicker tree and the silhouette that came out of the other side was not that of a small, rounded animal but one of a slight, tall human. I felt sick. Were they warning me, warning us that they were there, watching, and waiting?

Gabe brought his other hand around and squeezed mine. 'It's okay,' he whispered, 'We would not have been allowed this far if they were going to attack.' Gabe encouraged me forwards but my legs were wobbling weakly beneath me. I pressed all my weight into him and focused on taking the final few steps towards the house.

As we did, a dark shadow appeared at the door.

'Welcome,' the deep voice said. I looked up towards the towering shape.

'Come on in.'

Chapter 23

Gabe put himself in front of me as we stepped onto the porch and pulled his arm in to trail me close behind. I looked behind me again and saw random pairs of shining eyes, watching from a safe distance behind the trees. They knew what Gabe was and they obviously knew the kind of damage the immortals were capable of doing. They were prepared and not willing to take any chances.

I followed Gabe through the door and passed the tall, well built man who had invited us in. He wore a cowboy hat and his black hair was pulled back into a long ponytail. He stood only a couple of feet away from me as I walked through, and I involuntary flinched away from him, even though Gabe remained steadfast and bold.

We stepped into a small kitchen, which was uncluttered and basic. I still didn't remember it – any of it. The low lighting gave way to stronger lights, which shone through from the adjoining room, and as we walked forward the light through the wooden archway became brighter. Gabe had to duck a little to step into the other room but he did it fluidly, as if he remembered every part of this house. I gripped his hand as tightly as possible as I followed him around the corner, apprehensive about who would be in there.

Once we were in the larger main room, I looked around at the walls, the shelves, the cabinets and the tall bookcase over against the far wall. There were two small, narrow doorways leading off from either side of the bookcase. When I brought my attention back to the people in the room, I realised just how silent it was. No one, other than the man who'd asked us in, had uttered a single word. Gabe was watching me, as were the other two men, and the one who'd invited us in still stood in the doorway. It was as if they were waiting for me to say or do something. It felt odd. I was probably the most insignificant person in there. There were strings of smoke lingering in the air and I looked towards the small table in the centre of the rug, which held a couple of candles, an unusual looking pot and an ashtray with a pipe slotted into a holder.

'Please, take a seat,' one of the men said. He had thick, short black hair with grey streaks running through it. He wore glasses, which framed his high cheekbones and his wide jaw, and he had a thickset body, showing the spread of age. The man who sat to his right on the couch was older again, with almost totally gray hair tied back into a ponytail. He averted his eyes from both of us. The deep lines etched in his face made him look ancient. He was easily the oldest man there, by a long shot, and was the one who had been sitting outside the store earlier that day.

My eyes were forced to look away when I felt the tug of Gabe's hand as he turned to move over to a matching couch opposite to where the two men sat. We sat down on the soft, springy seat and I instantly edged my way closer to Gabe. As I did, I looked at the entrance side of the room, to see a TV set-up, a stereo and some shelves housing DVDs and videos. I kept swallowing, like it was a strange compulsive disorder, trying desperately to calm myself down and lubricate my dry throat.

The same man who offered us a seat started talking again. 'I'm Jason, one of the elders. This is Abram and that is Caleb,' he said, using his hand to introduce the old man next to him and the one in the archway respectively.

'So,' he continued. 'You are here, once again, and many years have passed since our people last saw you. Abram remembers you of old, remembers your time with the tribe and the events which took place. Therefore, he is the one we asked to be present, to confirm the record of the truth and of the events which took place when you were last at this house.'

Gabe seemed much more relaxed than I did and nodded in agreement. 'We have come for two reasons. We know we've been tracked by your warriors, and we knew you wouldn't stop until I left of my own free will. Firstly, I believe you know who sits beside me, and you need the proof of who she once was and who she is now. Secondly, you know she is the key to proving that she was a mortal when she was killed, and I know what you must do to have this proof although she does not.'

As I stared at him, Gabe turned to me and took hold of both my hands in his. 'Meg, Abram is here as a mediator. He has abilities which will allow the truth about your past to be known, and mine also, to prove once and for all that I didn't kill you and that you carry the soul and spirit of Aiyana.'

I looked into Gabe's eyes. Even surrounded by these strangers in the most unwelcoming of places, all my trust and love was with him again. He knew Abram. I could tell by the way he spoke and looked back at him. 'I'll do whatever it takes,' I said, with no idea what I was agreeing to.

'Are you sure?' he asked.

'Gabe. I'm done with having to run, having to look over our shoulders all the time. I want a peaceful life together and, for that, I would give, or do, anything.'

He nodded a few times and then slid off the couch onto his knees, tugging me with him. He towed me until I knelt in front of the small table and kissed my hand. Then, he let go of me and moved back to his place on the couch. I looked into the two men's faces as Jason helped Abram from the chair and into a position mirroring mine at the opposite side of the table. I gulped again and turned to look at Gabe for reassurance, which I got. Jason turned the tall lamp off and returned to his seat.

I had no idea what was going to happen next or what I would need to do. I sat quietly in the candlelight, waiting. Abram sat on a high cushion on the floor with his legs crossed over each other. The smell in the room was a mixture of sweet honey and a nutty, woody aroma with something else lingering that I didn't recognise.

When Abram started to utter what, to me, were meaningless words, he sounded like a natural narrator, someone who had stepped into this role in a historic Indian documentary. His voice was low, husky and warm. I looked back at Gabe again. He was sitting back in the couch, his hooded eyes watching over me, worrying, while he rubbed across his top lip with his finger.

The clink of the porcelain lid being taken off the old brown pot on the table brought my attention back to Abram again. He lifted the lid and pinched something between his fingers, lifting it from the dish and high into the air over the top of his pipe. I watched, fascinated at what he was doing, my eyes flitting from him to Jason and then to Caleb, who was now crouching down in the archway.

Abram had gone quiet now, puffing on his pipe and looking into my face. He leaned closer over the table, barely two feet away from me, and stared up to the ceiling muttering words I *did* understand this time.

'Oh keeper of our people, let us see the truth of our past, heard in the words of this spirit, of what has passed, and what is yet to come. I am the elder, Abram, and the wisest of my remaining people. What I ask, let our keeper bring it to life.'

I watched him closely as he inhaled deeply on the pipe and then blew the smoke quickly towards me, scattering the particles of shining dust into the channeling smoke. It hit my nose and I instantly pulled back. But it was too late. I'd inhaled whatever was hidden inside. Some kind of poison, I was sure.

Abram was quiet, as was everyone else in the room. The smoke forced its way down into my lungs and I started to cough to clear my throat. The taste was getting stronger. I could feel the residue lingering on my lips. Then, I began to feel dizzy, not right, as though I were suddenly coming down with something. 'Gabe,' I whispered, panicked as my eyes started to haze over, go blind.

I felt his strong hand press on my shoulder for a second but it moved away again. That was the only reassurance I was allowed. I blinked constantly and, every time I did, a new picture was formed in my head. An old movie playing inside my eyes with the picture becoming clearer and changing each time I closed my eyes.

My body went completely still as I concentrated on the images in front of me. By my final blink, I was standing outside this very house, facing the door, waiting for something.

'U-was-vee tasi-se-do, do you hear me?' I was perfectly aware of Abram's voice. I could feel him directing his words at me and I recognised the name he was calling, my old native name.

I nodded.

'Where are you, U-was-vee tasi-se-do.'

'Standing at the door,' I replied, having no idea what I was saying or why. 'But I don't think you're all inside.'

'Can you walk in through the door?'

I pushed myself forward without taking a single step, but I was easily moving to the door now in my mind. I stepped inside and gasped. 'This is not the same house,' I stated.

'Describe what you see,' Abram pressed.

'I see wooden dishes and some knives. There is a board with some bread on it, and some dried flowers hanging on some binding on the wall.'

'U-was-vee tasi-se-do, can you tell me where the gun is kept?'

I wandered in my mind over to where the wood-burning stove stood and tiptoed up to look. 'It's here, on the top shelf above the stove,' I replied.

'Good. Now, what is different in the house?'

'There is no archway. The house is all one, just a big old room. But both doors are still there, leading to other rooms.'

'Can you walk to the mirror?'

I looked around. 'I can't see one,' I said, puzzled, looking at every wall.

'Try to find it,' Abram's clear voice said.

I walked towards the right-hand door and opened it. It was a small room, with a little bed, some wooden toys and two paintings on the wall. Something stood out about the signatures on the paintings but I didn't know what it was. I backed out, the mirror being what I searched for, and headed into the other room. This was a larger room, with a bigger bed, a wooden table and, above it, a narrow tall cracked mirror. 'I found it,' I said, relieved.

'Look at the top of your left arm, U-was-vee tasi-se-do. What do you see?'

I noticed I was wearing a long heavy dress, made of thick cotton, with no sleeves. I twisted to my right so I could look at my arm in the mirror. 'I have a tattoo there.'

'What is the tattoo like?' he asked.

'It is like a faded brown paw print, with long claws and three symbols underneath.'

'Good. Now, I need you to listen carefully for me. Tell me what you hear.'

I listened hard but heard nothing. 'I can't hear anything,' I said.

'Give it time. Listen well now, U-was-vee tasi-se-do, listen further away. What do you hear?'

I listened again, as hard as I could, but still heard nothing. I kept blinking my eyes, trying to make the scene clearer. 'Wait. I hear voices outside, crackling wood.'

'Why don't you go and look,' Abram said. I heard a deep growl. It was not in my head, and didn't come from the Indian who spoke to me, but it was close by.

I walked back through the house and towards the front door. As I stepped outside onto the earth, I saw several men. They were saying things I didn't quite understand, moving towards me. 'There are men, angry white men; they're coming towards the house.'

'What is happening now, U-was-vee tasi-se-do?'

'No. What are you doing? Gabe, help me!' I screamed his name. 'Please...no!' Then I felt a hard, dull thud, followed by more thuds, and stabs and pains in my body. 'Please...no!' For a few seconds, everything went completely quiet.

'Lone rabbit?' Abram asked.

I stayed quiet. Now I was watching from above as they hit me, stabbed me and ran a sharp knife across my neck. I could almost feel the warm trickling as the blood flowed easily. Then I was on fire. 'Why did they kill me?' I asked, my voice barely a whisper.

It was their turn to be silent.

'U-was-vee tasi-se-do. You love Gabriel?'

'Yes,' I whispered, still watching over the horror that unfolded below me. The men were backing off now.

'Did he ever hurt you?'

'Never.' My voice became harsh.

'Are you sure he never broke your skin with his teeth?'

'Yes. I knew he was something different. He left me at night when he thought I was asleep. But he loved me and would never hurt me, or our son, or my people. You were all so, so wrong,' I finished. 'He was your ayo-ne-gev a-tusu-tasa,' I said, 'your white son.' The words came out fluently.

Silence followed again.

I was still picturing the scene unfolding and then I saw him running out of the edge of the trees, his hat falling off, and his frantic, ferocious scream as he reached me and fell down next to my burnt body. I had to let him see; see that I was gone for now, but not forever. I forced myself down, back towards Aiyana's dead body, and hovered in front of him, forcing all the wind I could summon to come out of my spirit and push into his face.

I'd done it. He stopped screaming and took short, sharp breaths. Then, he followed me with his eyes, following as I danced and floated around above him before I moved off for the final time, high into the air, where I would stay until the day came when I found my next soul, the body that I'd known for twenty-one years as Megan Anderson.

I felt myself smile. As my spirit floated high through the trees, Gabe's face stayed with me and I knew he would find me again…one day. I danced high on the tree tops, in the fading sun above the mist that lay low over the mountains, the familiar grey blue haze that gave this place its name.

'You will not hurt him now, or ever!' I demanded. 'I forbid you!' I said out loud.

And, then, my body dropped to the floor with a thud.

Chapter 24

I don't know how long I was out for but the first thing I felt were strong arms wrapped tightly around me, keeping me safe. My eyes opened slowly, blearily, and the now familiar room came back to me. I was lying on the couch and Gabe was leaning over me, the amber light warming the paleness of his face, making him look human. He smiled at me and leaned in to kiss my forehead. 'Welcome back,' he said.

I reached up and ran my fingers down his face. 'What happened?' I asked. I was aware of what my eyes had seen, of the things I had described, but not of how I'd been able to do it.

'There is a natural drug that entered your system through the smoke,' he said. 'It is something that has been used for centuries by the Cherokee and allows the spirit within to emerge, to show what it has seen, using the host as a means of communication.'

'Are we safe?' I asked.

'Yes,' he replied, smiling. 'They know everything now and while you were out I explained to them why I did what I did to save you from the bear. They understand what I had to do.'

I sat up and, surprisingly, I felt perfectly fine, as if the whole trance-like state had never occurred. All three of them were sitting there, looking at us, listening. 'Oh,' I said.

The atmosphere seemed different now, more relaxed. As Jason and Caleb chatted, Abram laughed easily with them, puffing on his pipe. 'There is one more thing,' Gabe said to me, and everyone went silent.

Gabe turned me so I sat next to him. 'You need to know something else,' he said. Everyone remained quiet.

I looked around at all of their faces, wondering what he was talking about. They all just smiled and watched me. Slowly, out of the corner of my eye, I saw something small moving and coming to a halt in the centre of the archway. I turned my head towards it and gasped out loud when I saw a small, silver tabby cat standing in the doorway, its tail flicking and its eyes darting up to the ceiling, watching invisible things. 'Is this a trick?' I asked, tears filling my eyes.

'No,' Gabe muttered into my ear.

'Ned?'

He walked up to me and jumped onto my knee, purring and paddling on my lap. He looked deep into my eyes for a moment and then jumped off. 'Ned, wait!' But he walked off into the small bedroom. 'How? What?' I didn't know what to say or ask. I looked towards the dark shadow of the open door intently and heard some soft thuds and the sound of movement from inside the small room. 'Ned?'

Seconds later a tall Indian man emerged. He must have been in his late thirties, not noticeable in his youthful skin but in his knowing, mature eyes, and was over six feet tall. He had thick black hair hanging freely over his shoulders and down his back. He looked beautiful. I looked past him, looking for any sign that Ned would follow him out. 'Who are you?' I asked. 'Where's Ned?'

The man said nothing. He walked towards me and knelt down in front of us. I looked into his face, waiting for him to speak. His skin was a kind of pale russet colour, not as dark as the other three men's skin, and in his eyes I saw flecks of green. He was not a pure Cherokee Indian. I shook my head, desperate for him to say something. I looked towards the door again, watching for Ned.

And then I looked back at him.

His strong jaw relaxed into a softer face. The weathering around his eyes was heavy, and then I looked at the dark greens, mixed into the browns of his eyes.

I moved slightly closer to him, staring, and then pulled back, inhaling sharply. I covered my mouth with my hand.

'You can't be,' I breathed, pressing a hand onto each side of his face. 'Isaac?'

The man smiled.

'But, Ned. How...?'

His voice shocked me even more. It was deep and gravely. 'When your spirit left, my people told me what they believed to be true, that my father had killed you. It was not their fault, they believed what they saw, but they were very wrong to think he could hurt either of us. I believed him to be a killer and I hated him.' He looked at Gabe, apologising with his eyes, and sighed before continuing.

'Time passed and I moved on with my life, but the hate remained embedded deep within me. Because of who my parents were, it was inevitable that I would become a shifter. But I had to wait. The tribe couldn't waste their lives following Gabe around all the time so, instead, the Cherokee would wait until your spirit found another being and then we could protect you once again.'

Isaac shuffled back and sat leaning against the wall before he continued. 'When we realised he had found you in Boston, warriors followed him and waited. But it was my sole decision to stay around you all the time, to protect and watch over you, so I found the best solution. A solution I knew you would not turn away, one that would melt your heart and allow me to get into your life. I shifted into a stray cat I had seen wandering the streets as I watched over your house...Ned.'

I was frowning, shaking my head slowly, first in disbelief and then in realisation. 'So, what happened when Ethan showed up? Where did you go?' I had been feeling such grief since Ned had gone missing. I needed to know what happened.

'I sensed him coming so I ran out of the door the second he opened it and far into the trees. He was more interested in waiting for you; he had no concern for me and no reason to suspect what I was. Fool. I watched through the window. I knew he wouldn't hurt you there, that he would take you to meet Gabe and the other vampire, so I shadowed you, and if needed to, then I could act.

'When I saw you both handling Ethan easily enough, I knew that Nathaniel would travel back to the council and tell them what had happened, unleashing their retaliation. So I had to kill him, buy you some time. As soon as Gabe saw me, I knew you would both be heading back to North Carolina for answers, so we had you tracked in case you changed your plans.'

I looked to Gabe, who still had his arm tightly wrapped around me, and then back to Isaac. 'I guess it sucked big time being put in a crate for a three-thousand-mile trip to California, huh?' I said, smiling at him.

The sound of laughter eased the room and it felt good. Isaac smiled and nodded. 'Not nearly as much as a crazy dog trying to lick your ass and chase you around the house. Seriously, the times I wanted to change back and kick his butt!'

I burst out laughing as the mental pictures formed. Most of them I'd already seen. Tears of relief and happiness streamed down my face.

Everyone was roaring with laughter and I almost choked, imagining the scenes he described. Even Gabe burst out laughing, a sound I loved to hear from him, and one I hadn't heard nearly enough. When I had calmed down, I replied: 'I'll tell Ember what you really think of him. You'll hurt his feelings!' And then I realised something more. 'I'm really going to miss Ned,' I said. And I would. I looked towards Isaac.

'Ned will always be here, inside,' he said as he reached to take hold of my hand. 'Maybe, if you and Gabe would consider it, you could move closer or at least visit more often? It would mean a lot to me to get to know my family again.'

I smiled widely and looked to Gabe, the question ringing in my eyes. 'I really don't mind where we live, so long as I have you, and Ember,' he said. 'In fact, I think it would be a great idea. It would be a fresh start for all of us. We've missed a lot of years together.' He smiled, looking towards Isaac.

I glanced at the other elders for their approval. Their smiles gave it. 'We have another issue to address first and then we can arrange it,' I said, the pertinent issue creeping into my head now.

'Well, even with *that* issue, you have the full support of our people,' Isaac said, looking to the elders for their agreement. They all nodded vehemently, obvious hatred in their faces. 'At least here, you have our protection as well as Gabe's.'

I didn't want to jeopardise anyone else – it was bad enough fighting for our own lives – but it also gave me hope that with their support, as well as the vampires' fear of shifters, maybe, just maybe, we could reach an agreement with the council.

'Do you mind if I take a look around outside, if it's okay with the others out there?' I asked, wanting to get some fresh air and talk to Gabe in private.

'Sure, they know everything is well now,' Jason said.

I stood and took hold of Gabe's hand and led us through the kitchen to the door. The air outside was cold and fresh and, when I looked up, I really did believe it was the place where the stars shone the brightest. 'Wow!' I exclaimed. 'Amazing.' I looked up to the sky where the inky darkness was peppered with thousands of stars, some faint, some bright, but all blending together to form a blanket of sparkling beauty, encircled by the trees. I carried on looking and rested my head back onto Gabe's shoulder. 'I remember this place now,' I said.

Gabe wrapped his arms around me tightly and I wrapped mine over his. It wasn't the heat of his skin that warmed me; it was the love he enveloped me in. We both stood looking up, with the first real sense of relief setting in. After a few minutes, I turned around to face him. He kept his arms wrapped around me, and I spread mine to cover the vastness of his chest, looking up into his shadowed face.

'So, what do you think about us moving here?' I asked. 'Would that be too weird?'

He thought for a few seconds and looked back to the sky. 'No, not at all. I think it would be good for us. We can start out with no history and get to know our son again. I think we have both suffered from losing him in the past.'

'But what about the council?' This was the final piece of the jigsaw, the last awkward piece to slot into place.

'I think I should arrange a meeting with them, alone. They don't know what else I am capable of. I could embarrass them. They will also know before long of our ties with the Cherokee and they know what they are capable of, so that strengthens our case. They will not want this escalating any further for fear of being exposed.'

I nodded, thinking over what he had said. 'Okay, I think you're right. But you are not going there alone. From now on, we never separate. I mean that,' I said. I had had enough death and violence and myths to last me a lifetime – even if that lifetime was indeed two to three hundred years – so I was damned if we were going to be apart again.

Gabe looked down at me and smiled. 'You always were a feisty one,' he said. He let go of me with one hand and moved it to cup my head. His eyes glistened and even in the darkness I could see the lines creasing around them, which I knew meant that he had completely lost track of what he'd been thinking and was now focused only on me. He leaned down and traced all around my lips with his, before they attached firmly in place.

The relief flowed through both of us and my breathing became a little erratic. I wrapped my arms over his shoulders and around his neck, forcing us to stay locked together. After a few minutes, we both paused, trying to contain our overwhelming urges, and giggled. 'Come on,' he said. 'Let's go tell them about our wedding plans. Then we'll excuse ourselves and head back to the lodge.'

I nodded, unable to say much. We walked into the main room, where the four men sat, smoking and chatting, just as a younger man ran through the kitchen and shouted out a word I didn't understand. 'dala-nusi!'

It suddenly felt like I had a rock wrapped tightly around me. 'Where? How far?' Gabe asked. I knew then something was very wrong. His voice had changed instantly.

The man was puffing, out of breath. 'Close. The warriors are defending on the edge of town.'

Gabe looked to the three elders and Isaac. They spoke quickly in Cherokee, which made me even more frantic. I didn't understand a word of what they said. As I watched them mutter things in turn, I looked to Gabe for answers. His eyes were jet black. 'Vampires?' I asked, my body starting to shake. I knew it was.

'Yes,' he said. 'They're here.'

There was more intense discussion between the men and I hung tightly onto Gabe, terrified that I'd brought our fight to them. *Please, please, no,* I thought, and the shaking started to increase.

'Meg, I'll get you in the car and run with you until you're out of town. You need to drive fast, head back into Cherokee or somewhere busy. They won't follow you where there are people. They'll stay and fight us.'

'I'm not leaving you here and I won't let these people suffer because of me,' I screamed.

Gabe took my face in his hands. 'Meg, we don't have time for this. I am stronger than whoever is out there, I know this, and the shifters are equally capable of fighting them. There are many of them here to help me. But you have a weakness and they're here for you. It's not safe for you here. Leave this fight to us.'

I hated that he was right. Hated it. But I also knew me being here was more of a hindrance than a help. 'Okay,' I muttered, resigned and frustrated by my own mortal weakness. I looked to the others. 'I'm so, so sorry,' I said, then turned with Gabe and ran out of the house. In the quiet, cold air, I could hear the distant noises. We were placed in the centre of it all and the far growls and shouts terrified me, closing in with me, no doubt, as the target.

Gabe almost threw me into the driver's seat and leaned in next to me, taking hold of my face and turning it to his. 'Meg, we will beat them. I promise you that. There are far more of us to fight them than they could ever expect. Now, you need to calm yourself down and concentrate. Drive fast, don't look back and head to a busy place. Okay?' I nodded rapidly in agreement and tried to calm my body down, forcing myself to deal with the situation. I had to be able to drive, to do as he asked. 'I'll find you or send a sign that it is safe to return, okay?'

'Okay,' I said, having managed to calm myself a little.

'Okay, now drive,' he said, kissing me hard for a few seconds before he slammed the door shut.

I started the Jeep, switched the lights onto full beam and forced it into gear. I skidded off and along the dirt track, with Gabe running alongside, looking around us into the trees. I opened the window a little since I couldn't get enough air into my tightening lungs. I kept pace with Gabe, concentrating only on the road and not on what might be hanging around in the trees, waiting for me, waiting for Gabe, waiting to attack.

I fought back the tears and shouted out of the window, 'I love you.'

With no hint of a loss of breath, Gabe replied, 'I love you more.'

Then there was a loud scratch against the passenger side of the car. I jumped from the seat and wobbled from the road a little, almost pushing Gabe into the trees as I did. I evened up the car, looking ahead into the road, and then into my passenger-side wing mirror and saw something that had no reason to be there. Running parallel with the car was the largest mountain lion I'd ever seen. It ran alongside, glancing between the road and the trees, searching as Gabe was.

I pressed the button to open the passenger side window. 'Isaac?' I shouted. I knew it could only be him.

'Yes, it's Isaac,' Gabe answered back. 'Now concentrate…and drive.'

I didn't dare go over forty knowing that, firstly, I would probably crash and, secondly, that I didn't want to lose my two protectors who ran with me. When I skidded onto the main road through Ravensfork, they still stayed with me, only they ran more discreetly through the shadows of the stores and buildings. But no one was around to see them. Once we reached the outskirts of town, Gabe tapped on the side of the car, and I knew it was time. I slammed my foot to the floor and looked carefully in each mirror to see both the shadows I loved. Gabe looked at me once, his black eyes shining, and Isaac looked towards me too, in unison with Gabe, both saying goodbye…for now. They branched off and away from me, turning back around towards town, to the fight they had to face without me.

I hated it. Hated the sight of seeing them head back into such danger with me being blind as to what was happening. Tears were streaming down my cheeks but I pressed on hard, with no real idea of how to get back to Cherokee. The shaking started again, becoming unbelievably violent and harder than ever before.

When I was about two miles out of Ravensfork on the main highway, I pulled across onto the shoulder, skidding to a halt. My legs were shaking so much I could hardly feel the pedals beneath my feet. I couldn't drive any further. I had to calm down, give myself a minute and pull myself together.

But *why* was I running from them? I hadn't needed protection before when Gabe fought with Ethan in the clearing. I'd used my fire to protect me then and it had worked perfectly. Was I really such a hindrance to them when I had my own special ability? I could help them fight and if one of them came for me, I could block them, distract them for another to take out. Maybe I could be a great aid to them instead. Maybe by letting them believe they could get to me, the one they really wanted, I could divert the vampires enough for Gabe and the shifters to kill them.

That was it; I had to go back. I couldn't run away now.

Chapter 25

I slammed the car into gear again and skidded around in the dust to face the direction I'd come from. I hammered it back towards town, the vibrating starting to subside as my fierce determination kicked in. I felt my sharp teeth break through and my vision became suddenly enhanced as my eyes changed into those of the night timer. It still felt drastically unfamiliar; I had only turned myself once before in the face of a fight.

I flew through town and turned off on the narrow lane towards the house again. I planned to park the car in the trees well before I reached the house, not bringing any attention to myself, and go the rest of the way on foot. Hopefully, everyone would be distracted enough with their own fights so that I could work out the best place to plant myself. Maybe let Gabe see I'd come back and tell him my plan. He would be angry with me, sure, but he knew what I could do. He would know it made sense.

I turned the lights off – I could see perfectly well without them – and slowed when I saw a gap in the trees, bouncing the Jeep over a small ditch to park in amongst them.

I slid out of the car, leaving the keys in the ignition, and went to hide in the trees. I listened and watched for signs of movement, sounds of where the fights were taking place, but heard nothing. I kept a wide distance from the house, running fast and keeping low. I looked across as I passed, and could tell everyone in there had moved on now. It looked deserted, the amber lights inside casting no shadows.

Every fifty feet or so, I would stop and inhale, hoping to get a whiff of a scent I recognised, but smelled nothing. I moved in a wider arc around the house, stopping and inhaling, and moving further on. I finally ran into a gap in the trees and stopped again. This time, I caught the faint scent of something familiar, but I couldn't identify it. I inhaled again, the smell becoming stronger, but I still couldn't place it.

I ran on, trying to follow the smell. It must have been one of the elders or Isaac; someone I had been around before. Whoever it was, was not yet embedded in my memory. I ran through the clearing and saw the first signs of movement. In the distance I could see what looked like a bear, limping away from me. It wasn't moving fast. I knew it must have been an injured shifter. I ran towards it with no fear inside me at all. I felt stealthy and strong and ready to help with the fight. I was a good twenty feet behind the bear when it stopped and swung its head round to face me.

I noticed the deep wound on its shoulder right away and when I looked down, there was a larger quantity of blood dripping from its paw. I looked around to check all was safe. I could do nothing to help whoever it really was but at least I could tell its injuries were not life threatening. I took my jacket off and ripped the sleeve from it easily, wrapping it tightly around the paw to stem the bleeding. The bear leaned against a tree and I pressed my hand to its face. 'Who are you?' I asked.

The bear's head dropped slowly and a deep growl of pain came through its mouth. As it did, the face started to change, morph right in front of me. The dense brown fur started changing into black, growing longer. Cracking sounds ripped in my ears as the face changed slowly from a bear into a man, and then from the neck down its whole body followed suit. Within seconds, I found myself standing in front of the man who had rushed into the house to tell us the vampires were here.

His shoulder was not bleeding so much and the sleeve around his foot had become loose in the transformation. I bent down and tied it tighter, stopping the trickle of blood that oozed out. 'You should have stayed away,' he said.

I looked into his scared eyes, terrified that he would be an easy target now that he was wounded. 'How could I?' I said. 'If I can help in any way, I will. Where can I take you?'

'You should not worry for me. I can easily hide here undetected from them.'

'Where are they now?' I asked. If I couldn't help him, I needed to go and help the others.

'They're all over the ridge, fighting down in the valley,' he said, pointing to the steep slope to his left.

'Okay, are you sure you'll be alright here?'

'Yes, now go,' he said. I pushed myself forward, into my crouch, and up towards the ridge.

The noises were getting louder. I could hear growls and cracking sounds…and voices. If I could hear voices, they must not be too far over into the valley. I slowed my ascent the higher I got and when I reached the top of the ridge, I peered over carefully, into the darkness where shadows were clashing and things were on fire. I scouted around, looking for familiar shapes or sounds, but they were wide-spread and I couldn't recognise anyone.

I flipped myself quickly over the ridge and started making my way down on the outer edge, keeping my distance until I could see Gabe or Isaac or one of the shifters. The lower I got, the more I lost sight of everyone. Up high, I'd had the benefit of being able to see what was happening, but now I was at eye level it was much harder. I ran from tree to tree, closing the gaps, but stopping to take notice, to watch and to listen.

By the time I'd got to the third tree in my advance, I stopped dead in my tracks. I saw a dark figure about thirty feet away, skulking forward towards the centre of the valley, where everything was happening. I watched on, keeping my breathing silent and not moving a muscle. If I recognised scents so easily, I knew the vampire stalking in front of me would, too. I thankfully went unnoticed and he carried on into the fray.

When I knew it was safe to move, I turned to the left and followed my own route, constantly inhaling and searching for someone, for anyone I knew. But I kept coming up blank.

I was beginning to feel lost and worried that my eyesight was far more inferior to the vampires around me. If I wasn't careful, I would become the hindrance Gabe had described. I seemed to be in the lowest dip of the valley now but was still well away from anyone else. I decided to head up the hillside again to try and get a better view of what was happening below. And if I couldn't see anyone this time, I would follow the original plan and head back to the Jeep and out of town, as Gabe had ordered.

The climb was steep at first but then evened out onto a plateau before the next ascent. As I ran low towards the next rise, I slowed my stride, looking up towards the distant, familiar dark-coated shadow further up the hill. He was standing facing me, fifty feet away; I knew he wouldn't speak until we were close enough to one another, to make sure no attention was drawn to us. He would be so furious and I struggled to force my feet forward. Now I felt bad. He would have to leave the others fighting and protect me until we got back to the car again.

I stumbled a few steps towards him, but he just stood looking at me. I glanced around to make sure it was still safe, knowing he was probably watching around me for attackers until I reached him. His coat was floating in the wind towards me from where he stood on higher ground and I could see nothing of his face in the darkness. He looked blacked out, perfectly hidden. And I couldn't smell him yet.

I was closing the distance slowly, carefully, as he watched on. Forty feet…then thirty. But then I stopped, completely still. Gabe's smell did not come through at all, but I did recognise the scent that wafted across to me.

'Use your senses, Meg, and watch carefully,' Abigail had said the night we left Manzano.

I looked at him; the smell was all wrong. The coat was shorter than Gabe's and the way his head cocked to one side as I approached was something Gabe had never before done. I gulped and tried to summon my temper, desperate for the tremors to start, to enable me to protect myself. But I *knew* his smell, I know I did. How could I feel so threatened when I *knew* him?

I felt so mixed up. It was all wrong but how could a familiar smell harm me? Before I could think any more, he started taking tentative strides towards me. I squinted hard trying to make out the face approaching me. He was tall and wide and strong-looking. His hair was short and dark; the starlight pushing through the dense trees told me that. I took a few steps back to keep a distance, until I could react, maybe run. Was he a vampire or an Indian? His steps didn't slow and I was soon retreating onto lower ground, into a wider space where the trees thinned out.

But he kept coming.

I felt angry. If it was someone who meant me no harm, then why did he not say something? The vibrating started and I began to lose my temper. 'Who are you?' I shouted.

He stopped just at the edge of the trees and said nothing.

'Who are you?' I repeated.

And then, he stepped into the clearing under the starlit sky.

'Luke!' I exclaimed. I knew his smell was familiar, but I hadn't in a million years expected him to be here.

I couldn't believe it. 'Luke, what on earth are you doing here? It's not safe!'

'I came to see you, Meg,' he replied. But his voice was harsh, with an angry edge.

'See me...why?'

'Because, sadly, you are not supposed to exist. When I changed, I lost it big time and I hurt you. I am still sorry for that. But you won't have me back and now that he's infected you, I can't allow you to live. Those are the rules, you see. No vampire can part-change a human.'

My stomach dropped and I knew I was in trouble. 'I have no idea what you're talking about, Luke. I'm still just me.' I had to buy some time.

He laughed out loud. 'Good try, but I know the whole story: about Ethan and Nathaniel, the shifters and your vampire boyfriend. Tut-tut Meg.'

I was in shock. Shocked that the man I'd once loved was now a vampire intent on finishing me off. Then I got a slight whiff of another familiar scent. It was not very close but it was there, and getting closer.

He smelled it too.

'Times up,' he said, smiling.

And I knew it was.

I held my ground and tried hard to summon the fire from within me, tried hard to be angry. But I knew he could cross ground much faster than I could draw on my power and give Gabe the vital seconds he needed to reach me.

I couldn't do it.

I stood still watching Luke and it all happened as if in slow motion. He launched towards me and I closed my eyes.

And then two scents hit me at the same time. I turned my head over to the left and slowly opened my eyes. I breathed in, inhaling their beautiful scents, and looked at their treasured faces.

Gabe was racing towards me, and on his flank was a mountain lion. My boys.

Gabe's face was completely black, full of torment and rage, but the glistening in his eyes was focused completely on me while Isaac's eyes were on Luke. I did the one final thing I wanted to do.

'I love you,' I shouted to them both, and a solitary tear fell onto my cheek. Then, I felt the strike.

It was a hard, fast blow, straight into my throat. And in the warmth I felt flowing down my chest, I knew I would die.

I started to fall to the ground but kept my eyes focused on Gabe. His voice was screaming silently as my senses gave in and my body fell heavily to the earth.

He started to fade from my sight.

I fought hard to keep him there.

But I lost.

And then it went endlessly black.

Nothing.

Nothing

Endlessly nothing.

Chapter 26

I woke to the sound of the alarm. It got louder and louder, and eventually my hand fumbled for the snooze button. Just another ten minutes, that's all I asked.

I fell straight back to sleep, easily tuning out the noise and bustle of the city. The ten minutes felt more like ten seconds and then off it went again, shouting at me impatiently. I hit the off button, and rubbed my balled-up hands over my eyes, seeing speckles in the darkness as I rubbed and rubbed, trying to force them to open. I turned my head to the right and rested it on the pillow, stretching out and looking towards the solitary curtained window, listening to the sound of heavy rain outside. 'Great,' I muttered to myself, croakily.

I forced myself out of bed and into the bathroom. The shower always did the trick, waking me up and enabling me to resemble some sort of human being. With my hair in a towel, I walked into the closet and grabbed my black trousers and light blue shirt, before heading to the kitchen for breakfast. The damp and dark weather encouraged me to make some effort so I cooked a pan of hot oats and poured on thick syrup.

After breakfast, I rushed back to the bathroom and grabbed my hairbrush, yanking it through my long black hair, knowing I was, as usual, running late. I gave up halfway through blow-drying and slung it into a rough ponytail. My makeup only took five minutes, and with a slick of mascara to make my eyes actually look awake, I got dressed, fed the cat, grabbed the checks for the bank, and stuck everything I needed into my purse. Martha, as usual, followed me to the door and, as usual, I picked her up, kissed and fussed her head, and placed her on the telephone table, running my hand through to the tip of her tail as I walked out of the door.

My rented apartment was on the fifth floor of a reasonably modern block and was a small one-bed, one-bath place. Even though it was in a fairly desirable area of Manhattan, with great security and amenities, it barely gave me enough room to swing a cat, much to Martha's delight.

I switched my cell on as I waited for the elevator to arrive, stifling a yawn. After a few minutes, I was on the ground floor and heading towards my mailbox located in the long hallway by the main entrance. I fiddled with my keys until I found the right one and then stuck it in box number 519. As I twisted the key, I looked across to the plate glass doors and the hammering rain outside. 'Urgh.' The weather in New York at this time of year was cold and miserable, and the rain only served to worsen my already bad mood.

When I looked back into the box, I saw a handwritten envelope on top of what looked like two bills. I frowned and reached in to take everything out. In perfectly neat black ink, on the front of an expensive-looking envelope, was my name.

Erin Robinson

There was no postmark, no address, just my name. I knew it had been hand-delivered.

I opened it up and pulled out a thick piece of cream card and a key. Written on the card in the same black handwriting was the name of the bank I used, along with a six-digit number. That was all. I paused for a moment, wondering if there had been some mistake. Then, I looked at my watch, realised I was going to be seriously late and ran out into the pouring rain.

The subway was only a five minute walk away and, with two further changes, I would be within a short walking distance of the massive skyscraper which housed my office. I worked as an editorial assistant for a wildlife magazine with a reasonably large circulation. We took up the entire nineteenth floor, relatively low down and

insignificant compared to the upmarket fashion and business magazines, which were located on more exclusive upper floors.

I headed through the main doors only a few minutes late, and then
through security, before waiting at one of several elevators with
couture-dressed and exceptionally gorgeous men and women.

I exchanged the usual morning greetings as I made my way
through the office and sat down at my desk, hitting the 'on' button on
my computer. I pulled the blinds to let the dreary light in – it was
better than nothing, at least I had a view – and started gathering things
from my bag. I took the envelope containing the key out and placed it
in the top drawer of my desk, shutting it away out of sight.

All morning my mind wandered, mystified. I tried to focus on my
tasks but it wasn't going well. I had originally planned to stop by the
bank on my way home but I knew I wouldn't get through the day
mentally unless I made the trip in my lunch hour.

I pressed on, answering emails and calls, and liaising with one of
our freelance reporters. He was on a wolf release program in Idaho,
which was, sadly, causing quite a stir with local ranchers. It was just
after eleven when Oliver first showed his face, smiling widely as usual.
Oliver was the chief editor, who I had been on several dates with over
the last few months. We hit it off as friends when he started at the
magazine five months ago and things were slowly moving forward.
Like me, he was passionate about wildlife conservation and was a real
outdoors type, someone who liked to get away from the city as much
as possible. We were a good match.

'Hey, how's it going?' he asked, making his way towards me.

'Hey,' I replied. 'Are you slacking already?' I added.

'Sure am. So, would you like to go out for lunch today, I'll treat you
to a crayfish enchilada.'

'Erm, well I was going to head to the bank actually, and also pick
up a few things I need. I can grab some take-out though and bring it
back?'

'Oh, okay. That'd be great. Anyway, better get back before the boss
catches me!' he whispered, a now-familiar twinkle in his eyes.

'Okay, see you later.' He gave me a lingering look and, after a few seconds, I turned back to my screen, grinning. 'Erm, I don't think the *boss* should be staring at staff *that* way,' I said, refusing to look at him. I couldn't stop grinning. I felt like things were heading somewhere with Oliver.

With a little over an hour to go, I threw myself into my work and tried to be patient until I could get out. I kept sliding the drawer open, looking at the card attached to the key, and shutting it again.

Lunchtime came five minutes early today; I could wait no longer. I threw the key in my wallet and headed out. Thankfully, the rain had stopped, for now. The bank was only a couple of blocks down and I headed there before I did anything else. I wrote out the deposit slip and walked to the line for the teller.

'Hello,' she greeted me.

'Hey. Can I pay these checks in please?' I waited anxiously until she'd tapped all my details into the computer.

'Okay. All done. Is there anything else I can help you with today?'

'Actually, there is. I found this key and I can't remember what it's for. I wondered if you recognised the numbers.'

The teller looked over the key. 'Sure, it's for one of our safety deposit boxes. If you head over to customer services, they'll help you out.'

'Oh, great. Thanks for your help,' I said, turning and making my way to the desk. That had seemed easy.

I went through the same pleasantries with the man on the customer services desk, who asked me for two forms of identification to gain access to the box. It was, apparently, a low-security box, whatever that meant, so it was pretty easy to gain access to.

He took me through two secure doors to a small room full of numbered safe type boxes. 'Okay,' he said, walking further into the room. 'D18-240,' he repeated to himself.

I followed on and gulped as intrigue affected my nerves. 'Here we go,' he said, slotting the key into the door. 'Feel free to use one of the desks and when you're done, just return your drawer and press the buzzer. Someone will let you out.'

'Thanks,' I muttered as he walked off. I took a deep breath and twisted the key round twice in the heavy lock. When it finally clicked, I pulled hard and the door came open.

Inside the tray there was another solitary envelope but it had no thick keychain rutting out through the paper this time. I pulled the tray out, my hands shaking, and took it over to the desk. The envelope was the same type as the one which contained the key – thick and expensive.

It had my name on the front in exactly the same handwriting, the same ink. I turned it over and cautiously tore it open. Once I'd opened it, I peered in and saw two pieces of thick paper neatly placed inside. One was a piece of card, tatty around the edges and worn looking. The other looked newer, more modern, and as I slid them both out I saw that the newer one had Kodak printed on the back.

I turned them over and frowned.

The first old photo looked like something you'd buy on holiday, a memento of your trip. I squinted to look at the faded faces. They pretty much all looked to be of Indian origin, except one, but the reproduction was poor, the photo worn. A group of people stood looking into the camera in front of a building named 'Cherokee General Store'. I turned over the photograph and saw '1912' written in faded ink.

I turned to the next photo. It was bent and tatty too, as if it had been looked over time and time again. It was much more recent, though, maybe five or so years old. It was hard to tell. A fluffy black and white dog sat contently on the sand in front of a pale, gaunt, dark-haired man and a pretty, green-eyed, dark-haired woman sitting close together on a large rock. His arm was wrapped tightly around her shoulder, pulling her into him, and she smiled widely at the camera.

I shook my head. I had no idea who the people in the photos were or what relevance, if any, they had to me.

I returned the box and left the bank hastily, the photos tucked carefully into my purse. I headed to buy lunch to take back to the office and walked back to work, my mind lost in thought.

I felt uneasy as I travelled up in the elevator. When the bell dinged to announce I was at my destination, I rushed out before anyone else and hit a solid wall, the air from my chest rushing out. I looked up into a handsome face. He was holding gently onto my arms to steady me. 'Sorry,' I muttered, stepping back so I could walk around him.

I started walking quickly towards the editorial suite, but slowed to a stop, my mouth starting to gape open.

I rummaged around in my purse until I found the envelope, pulled both photos out and stared at them.

I scowled, trying to put the two together.

I was sure…

I looked around towards the elevator and raced back until I stood in front of it.

Just as the doors were about to close, the darkest eyes locked onto mine.

And he smiled.

The End

memories for her. Antheia had been glad to take the girl in, saying her home was too quiet now that Rheia and Charis were gone.

A voice called from the trireme. "We're all aboard, Trierarch Loukios, and the tide is turning."

"Barely in time," Antheia muttered to her son before leaning over to kiss her husband on the cheek. "May the winds be favourable."

"I wish I could come with you," Rheia said as she ran a hand along Alexandros's jawline. He turned his head to kiss her palm and she blushed, stepping back so he could pass. "I'd like to see that box sink into the deep with my own eyes."

"Me too," said Parthenia, glaring at the sailcloth.

Loukios made a choking sound. Laughing, Antheia linked her arm through her daughter's. "I think you've upset the status quo enough for one week, Rheia," she said, her voice dancing with laughter as her husband turned away, grumbling about "the women" ganging up against him.

"Oh no, *Mammidon*," Rheia said, smiling as she watched Alexandros stride up the gangplank after her father. "I've barely started."

THE END

but her father held his hand up. "I know you were already married in the house—" Rheia fought to keep her face still at that "—but your mother would love the chance to feast you both."

"Let's do it," Alexandros said, beaming down at her. "I know summer weddings aren't as propitious as winter ones, but the city could use a celebration after so much grief."

"If that's what you wish," Rheia said meekly, squeezing his hand to let him know she wasn't angry, despite her reluctance. She looked at her father. "Do you think *Mammidon* would be happy to organise it, though? I'm planning the construction of a new temple to Eidoneus."

"Bringing back the old gods is important. And she'll be thrilled," Loukios said, relief easing the tightness around his eyes as he looked over Rheia's shoulder. "Here she comes now."

Rheia turned to see her mother striding onto the docks, Parthenia at her side and a shamefaced Aias at her heels. "You're lucky we got here in time," she chastised the boy as they wove through the crowd.

"Yes, *Mammidon*," Aias said with a sigh. His eyes brightened when he saw Alexandros. He'd declared he wanted to be a healer-priest instead of a soldier, to not only Antheia's but, surprisingly, to Loukios's relief. "Well met, Brother."

"Well met, Aias," Alexandros said, his expression serious.

Parthenia gave Rheia a quick smile, adjusting her veil over her hair. She'd chosen to stay in Oreareus instead of asking to be returned to Carmea as the two boys had—but the House of the Beast held too many unhappy